PRAISE FOR WINDHOME

After an eight-year hiatus, Landon (*The Dark Reaches*) returns with a complex fourth novel that combines dystopian and first-contact themes. // This is a quiet, tense book, saturated with dread.
— *Publishers Weekly*

This striking tale of survival and fortitude in an icy, alien world by the author of the "Hidden Worlds" trilogy is recommended for readers who enjoy character-driven stories.
—Kristi Chadwick, *Library Journal*

...Landon's worldbuilding skills shine. While the action is strictly between the humans and the natives, the setting is easy to envision and believe...// Overall, this isn't a necessarily happy story, but it is satisfying and leaves wide the possibilities for the next book.
—Karen Sweeny-Justice, *Romance Times*

Windhome delivers a page-turning epic journey of human survival through a maze of alien politics and environmental challenges. Its cultural worldbuilding is fascinating, detailed, and nuanced in a way that may remind readers of George R. R. Martin, Poul Anderson, or C. J. Cherryh. We should see more from Kristin Landon.
— G. David Nordley, author of *After the Vikings*

ALSO BY KRISTIN LANDON:

The Hidden Worlds
The Cold Minds
The Dark Reaches

WINDHOME

Kristin Landon

Candlemark & Gleam

First edition published 2017

Copyright @ 2017 by Kristin Landon

For information, address
Athena Andreadis
Candlemark & Gleam LLC,
38 Rice Street #2, Cambridge, MA 02140
eloi@candlemarkandgleam.com

Library of Congress Cataloguing-in-Publication Data
In Progress

ISBN: 978-1-936460-79-3
eISBN: 978-1-936460-78-6

Cover art by Julie Dillon

Book design and composition by Athena Andreadis

Editor: Athena Andreadis

Proofreader: Patti Exster

www.candlemarkandgleam.com

In loving memory of my parents

ONE

From the journal of Vika Jai:

They say the sound of the wind in this country never stops. Those who are born here live all their lives hearing its voice. Long ago, the old stories say, the wind drove back the sea, piled stones into mountains, and scoured out a great valley in the heart of the land. Then the wind spoke the land's name: Shothef Erau. In the language of this world that I know best—the one that my heart now speaks—that name means "the wind's home." Windhome. And they say that all the winds of this world are born here.

Summer here is brief and somber—dust, dry breezes, and small, pale flowers. Winter is deadly. The people of Windhome are strong, tenacious, born for the cold. But even they fear the wind of winter: the world-wind, the weather-mother. They fear it, or they die.

In this wide country, on this cold world, so few people remain. Their lives are for each other. Their families are close. Their love is strong and full of patience. But their rules, though few, are not to be broken. And their justice can be bitter. I have seen it. I will never forget.

Still, sometimes, in the long hours of night, I lie awake listening to the world-wind. Stories tell of voices in that wind: the voices of those who have been cast out, and of the unavenged.

But I am of Earth, and to me the wind's cry is wordless. There are no messages there for me. He is gone, into fire, into death. Even his ashes are gone—scattered in darkness. Borne to the sky on the world-wind.

She woke to fire, and lancing brightness—to hissing, and roaring, and the sluggish drumbeat of her pulse. She woke wordless and without memory, knowing only that she was alive, and in pain. Waves of heat beat at her naked body, its flesh raw as a burn. She was spinning, swooping, diving. Even the redness she saw through her closed eyelids brought tears. When she opened her eyes, the light stung like needles. She took a breath to cry out. But only a whisper came.

Something touched her, something hot. A hand on her shoulder. "Vika."

Vika. Who was Vika?

"Vika, we're in microgravity. Just like training. You're strapped down. You're safe."

"Where," she rasped. Then "*Where?*"

The hand let go of her. "We—we made it." A woman's voice, unsteady.

Wrong voice. She coughed. "Who?"

"Keep still," the voice said. "I've finished the revival protocol. I'm dimming the lights. Try to open your eyes."

Through slitted lids, she saw that the light was weak now, and yellow. Someone floated between her and the light—long arms and legs, in gray, familiar, familiar gray.... Strange pale face. No hair. *No hair.* She remembered—people shaving off each other's hair, laughing at each other— Other memories. People crowded around a table, in a little room, the light all blue. Drinking out of little cups—laughing— spilling the, the, what was it they were all drinking, something fizzy.

And now— *Wrong person.* "Eleni," she said.

"No," the pale person said. "I'm Anke.... Don't talk now. You're getting food, in your veins, and medicine. You'll feel better soon."

She coughed again. Chest aching. "Where's—Eleni?" The kind face, the warm hands. The right one. Her voice was clearing. Plastic taste in her mouth. A word she remembered now—*cryofluid*.

"Everyone is resting," the wrong person said, jerking a blanket tight against her body, then clipping it down, holding her down, *holding her down* with her arms inside. She struggled, *too weak*, but the person patted her and said, "You rest, too. Until I come for you." Vika took a breath to say no, but the person, Anke, had already left. Silence, and cool air that smelled like a—hospital. Familiar, not familiar....

Eleni would tell me what's wrong. Time was wrong. Jerking from thought to thought, and how much time in between—

Then, between one breath and another, she knew where she was. And why. And who had just tied her down.

Vika took a sharp breath. *Fuck this.* Rage helped her move. Weak, shaking, she freed herself from the cot, gripped it hard to keep from floating away. Locker over there. She stretched out an unsteady arm and got it open. Folded cloth. Clothes. She tore a clean coverall out of the pile, a few others floated out, she ignored them. Struggled to dress, hampered by the thing taped to her left arm. *IV pump*, the words appeared in her mind. Medicine, sugar, good thing. *Don't tear it off.*

She managed to get into the coverall one-handed, holding on the whole time. Her muscles ached, her bones ached, every motion made her spin. But she was cold. And this body wasn't hers, so sallow, so thin. *Hate this.*

"Vika!" A man's voice, sharp. "You should be resting."

The coverall sealed, and Vika pulled herself around to face him. She blinked at him. Someone else she'd forgotten. A lean, brown-skinned man, hairless of course, dressed like her, like Anke.

Then he frowned, and *jolt* a name came to her. Pierre—he was Pierre.

And then *jolt jolt jolt* more memory came, shaking her body, making her whimper. The man, Pierre, took hold of her arm and it was like a shock, she jerked away. This little room—the med bay. That man—Pierre Gauthier. Third on the command crew, under Fadma and—Dane. Not a man she knew well. Not a friend.

Jolt. More names. "Pierre," she said. "Where is Eleni? And, and

Nia. And Isamu." Why was she afraid to say their names? "We're here," she said. "She, Anke—" —*Anke van Houten*— "she s-said we made it." She looked at him, at his eyes smoky as ash. "Where are they?"

Pierre took a breath to speak, then hesitated. His brown skin had a faint tinge of green—from the blood replacement, Vika remembered now, that taste in her mouth. Cryofluid.

Cold sleep. *Forty years of cold sleep.* She remembered how afraid she'd been. Then *jolt* and she knew this was a ship, the *Assurance*, she knew she had lived through all those years, she knew she was facing Pierre, Pierre who never said much, who had an odd accent— *Québecois*—who hadn't grown up in the Covenant, why was he here, why was he here if Isamu was not—

He was near her again now, had hold of her hands, his hands were warmer than hers. Thin hands, he was thin like her. *Cold sleep.*

But beyond that— She looked up at him, into his face, and frowned. *He's afraid. He's really afraid.*

He frowned back. Hiding fear. "Come with me."

Maybe he would take her to Eleni. Eleni, always so kind. *She'll answer my questions.* Vika followed Pierre out through the open hatch. Awkwardly at first, she pulled herself behind him along one of the ladders in the dimly lit central passageway. Heading forward. She felt strange, as if she were moving someone else's limbs. And this—microgravity—confused her. When she last passed this way, when the *Assurance* had been under drive, forward had been *up*. She remembered that much.

Pierre reached the only hatchway that was spilling light into the passage. A sign next to it said RESEARCH BAY. Vika took hold beside it and looked in. Familiar, this place. *I've worked here.* The compartment was walled with screens, most of them dark. Anke floated near the hatch, her pale, quiet face lit by her own workscreen, her thin fingers tapping against the input plate. She did not look at them.

Cold touch on Vika's spine. *Anke. Pierre. And me.* Three of them alone—not even one other of the team. Sixteen men and women—

Oh, no. Aghast, Vika looked fore and aft along the passage.

Darkness and sealed hatches. She took a breath to speak, but Pierre had already passed through the hatch. Vika swung awkwardly after him through the opening and caught hold of a loop just inside, one question trapped in her throat.

Pierre flicked a glance at Vika, then looked at Anke. "Tell her. We have no time to be gentle."

Anke turned to Vika. Her chin lifted. "Vika—our colleagues, the rest of the team—they're gone."

Gone. Vika tightened her hold and looked at Pierre. His eyes were dark, strange. She shivered. "You mean they're dead?" Voice like a thread. She had to take another breath. "They're *all* dead?" The words hollowed her out as she spoke them.

"Worse than that," Anke said. "They're missing. Gone without a trace. All but Isamu, and he—"

"Isamu is dead." Pierre's voice was quiet. "Anke found him when the system revived her yesterday—because she was the backup medic. And she revived me."

"Because he's the backup commander," Anke said in a low voice.

"No," Vika said, her voice high and strange in her ears. "Oh, no, no." She stared at Anke. A dozen people. *Missing.* More names crowded into her mind, too late. Fadma Taouil, the pilot, the captain. Eleni Sadik—the doctor, the kind one. Dr. Alexei Kozlov, their team leader, the wise one. *Gone.*

And Murakami Isamu, the nearest to a friend she'd had on the team—Isamu was dead.... "How did it happen?" she said. Her eyes burned, tearless. "How *could* it happen?" Sealed in this ship for all those years of cold sleep, alone in the dark between the stars—

"Our teammates' cryopods are gone," Pierre said. "Cut off at the base, very cleanly. Removed. I cannot tell how. Or—or by whom."

"By *what*," Anke said harshly. "Pierre says it happened just over a year ago. Something about pressure changes in the environmental logs. Something came aboard. And left. Left us behind."

Vika looked away, at the bulkhead, the dark screens, at anything but their faces. "So...what do we do now?" Then, a little wildly, "What *can* we do?" *Three of sixteen?*

"We go on," Pierre said. "We salvage what we can of the mission." He sighed. "Anke. I have more to check in the lander. Vika must be ready to work in an hour. Give her more drugs, give her tea, anything. I'll see you both in the common room at twelve hundred. We'll plan our work for the rest of today. We need complete data before we decide the landing site." He launched himself through the hatch and vanished into the dark.

Vika floated there, her thoughts scattered, touching and revisiting one impossible fact after another, implications unfolding slowly in her mind. "Anke. How can we do this?"

"Ask Pierre," Anke said abstractedly, already turning back to her workscreen. "I've got work to do. There's no data system like this on the lander."

The lander. Why did that matter? They wouldn't be using the lander for weeks yet. Vika swung to face Anke's screen. She could not tell what it showed. A rough, broken gridwork of bright colors, overlaid on a contoured gray surface. "What's that?"

"Ruins, from this world," Anke said. "Scans from the old probe, built up over the years while we were coming here." She looked up at Vika, her face lit by the screen, angry. "Do you remember anything yet? The ruins. This world was attacked, six centuries ago. The civilization here almost wiped out. Not all the way, like at Kishar, but almost as bad."

Vika frowned. "I remember. I do remember."

"And so they sent us here. To find what happened, to protect Earth."

"I know," Vika said. "I know that. Tell me what this is, on the screen."

Anke stared at her for a moment, then said, "This is the most important site, in the south of the main continent, near the mouth of that big river. It must have been their largest city once, maybe three hundred thousand. Good infrastructure, all rubble now. No standing structures left."

"Why not?"

Anke looked impatient. "See the rings here and here? Craters. Full of water now. A crater where the dam was, too. Bombs. Or big impacts. But I think bombs. We know they used bombs on Kishar."

Vika shivered. "So all of that might be—radioactive?"

"Pierre says we can't tell from orbit. It might be, even after all this time." Anke frowned at the screen. "But we could probably work there for a short time. It's not as if any of us will be having children." Anke caught Vika's wrist, measured her pulse. "Are you thirsty?"

"No." Vika shook her off and floated to her workstation against the far wall, reached out to unclip her datapad from the bulkhead beside it. Then hesitated. She remembered leaving it there—forty years ago, the night it was her turn to go into the sleep. She remembered slipping it into its holder, afraid, jittery, but imagining this moment....

No. Not this moment.

She took a breath, then tapped open the top layer of her files, swiped one onto the screen. While the grid populated with new data from the orbiting probe, she said, "You keep saying we don't have time. Mission protocol says at least forty local days in orbit, gathering data, before we make the first landing."

"That was the old mission," Anke said flatly. "You'll find out at the briefing."

As Vika expected, Pierre was the last to arrive in the common room. Anke had said that none of them were ready to digest food yet, so she and Vika were sipping bulbs of warm water with electrolytes. It tasted terrible. Anke, one arm hooked through a loop on the bulkhead, seemed absorbed in her datapad, but she looked up when Pierre entered and took hold on the bulkhead opposite the two women. He gave Vika a searching look. "Anke, how much does she remember now?"

"I think the amnestic phase is over," Anke said.

Pierre faced Vika. "We've reached our destination. We are in orbit. But there are—complications." He seemed to be struggling for words. His Standard had never been as strong as everyone else's. "The ship is damaged. We can't follow the mission protocol."

Vika set her water bulb on the bulkhead, the little magnets making a faint click in the silence. "The—those—what came aboard. They damaged it?"

Pierre's lean face looked grim, half-lit by Anke's screen and nothing else. "I thought we were all right, at first. A hole burned through the outer door of the aft airlock, that was all. I would guess that—they— sealed a docking tube there. But when I looked further—" He stopped for a moment, then said, "The environmental systems have been interfered with. Some kind of hardened black coating mingled all through the main boards, mixed in with them. I can't remove it. The systems are frozen, nonfunctional." He shook his head. "Recycling efficiency is inadequate to sustain us more than a few days. And we cannot trust any of the ship's systems—I won't have time to inspect everything on a ship this size, alone." He lifted his chin. "So we must land *now*."

"Pierre says we have two days," Anke said flatly. "Two days to prepare for landing."

Vika looked from one to the other in shock. "Two days? That's impossible!"

"The lander is pre-stocked with supplies, or it *would* be impossible," Pierre said. "But we must abandon ship within forty-eight hours. Which means settling on a landing place."

"Which Pierre and I can't seem to do," Anke said bitterly. "He insisted that we needed your input. You're the biologist." She gave Vika a dark glance. "The one we have left."

Vika looked at them both, feeling the distance between them. She remembered hearing that they'd been lovers for a while, late in training, but that it had ended quickly. She struggled not to swear.

"Pierre," she said. "Both of you. Do we still *have* a mission? Will the ship even be able to relay our data to Earth?"

"For a few years," Pierre said. "I can't be sure beyond that."

"A few years," Vika said. "So we have time to learn what happened here. Look for scraps of the attackers' technology. Learn from the—the survivors what they know. And tell Earth." She looked from one to the other. "We *can* go on."

"Of course," Pierre said. "We must. But the mission has changed. We have enough fuel for one landing. Without the ability to refuel, we will be able to move the lander once, maybe twice, from point to point on the surface." He looked away, frowning. "But, we have a pilot, a biologist, and an expert on ruins. We can go forward with that." He turned to Vika. "Can you confirm the original probe data on the life here? Is this a seeded world?"

"Yes," Vika said, irritated. "The colors of the vegetation, the chlorophyll—it's all consistent with Earth life, and the biota found on—" She stopped.

"On Kishar," Pierre said gently. "The first of the attacked worlds that our people found." Vika grimaced.

"So it won't be starvation that kills us," Anke said. "Cold, maybe. Or the inhabitants—if they have records of the attack, they may think we're their enemies come again." She turned to Pierre. "I still say we need to land by the ruins. Kishar—that happened so long ago, there's almost nothing left. Here we can study at least one actual attack site. A recent one."

"That might tell us how it happened," Vika said. "But not what it *meant*. What it was like. Our people need to know that, too."

"Stories," Anke said dismissively.

"No." Vika looked at Pierre. "Evidence." *The people.* The people of this world were the key—whether Anke or Pierre saw that or not.

Late in the ship's night, Vika floated alone in the science lab, taking her turn at the big main display, glowing with images and data. Pierre and Anke had gone over most of them in detail. Pierre wanted safety; Anke wanted her ruins. They argued over the method of destruction, the chance of residual poisons, radiation, unknown threats.... And all the while lingering cold sleep made them all likely to drop off to sleep without warning, sleep intensely for a few minutes, then rouse confused. It wasn't helping any of them think clearly. Or keep their tempers.

Vika rubbed her eyes. Pierre had gone off to make sure some necessary thing or other was safely in the lander, and Anke was off gathering the next round of IV nutrient packs and post-sleep injections. Nasty ones—stimulating their bone marrow to pump out blood cells faster. Vika's bones still ached from the last one. But Anke said they'd need their strength when they landed.

Soon now. Too soon. Her heart lurched when she remembered what her first task would be: first contact. *To face the aliens, alone.*

She studied the main screen. Just now it glowed with a wide view of the world on which they would live out their lives. "Chara c" in the catalogs. Beta Canum Venaticorum c. The Task Force for Exploration had given it some noble name or other, that no one on the team had ever used.

A world bitter and beautiful. A white dazzle of ice spread from each pole halfway to the equator. Around the middle was a band of gray-blue ocean, dotted with barren-looking islands. The one significant continent, north of the equator, lay centered in the view: wrinkled gray-and-white mountain ranges, a few side valleys feeding into a great river plain dull green with vegetation. Farther north, the land blended with the ice cap.

Vika rubbed the back of her neck, took a breath of the cool ship's air, with its faint tang of metal and plastics. It did not yet smell stale.... No, they must land somewhere in that river plain, where most of the people were. Winter would come soon; and the winters here were dangerous. This world's year, like its day, was longer than Earth's. The seasons varied with the planet's eccentric orbit. Summer came briefly to the whole world all at once, when it made a swift passage closer to its sun. Winters were long and bitter everywhere. *No.* Marooned down there, they would certainly die without help.

She expanded the image of the river plain. All of this was like the interstellar probe images she had studied in training—studied so intensely that she had sometimes dreamed of them. But now that it was so near, only a few hundred kilometers below their ship…it was no dream. A harsh world. *And full of secrets.* Vika rolled her shoulders, moved her head to ease tight muscles. This sick feeling was more than just the cold sleep reaction, more than just grief. She guessed—no, she was certain that there was danger down there

Vika closed her eyes again, remembering a dream. Blue light. A thin whistling sound. Bitter cold on her bare skin. She'd known that dreams happened in cold sleep—the slow dreams of four degrees Celsius. But this one—maybe it had been real. She held her breath against another surge of nausea.

Yet there, below, lay the first living alien civilization humans had ever found. At that thought, she felt a tremor of excitement again. She flipped through some of the river-plain views again, working her way north along the river. Plenty of level land to set down on, but where exactly made the most sense? Anke's orderly sequence of images, thickly tagged with notes, showed some ancient, overgrown roads, and two precisely round lakes along the southern stretch of the river—more craters. As for the survivors' descendants—the only signs of them were wandering threads of dirt roads, scattered patchworks of pastures and fields, small clumps of buildings. A few widely separated towns. These people had restored nothing of what they had lost.

She scrolled through one huge, almost cloudless composite image to the spot that she'd drawn to Pierre's attention earlier. A group of big open fields, a couple of kilometers from a major cluster of buildings protected by a double wall and surrounded by smaller fields. And it was only thirty-eight kilometers by road from the largest of the river towns. Vika pondered it. They would draw attention from those buildings, right enough. They could make contact from the safety of the lander. With luck, in time they'd be allowed shelter there. They could reach out to the larger center nearby, once they'd learned the local language.

Vika knew she would end up taking point on that; she had trained as backup for Lucas and Nia, the contact team. Both gone. Since she was a child, she'd loved learning new languages. Anke had once said she did too, but only to read. And Pierre's Standard was still stiff, still accented with his Métis French.

Just the three of them left to do this. She held still against another wave of sorrow. In the quiet of the ship, the others would hear her if she cried; and she did not want them to hear her. She rubbed her eyes again. *Rest for a few minutes.* The next two days would be hard ones. She waved her screen dark, slid her datapad into its slot on the bulkhead, and worked her way carefully to the hatch.

The passageway was dimly lit for safety, but Vika stopped and held on. There was light from the med bay where Anke was working. But beyond it, far aft, blue radiance spilled from the sleep bay. What could Pierre be doing there? She pulled her way aft along a ladder until she reached the hatch and stopped, swaying, in the opening.

Pierre was there, alone, his back to the hatch. Floating beside one of the remaining cold-sleep pods—the only one showing the pulsing blue light that meant it was powered. Isamu's pod. Now his grave.

As she took a breath to speak, Pierre touched a control on the side of the pod. With a hiss, vapor plumed from the slit along its seal. Then the cover split and folded back into the sides of the pod. A light flicked on, illuminating what lay inside. And Pierre recoiled, almost losing hold.

She launched herself forward, over the neatly sliced metal stubs where the missing pods had stood. Pierre looked up in startlement. "No, Vika!"

She took hold beside him and looked at what lay in the pod. Stared at it, paralyzed. Though her stomach was utterly empty, years empty, nausea almost overpowered her. She swallowed hard, again and again.

Isamu had been laid open and cleaned out, neatly and completely. His abdomen gaped; his rib cage, sliced through the sternum and splayed, was hollow, too. His spine glistened, knobs of yellow-white. An arm and a leg had been flayed, and the bones of his face laid bare. And from the brow up was nothing. They had removed the top of his skull, and taken his brain.

There was no blood, of course—only cryofluid, clear and greenish, frozen now that there was no need to protect Isamu's tissues. The cuts through flesh and bone were impossibly clean and straight.

"That's enough," Pierre said harshly. She looked up at him, saw the anger in his eyes. "You didn't need to see this."

"Isamu was my friend," Vika said. Something tiny and glittering was floating in the air in front of her face. A tear. She rubbed her eyes and the rest of the tears spread out, cool over the skin of her face. "Why are *you* looking at him?"

Pierre touched a control, and the pod closed and sealed again. "Because I must," he said.

"Because you're in command," she said slowly.

"Of course," he said. "I am the only survivor of the ship's technical crew. The only surviving pilot. Dr. Kozlov planned for all contingencies."

Pilot. That had been Pierre's work assignment before the team formed, she knew—but that had only been cargo runs from Earth orbit to the Moon, or to the LaGrange points. "Did Dr. Kozlov plan for *this*?" She opened her hand, indicating the two of them, the ship, everything.

His eyes were dark. "Something like this. Because of the dangers of so long a cold sleep, he analyzed many possible combinations of survivors. And left detailed orders, which we will discuss tomorrow." He touched Isamu's pod. "For now, I have a duty here. And little time."

"Reintegration," Vika said. "I would like to stay."

Pierre hesitated, then said, "Of course. It will be brief."

"Shouldn't Anke—"

"She has no interest in such things." His voice had an edge. Vika said nothing more.

Pierre took out a book—an actual book, small and thin-leafed—and read aloud from it in French. Something Vika didn't recognize, about green pastures, and a shadow. He put the book away without explanation. Then he took out his private datapad, touched a file, and began the familiar Reintegration service.

Vika let the words run past her and studied the sealed pod. For Isamu, as for all of them, there would be no true Reintegration. Gaia, their mother, had lost them. Vika knew she should grieve over that. But it seemed a strangely unimportant loss, among all the rest.

In the cool blue shadows, Isamu's pod was white and smooth. For a man who had been full of laughter, of the colors of life, it seemed a lonely place to lie forever. And the others—where were they now? Vika had decided that it would be best if they were dead. They *must* be dead, whatever Pierre imagined or hoped. Taken apart like Isamu, most likely.

Blinking back the pointless tears, she made herself listen again to Pierre. He was finishing the last meditation, the one for peace in the mourners' hearts. He ended and let the datapad go dark. "That's done," he said. "Our last duty to Isamu."

"Except to remember him," Vika said quietly.

He frowned. "Of course.... Well. We're awake; we should be working. Anke will have your next round of medications ready."

Taking the hint, she slipped through the hatch and pulled herself toward the med bay. Her thoughts were grim. The plans and protocols they'd all worked so hard on during training—their safe, careful approach to the world below—none of that applied anymore. The next few days would decide everything.

Morning, for all the difference it made in the haze of Vika's tiredness. After their silent breakfast in the common room—the first food Anke had allowed them, a glop of rice mixed with sweetened water—they gathered at one end of the too-long table, belted into chairs. It was meant to be a comforting simulation of life under acceleration. It felt awkward, artificial. And Pierre took the seat at the head of the table, the one that had always been Fadma's. So this was going to be formal. Vika glanced at Anke, who looked as tired as Vika felt.

"This is the latest transmission from TFE Command, received nine days ago," Pierre said, and flicked it from his datapad onto a wallscreen. News from Earth. Twenty-six years old, of course. Vika watched as the blandly attractive TFE communications agent read it out, accompanied by visuals. The sound was flawless, the crisp images chilling.

There had been five more megacyclones in the northern hemisphere this year than last, and sea level rise was threatening to overtop the massive dam at the opening of the Mediterranean. The Semi-autonomous District of South Asia (Vika flinched—*home*) had named three more coastal cities for permanent evacuation within fifty years, and the water crises in Africa and central Asia were deepening. The UN Office of Climate Monitoring had advanced the year when Earth would cease to be capable of supporting its projected population—even reduced as it already had been by rigid population control and by the endless toll of natural disasters. The crash was now barely three centuries away. As a result, planning for exploration and colonization missions had expanded to meet the challenge. The agent's warm voice was reassuring. "The children of Earth will find new homes, and new challenges, on other worlds."

"They're still keeping it secret," Anke said. "The real reason we're here."

"They will as long as they can." Pierre looked grim. "Better lies than panic."

Now the command update, from a young man as pretty as the young woman: a series of cheerful reminders to the assembled crew to rely on each other as they had trained to do, and to always work with a good heart for the safety and prosperity of the homeworld.... Vika stopped listening. In the middle of the night she had gone to her bunk and dutifully viewed the last two or three of the small queue of communications from her mother and father. They were well, they said. They looked older than Vika had expected. Thinner. Smiling stiffly at the imager.

Her father had tried. He at least had always tried to keep communication open after she broke their hearts by choosing this mission—robbing them of their one hope for a grandchild, perhaps even a grand*son*.... By now, of course, they were likely dead of old age, or one of the savage new cancers. Vika had tried to make herself feel it as real—as a reason for grief. But she could not. It was not like losing Isamu.

The recording from TFE ended, as all of them did, with the Task Force for Exploration logo and a bright fanfare. Their duty to Gaia, humankind's endless future, limitless vistas. Joyous young men and women marching under the green and blue and white of the flag of Earth. Pierre shut it off. "You see," he said. "Earth needs our data more than ever. They are vulnerable to the same threat that devastated this world only a few hundred years ago. The new worlds they settle will be even less able to defend themselves." He looked from Anke to Vika. "Even weakened as we are, we must still learn all that we can. We can't know what small detail might be the clue that keeps our people safe." He set his fists on the table. "We three—we *must* complete the mission."

Anke gathered herself. "You still refuse to accept that *we three* are an experiment," she said, speaking carefully. "We were left alive precisely because those things that boarded us want to study us in the environment of our mission. Our ship was disabled to force us to land. They want us down there so they can study our actions, and judge us. Judge Earth." She took a breath. "And plan their attack."

"And you know this—how?" Vika heard the tension under Pierre's calm voice.

Anke frowned impatiently. "It's the only explanation that makes sense. Maybe they detected our first probe, all those decades ago. Maybe they were expecting us. Watching us. Maybe even now."

"From where?" Pierre's voice had an edge.

"I don't know," Anke said. "Somewhere in this system. Hidden, so they won't interfere with the experiment. Until it's time to end it."

"Listen to me," Pierre said, his voice rough. "We *will* explore this world. We *will* discover what happened here, and how. And when we've learned enough, when our report is complete, we will transmit it to Earth."

Anke, pale with anger, faced Pierre. "What would you say our chances are?" she said to him. "Your *professional* assessment."

He sighed. "We do have a chance. But I need your best work, yours and Vika's. Your most careful attention to the problems before us. Not only the mission—the indigenous race will be frightened of our landing, may believe we are their old enemy returned. We'll be at their mercy."

Anke laughed. "If they know what mercy is." She looked at Vika. "I don't envy you—having to face them first."

"I'll be ready," Vika said steadily. *By the time it happens, I will be.*

They all worked hard for the rest of that day, the last before landing. The bone aches and abrupt sleeps of recovery faded. And at their noon meeting, Pierre chose the landing site that Vika had suggested, over Anke's objections. Not the ruins. The people. Which meant Vika would certainly face them tomorrow.

Pierre was carrying out a complete check of all their equipment in the lander, in hopes of spotting any tampering. Vika endured Anke's resentful silence alone as they worked to transfer the probe's data and their own to the lander's systems.

But all systems, all supplies, tested out. After their evening meal, as they finished the last coffee they would ever taste, Pierre reviewed the results.

He took his time, as always, but at last he set the datapad aside. "This is the final set? Then all appears to be correct."

"Every system but one," Anke said.

Vika looked at her in surprise. "Which one?"

"The comm implants," Anke said. "We need to remove one of them and check it under the scope."

"But they were placed in us on Earth," Vika said, hiding her fear. "And there's no sign that any of *us* were—interfered with."

"The diagnostics show no change in the implants' function," Pierre said. "And our body scans show normal placement. Paranoia should not drive us—"

"We haven't *seen* the implants," Anke said. "Pierre, as medical officer, I must insist on this." She looked at Vika. "Pierre is our pilot. We can't risk infection or a fever, not with him. So I'll remove yours."

Vika winced. Pierre sighed again. "Very well. I will examine the implant. Once it is cleared, you will replace it. But this is the last delay. I've made the landing calculations. We launch tomorrow at 1750—it will be midafternoon at the landing site, with good light."

"And the weather looks good," Vika said.

"All will be well," he said, and smiled at her. But his smile looked hollow.

"Hold very still," Anke said, and Vika heard the faint hiss of the scalpel beam moving in the numbed flesh under her jaw. Vika's sweating hands gripped the edges of the medical pallet, her muscles so tight they ached. She had lost count of her breaths. A hundred, Anke had said. She caught a whiff of smoke. Her own flesh burning. She steadied her breathing against a qualm of nausea.

Anke worked on. "Clear that, Pierre." A wet, sucking sound. "No, all of it—I don't want it floating into my eyes." Vika winced at sudden pressure in the numb wound, metal against bone. "I see it," Anke said. "I'll have to lift it a little so I can dissect it free. Steady, Vika."

A hard, aching tug, and a sharp thread of pain. "One more," Anke said. "There. Take it, Pierre." Anke's face moved into view above Vika's. "It's done. But hold steady, I've got to cover the wound."

When Anke was finished, Vika turned her head. Pierre was hunched around a datapad linked to the microscope field that held the implant. His lean shoulders were tense. Vika licked her dry lips. "What is it? What do you see?"

He turned to them, frowning. "Look."

Vika released herself from the pallet, and she and Anke floated over to see the datapad. The magnified implant was clear on the screen, a complex, irregular gray object, its biopolymer surface meant to protect the wearer's body from the comm device inside. But at one end she saw a glob of something smooth, glistening pink, adhered to it. Tissue? But nothing was supposed to be able to attach to these.

"See." Pierre touched the pad and the image rotated. The pink substance covered most of the other side, a hard, smooth layer.

Vika's stomach turned. "What is it?"

"I don't know," Pierre said. "From its appearance, it grew there. But it is not flesh." He sounded weirdly calm. He tapped the pad and the image changed to an internal scan, the pink material highlighted so they could see its extent. Threads of the material reached deep into the communicator. "I can't judge what effect this invasive material might have. But it's clear that this device, too, has been modified."

Those things *had* touched her. Vika took a steadying breath. "If they did that to me—"

"We must assume they did it to all of us." Anke's fingers were pressed against her jaw, just where her own implant was. "And we now

know that they were able to—interfere with us without leaving a mark."
She looked at Pierre. "Our implants will have to come out as well."

Pierre looked bleak. "That leaves us dependent on hand comms,
which can be lost. And we lose our ability to track each other."

"The alternative," Anke said hotly, "is to leave alien technology
inside our bodies. Technology whose purpose we don't understand. It
may let them track us, monitor us, perhaps kill us at will."

"Oh, I agree," Pierre said. "The risk will be a little worse. But it
was already very great." His pale face set hard, he clipped the datapad
to his equipment harness, beside the container that held Vika's
implant. "I must examine this in the lab, and then we'll remove the
other implants. I observed this procedure—I'll do yours. And then we
will proceed according to our orders."

Vika watched, her hand on her aching jaw, as he slipped away
through the hatch. Then she looked at Anke. "We'll be all right once
we're free of those things."

Anke looked at her. "Oh, certainly. Assuming this is *all* they did to us."
Vika could find no answer to that.

Toward midnight, Vika assisted as Pierre removed Anke's implant,
and a few minutes later as Anke removed his. Then they rechecked the
inventory of the lander's cargo. With only three people rather than
sixteen, Pierre had decided that they could load in much more than
just the mission-specific supplies and equipment that were already in
the lander; at his insistence they bundled in all the clothing and food
that remained in the ship's supplies, securing it in and around the
empty acceleration couches. And of course, all the weapons—small,
chemically powered guns that threw heavy slugs of metal. Aboard the
lander, Pierre locked them away carefully.

Vika still struggled against fear. The dreams—once they were
free of the ship, she hoped, the dreams would stop. Vika's thoughts

now were of Dr. Kozlov, of Isamu and Lucas and Nia. Her friends, her colleagues, far more than Pierre or Anke. Gone. Or—again, the thought she could not push aside. *Or they're still alive somewhere. Afraid and in pain.*

Silence in the ship, in all the empty places. Silence in the dark passageways, and in the cold pod where something lay frozen, shut out of sight forever.

Silence in the cubicle where Anke slept restlessly, floating, lightly tethered, her long hands twitching. And dreamed of water rising, rising, stealthy and cold. Dark water swirling. Touching her feet. And over her head, the locked hatch. The water rose.

Silence in the narrow compartment where Vika dozed, sweating in her sleep bag. Dr. Kozlov embraced her again, warmly, more than warmly. He was her lover, as he had never been. She turned and muttered in the heat and darkness, and in the dream his hands caressed her body, gathered her against him. And just as he took her, his lips against her own turned hard, bare, and she pulled back and looked into his face. But he had no face, only gleaming bone, like Isamu. Just the same....

The boarding bay was also silent. Pierre slept dreamlessly, a datapad still glowing, turning slowly, slowly in the air near his hand, a pad with a checklist nearly filled. But even in the place without dreams, he was afraid.

Two

Vika endured the jouncing, juddering descent from orbit in a fog of nausea and fear. Landing was a jolt, then echoing silence. The lander creaked and popped as its metal skin cooled. It would never lift to orbit again. They were one more irreversible step from Earth.

She released her straps and lay rubbing her hands together—they ached from gripping the sides of her acceleration couch during entry. Ahead of her she saw Pierre deftly locking down the control board. Beside her, Anke lay still, her eyes closed, breathing with careful steadiness. Here they were, and here they would stay. The *Assurance*, left in low planetary orbit, had only one purpose now: to transmit what they learned here back to Earth for as long as the ship's power lasted.

And so it was time to get to work. Vika unstrapped and sat up slowly. She and Pierre had chosen this landing site with care: a small cultivated area tucked into the hills above the main river valley, within easy distance of a cluster of buildings that might be a village, and two days' walk northwest of the largest town on the continent—possibly fifty thousand inhabitants. Vika watched as Pierre swung his booted feet to the deck, leaned forward and sighed. He had actually shaved his face for this, but the black stubble on his scalp still made him look untidy. He struggled to his feet, hunched in the cramped space, and shuffled to the hatch. The release was manual, a bare-bones device—no power-draining automatics. He looked bleakly at Vika and gripped the handle.

The hatch chuffed open, then groaned as Pierre slid it aside. Daylight filled the lander, and with it came a gust of air, fresh and vividly cold. It had a green, pitchy smell, sharp enough to taste. From Vika's couch she could see only a slice of deep-blue sky, with a lacework of high cirrus clouds racing past.

Pierre leaned out. Vika moved her tongue, trying to form a question, but Anke spoke first. "So?" she croaked.

He shaded his eyes with his hand. "None of the intelligent inhabitants in sight. I would guess this is a pasture. I see a stone fence, and some large animals at the far end."

Vika rose—the gravity felt far too strong, unnaturally so, though she knew it was slightly less than that of Earth. She made her way over to join Pierre. The lander stood on level ground at the top of a sloping field of tufted, grayish grass, closely cropped and fenced with neatly laid gray stone. The animals—fifteen or twenty brown, low-slung quadrupeds, with spiky two-branched horns—crowded against the fence a hundred meters away, heads tossing restlessly. They were big, bigger than cattle on Earth. She wondered what they would do when she was down there among them. And what the aliens would do, confronted with beings from the sky. They would have every reason to be afraid.

Past the fence was a belt of squat, blue-gray trees that looked like conifers, branches tossing in the cool, steady wind. Beyond that, the little valley rose again toward a wooded ridge. To the west, she decided. The whole scene looked like a history holo, if she overlooked the odd hunched trees, the gray tinge in all the foliage, the gaudy, impossible blue of the sky. "It's beautiful," she said.

Pierre glanced down at her. "Now it is. But summer will be short." She grimaced and turned to look at Anke, who had slid open the shutters on the viewport opposite the hatch. Through it, Vika glimpsed a hillside, covered with evenly planted trees. Their leaves were a deep purple-black.

The inhabitants certainly knew they were here; the landing jets would have been audible for kilometers, the flame brilliant even in daylight. Vika steadied herself with a hand on the bulkhead next to the hatch. She felt wobbly, even after the full cycle of preacclimation drugs. They'd landed. Their mission was beginning—a much harder one than they'd trained for or ever imagined. The three of them were alike in only one thing: they'd given up literally everything for the work they were about to undertake.

Now they had to make it worth their comrades' sacrifice. Vika straightened and turned away to prepare what she would need for her first task: to stand face to face with the aliens.

Kelru stared up at the sky, his hands pressing his ears shut, his claws digging into his fur. The white flame descended. Not toward him any longer—further east, in the direction of the sisterhold. Thunder shook his bones, built, built—then ended. Slowly he removed his hands. In the sudden silence even the *klakurr* were still. Kelru's mount crouched low under him. The fur stood erect along its neck. "Be easy, Thonn," Kelru said, and clicked comfortingly. A lie: he was certainly as frightened as the beast. "Up!"

As Thonn reluctantly rose again beneath him, Kelru kept his eyes on the eastern sky. The flame had gone down behind the shoulder of the next hill. At the men's college in Kheosseth, Kelru had heard of stones that fell from the sky like that, with fire. So this did not necessarily mean that the Destroyers had returned....

But if it had been a stone, why had it *slowed* as it fell?

He scratched his nose with a claw. Now, he knew, his friends in Kheosseth would want him to be their ears, their noses, their eyes. He had come here, dangerously close to the Thanen River sisterhold, to meet with a group of the farmholders and encourage them to send at least a few half-grown boys from this year's outdriving to Kheosseth to learn, instead of turning them out onto the road to wander until they found place as men. He and his cousin Nakhalru had agreed that this kind of recruitment was necessary, if there was ever to be a strong coalition of educated men to stand against the Old Anokothu and their followers.

But it was a risk, coming here—it would anger Dethun, and she had many men in sworn service protecting her sisterhold. And patrolling near it. They, too, would come to investigate this thing that had happened.

No time to waste. Kelru sniffed the air again, looked up and down the road. It was a task he knew he carried well, to pass through danger and slip away again. So, then. He would go and see this stone from the sky for himself—yes, even in the shadow of Dethun's walls. And then—if these were not the Destroyers come again, but something else—he would escape with the news.

When Kelru was a boy, still in his birth family, one of his fathers had taught him that some events, and some truths, carved a new streambed for time and history. If this was such a moment, and the flood swept him away—well, it would be a death worth singing about.

If anyone was left to sing.

Kelru urged his mount forward along the road, toward the place where fire and thunder had touched his world once more.

In the lander's hatchway, Vika tensed. "I see something."

Pierre and Anke both sat up straight from their work rechecking the travel packs they would carry from the lander. "Where?" Pierre demanded.

She pointed. "There. Under the trees at the bottom of the pasture."

They joined her at the hatch, and she handed them their scopes. Vika trained hers on the shadows under the gray-green conifers. She swept slowly back and forth, wishing the scope were powered and set for infrared. But the optics were plain glass, built to last decades. Nothing, nothing...*there*. She backtracked. Its outline— "Humanoid!"

Vika felt a shiver of excitement. Humanoid, and cautious. Not, in this moment, aggressive. Perhaps because it was alone?

"I see it," Pierre said. "Not just the same biochemistry, then. Perhaps a shaped intelligence as well." Cultured by unknown outsiders, as humans had been in the dark, lost past.

Anke caught her breath. "It's coming over the fence."

Yes, its body outline was humanoid—tall and powerful. But when it turned its head briefly, Vika could see that it had small erect ears, and a short-muzzled face that was substantial and strong-looking. Not like any Earth animal—something other. It seemed to be wearing a coat made of animal fur, like something on Earth before the Covenant. She looked again. No, the fur appeared to be its own, sleek and reddish-brown.

It moved through the animals, seemingly unconcerned, and they yielded to it. When it walked into the sunlight Vika saw that it wore no clothing, only a strap around its waist, and another angled across its chest. But it carried a long, powerful bow, held it with an arrow nocked on the string—an arrow that must be close to a meter long. She itched to get a better look.

"See that," Pierre said. "If bows are their best weaponry, we have them well outgunned."

"That's a longbow," Anke said from behind them. "You shouldn't underestimate it. Especially one that size."

Vika nodded. The huge bow was in proportion: the reddish-furred alien had to be well over two meters tall. It had no tail, as far as Vika could see. Its eyes faced forward, and it strode forward calmly and deliberately. She was struck by its dignity in the face of the unknown.

About thirty meters from the lander, it stopped and stood looking up at them. Pierre turned to Vika. "It's time."

"She should at least be armed," Anke said. The stubble of her fair hair looked white in the sun. Her pale eyes were intent, her strong jaw set firmly. "Surely, Pierre. Look at that thing. It's twice her size."

Pierre turned his head, and Vika followed his glance at the weapons locker. "No," Pierre said. "We must not go armed into their reach."

"Pierre's right," Vika said. "If the people here want us dead, we'll die. With a fight or without one." She looked out at the approaching alien. *Now it begins.* "I'm going down."

Vika heard Anke take a quick, angry breath—then let it out. "Good luck, then. You'll need it."

Vika felt hollow, unreal. But her hands were steady as she clipped her datapad to her equipment harness. Then she rose and moved to the edge of the hatch. She folded out the landing hoist, and Pierre helped her into the sling. "Hold tight," he said. "Cross the burned ground quickly. And don't worry. You will do well." He gave her his version of an encouraging smile. *Don't screw up.*

She frowned at him and said, "Watch for my signal."

All through her descent she was conscious of the alien watching, of the bow ready in its hands. Now she was down. She stepped over the black, stinking burn from the landing jets and onto grass, closely cropped, mounded here and there with pungent animal dung. She smelled smoke, and dirt, and ammonia. The alien waited, still without taking aim. But she saw its ears twitch as the wind carried her scent toward it. Behind her she heard the faint hum as the sling ascended. No retreat. *But this is what I came here to do.* She had expected to be afraid. Yet all she felt now was clear focus, and a tremor of excitement.

She walked down the gentle slope, picking her way among droppings and tufts of grass, mud from recent rains. Five meters away from the alien, she stopped.

The alien regarded her, still with that apparently unshakable calm. She looked it over more closely. It might possibly be male, if such an analogy could be made here. A working hypothesis. The alien held the bow steady, left-handed, and waited.

"I come from a planet called Earth," Vika said. She spoke in Standard. She must not sound excited, must not provoke this being. She closed her fists to keep her hands from visibly shaking.

"*Shothef av'n snng,*" the alien said. "*Shothef nadaeth, sugfroheh.*" The voice was deep, husky, strange. They stared at each other. The alien's ears twitched. Then he made a fist and thumped his chest. "*Kh'doeh sennoeth kelru.*" He waited, then repeated the gesture. "*Kelru.*"

The word might be greeting, but more likely it was his name. "Kelru," she repeated, and then copied his gesture. "Vika."

"*Veekahh.*" Her name in an alien voice. She felt herself flush with excitement. A connection. A beginning.

Now, her eyes on the alien, she reached slowly for the packet of pictures clipped to the belt of her harness. He watched her hands, but made no move.

She unfolded the packet and took out the pictures. The first, made a few hours ago, showed herself. Unsmiling, looking straight into the imager. *Procedure: Establish that the images represent physical reality.* She walked forward slowly, holding up the square of plastic.

He came to meet her, bow still half-ready. She offered the picture. He lowered his bow slowly, then took it and the arrow together in his right hand and accepted the picture with his left. His fingers did not touch hers. He had long, strong-looking hands, with three fingers and a thumb ending in sharp claws. His palms were bare skin, brown and deeply creased.

She pointed at the picture, then at herself. "Vika."

He peered at it, and then at her, tilting his head slightly to one side. The gesture looked quizzical. His eyes were red-gold, as fathomless to her as the eyes of an animal. But this was not an animal.

She held out her hand, and he gave her the picture. His ears twitched again. She wondered what it meant. Curiosity, she hoped.

They ran through the rest of the pictures the same way. This planet, gray and silver. Then Earth—the land tan and gray and fading green; the ocean flecked with vivid green seaweed farms; no ice caps at all. Their ship. The lander descending. Herself again, then Pierre and Anke. And that was all.

As the alien—Kelru, she ought to call him—finished studying each picture, he returned it to her. When she had the last one, she folded up the packet and clipped it to her belt. Kelru watched her with level interest. The sun beat down on them both. Sweat trickled down her neck.

Then she spread the fingers of her left hand carefully at her side, the signal that would bring Pierre and Anke down. Her work was just beginning, but this moment was over.

And here was Pierre already, picking his way down the slope from the lander. Anke, she saw, stood by the lift, guarding their packs. Not visibly armed, Vika saw with relief.

Pierre stopped beside Vika. She sensed his nervousness—as tall as he was, he had to look up at the alien. Kelru repeated the gesture he had made before, and named himself. She elbowed Pierre. "Say 'Kelru.' Then do what he did and name yourself."

Pierre complied. "What is he, do you think? A hunter?"

At that instant she heard a strange buzzing *churr*, and the shaft of a huge arrow trembled in the ground near her foot. Staring at it, she stumbled as Pierre seized her arm and jerked her back, away from it. The alien called Kelru had already moved to the relative shelter of one of the landing struts. They followed, and Anke as well.

The alien's ears were flat back. He laid the arrow on the string of his bow again. Motion, shadows. The animals at the foot of the slope stirred. Vika saw seven, no, eight more of the aliens, spread out in a line, striding up the slope toward them. All but one of them were armed with bows. They were unclothed like Kelru—just straps for knives and pouches, and for quivers of arrows. The one in the lead, stocky and gray-coated, wore only a silver-hilted knife in a sheath at his side. At the spot where the arrow had struck, they stopped.

Kelru looked down at Pierre and her. "*Dokhosk*," he said, and tossed his head toward the lead rider. "*Ganarh*." His voice sounded different, harsher. He half-raised his bow, and Vika saw the muscles of his arms and shoulders bunch under the dense pelt. He was ready to aim and loose. These must be his enemies—dangerous ones, if he would turn his back to the humans in order to face them.

The gray one raised his arm straight up, hand clenched in a fist, and spoke in a clear, deep voice. His followers spread out and encircled the lander. Pierre put his arm around Vika's shoulders. She twisted a little, and he dropped it back to his side.

Another order, and three of the bowmen nocked arrows on their own strings, half-raised their own bows. The lander's strut gave them no protection now, but Kelru did not move as the gray leader approached. The sun went behind a cloud; the wind was picking up.

The leader kept his eyes on Kelru as he walked, his ears flicking forward and back. Vika noticed a black ring punched through one of his ears, maybe tarnished metal. He spoke—to Kelru. "*Khadai!*" He gestured downward. The bowmen stood ready behind and beside him.

Kelru planted his feet and started to raise his bow.

The gray one spoke sharply, and beyond him, in a smooth motion, his bowmen aimed at Kelru. Their arrows, gleaming yellow, had savagely barbed metal tips.

Kelru froze. Then, slowly, slowly, stooped and laid his bow in the mud.

The gray alien stepped forward and held out his hand. Kelru drew his knife, stopped a moment, then reversed it and handed it hilt-first to the gray one.

"*Ai,*" the gray one said, with what sounded to Vika like satisfaction. Then he stepped on Kelru's bow, pressing it down into the mud— stepped forward over it and walked a slow circle around the three of them, sniffing the air.

Then he threw back his head and called out in a strange, high voice that pierced Vika's skull. And from far away, in the direction of the distant buildings, a second voice answered.

There was another answer as well, from the trees below the pasture: a deep, rumbling cough. Ganarh looked downslope, shading his eyes with a hand, and spoke. Kelru seemed at first not to hear; but then he raised his voice and called. One word: "*Thonn!*"

The shadows under the trees moved, resolved into a huge, shaggy, long-bodied beast—dun-furred, with a sinuous neck and a broad, flat head. Vika's eyes widened. Surely that *thing* would not come into the pasture— But it strode over the fence, almost flowing, and paced up the hill toward them. The pastured animals scattered in panic, hooting. Vika and Pierre shrank back as the huge beast passed near them. When it reached Kelru it stopped, prodding his chest with its nose. It wore a saddle, with a couple of leather packs slung up behind, but no other harness.

The creature's enormous head turned, and it regarded Vika and Pierre from two meters away. She drew back, rigid, as it bared its teeth and snorted. Strong jaws, a carnivore's teeth, mad cinnamon eyes. She heard her own breathing, shallow and quick. She could not look away from its eyes.

Then Ganarh raised his left arm toward the gathering clouds and shouted a command. The bowmen moved closer. Vika saw Kelru tense, his hand moving to the empty leather sheath where his knife had been. Instinctively she tensed, too.

But Ganarh turned away, bent and picked up Kelru's bow from the mud. He raised his fist again and called, "*Nata'akhanai!*" Then he swept his arm forward, down the slope, and strode off. His bowmen followed, urging the humans and Kelru ahead of them on foot. The beast followed as well, close behind. The stubble on Vika's scalp prickled as its hot breath touched her. She had to hurry her steps to keep up with the tall aliens, and with Anke and Pierre.

The sun vanished behind darkening clouds, and a chill rose from the damp ground. Vika chose her footing carefully. The unmortared stone wall, chest-high to her, was old, crumbling under her hands, scraping her as she climbed unsteadily over it with a boost from Pierre. A rutted, muddy track led away through more trees, toward the cluster of buildings. Something gave voice in the trees along the path, a harsh *krek-krek-krek*. She heard little noises in the thick scrub as they passed: *chip-pop, chip-pop*.

As they walked she heard the wind in the trees, the hissing breath of Kelru's beast close behind, the solid thump as its lashing tail struck the ground. She glanced back at it, and its eyes glittered at her, its black tongue lolling. Then Kelru moved up beside her, and spoke to the beast behind them. "*Thonn. Uvekh'a.*" And the creature dropped a little farther behind. Vika took a slow breath of relief and smiled up at Kelru.

And he looked at her sharply, the fur on his neck rising. Oh. She had bared her teeth at him. She covered her mouth with her hand, and he snorted and moved away.

Pierre looked back at her, his expression a warning. Ahead, in the deepening gloom, a stone wall loomed. Shelter—that was good, she could smell a storm coming—but what else waited there? A narrow gate opened, and Ganarh strode through. Pierre and Anke followed, then Vika and Kelru. Now she smelled stone, manure, woodsmoke—smells almost familiar, but so strong after subjective months on shipboard that they seemed artificial.

They stopped in the center of a small, muddy courtyard. Vika looked around. Walls of yellow stone, walls of weathered wood loomed, broken by a few narrow vertical windows. Aliens were closing a heavy, iron-bound wooden gate behind them. Before them was another such gate. Ganarh walked up to it and spoke in a low voice.

Now the second gate opened slightly, and someone came out. Two of the aliens, smaller than Kelru or Ganarh, empty-handed, completely unadorned. One said a few words to Ganarh.

He and his bowmen turned away and left through a side gate, taking Kelru and his riding animal with them. Kelru looked back intently as he moved off, and for a moment his eyes met Vika's. She felt a strange pang of worry, almost of loneliness. She hoped they would not harm Kelru, the only one of these beings to offer her his name.

Now the inner gate swung wide at last. "Here we go," Pierre muttered.

The two smaller aliens led the humans forward into another courtyard, narrower and deeper than the one outside. A third closed the gate behind them and barred it—barring Ganarh and the others out. Vika frowned.

Wooden buildings surrounded this inner courtyard, high, heavy-beamed, built at odd and precarious angles. They seemed to lean over her, casting shadows that might hide anything. The narrow windows showed no light. Far off, in the blackening sky to the south, thunder grumbled.

Their guides urged them up a flight of wooden stairs just too high to be easy for humans to climb. Pain stabbed through Vika's legs and back, long-unused muscles protesting.

At the top, she followed the others through a tall, arched door. Inside, shivering with chill and nerves, she looked around, forcing herself to observe. The room was an uneven rectangle with a low beamed ceiling, neat and whitewashed. The windows let in almost no light; a fire blazed in a low-arched alcove of rough yellow brick. There was no furniture but a low table near the fire. The wooden floor around it was scattered with thick-furred animal hides.

Then a strong, cool hand clamped Vika's wrist. The larger of the two aliens tugged her closer to the fire. The other appeared beside them, holding a small bowl of brown glazed clay. And then drew a knife, a slender, straight blade, and handed it to Vika's captor.

Vika took a sharp breath in reflexive fear, but she kept still. She said, steadily, "It's all right. Don't move. I think they only—" And she gasped as the knife gashed the side of her right hand.

The grip on her wrist stayed steady. Vika's blood dribbled into the bowl. She looked away from it, looked up at the alien who had cut her. The dark, wide-pupiled eyes turned from the bowl to Vika, met her look. Then the alien released her.

Vika backed toward the other humans, holding part of her sleeve wadded against the cut. "Are they going to drink it?" Anke sounded sick. Vika swallowed, her throat dry.

The aliens did not drink the blood. They studied it in the light from a window, sniffed it carefully. Finally the smaller one spoke a word to the other, then pitched the blood into the fire, where it spluttered and steamed.

Vika pressed the wadded cloth harder against her cut. The blade had been so sharp she had barely felt it, but now the wound throbbed with her quick heartbeat.

Anke said suddenly, "I think these two are female."

Vika took a closer look at their hosts. It could be true: they had teats, so small that their dense fur almost hid them—four, in two rows. Call them female, then—which meant she had probably guessed right about Kelru.

The larger alien stared at them, then spoke a sharp sentence. The other lit a small, sooty-globed oil lamp and, carrying it, led them out another doorway, up one more flight of steep stairs, to a narrow, arched door. She pulled it open and stood aside. Vika followed the others in. This was another asymmetrical room, musty-smelling, with a small unlit fireplace in the center of the longest wall, opposite two narrow windows. Two rough beds covered most of the floor—wide, shallow boxes holding sack mattresses. By the empty hearth stood a low table. Thunder rumbled, nearer and louder.

Then the alien female gripped Anke by the arm and started for the door. Caught off balance, Anke stumbled after her. "Pierre!" She sounded more angry than frightened. But before Vika could move, before Pierre could reach the door, Anke was gone. The door closed heavily behind her. Then Vika heard the grating sound of metal sliding on metal, and a crash as the bar slid home.

THREE

Pierre flung himself against the door an instant too late. The heavy timbers barely shifted, firm against the bar outside. He was locked in. Trapped. And his team—his remnant of a team—was divided.

What else did you expect? The thought was bitter, familiar. He pushed it aside. No time for despair. *Tend to your team.* He spread his hands against the rough wood of the door, gathering his strength, and turned.

Vika was watching him, her dark face still, her cut hand curled against her chest. He sighed inwardly. With forced gentleness he said, "They won't harm her, Vika."

"You don't know that."

"But there is nothing either of us can do," Pierre said. "Unless—" He went to one of the windows, ran his hands along the frame. The window was narrow, glazed with thick, rippled glass set in small square panes, now spattered with the rain that had just begun to fall. Through it he saw only vague dark shapes, walls or other buildings. The window was firmly set in its frame, and the metal strips between the panes formed a tough, dense grid. As Vika joined him there he said, "It's not made to open. And we can't break this."

She frowned. "Even if we could, they'd only be angry. And we need their help, Pierre."

He studied her as she stood looking out at the fading light. Her chin high, her expression remote. Did she feel the same secret relief as he—that for now they had no more choices? They would *have* to rest....

Then the door rattled open again. Pierre turned to face it, hopeful—but it was not Anke. One of the female guards stepped into the room, knife at the ready. Then a second female entered, calmly. Tall, like all of these people, and long-boned, with fur so pale it was almost white. She did not meet their eyes. She carried a tray with a pile of what looked like bread, and two bowls. Pierre swallowed hard as the scent reached him: meat in hot broth, with a scent of some resinous herb. The alien bent, set the tray on the low table, then straightened and left with the guard. They heard the bar close again.

The warm aroma filled the room. In spite of his disappointment, his worry for Anke, Pierre felt his mouth watering—once again, his body stronger than his will. The aliens had kept the packs Anke brought from the lander, so they had no rations of their own. Vika went to the table and knelt there on the rough wooden floor beside it. Pierre hesitated, then joined her.

The bowls held a kind of stew, thick with rubbery chunks of meat. Pierre picked up a bowl and one of the two carved wooden spoons. Once again he was glad that he was not Gaian, not of the Covenant. His family had supplemented their minimal income, dissidents' subsistence, with illegal hunting in the dying forests near their village. That meat had kept them from hunger for much of the year. He ate easily, but noticed Vika picking through the stew to avoid the meat. He wondered, with brief irritation, when she would realize that Gaian squeamishness had no place here.

The food was good, with the rich, real taste Pierre remembered from Earth. The stew was filled out with mealy yellow tubers and thin threads of cooked greens; the flat rounds of hard, coarse bread were chewy and substantial.

By unspoken agreement they left some of the food for Anke. By the time their share was gone, it was dark. There was no lamp, and no wood for the hearth. No sign or sound of any other being near this room. Rain drummed on the glass of the windows, and the walls gave off a deepening chill. After a silence Pierre said quietly, "Vika, get some sleep. I'll take first watch."

He saw Vika hesitate. Then she loosened the belt of her coverall and lay down one of the beds. Straw crackled under her as she covered herself with one of the rough-woven brown blankets, turned over with her back to him. And lay still.

Pierre closed his eyes. *Thank God.* He had reached the last thread of his strength.

He rubbed his hands together to warm them, took a breath of the chill air. A warm summer night for this world, no doubt. He took a blanket from the empty bed, wrapped it around himself, and settled on the wooden floor against the wall opposite the door. He waited, and listened, until Vika's slow breathing assured him she was asleep.

Then he rose to his knees soundlessly and turned to the wall. He knotted his hands together against it, and rested his forehead on them, feeling them tremble as his whole body trembled. He tried again to pray, as he had tried every night on the ship, every night since this nightmare began. But again he could not overcome the feeling that God was too far away to hear him. No. Pierre was too far away. He had come too far out among the cold stars, into the night where faceless things waited and watched. And they had found him. He and the others had been helpless against them. As Earth would be helpless—and the children of Earth.

At that thought he remembered. His hands remembered the dark silk of his son's hair; he remembered carrying him to bed, his warm slumbering weight. The last time he had seen Thierry, though he had not known it then. Gabrielle, smiling politely as she let him out—she had known.

He remembered the last days in Denver before the team left for the Moon, to join their ship in lunar orbit. Waiting for Gabrielle to bring their son to see him off. Waiting, waiting.... And when he had called her personal code—

Gabrielle's face appeared, her eyes narrowed. "What do you want?"

"Where are you? Where is Thierry?"

He saw her firm jaw tighten. "I won't tell you."

Anger, and the first sick comprehension. "Gabrielle, I leave tomorrow! I have the legal right to see him."

She shrugged. "Then find a lawyer."

He kept his expression steady. "Gabrielle. Please!"

She did not look at him. "You chose to leave Earth."

"You left me first," Pierre said hotly.

"For a man who loves Thierry," she said. "Who gives him what a father gives."

"I am his father." Pierre's voice shook. "I was there whenever training allowed it. Whenever you allowed it."

"Thierry is five years old," she said. "In a year or two he'll forget you entirely—if I protect him now." She looked straight at Pierre. "If you really cared for him, that is what you would wish for him, too."

"But when he grows up, he'll ask who I was," Pierre said. Anger strengthened his voice. "My name is on his genetic record. He'll want to remember me. And he will hate you for this."

"Perhaps," she said. "Or perhaps you'll be just a name to him. A man who didn't love him enough to stay and watch him grow up."

"I signed onto the team after you left me," Pierre said. "He was only a baby. I wanted to hurt you, not him. I didn't know." He could not keep the anguish from his voice. "I didn't know what he would mean to me."

"That was a mistake," Gabrielle said calmly. "And not your only one. Goodbye, Pierre. I'm canceling this code." And she was gone.

In his silent prison Pierre sank down until he was sitting on the cold wood floor. Gabrielle had emptied him. She had left him only rage. Time and the mercy of God had eased that; but now Pierre had nothing left. Nothing but the mission. He sat with his eyes open, staring into the darkness. To make that loss, all their losses have any meaning at all, the mission must succeed.

While he had slept in darkness, only a year ago, *they* had looked down at him. But they had chosen to leave him alive. And Anke, who had taken him to her bed a few times in the last weeks before launch—who had no use for him now, but still haunted his dreams. So like Gabrielle in her hard, clear thought, her careless beauty, her mercilessness.

And they had left Vika, too—who was so young. Too young—barely twenty-five. He could just see her, a small dark shape, quiet in her blankets. Though she hid it well, she must surely be frightened—and he did not know what comfort he could offer her. *Or anyone.*

The straw of her bed rustled as she turned restlessly. Pierre sighed and leaned his head back against the wall.

It was then that he heard it—a high, sliding wail, not far away. A voice. A wavering chant, rising to a shriek, like Ganarh's brief call earlier today. But this went on and on. It paused, then began again—the same sequence of notes, the same timing. Alien music? But it was too loud, too piercing. It paused again. He saw Vika sit up.

Then he heard a new voice—faint, distant—take up the same chant. Far off in the night. It repeated the notes twice, then faded into silence.

"They're spreading the news." Vika's voice was steady. "Toward the city, I think."

Pierre did not answer. Soon he heard her lie down again.

He kept his breathing steady, but it took all his strength. On Earth, he had thought this mission would be a worthy challenge—that the work he could do as part of the team would benefit them all.

But now he had a much harder task, one he had not trained for. Now he wanted to cry out against God, against the universe: *unfair, unfair—*

He should never have come. He should have stayed with his son. Kept his son safe for as long as hope lasted, to protect what there might be of his future, on a world that was dying.

Yet now he must lead Anke and Vika in carrying out their mission. Three people, ill-assorted, ill-prepared to carry the whole mission on their shoulders— It might well end in failure, as it had begun. Failure, disaster, death—and against those, only their best effort. And the blind hope of their hearts.

It would have to be enough.

Pierre tightened his hands, caught his breath, and began again to pray silently. Empty words cast into emptiness. He was alone.

Muffled sounds outside the door woke Pierre at dawn. He raised himself on an elbow and scrubbed the sleep from his eyes. *Cold.* The windows showed only the featureless gray of a foggy morning. Vika, on watch, stood at one of the windows, a blanket wrapped over her coverall.

The bar shot back with a clank, and Pierre was on his feet before the echo died. Vika turned as the door swung open. A muscular, gray-furred alien female came in. Leading Anke by the arm.

Pierre's breath left him for a moment. "Anke. Thank God." He went to meet her, took her cold hands in his. One was roughly bandaged. "Are you hurt?"

"No," she said quietly.

Vika looked at her with concern. "What happened?"

Anke shook her head. "An examination, that was all. They took the blood, then looked me over, and they argued with each other. Watching me the whole time. There was a bench with some kind of fur on it. I fell asleep."

"So perhaps they mean us no harm," Pierre said.

Anke was looking beyond Pierre. "Though now it seems they want *you*."

It was true. The big red-furred alien was gesturing him toward the door.

No point in hesitating; she was certainly large enough to compel him. "I'll go," he said harshly. "Anke, get some rest."

"When I need it," she said evenly. "Look after yourself, Pierre."

Still wearing the rumpled coveralls he had put on in orbit more than a day before, Pierre preceded his guard down the stairs, then out into the courtyard. There, two more females fell in behind them, heavy sticks ready in their hands.

Pierre looked all around as he walked. The thick, clammy morning mist shrouded everything, muffled all sounds. Trickles of water ran down the gray wooden walls, greasy-looking in the weak, cold light. No other aliens were about.

His guards took him through a passage under a building and into another courtyard, a loosely arranged garden filled with clumps of stiff, lacy plants, some with small wan flowers. They mounted more high steps and passed through a high, square double doorway.

The room beyond was large, and full of aliens. Like the ones he had seen yesterday, they were unclothed, although most wore belts with pouches or pockets. They stirred as Pierre came in; a few even cried out, strange wailing exclamations. The voices were baritone, tenor, no higher. The sound echoed in the hard, chilly room, with its high ceiling. He smelled old wood, and dust, and damp fur.

Pierre looked around, seeking Kelru. He did not see him, or Ganarh. At the far end of the room, in an angled alcove, a great hearth stood empty, swept clean. A heavy iron rack of oil lamps, unlit, hung from a ceiling beam. Narrow windows lined one of the long walls. The other walls were plaster, covered with flaking murals in faded red and blue and green. The place felt old—built centuries before the attack, maybe. He tried to make sense of the jumble of images, the strange depiction of perspective. Stiffly posed aliens holding unidentifiable objects. Spiky masses of vegetation. And, many times over, a sun emblem—plain as a child's drawing, a circle with eight rays.

A small, dark-furred female moved forward to meet him. And she wore clothing, the first Pierre had seen—a plain sleeveless shift or robe of dull green cloth. She guided him to face a bench that stood alone in the center of the room. Seated on it was another female, her fur reddish but touched with gray on her face and above her eyes. Old, then. She was broad-shouldered and substantial. Her sleeveless robe was deep green, unbelted, and covered her to her ankles. She sat with her big hands resting on the thick head of an elaborately carved stick, which looked to him like something ceremonial, not a necessity. Her authority was palpable; every eye in the room was on her.

She looked him over for a moment, her red-gold eyes unreadable. Then she thumped her chest with one hand and said, *"Kh'doeh sennoeth Dethun."*

But when Pierre repeated Dethun's name, she bared her teeth, and the room went still. Pierre blinked. The dark-furred female nudged him and hissed, *"Dethun khesit."* Obediently Pierre repeated the name and the other word—a title, an honorific?—and Dethun seemed satisfied. She spoke in her own language, then stopped, as if waiting for a reply. When none came, she turned to the other aliens and spoke several times, receiving brief answers.

She turned to Pierre and spoke again—several short sentences, rapping her stick ceremonially on the floor after each. Then she rose to her feet—she was taller than Pierre—and strode from the room, carrying the stick lightly in one hand.

When the door closed behind her, a hum of voices rose. Some of the aliens hung back, still watching, but others closed in around Pierre. They seemed curious, amazed, tentative. Perhaps their examination of Anke had removed some of their fear.

But there were other tests to come. Three or four aliens led him to an alcove in which a tall window stood open to the chilly morning light and air. He smelled conifers, heard them rustling in the steady wind, and a vivid memory of his childhood home stabbed through him.

In the light, the aliens carried out what seemed like a physical examination. They began with the same test they had performed on Vika. He managed not to wince. When they were satisfied with his blood—whatever it was they were looking for—they washed the cut and bound it up carefully.

They measured him against a marked stick, prodded his limbs, peered into his eyes. Pierre bore it stolidly. The aliens listened to his chest with cones of polished wood, felt his pulse in many places with sober attention, looked at his teeth and into his ears. Yet always they were courteous.

Until they undressed him. They went still then, staring at his naked body, their eyes narrowed. Their ears were laid back flat, their teeth bared. Pierre looked from one to the other.

One of the examiners spoke in a tight, trembling voice. He heard a stir behind him, and turned, his heart racing. Some of the alien females were hurrying from the room. Then two of the large females with sticks appeared in the doorway. Staring at him. Hastily he picked up his coverall and dressed again, and his examiners made no objection; they had stepped away from him.

The outer door opened, and Dethun strode in, gripping her heavy, metal-shod stick like a weapon. She gave Pierre a long, piercing look, her ears laid back flat. Then she said coldly, "*V'elda't aru*." The stick thumped once on the floor. Immediately, two big females caught Pierre by the arms and twisted him around to face Dethun. She advanced on him, her teeth bared, and raised her stick. He met her eyes, and saw his death there. He tried to wrench away to lessen the blow, but they held him too strongly. A white explosion of pain, and then nothing.

FOUR

n the room that was their prison, Vika stood across from the door, waiting, listening. Night was falling. Anke sprawled on one of the beds, her eyes closed. Twice, in morning and evening, that door had opened; both times it had been a woman bringing food and water. Each time Vika's hope had diminished a little. If they'd still had their comm implants—

"Vika." Anke's voice was quiet. "You need to be realistic. Something's happened to Pierre."

"He'll come back," Vika said.

"We need to make our own plans," Anke said. "Go ahead without him."

Vika turned and faced her. "At the start of training, I swore an oath. And so did you. Freely and in clear conscience, that's what we said."

And Anke sat up. "I did not take the oath freely," she said flatly.

Now that had to be a lie. Vika could not read Anke's expression in the deepening shadows. "Dr. Kozlov always talked about how eager you were to join the team. After all your artifact studies, your work on those foundation carvings, he said—"

"He lied," Anke said. "I was forced to join."

"But that's not possible," Vika said, frowning. "No one is compelled. It's in the Covenant—you *can't* be compelled."

"I was compelled," Anke said. "I had my alien studies work at the institute in Denver—friends, a life— But if I'd refused this mission, Dr.

Kozlov's friends in TFE Command would have posted me down from Denver. Right out of the Task Force for Exploration, for good. They made that clear. No more teaching, no data, no access to artifacts."

Vika stared at her, startled. "Why would they have to threaten you? There were waiting lists for all the teams. Dr. Kozlov could have gotten—"

"No." Anke's face was unreadable. "There was no one with my knowledge. He wanted *me* on this mission. And he always got what he wanted. He manipulated people. Including you."

Vika sat down on the edge of her bed, facing Anke. "That isn't true." She tried to sound calm.

"And you let him. Kozlov liked followers. He built himself a whole team of followers. That's why we're in trouble now. And why you can't even see it."

Vika knitted her hands together and looked down at them. "I'm here," she said curtly. "I'm going to do the best I can, whether or not you care to help." She looked up at the shadow that was Anke. "If Pierre is alive, I'll find him. If he's dead, then—I'll learn to talk to the people here, and I'll go on from there."

"So you still believe in Kozlov's master plan." The contempt in Anke's voice was clear.

Vika rose and walked to the table, poured herself some water, and drank it slowly, tilting her head back, her eyes closed. She felt her heart slowing. As she had been taught, she visualized the aggressor biochemicals clearing from her blood. "I'm going to bed."

No answer.

Vika weighed the water jug in her hand. It had been refilled every mealtime so far; there was water to spare. So she filled her bowl again, took off her coverall, and washed herself as well as she could with sparing handfuls of cold water. Her whole body itched—hair growing in again. She hung the coverall over the bench to air out and climbed into her bed. Huddled down in the coarse blankets, she slid her icy hands into her armpits to warm them.

Anke still didn't move. The room was so quiet that Vika could hear the other woman's breathing. From time to time her breath caught. It almost sounded as if she were crying, silently.

But the way between them was closed. Anke had closed it.

Vika lay still and tried to go to sleep. It took a long time.

Pierre struggled in a nightmare of cold sleep: His arms and legs heavy, aching with cold. Square blue lights hovering. An inhuman voice, silver ice hissing in his ear. Isamu's corpse glistening, the cuts fresh. Cryofluid a greenish fog that half-obscured him.

Pierre woke with a gasp. Darkness and cold— He tried to sit up. The pain in his skull, instant, lancing, forced him down again. He had to close his eyes, breathe carefully, to keep from vomiting.

Then a deep voice spoke words he did not understand, and a cool, strong hand touched his chest. Fighting back panic, he opened his eyes. Nothing. Was he blind? He tried to move his eyes, tried to see something, anything.

There. A dark-blue glimmer, a distorted square above him. Cold, like the blue lights. Fright made him choke, then cough retchingly. Black pain bloomed in his head.

The cool hands raised him, supported him sitting upright. Gently they turned his face away from the light, helped him lean forward while he vomited helplessly. When it was over he felt a little better, the pain duller. The deep voice spoke again. "*Thu'arrd.*"

"I don't understand," Pierre said, in French, because it did not matter. Something hard and cool brushed his chin, and when he raised his shaking hands he found it was a drinking bowl. He sipped cautiously. The water was so bitterly cold that his throat ached, swallowing—so cold it had splinters of ice in it. But it cleared his head a little.

He realized he was with one of the aliens. In a room, a very cold room, at night. Stiff dried plants crackled under him when he moved. They had a pungent, dusty scent like old dried sage. He was wrapped in a thick, thorn-coarse blanket that smelled like greasy wool. And he could see more clearly now: the square angle of light high above was a window, unglazed, and the blueness through it the frosty stars. He touched one of the arms supporting him. His fingers sank into short, dense fur.

At the touch, his helper lowered him to the straw again. Pierre could just make out a dark shape against the starlight, a head bent down to study him, ears erect, flicking slowly, contemplatively.

With careful fingers Pierre felt the sticky lump over his ear. It itched more than it hurt. He rubbed his stubbly face and coughed again. Then unsteadily he touched his chest with one hand. "Pierre," he said, his voice thick and raw.

"Kelru," the deep voice answered.

Kelru. The one who had met them when they landed. Who had been taken away under guard when they arrived at this place. If that was where they still were.

Anke and Vika must be terrified, alone, not knowing where he was, whether he was even alive. But there was nothing he could do now. The pain in his head pulsed whitely, and his eyes watered.

He should not sleep, not with a head injury. But he was so tired. And there was nothing he could do now.... He sighed, shifted uncomfortably on the straw, and settled back to rest.

And the alien laid his hand lightly on Pierre's chest. Pierre's last clear thought was to realize, sleepily, that Kelru must want to be sure that he was alive. That was comforting, because it meant Kelru did not want to kill him. It was good to know that *someone* didn't.

Long past dawn, the stranger still slept. Kelru watched him patiently. The stranger's breathing was steady, and his odd, quick little heartbeat pattered away under Kelru's palm. But it was disturbing that he had not awakened again, so late in the day.

And it *was* late. Dethun was letting Kelru wait, hoping he would worry. He'd expected that; she was showing her teeth. Leaving him penned up with one of the strangers—a sick one, at that. Perhaps she thought it would help her cause in Kheosseth if she inconvenienced or offended Kelru.

He scratched his neck. Looking at the stranger made him itch. Why, by the Old Man's Eye, had the strangers shaved their fur off before they came here? To look even uglier?

His ears flicked back as he studied Pierre. A truly odd name, not one a person could say properly.... These creatures hardly needed help looking ugly. Puny things with high voices. Dish faces and no noses at all. Extra fingers. Anything born like that among the Anokothu would not have drawn its second breath.

And Pierre's family—the two women. Obviously his mates, as he lived with them freely. A new family just beginning usually included only one woman. An old family dying might be the other way. But these people were young, Kelru would set his palm to that. He snorted. It was an odd thing. And somehow he guessed that Pierre would not wish to discuss it.

Yet Kelru had watched them, and he was sure of one thing at least—these strangers were *people*. Thinking, speaking, feeling people.

Kelru's ears twitched with anticipation. The arguments this winter were going to be fine. Were the Anokothu wrong about that as well? Was there, after all, no single ordained form for a person—for a being with breath, and reason, and a place in the order of life?

The Destroyers had reason, the stories said, but not breath. No one had seen them, not in living memory. The survivors of their coming had left only crude pictures and descriptions. Still, even Dethun must know that these strangers were not Destroyers. Their blood was red like a person's blood, and they had breath. And this one kept his form even when he slept.

Kelru sniffed. Yes, many excellent arguments were ahead. Perhaps even duels. He wondered what Dethun thought of the stranger women. Of all of this. Her tidy world was all spilled and tangled, and there was no one she could command to put it right. No records to consult for guidance; no custom, no tradition for *this*. Kelru's lips lifted from his teeth in half-animal pleasure at the thought of Dethun shaken, disturbed, by anything.

At midday, as the sisterhold was settling to sleep through the heat, Ganarh himself came for them, with a couple of his guardsmen. Dethun's summons at last. Ganarh's mouth was shut tight as a firecone, but Kelru knew what this meant. He would be freed—after a lecture from Dethun.

And the stranger? Well. No sense in wondering, when time would bring the answer. Most likely they would kill him. Unfortunate, but as a male, Pierre threatened Dethun's ordered refuge far more than his two mates did.

When Kelru roused him, the stranger seemed confused—he wanted to stay wrapped in his blanket. As if he could be cold in summer! The blanket made him look even more like a huge, misshapen infant. Kelru got it away from him, but then Pierre shivered until they reached the stifling heat of the outer courtyard, airless between two stone walls.

It was a short walk to Dethun's chosen meeting place. Kelru knew her—he had known she would have one, in spite of the sisterhold's laws against admitting outside men within the walls. And he had known she would choose this time, when almost everyone was resting indoors. She liked her secrets.

He remembered when she had been his mother. She'd kept secrets even then, from him, and from his fathers....

They passed a rack of long hanks of woolen yarn, dull red and damp, the fresh dye pungent in the heat. And beyond it a stack of bales of woven cloth, ready for market. There must be a pack train due soon. An old dyer, her silver fur fantastically stained, straightened

from one of the piles to watch Pierre go by. Kelru pricked his ears at
her politely. "Ugly, isn't he, Aunt?"

She hissed and turned away, and Ganarh bared his teeth. Kelru
did not risk speech again.

The door in the wall was hidden in a dark corner, the passage
beyond it narrow and low. Kelru felt a moment of shock as he realized
that they had turned inward—that they were now within the *inner*
wall. The wall no man, not even Ganarh and the other male guards,
should ever pass.

The passage led to a small room with no windows and one other
door. Waiting there in the heat, in the light of a single lamp, were the
stranger females. And another, one of Kelru's own people. A woman,
and young. He quickly turned his eyes away from her, but he could
scent her, a fresh clean smell like *esketh* or some other mountain herb.
And in that glance he had seen she was small, dark-furred like a South
Coast woman, with the bright eyes that meant a strong will.

Clearly Dethun set many rules aside in this room. Of course this
woman was nowhere near the time of the Red Mind, or she would not
be here. She was no threat to his peace, or he to hers. But the insult to
her, under Dethun's orders....

And now Pierre had started toward the two women! Who stood
staring at him out of their strange flat eyes. "No, no," Kelru said,
annoyed, and dragged him away from them. By the Eye, were the
females going into whatever passed for the Red Mind in their kind?
The stranger needed some lessons in formal restraint. Until then Kelru
would sit on him, if that was required.

No, Pierre settled back into his place, and only just in time—the
door opened, letting in a splash of harsh sunlight, and Dethun came in.

Everyone stood up. Ganarh stepped forward into the room
and took up his place at Dethun's left, facing Kelru and Pierre. His
knife gleamed in his scarred left hand. Kelru knew just how lovingly
sharpened it would be.

Kelru looked at his mother, who did not look at him. She had aged—she was toughened, dried. He counted the years—five now since he had last seen her. That bitter meeting in Kheosseth, where for the last time he refused to take service with her. Where she had named him as unfamilied, purposeless. A follower, because he would not follow *her*.

He had forgotten, in those years, the physical impact of her presence. Aged, yes. But, tall for a woman, and heavier than ever, she carried pride and power in every line of her body. Now she met his eyes and said, "Kelru," in her rich familiar voice. She had never liked his man-name. She had never liked anything he chose for himself.

Now she stretched out her left hand toward him, palm down. Courtesy demanded that he respond, and prudence as well—all power in this room, in this sisterhold, was hers. And Ganarh was her chief weapon, ready and sharp. Kelru stepped forward and crouched, though not so low that she could touch the back of his neck. She did not try to claim that dominance; she merely touched his shoulder, and he rose and stepped back.

Dethun turned at once to Pierre, who seemed to try to pull himself upright. She looked him up and down. "What have you learned about this?" she asked Kelru.

"Only that his name is Pierre," Kelru said, struggling a little with the name.

"He came from the sky. He's from the Destroyers," Dethun said. Dethun's young attendant stirred uneasily, but she did not speak. Dethun went on, "The females I can study, and perhaps find a use for. But this one is male. Grotesque, they say. And I permitted him inside the sisterhold, among the women here."

Kelru could see where this was heading. And also—well, he liked Pierre. "He's no threat to a woman of our people."

"That doesn't matter," Dethun said. "I made a vow to the women under my care, that they would have peace here. This...man made me false to them."

"A pity," Kelru said. "Turn him out, then. With me."

Her ears went flat. "No. I will not have such a thing go free where it can do harm to anyone."

"You aren't responsible for anyone outside these walls." As head of the Council of Lady Mothers, she had influence—a great deal of it—but no direct power except within Thanen River sisterhold.

"But we are inside them now," Dethun said. "Again, no." She turned to her right. "Ganarh," she said calmly, "kill it."

The young woman drew in a hissing breath. Kelru stared at Dethun, shocked. "Not here," he protested. "Not in front of his bondmates."

"It will do them no harm to understand my power," Dethun said.

Ganarh's men took hold of Pierre, who struggled in their grip. Though Kelru saw that he kept his eyes steady on Ganarh—maybe he *was* more than a boy. Ganarh stepped forward, looking pleased, his knife glinting in the lamplight.

Kelru let his ears go flat, let his fur rise. Then he stepped forward, between Ganarh and the stranger. He took Pierre's left hand in his own. Pierre looked up at him, his expression impossible to read. Kelru said, "By blood shared and a shared prison, by water shared and common food, I claim this man as a brother." He embraced Pierre lightly, touching his face to one shoulder, then the other.

Dethun cried out angrily, "No! I forbid this!" The younger woman raised her head and stared at Kelru, her dark eyes gleaming strangely.

"To kill him is wrong choosing, Dethun," Kelru said. "These people have knowledge we've lost. What this one knows might bring us all back to plenty and peace, to the days before the Destroyers."

"Or wake the Destroyers and bring them down on us again," Dethun said.

"The Destroyers have slept for many sixty-fours of years," Kelru said. "It's done. I take him as I said. Keep the women, for now. But my friends and I will help Pierre petition Vakhar for their release." *You want to use them for your political gain. To frighten the Council, to strengthen the arguments of your Anokothu faction—to break the balance. Even Vakhar will see that.*

"Vakhar will rule as I ruled, and more," Dethun said. "He'll order them all to be killed, and their skyship destroyed, and all they have touched to be burned."

"He may," Kelru said, spreading his hand palm-down in the gesture that meant *But I think not.* "For now, though, as you cannot kill my brother, who is your son—" he saw her eyes narrow at that—"you must free us both."

Dethun bent her head as if in thought. Then raised her hands to her face and clawed herself, carefully, slowly—the gesture of deep and formal grief. Blood ran quickly over her reddish-brown fur. Kelru took a deep breath. Grief—because he, too, would now die? But he kept his eyes steadily on hers.

She spoke in a pain-tight rasp. "Do as you've chosen," she said. "Follow the scent that has caught you. It will take you to your death."

"And free your family name from the son who shames it," Kelru said. "I cannot begrudge you that."

Dethun turned to Ganarh. "They are to go," she said. "With exactly what they brought, no more." Her voice rose. "They are to go *now.*" Blood dripped from her cheeks, staining the green shift. The smell filled Kelru's nostrils, fed his anger.

Ganarh slowly sheathed his knife, his eyes on Kelru. His men let go of Pierre and stepped back. Kelru had to catch Pierre's arm as he swayed on his feet. He had a new smell to him, sharp and salty, and his naked face was wet.

"Prepare for their leaving," Dethun said to Ganarh, who ducked his head again and left, followed by the two guards. Dethun gave Kelru and Pierre a last bitter look, then whirled and went out through the far door. The other woman followed, shooing the strangers along ahead of her. The little creatures looked back at Pierre, their flat eyes wide, piping in their high childlike voices. They sounded distressed. Kelru wondered if they guessed what had just happened. If they had yet begun to understand Dethun's power, which now held them fast.

He looked back along the passage. *His* way to freedom was open.

He would take it.

Kelru kept his hold on Pierre until they were out in the courtyard again, in the smothering, trapped heat. His mind was full of plans, and other thoughts less rational. Dethun's rage, her humiliation—so great that she had almost given words to it, set her honor to it—that thought filled him with an almost shameful satisfaction, a child's satisfaction—touched with grim humor.

Yet he'd set his own honor to something this day, and now he would have to fulfill it. He slowed his steps to ease Pierre. There was so much the stranger did not understand—it would be harder than teaching a half-grown boy just turned out of his birth home. Pierre's mind was a man's, clearly. But full of wrong thinking, wrong actions. Wrong teaching. It did not follow that he was dishonorable. But his ignorance was certainly offensive.

Kelru's ears flicked forward in a smile. Let Pierre learn to speak as people did, and then a few eightdays' teaching would set that right. Kelru would see to it.

When they came in sight of the gate, Kelru's heart went light within him, like a spark taking to the wind. Ganarh had followed Dethun's orders. His great beast Thonn stood there, one of Ganarh's men settling his saddle, another slinging Kelru's packs and his bow behind. As the men stepped back, Thonn raised his shaggy dun-gray head and snorted at Kelru's scent.

"I'm pleased to smell you, too, cousin," Kelru said and went to him, sniffing with laughter as Thonn stretched his mouth in a yawn of pleasure. Shreds of meat were caught between the beast's teeth—so they'd fed him. Absently Kelru picked the meat out with his claws and ate it. Thonn's black tongue caressed him, and the fire-heat of his breath. Kelru turned then and saw the stranger.

Pierre looked yellow, not brown, and the black prickles of new fur that covered his face and head stood out sharply. He stood well back from Thonn. One of Ganarh's men sniffed and prodded him forward. "Get this thing out of here," he said to Kelru.

Dethun's tame man, content to serve at a sisterhold, guarding the walls, never seeing Kheosseth or learning a new thing from one year's end to the next. "Manners," Kelru chided him. "Remember whose son he is."

The word had spread already, Kelru saw from the silent flickers of amusement among the men. Only Ganarh kept his ears still. "Half the day gone," he growled, "and no shelter on the road for unfamilied men. You'll sleep with wide eyes tonight."

"The *kharag* are lazy in this heat," Kelru said, letting his glance linger on Ganarh's men slouching in the shade. "The pack females find plenty of carrion. No need for the males to hunt." Ganarh bared his teeth, but said nothing.

Kelru turned away and checked his saddle-pack. His knife was inside it—he sheathed it at his side with relief. His old spare *thessach* was still there, too. In the day Pierre could wear it with the hood up to cover his strangeness, and it would serve him as a blanket at night.

Ah, and no one had touched his stock of dried meat and powdered tubers. They could sleep; they could eat. Satisfied, Kelru helped Pierre mount in front of Thonn's saddle, just behind the beast's shoulders, and then swung up behind him.

As they started forward through the gate, Kelru could feel Pierre's fear in the rigidity of his back. But he kept silent, and his breathing was so steady that he must be controlling it.

Kelru bared his teeth. Good enough, for a beginning.

FIVE

Thiain hurried to catch up with Lady Dethun's long strides as they crossed the courtyard toward the outer stairs to Dethun's refuge—her private study. "Khesit," she stammered. "Khesit, the strangers are still—"

"Put them back in their room," the Lady snarled over her shoulder. "They can rot there."

Thiain turned to the guards and gestured for them to follow the order, then, gathering up her long linen shift, clambered after Dethun up the wooden stairs to the cool, musty dimness of the study.

Dethun walked to the dark hearth, spun, and faced Thiain. The blood on her face— Thiain made herself look down. *Defeat always makes her dangerous.* "How may I serve you, Khesit?"

Dethun said nothing for a long time. Thiain heard her quick angry breaths begin to slow. *Her son has defied her. Before her own servants.* The one in whom she had once placed so much hope. Surely she would not forgive him for this.

"Kelru has the stranger Pierre," Dethun said in a low voice. "His to use with those friends of his in Kheosseth. His to set before Vakhar and argue that because this new thing has come to us, all our ways must change." She knotted her left hand into a fist, then with a clear effort, relaxed it again. "But he cannot use that creature until—"

"Until what, Khesit?"

"Until it can speak," Dethun said. "Until it can understand."

Thiain kept her eyes down. "Yes, Khesit."

"And we have its mates," Dethun went on, with more energy. "My son, an unfamilied man—he won't understand the importance of that."

"If it *is* important," Thiain said. "They're so strange." She moved to pour Dethun a cup of cool, watered wine, and set it on a table near the Lady's left hand. Then set herself, as always at times like this, to watch for the first hint of the next thing she might desire.

Dethun grimaced, but picked up the cup and sipped. "I don't know these creatures," she said. "But I *must* know them. Then I'll know how best to use them." She stood a moment, looking at Thiain. Then said, "And so you will teach them to speak."

Thiain shrank within herself. Face those *things*? Try to talk to them? "Khesit, I—"

"You are not afraid," Dethun said firmly. "You've never feared anything. You made your way here alone, in winter, when you were still a very young woman."

Thiain's belly ached at the memory. The merciless cold, and her body still raw and sore from the miscarriage. Not knowing whether the sisterhold would grant her refuge before her bondmates found her, forced her home to try again, fail again— *Of course I was afraid.* "Khesit, I don't have the skill to serve you in this way," she said woodenly.

Dethun sighed. "I wanted you to see the stranger women before I asked this of you. Otherwise—" she tilted her head— "Otherwise I would never have made you witness what just happened. I did it because I know that you *can* serve me in this way. You have the strength. It's why I wish you to be the woman who stands where I stand, after I am dead."

Thiain met her eyes. "May that season never come, Khesit."

Dethun's ears flicked back. "Will you do as I ask?"

Thiain hesitated. Then bowed her head. *This is my only refuge, and so you own me.* "Yes, Khesit." But she thought with revulsion of the strangers—their naked skins, their weak voices, their strange flat faces.

"Teach them to speak as we do. Then teach them to think as we do," Dethun said. "The male—he'll live among Kelru and his friends, the students and unfamilied men. They have their way of seeing the world, and the stranger will learn it. So we must teach his mates to see the world in *our* way. As Anokothu see."

Thiain raised her head and met Dethun's eyes. "You mean—teach them to fear."

Dethun's eyes narrowed slightly. Then her gaze lifted to the wall beyond her worktable, to the old hanging there that showed jagged fire striking down from the starry sky. Frozen figures of people running, falling, burning. "I mean for you to teach them of the Destroyers," she said roughly. "Show them the records of those days. Teach them the danger they bring to us by coming here. If we teach them properly, then *our* strangers will speak against Kelru's at the Council this winter." She turned and faced Thiain. "But they must know how to speak well."

Thiain looked down at her hands, calm again. *No weakness before the Lady.* If Thiain lost her position here, no other sisterhold would take her in—Dethun would see to that. "They will know, Khesit."

"Good," Dethun said. "Begin now."

Thiain looked up, startled. "Now, Khesit? It's time for me to sort your letters, and then order your supper."

"Those are no longer your tasks," Dethun said.

Thiain could not hide her shock. "But, Khesit!"

"Enough." Dethun's ears flicked back again—another flash of anger. "Gheren will do to serve me until this is done. I can trust only you with this." With both hands, she took firm hold of Thiain's shoulders. "Befriend them. Teach them to trust you. You may give them whatever they ask short of freedom. By this winter—" Her grip tightened. "By this winter, they must be mine."

Locked away again. Vika stood brooding at the window, blind to the brightness outside. They had seen Pierre—pale and weak, but alive. For a moment Vika had thought he was being freed, returned to them. And then Pierre had come within moments of being killed at Dethun's order.

She folded her arms tightly, as if that would contain her worry. To have Pierre forced away with Kelru was better than having him killed—but where was he being taken? Would they ever find out? Whatever she might think of him, he was one of only two other humans in the world. And the other—

"It was never going to work, you know," Anke said behind her.

Vika turned. Anke sat hunched on her bed, her datapad, dark, unregarded in one hand. "The mission isn't over," Vika said. "We still have to try."

"And yet the odds against us keep going up," Anke said. "I don't think we'll ever be allowed to leave this place."

The thought of a lifetime in this room, with only Anke to speak to, made Vika's chest feel hollow. She took a breath—and then heard the familiar rattle as the bar on the door was drawn aside.

Anke rose to her feet and moved to stand beside Vika, facing the door. When it opened, only one woman came in. The woman who had been at Dethun's side in that hidden room: unusually small, smaller than Anke, with dark fur and clear black eyes. She turned and closed the door. No one outside barred it. Then she turned back and faced them. Touched her chest lightly, and said, "Thiain."

Vika straightened, repeated the gesture, and said, "Vika." At a nudge, Anke, too, named herself.

Silence for a moment. Thiain did not move closer, or speak again. *She's afraid*, Vika thought. *And why wouldn't she be?* Vika bent and fumbled under her blanket and found the packet of pictures she had used with Kelru. Turned and faced Thiain, the image of herself held up. She saw the woman's dark eyes brighten with interest.

Vika took a breath. It was a beginning.

Vika liked the days that followed. Thiain came to them in the morning with their food, and remained all day. She always brought a bag with a collection of objects in it—kitchen tools, sewing tools, a distaff and spindle, fruits and vegetables—and they would examine them together, with Thiain showing their uses. Thiain would name them, and the two humans would repeat the words until they knew them. From there to simple verbs—*give, take, pick up, put down; eat, drink, spin.* Vika absorbed them quickly, Anke a little less so—but every word was a step toward what they needed: communication. And Thiain seemed willing to pursue this as far as she could.

Door. Fire. Open, closed, hot, cold, water. They learned that this world was called Shothef Erau: the home of the wind. Windhome. And the wind blew almost incessantly in this broad river plain. Vika did not try to teach Thiain any Standard words, or show her one of their datapads—too much, in this culture whose technology had been crushed only centuries ago. And she and Anke could not risk losing what little equipment they had.

After eight days, Thiain began to take them, with an escort of two female guards, around the courtyards, gardens, and kitchens. She showed them berries and tree fruit just beginning to ripen in the relative warmth of early summer; a strong woman hacking apart the carcass of one of the *ashanoi*, the herd animals; other women baking bread in ovens built of stacked stone. Everything had a name, or more than one. Vika made herself remember them, noted as many as she could remember and their meanings in her datapad every evening. Anke did the same.

In a distant corner of the complex, Thiain showed them a courtyard with pens where small woolly animals, *khaltenu* she called them, were jammed in together, crying out in voices eerily like those of frightened children. Strong-looking women lifted them out one by one, skillfully stripped away their matted brown and tan fleeces, then returned them to another pen where, eventually, other women herded them away.

Everyone worked. Even Thiain worked while she was in their room, deftly spinning fleece from a distaff into thin yarn for weaving, pausing every meter or so to wind it onto the weighted spindle by rolling it down her thigh. She did it smoothly and automatically, while she listened to them and as she spoke.

After sixteen days, Thiain brought them their packs, and Pierre's. Someone had rummaged through them, that was clear, but nothing was missing or damaged. Sealed into featureless metal boxes, the equipment was also undamaged. Vika did not open or use any of it in Thiain's presence. But she began to work, late at night, to analyze samples of the plant and animal parts that she was able to collect on their walks. Accumulating raw data she could not examine further, that was all, but it was a start. Every night's work uploaded to storage on the lander added to it.

And it kept her from worrying about Pierre. As soon as Vika could, she had asked Thiain where he had gone. But Thiain would not, or could not, answer.

Close to midsummer, Thiain appeared in the late evening when they were preparing for sleep and said, "Come with me. Both of you."

Vika looked uneasily at Anke. No reason to suspect danger, but—

"The Lady Dethun is waiting," Thiain said firmly. "Come with me. Now."

They made their way through the shadows to the courtyard where the great hall was, and then up steep wooden outdoor stairs to a room near the hall. Dethun waited inside, standing, her back to a dark hearth, at her side a worktable scattered with rolls of paper, a finely engraved cup made of dark metal, what looked like writing implements.

Dethun faced Vika and Anke. "Can you speak like people yet?"

"We can, Lady Dethun," Vika said carefully. Anke echoed her.

Dethun looked past them at Thiain. "Can they read?"

"A little, Khesit. Just words I write for them."

"They need more than that," Dethun said. "So I will provide it." She turned to Vika and Anke. "What do you know of our history?"

"Only what we have seen from studying your world from above," Anke said. "There was—much destruction, in the past. But you have begun to rebuild."

"We have rebuilt," Dethun said. "Rebuilt the way of life that we should never have gone beyond. You need to understand this. You need to learn."

Vika bowed her head as Thiain always did when the lady was instructing her. "Yes, Lady. What must we learn?"

"Why we live as we do," Dethun said. "In this land, in Windhome, we tear life from death's claws. We don't *hope*." She almost spat the word. "We survive by right thinking, and by joining together, and by obeying the Rules of Winter. Maybe you strangers have no enemies, need no rules. Maybe you're like my own people long ago, laughing over their toys, doing as they pleased—until the Destroyers came." She straightened, her ears still. "They will come to your own world, in their time."

Destroyers. The word chilled Vika: it carried inflections that meant it was not to be spoken lightly. Not a holy word: from all Vika had been able to learn, these people held nothing holy. Not a holy word, but a word of fear. "We do not know the Destroyers," Vika said uneasily. *The dreams—*

"Attend, then," Dethun said, with a gesture that Vika had learned was a call for silence, superior to inferior. "Many sixty-fours of years ago, while we lived in our foolish ease, the Destroyers came from the sky with thunder and fire—as you did. When they came, they destroyed our cities, some greater than eight Kheosseths. Those cities became holes in the ground, and then lakes whose water is still death to drink. All the people in the cities died. *All*. Those who lived elsewhere the Destroyers hunted in darkness, in the winter cold, from farm to farm and from valley to valley. They killed all they found—old women, and young men, and babies in their baskets." She spoke with passion and authority. "And then they were gone. It was many years before we came down out of the mountains, those of our ancestors who lived. And many of us still remember what our people learned then—that we must live humbly, and quietly, at the mercy of the Destroyers."

She moved to Vika, loomed over her, shadowing her from the lamplight. "I protect and shelter you both as I do Thiain," she said, "because I wish to understand you. And for you to understand us."

"We wish that as well," Vika said firmly. The Lady turned to Anke, who said, "I would like very much to learn more of that time."

Dethun studied them for a moment, then turned to Thiain. "Show them the records. Bring them here every afternoon. Sit with them, and teach them as they need. I want them to understand everything they see. *Everything*."

Vika and Anke looked at each other, and Vika was sure they were having the same thought. *These people are divided. She's trying to win our loyalty—to make us her tools.*

Thiain bent her head deeply, picked up one of the lamps burning on Dethun's worktable, and turned to Vika and Anke. "Follow me."

They left Dethun's study, not by the stairs, but through an inner door, which Thiain unlocked with a heavy iron key hanging from her belt. Dethun did not accompany them. Thiain opened the door and walked ahead of them. A larger room, windowless. High, and chilly, and smelling of—

Books. Paper books, old ones. She and Anke looked at each other in doubt, and wonder.

Thiain set the lamp on a table at the center of the room, and now that the light was steady, Vika saw high, wide walls of wooden niches on both sides of the room, and at the far end. Some were so small they could hold only a single roll of paper. Larger ones were crammed with rolls, or held neat stacks of paper that looked as if they might be bound together. Vika shivered. This was more than she had ever dreamed of finding here. "A library," she said softly in Standard.

"A big one," Anke said, and there was awe in her voice.

Thiain turned to them. "There is no better collection in the world. The Lady has brought records here from almost every sisterhold, and even copies of the entire collection from the Council archive at Kheosseth. She keeps them safe, studies them, and shares them with other scholars when they request it." Thiain faced them. "In this room," she said, clearly and carefully, "you will learn much. You will read much about us. I will help you, and answer your questions."

Vika glanced at Anke, whose eyes held a fierce light she had not seen in weeks. "Finally," Vika said.

And Anke, turning to Thiain, said in Thiain's tongue, "Thank you."

In the days that followed, Vika and Anke still heard nothing of Pierre; but Vika, at least, persisted in hoping that he would get word to them somehow. He did not, of course, have a comm, or his datapad; those were both still in his pack, which they kept safe in their room.

They spent their days in Dethun's library; the precious papers, as far as Vika could tell, never went beyond Dethun's study. Vika imaged them onto her datapad, which Thiain appeared not to observe.

There was so much to absorb. The stacked rolls of manuscript in the walls of niches had turned out, some of them, to be records dating back to the time of the attack, or shortly thereafter. They were written on paper—some coarse and handmade, some smooth as if milled—covered with dense, spiky, difficult characters, or hand-drawn images that were often difficult to interpret.

But Thiain proved to be an eager teacher. As Vika's command of the language improved, enough that she began to sense nuance in others' choice of words, she saw that Thiain was as curious about Earth as Vika was about this world. But Thiain's curiosity was tightly leashed. She never let a discussion of Earth go far, and she never permitted them to explain any Earth technology. And at some of their questions, Thiain would look down at her hands, her ears still, and let that silence be their answer. Vika began to learn as much from Thiain's silences as from her words.

Anke, too, was beginning to speak and understand clearly. The language of Windhome was heavily inflected—inflections for negation and affirmation, for the time and duration of actions, for the age and status and sex of the speaker, for irony, for disbelief. There were even inflections for ethical rightness or wrongness; in some matters these judgments could be made by the speaker, but in others rightness or wrongness was invariable, absolute—and to speak in the wrong mode was a fearful mistake. Thiain was patient with them both, but Vika knew she was often shocked. She did not encourage them to speak in the Lady's presence.

Their progress was also slowed by gestural problems: Thiain's people conveyed a great deal with the movements of their ears. Human facial expressions meant nothing—except, of course, that an open smile was an open threat.

Vika and Anke had fallen into a way of working together that was almost comfortable, though they spoke only about the writings. The work itself was enough. And Vika sensed the beginning of what might be called a friendship with Thiain—whose curiosity ran in the opposite direction, but seemed as strong as her own. Though she never spoke of it.

A little past midsummer Dethun granted their request to return to the lander to fetch their winter gear—and, Vika hoped, a few more pieces of lab equipment. But in the end only Anke was allowed to go—Dethun ruled that Vika should not leave her work in the library even for this; she was not as far advanced as Anke.

Anke had returned with some useful equipment stuffed in among the parkas and winter boots; but clearly she hadn't recognized everything on the list Vika had written out for her.

Access to more equipment did mean that Vika could now assay her biological samples, running genetic tests and comparing Windhome biochemistry to that of Earth. And Anke now had archives of some of the large image files from the orbital surveys, and from Kishar, that were difficult to access remotely.

Vika had found no surprises: compatibility with Earth and Kisharan life was almost complete. Life on all three worlds had been, not just seeded, but directed in much of its early history.

Vika and Anke spent their days with Thiain and the records. Or, when the Lady required use of her library, they hunted for new specimens of weeds and small insect-like creatures in the gardens and storehouses. The tedious and repetitive tests continued to absorb most of Vika's time in the evenings, when she and Anke were barred into this room and left alone.

Vika's biology work had to be carried on in secret, so far as possible; other than Vika's datapad, they never used any of their instruments when Thiain was present. Vika got little sleep in these days, but was so deeply absorbed that she hardly noticed.

They began to know this place—called *thololkhun*, "sisterhold." It was a jumble of courtyards, dormitories, kitchens, stables, warehouses stuffed with bales of wool. In one cavernous hall, women worked at carding the wool, spinning it into sturdy thread, and weaving it into cloth. Beyond that hall was a dyeworks for the finished yarn, partly outdoors because of the stink.

About three hundred women lived within the inner wall. Some of the older ones were scholars or teachers like Dethun, though subordinate to her; some young girls were students sent here by their families for an education. But most worked at the industry of the sisterhold: turning the wool from their flocks into the tightly woven wool cloth used everywhere for winter clothing, blankets, rugs, tents for travel.

Some of the men who stood guard on the outer wall also worked beside many of the old women in a little hospital just outside the gate, which was open to patients of both genders. But no male ever intruded within the inner wall. Thiain never spoke of what had happened in Dethun's secret room. Vika had asked about this rigid separation by gender and was answered only by one of Thiain's silences.

Vika and Anke discussed it in their room at night, however. This segregation of the sexes was a pattern that had existed in Earth's history as well, though the Covenant now forbade it. Here it did not seem to be a religious custom—even in the writings, they found no hint of any religious belief, not even a science-based system of ethics like the Gaian precepts now followed, with varying degrees of fervency, on Earth.

One afternoon when Vika and Thiain were walking through one of the small courtyards on their way from the herb garden to Dethun's library, they passed a door barred on the outside, with a stout old woman seated on a bench beside it, spinning. Thiain seemed startled and sniffed the air, then caught Vika's arm and hurried her toward the gate at the other end of the yard. As they passed the door, it rattled from a heavy blow struck from inside. And a woman's voice, muffled, gave a long, strangled cry. It was a voice stripped of words and thought—it chilled Vika. She looked back over her shoulder. The old woman had not moved from her place on the bench. So this was an ordinary thing....

"What was that?" Vika asked.

"Nothing we speak of in a public place," Thiain said. "Come. The Lady is waiting."

She would say nothing more.

Dethun waited impatiently for the strangers' work in her library to end. She had not understood, when she formed this plan, how disturbing it would be to see those hairless beings, with their naked, worm-fingered little hands, pawing over the books and papers that were in her charge. Thiain was with them, of course, and would prevent them from doing any damage, rousing any trouble.

But today there had been the incident in the courtyard.

Dethun sighed. If this damned late-summer heat would only ease. She rose from her worktable and poured a cup of water, drank it down. Thiain's personal cowardice was manifesting itself again. Clearly Dethun had been giving her too much freedom with these strangers. What other vital matters had she chosen to pass over with them?

At last the old bell across the main courtyard rang the call to supper. Shortly afterward the inner door opened, and Thiain emerged with the two strangers. They were chattering to each other, rudely, in their nonsensical language, but broke off when they saw Dethun standing there. "Thiain," Dethun said. "Tell Tevian at the foot of the stairs to take these back to their room. I wish to speak to you."

Thiain looked apprehensive, but she reappeared quickly, closing the outer door behind her. "Khesit," she said. "How may I serve you?"

Dethun, seated at her worktable, let Thiain stand there wondering for the space of two breaths. Three. Then she said, "Why is it that the strangers know so little of our lives? Are you so poor a teacher?"

"I had hoped not, Khesit," Thiain said carefully. "How have I failed you?"

"This afternoon," Dethun said, spreading her hands out flat on the worktable in front of her. "When the little dark stranger passed too near to the room where—who is it? Oh, yes, Kiathen—where she is suffering the Red Mind. And the stranger did not understand what it was! How is that possible? Are you too filled with shame at your own failure to speak of it?"

"I am not ashamed, Khesit," Thiain said steadily. "I, I didn't think it was necessary, just yet, to discuss—"

"It is an ordinary thing," Dethun said. "Even what happened to you—that is ordinary. I can think of forty other women here who've passed through the same."

"Yes, Khesit," Thiain said, but Dethun saw that her eyes had narrowed a little. She was betraying anger to Dethun's face.

Then let her be punished appropriately. Dethun let her ears flick back and saw Thiain flinch. *Good.* "Tomorrow morning," Dethun said, "before anything else, you will explain this matter. Completely and truthfully. You will hold nothing back. They must see what our lives are, here. They must understand what the Destroyers did to us. The evil we have lived with down all these long years." She leaned forward in her chair. "Do you understand?"

"I understand, Khesit," Thiain said quietly. Her eyes were properly downcast now.

"One more matter," Dethun said. "Find Gheren and tell her I will dine in my workroom tonight. She will attend me."

And here were the narrowed eyes again. But Thiain said only, "Yes, Khesit."

"I would be sorry to make this a permanent change," Dethun said. "Do you understand that as well?"

At that Thiain met Dethun's eyes. "Yes, Khesit," she said, but her rigid stance said much more.

"Go," Dethun snarled, and reached for a stack of letters. But after the door had closed, she sat for a long time, looking thoughtfully into the shadows.

Six

At sunrise, cold with anger and dread, Thiain stood outside the closed door of the stranger women's room, remembering the Lady's words last night. *It is an ordinary thing.* As if there were never any pain in it for anyone; or as if speaking of it should mean nothing to Thiain. Perhaps Dethun had forgotten. She had many other concerns....

Be done with it. Thiain carefully unbarred the door, then stepped in quietly and stood studying the strangers. Anke's eyes were closed, but she was awake—that was clear from the way she was breathing. But Vika—*she* was truly asleep. Such a small person—she looked like a child curled up there.

Except that a child would never sleep alone. With her womb-sibling, or a parent or two, or a pile of other children—never alone—

She straightened. *No. That life is over. I serve the Lady now.* Reluctantly, she stepped forward and woke Vika with a touch. And as she expected, Anke sat up as well.

Vika sat for a moment rubbing her odd flat face, then got out of the bed and picked up her clothing. As she dressed, Thiain looked with pity at her small, brown body, almost hairless—the black fur had grown back in only a few places. And she really did have only *two* breasts. These people were so scant in everything. In the pleasant coolness of the late-summer dawn, Vika was actually shivering.

Thiain moved to the fire and stirred the embers out from under the unevenly piled ashes, knelt and blew on them, then quickly added some kindling and a small, dry log to get them going again. These women never banked the fire properly. When it began to blaze up, she moved aside and let Vika, and Anke, who had also risen and dressed, warm themselves a little. *Poor things.*

Thiain took a deep breath and said, "Vika. You had questions yesterday. I didn't answer them, because it isn't a matter we discuss outside our own families. But the Lady has told me to answer them."

Vika turned her back to the fire and studied Thiain. "You mean, the locked door," she said. She lifted her chin. "We came here to understand your people better. We need to understand what that was."

Thiain clasped her hands behind her back. "That was the Red Mind."

"An illness?" Anke asked.

"No," Thiain said. "A thing that comes to women, once a year perhaps, or more often if we're not mated." She looked into the fire. *Get it said.* "It means that we're ready to mate, and conceive. And when it happens, we—women—we think of nothing else, want nothing else, but to mate." She looked at the stranger women. "This does not happen with you?"

"No," Vika said. "Not at all. Our natural cycles don't drive us like that. And we can control them."

Anke was frowning. "So all this, the walls and the guards outside, and all the rules—are they just to keep women safe? So they won't fuck?"

A word that applies to only animals. Anke certainly knew that. Thiain made herself answer calmly. "You misunderstand. The women here are unfamilied. Many by choice. Some not." She looked down into her cup. "A mating forms a bond, at least among decent people. And usually children are born from it. It creates a family, if one was not there before. So if a woman—wishes to be free of that kind of bond, that kind of burden, she must not mate. But out in the world, away from a sisterhold, an unfamilied woman has no choice. When the Red

Mind comes, there's nothing, no one to restrain her from obeying her body. And any man who scents her will fight to mate with her. The Red Mind takes them as well."

"So that is what the walls are for," Vika said slowly.

"Yes," Thiain said. *Finish telling her, answer her questions, and it will be done.* "Only in a sisterhold can a young woman have a free life—study and work as she chooses. And when she is older, past the Red Mind, she's still more free—she can even go among men, as Dethun does."

Anke tilted her head to one side. "Did you choose this life?"

Thiain looked away and mastered her breath. "Not—at first," she said. "I was familied. It's our way. I lived with my mother and sister-mothers and fathers, and when I was near the time, they sent me here for two years, so I could learn in peace and grow older, and be ready to mate and bear children when I returned."

Anke's face twisted. "To the same house you were born in?"

Vika said, "Just listen, Anke." They looked at each other with the displeasure they showed so often. They were not sisters, that was clear.

I can't bear this. Thiain rose restlessly from the table and went to the window, leaned there with her back to the light. "I missed my family," she said. "I wanted to be a familied woman, with children of my own. I went home before the Red Mind came the third time." She kept her eyes on Vika's, to help her draw the memory from her mind, not her belly. "My mother and my three sister-mothers welcomed me. I slept with the other women instead of with the children. I did a woman's work on the farm and in the house."

"And when the time came, you mated," Vika said. Thiain had learned to hear emotion in her voice, sometimes; there was none, now. It helped.

"I mated," Thiain said. "I was glad of it." She remembered it still—the joy of that intense, rising hunger, the greater joy when it was finally fulfilled. How powerful she had felt, in the pleasure of wanting, and taking, and wanting again, in the humid dark of the mating hut, by that fire. Sleeping in a tangle of furs and men's strong, warm bodies, then waking to the hunger again.

And after, when they were not just *men*, but once again Tolokh and Anodh and Nekhesh—afterward, they had become her bondmates, fireside companions, bedmates for warmth. They talked eagerly of the children who would be theirs....

Anke still looked troubled. "But wouldn't one of those men have been your own father?"

Answer all their questions, Dethun had said. "No," Thiain said. "Old men are kept from young women's matings. The senior mother sees to it. It's easy to make them drunk. Or they take their beer down to the farm gate to, to guard the house. They aren't so eager as young men, or so quick to tell when it's time." She folded her hands on the table. "So, I mated, and in the spring I bore two sons. But they were not whole. Not formed right. One took only four breaths—I counted them. The other—" She saw that Vika was close to weeping, and welcome anger rose inside her to carry her through the last of it. "The other was shaped wrong. This happens with us—the poison the Destroyers left, still marking us, down the generations.... And so my mother showed him to me, and I said, let it happen as it must." She waited a moment for her voice to return, and said, "And so he died."

"You mean, he was killed," Vika said, in a thin voice. "For being... shaped wrong."

"It's our way," Thiain said, the anger still strong. "This world is hard. We can't help them. Often they can't even eat. Ending it quickly is better."

Vika shook her head in the gesture Thiain had learned meant *no*. But Anke only looked down at the table and said, "I understand."

No, she doesn't. Thiain went on, "After that, without children to suckle, I came into the Red Mind sooner, and I tried again. But I lost them both very early, long before they could have breathed outside me."

"I'm sorry, Thiain," Vika said.

"I grieved," Thiain said. After a long silence she went on, "But I saw the look in my mother's eyes, the second time. I'd failed my family. So, when I could, I—left, alone, and returned here. Where I'm safe, and have work to do."

"You're bitter," Anke said calmly. These people seemed able to speak calmly about anything.

"I'm at peace," Thiain said, her voice as strong as she could manage. "This is my life. I chose it. And the Lady is kind."

At that Anke muttered something, and Vika looked at her angrily and said, "This is hard for Thiain."

Anke stood up and, rudely, turned her back for a moment. Then turned back and said to Thiain, "It could be different. And you know it." Her flat face had turned pink, and her pale eyes glittered. "Some of the records, where they talked about life before the Destroyers came. You've read them, too." Vika said something sharp in their tongue, but Anke kept her eyes on Thiain, waiting.

"Yes. We did not live like this," Thiain said. "There were medicines then, to control the Red Mind. A woman would come to it only when she chose. She could even go out into the world and *choose* her family. It was—much different."

"It can be that way again," Anke said, sitting down again. "Our people can help you rediscover those ways."

Thiain remembered the right words, the Lady's words. "That would be the first easy step on a wrong path," she said. "Choosing a softer, easier life. Going down that path was what brought the Destroyers down on us." She knew this lesson well; it was the heart of all the Lady's teaching. "Our way is good enough. Most people are safe. Most women have healthy children. Most families are happy. Men and women are bondmates, brought together by mating, and children, and the work of their farmhold."

"What happens to the boys?" Vika asked.

"When they're close to becoming men," Thiain said, "they're driven out from their families to grow to manhood and find their way in the world outside. In the end, most find a family willing to take them in, a place where they can mate and become fathers." Or they died hunting, or working in mines. Or in fights, as her dear womb-brother Nerigh had, the year they were both fifteen.... She looked at

Vika. "Others—others live on unfamilied. They find work, or they study at the men's college." She sniffed.

"And you don't think much of them," Vika said.

"Dabblers," Thiain said, with another shrug. "Men who wander. They're cut off from the land where they were born. They haven't found another family to take them. So they invent things to care about. Politics and philosophy at the men's colleges, for those whose birth families are rich enough to send them. For the rest, scuffles over herding ranges and hunting grounds." She snorted. "But it's all above their noses. Their bellies don't belong to the land, so their minds don't, either. They change like the clouds, one fashion to the next."

"But women—" Anke said.

"Women keep our history," Thiain said. "We remember—here in the sisterholds, and in our homes. Our lines go back through our mothers and their mothers, on the same land. We understand everything with our bellies *and* our minds." She turned to Vika. "What else do you want to ask?" She could not keep a note of challenge from her voice.

"Nothing just now," Vika said carefully, looking straight at Anke.

"Then we'll go to your work in the library," Thiain said. "And we'll talk of other things."

Anke looked up at her and said in a low voice, "For now."

Autumn arrived. So far as Vika was concerned, it might as well have been winter. Vika and Anke's work continued—days spent in Dethun's library or gathering biological samples, and evenings locked in their room, where Vika continued sequencing and structural work and uploading the results to the lander. Anke began a massive cross-referencing of the records they had scanned in so far: presumed location, approximate date, family names of victims and survivors, orbital images of sites, and, most interesting to Anke, a detailed comparison of descriptive terms for the various types of attacks. Anke said it was beginning to give her an idea of how Windhome people assessed the unfamiliar, and it might make some of the fragmentary records more comprehensible and possibly even useful.

No word or rumor of Pierre reached them. Vika worried, but there was nothing she could do. On a frosty evening several eightdays after the autumn feast, long after the evening meal, Vika pushed away her datapad and rubbed her chilled hands together, then stretched them out to the fading fire.

It was long past dark, and the season had definitely turned. *Frost again tonight.* Even near the hearth, with the fire flaring and dancing with the wind in the chimney, Vika worked in her parka. She was about to suggest shutting down for the night when they both heard a heavy tread on the wooden stairs leading up to their door.

Vika flung a rumple of blankets over the portable biolab on her bed just as the bar outside was slid aside. Anke sat up straight, and the door opened.

This was not Thiain; this was a woman Vika did not know, one of Dethun's female guards. She cradled a knotted staff in her hands, and her red-brown eyes were remote. "Come," she said. "Both of you."

Vika and Anke looked at each other, then pulled on their parkas, stuffed their feet into their boots, and followed the guard out. Vika asked, "Where are we going?"

The woman said only, "Hurry." As they left the building, Vika shivered in the sharp night air. She looked up beyond the dark, steep-pitched roofs at the frosty sky. The winter star—Arcturus—burned low over the roofs to the east, a bitter, reddish-orange spark, far brighter than it appeared in the skies of Earth. Thiain had taught them its name here: Tlankharu, "old man's eye." It ruled the night sky in the depth of winter.

As Vika had expected, it was Dethun who required their presence. The guard deposited them at her study door, and they entered at a call in an unfamiliar voice. At Dethun's worktable a white-furred old woman stood sorting papers from the table into a big leather case. She glanced up at them and gestured them toward the fire. The stillness of her ears was a warning.

Dethun stood near the fire, grim and heavy in a gray woolen overdress, gripping a curled sheet of fine beaten-flax paper in her claws. And Thiain waited at her side, silent, her eyes downcast.

"Dethun Khesit," Anke said carefully, and bowed her head; Vika did the same. When she looked up she saw that Dethun's ears were flat back, the fur of her neck and head erect. Her eyes burned. She looked from Vika to Anke and back, and spoke at last, "I should have you both killed," she said. "You didn't come here to learn. You came to bring us death."

Vika stared up at her in shock, searching for an answer. She dared not speak a word of blunt denial to Dethun; to do so would be insolence, risking a blow. She turned to Thiain. "Who has said this?" But Thiain only looked away.

Dethun raised the paper in her hand. "I have a letter from my old friend Vakhar," she said. "Who helped me achieve this place after I came into my age and my freedom. Vakhar heads the Council of Eight, whose voice speaks for Kheosseth. He writes angrily to me. He blames *me* for what my son has done. And the other one of you strangers, who lives in my son's house."

Anke jerked. "Pierre!" Her voice was sharp. "Pierre is alive? Khesit."

"He breathes, they say," Dethun said. "I was ashamed of my son for taking this stranger to himself. But now it's far worse. Kelru has placed a petition before the Council: that the stranger Pierre be permitted to travel in forbidden places, to ask impertinent questions, to move freely through our lands and farmholds. To speak to anyone he chooses!" Her voice deepened and strengthened. "Kelru's friends have corrupted him. And so has this—this Pierre. This friend of yours."

Vika took a calming breath. "Khesit, we seek only to understand what has happened to your world. How you, and my people, might protect ourselves. And whether Anke and I can be of use to you."

"Vakhar believes that you are spies of the Destroyers," Dethun said.

"Vakhar doesn't know us, Khesit," Vika said.

"If he thinks we're spies of the Destroyers, he'll simply refuse Kelru's petition," Anke said. "Won't he?"

"There are eight men on the Council," Dethun said. "A few of them, some who should be wiser, agree with Kelru. They want to learn what Pierre can teach them. They don't *fear* Pierre! Vakhar cannot be certain of speaking for them all, and so he cannot speak against Kelru with the full power of the Council. Not yet." She held up the letter in one strong, furred hand. "Before your coming there were some who said the danger is over—that the Destroyers are gone, and we can now live as we choose. Now those same ones are saying, *See this Pierre, hear of his world. Hear of their wealth, and their power, and their easy lives.* Yet the Destroyers have not come there. And so, these men say, the Destroyers are gone."

"We came here only to learn," Vika said, almost stammering in her struggle to find the words. "About you. And your history. If—" Just in time she stopped herself from saying, *If what you say is true.* "If the Destroyers return, they would be a danger to our world, as well."

Dethun's ears flicked restlessly. "We who remember—" she used an old phrase, *ano kothu*— "we believe that the Destroyers are still here, sleeping under ice, waiting. And so *we* will never forget. Our people still suffer from their coming, from the poison they spread. Women like Thiain, who give birth only to defective children—we Anokothu hear them weeping, year after year. The Destroyers must not come again." She looked up at Vika and Anke. "And so we must not live as we once did. As your people do."

"Khesit," Vika said carefully. "What does Vakhar want from you?"

"Your deaths," Dethun said calmly. "In return, he pledges to arrange for the other one's death—the man's."

Words fled. Vika stood shaking her head, and then said unsteadily, "But none of us have done him any harm."

Dethun raised a hand. "Now be silent." Her voice deepened and slowed. "I haven't agreed to this, and I will not. Vakhar forgets, or does not know, that Kelru has claimed Pierre as a brother. Killing Pierre would lay a blood matter between the Council and Kelru. And I wish to bring Kelru nearer to Vakhar, not to drive him away." She gazed into the fire, her expression brooding. "I've chosen another way." She faced them again. "I will go to Kheosseth for the winter. Now, well before the Council sits. And I'll take you both with me." Vika saw Thiain look at the Lady sharply, her ears upright with surprise. The Lady went on, "You must persuade Pierre that Kelru's path is the wrong one—and separate him from my son. That will be your first task in Kheosseth." She looked from Anke to Vika. "Do you understand?"

"We understand, Khesit," Vika said, with a sinking feeling. "But what is the other task?"

"When the Council meets, I will take you before them." Dethun's deep voice trembled. "I will testify that you are not Destroyers—but that your coming means that the Destroyers are stirring, or soon will be. And thus this is no time to turn from Anokothu ways, to follow foolish ideas into danger and death." In the dimness her eyes glittered, amber-red as Tlankharu in the chill face of night. "The Council must return to wisdom, and agree to repair the damage Pierre has already done. Then my son will be safe. He will take a man's place in the world, as he was meant to."

"And Pierre?" Anke said. "What will happen to him?"

"We will discuss Pierre," Dethun said, "when you have succeeded. Not until then."

Vika bent her head in acknowledgment, and saw Anke doing the same—it was the only gesture open to them when Dethun spoke in that mode. But far down in Vika's mind, she felt a cold stirring of dread.

SEVEN

Vika shivered in the raw pre-dawn air, pulling her woolen thessach more tightly around herself. A gift from the Lady, dyed the pale, spring green of Dethun's sisterhold: an enveloping, hooded cloak with sleeves. It could be tied closed in front against the wind. Anke wore one like it—a public obligation laid on them both. But the thessachs were warm. And, with the deep hoods up, concealing.

She and Anke trudged along silently through the frozen mud of a Kheosseth street, following Ganarh and escorted by four of his bowmen. All around them, Kheosseth slept, hiding itself and its people behind blind walls, shutting out the sky.

By messenger, Dethun had arranged for the human women to meet Pierre and Kelru at a public square near her city house—Kelru must not even approach Dethun's outer door, marked as it was with a slash of red paint because Thiain, a young woman, lived there. Even Ganarh and his men, who would guard the Lady through the winter, were not allowed inside that door; they lived and slept in a narrow watch-room just outside.

Now Ganarh stalked along stiffly ahead of them, grim and silent as ever. He had made it clear to both the humans how strongly he disapproved of this entire adventure—of the Lady wintering away from Thanen River sisterhold yet again, and of the stranger females who he felt had driven her to it. They rounded a corner and he snapped the order to halt. A broad, open square lay before them.

At this hour it was still empty of people, a blue-shadowed expanse overlooked by low houses built of wood or yellow brick. On the far edge, one low window glowed with firelight. Another watch-room. Some woman there must be in the grip of the Red Mind....

Vika looked upward. The bitter dawn sky was clear and colorless. Only the brighter stars still pricked through. High in the eastern sky, Tlankharu gleamed steadily, inimically, as bright as a planet. She shivered, and looked down.

She saw two people walking toward them from the far side of the square—a tall man and a boy, she could see from their belted thessachs. No, not a boy—with a surge of relief she saw that it was Pierre. And the tall one was Kelru, of course, his thessach midnight blue. As they drew nearer she saw that Pierre's eyes were alight, though he did not smile. But in the pale, early light, she could not read Kelru's expression even when they drew close. His bearing shaded subtly from erect grace to stiffness as he faced Ganarh again.

Ganarh sketched a gesture of greeting. "Kelru."

"Ganarh." Kelru looked at Anke and Vika. "You're both welcome," he said tentatively.

"You make us glad of the journey," Vika said.

His ears twitched. "You speak well."

"Better than I do," Pierre said in the same language. "I am glad to see you both." He was smiling slightly now. Vika studied him. Of course she had known his black hair would be back, short but thick, as hers was; but for some reason she had not expected the dark beard framing his sharp-boned face. It suited him.

Ganarh stirred impatiently. "Let's get this done. Kelru, do you accept responsibility for the safety of these women until I return for them?"

"I do," Kelru said. "As does my brother." Pierre bent his head deeply in the sign of formal assent. Ganarh wheeled without another word and stalked away, followed by his men.

"Home now," Kelru said, "and fire, and food." His eyes were bright with welcome.

It was a long way to Kelru's house in the southern part of the city. As they walked, Vika looked around curiously in the rising light. The houses faced onto inner courtyards, turning their blind backs to the street, showing only high, strong gates of thick wood. The shadowed streets were narrow, mostly plain dirt, though a few stretches were paved with brick.

As the light grew, they climbed a twisting side street and stopped before a courtyard gate. Kelru opened it and led them through a passage walled in wood, into a small, bare courtyard. Vika looked around. The building surrounding the courtyard was only three stories high—not much, when the snow would soon lie meters deep. Five or six stairways led up from the courtyard; Vika guessed that there must be five or six separate dwellings, broken up from a larger house that would have sheltered an entire family.

The ground floor of all the houses seemed to be stables—judging from the smell—and storehouses. They followed Kelru up one of the stairways. The worn wooden steps creaked under them as they climbed. Kelru unlatched the door and led them inside. A tiny anteroom smelled of mud and leather. Beyond was a dim, chilly hearthroom. The fire had been banked; Kelru knelt to stir it up. Vika put back the hood of her thessach and looked around, but it was too dark to see much—the few windows were the usual glazed slits.

Pierre lit a spill from the fire and used that to light a lamp. "Let me look at you both," he said to Anke and Vika, still in Kelru's language.

"Pierre, we need to talk," Anke said, in Standard.

Pierre frowned at her. "Not now," he said, then went on in the language of Windhome. "Speak as I do. We are guests here." He set a pot of water on a hook over the fire, and arranged a worn fur rug near the slowly increasing warmth.

Kelru went out. Anke sank down onto the rug. "May we speak our own language when we're alone?" she asked acidly.

"Of course," he said in Standard. "But as a courtesy, we won't if anyone else is near." He smiled. "I need the practice. It is a hard language."

Vika studied him. The spiky hair and untrimmed beard gave his lean, expressive face a wild look. He wore Windhome clothing of undyed gray-brown wool—a man's knee-length tunic, belted with worn leather, over baggy trousers and patched felt boots. "You fit in," she said.

"It has not been easy," he said. "But you—you've been well?"

"We—were concerned about you," Vika said. *Afraid for you.* "But we've been busy. Pierre, Dethun's let us use her library. Hundreds of manuscripts, some of them from immediately after the attacks."

"I look forward to hearing of it," Pierre said mildly. "I, too, have been learning."

"I hope so," Vika said. "Has Kelru told you about the Destroyers?"

Pierre gave her an odd look. "Of course he has. And he warned me about Dethun."

Vika took a breath to speak, but Pierre laid a warning hand on her arm. Heavy footsteps coming up the stairs. Kelru shouldered open the door, letting in ice-cold air and a stream of pale sunlight. He carried a clay jug wrapped in a cloth. "I borrowed hot water," he explained as he kicked the door shut behind him. "That pot on the fire will take too long." He handed the jug to Pierre. Then from a high shelf he took a small gray stone flask and unstoppered it.

"You should have put the pot on before we left," Pierre said.

Kelru stopped in the act of pouring from the flask into the jug. "And if Ganarh had decided to give a speech this morning?" he demanded. "My best copper pot, boiled dry and cracked."

"Your only copper pot," Pierre said gravely.

Kelru turned to Vika and Anke. "See how he laughs at me for being poor!"

"He is unworthy of your name," Vika agreed.

Pierre gave her a fierce look. "What I have is Kelru's."

"What you have there is my neighbor's," Kelru said, as he took the jug and deftly filled four bowls. "Don't break it."

Vika accepted hers, lifted it toward Kelru in thanks, and sipped from it at once, as Thiain had taught her—different rules for tea and alcohol.... The hot drink was good—not sweet, but flavored with sweet spices. And something like brandy. She sipped again and stretched her numb feet out toward the fire.

When they had all been served, Kelru said, "Now. We have matters to discuss."

"Kelru," Pierre said, "Dethun has told them about the Destroyers. She has shown them the records she keeps at the sisterhold."

"Ah," Kelru said, his deep voice hard now. "Dethun's records." He turned to Vika. "You must know that she plans to use you for her own purposes."

Vika looked up at Kelru. "And what are *your* purposes?"

"My friends and I oppose the Old Anokothu," Kelru said. "We oppose all who believe that our people are best kept in silence and ignorance. In darkness without hope." His voice was quiet, but his body's stillness, his unmoving ears meant intense emotion, rigidly controlled.

Vika had learned that from watching Thiain. She shook her head. "This isn't—" She stopped, took a breath to steady her voice, and went on, "This is not our battle, Kelru. We came to this world to learn about the Destroyers. Dethun can help us, and she has."

"I know her," Kelru said. "If she offers help, she requires something in return."

"Yes," Vika said. "She has asked us to support her when she speaks before the Council of Eight. She opposes your petition to allow Pierre freedom to carry out our mission."

Kelru looked troubled. "And will you support her?"

"Anke and I have gotten through barely a third of her records," Vika said. "We need to resume our work. It's vital. We must have her help."

"But the price of it," Kelru said, "is more than you may know."

Vika looked up at him and let her eyes meet his—in this world, the gesture of good friends, or bondmates. Or enemies squaring off, knives drawn.... "Dethun warned me that you oppose her in this," she said.

"And many other things." Kelru's gaze did not shift. "She does not simply lead the Lady Mothers of all the sisterholds. She is also influential with the Old Anokothu. And the Old Anokothu have always been a strong voice before the Council of Eight. Even on it."

"I see." Vika got to her feet, though even then she had to tilt her head to look up at Kelru. "And how will you defeat her? She tells us that your laws are on her side."

"Let *me* explain," Pierre said. He looked earnestly at Vika. "Kheosseth is not like the sisterhold. There the Lady speaks, and everyone obeys, or they must leave. Here the Council of Eight is charged with enforcing the laws of the city. Some of them Anokothu laws. But the Council's power is not so absolute." He set down his bowl carefully. "The laws against the old knowledge have not been strongly enforced for several generations. At the men's college here in Kheosseth, and even at some farmholds, many now disagree with those laws. And with Dethun and her allies."

Vika faced Pierre. "How will it help us to become involved in this—" she used the Standard word "—*political* struggle?"

"The Lady intends to use our coming to frighten her people," Pierre said. "To make the Council renew the old laws, and make them stronger." He glanced at Kelru. "To make herself stronger, some say." He looked at Anke. "The fact is this. She does not care what you say in front of the Council. She only wants them to see you up close. To see that you are not of this world."

"To be afraid," Kelru said. "And to choose a path that will increase her power. And put you two in danger."

Anke tipped the jug into her bowl again. "What will they do?"

"I think they will not touch Pierre," Kelru said. "I have a brother's right of vengeance for him, and they know I would use it. But you women aren't of my family. And I cannot adopt you as I did Pierre.

If the Council returns to old ways and listens only to the Anokothu, they might kill you. Or they might order your exile. Now, with winter coming, it would be the same."

Vika looked up at him, shocked. "Is Dethun's word empty, then?"

"Her word is not empty," Kelru said. "But you must listen exactly to it, for she keeps it most exactly. She gives no less, but also no more, than she has promised."

Vika frowned at him. "She said she would protect and shelter us as she protects and shelters Thiain. Those were her words."

"But what does that mean?" Anke asked. Vika looked at her in startlement, but she went on. "She brought Thiain with her into a room full of men, when she sent Kelru away. Was that protection? And now she brings Thiain to this city, for her own purposes. Is that shelter?"

"No," Vika said slowly. "No, but—"

"But the Lady has her reasons," Kelru said quietly. "And we must all trust her."

Vika sighed inwardly and turned to him. "You and your friends— do you believe the Destroyers are no longer a threat?"

He stood looking down at her, his drinking bowl cradled in his hands. "We don't believe that we should live in fear forever. Many sixty-fours of years later we still live like *feotheg* under a snowdrift, hiding, afraid of sounds and shadows. How long must we huddle in the dark before we go out to see if the klakurr has flown away?"

"And what if it hasn't?" Vika folded her arms. "We have reason to think the danger is near." She looked at Pierre. "Did you tell him what happened to us?"

Pierre frowned. "Of course I did. But that is not the point."

"That is exactly the point!" Vika's voice sharpened. "We aren't talking about shadows. They've touched us all. It would be stupid to pretend that we're safe, that any of us is safe."

"Or that our own world is safe!" Pierre said hotly. "That is why Kelru's petition must not fail. If it succeeds, we can carry out our mission. If it fails—" He shook his head.

Kelru set down his drinking bowl. "Speak to her in your own tongue, Pierre," he said. "I'm going for wood." He left silently.

"Go ahead," Vika said in Standard, when the door had closed. "Explain why you want to isolate us from the power structure here. To destroy our credibility with one of the most powerful leaders of this society."

"It's simple," Pierre said, his face dark with anger. "To finish our mission, we need freedom of movement. Which the Anokothu, if they prevail, will never grant us, no matter what Dethun may have promised you. That is why I need you here. Not serving Dethun's purposes." He shook his head. "Not under Dethun's control!"

"You should read the records before you decide this," Vika said, cold to her spine. "I can transfer you scans of everything we've studied. We know a great deal about the Destroyers now, Anke and I." She turned to Anke. "Tell him."

Anke rose to her feet and poured herself another bowl of the spiced drink, then turned and faced Vika. "Vika, your emotions are clouding your thinking," she said. "The Lady decided which records we would see, and told us what to think about them. She made Thiain tell us her story." Her expression was gentle. "I think she knew the effect it would have on you.... But I don't trust her. Neither of us should trust her. Now that we're here, we should stay." She looked at Vika seriously. Her fair skin was flushed by the fire's warmth, and she held her bowl lightly in her long fingers.

Vika took a breath, another, forcing down rage. "But our work isn't done!"

Pierre stretched out a hand toward Vika. "Vika. You should listen to Kelru. He knows Dethun."

Vika turned away. "His word, her word—"

Pierre sighed. "Never mind words, then. Watch what people do."

The fire flared in a gust of bitter air as Kelru came in with a load of wood. Vika turned to him. "And *you*, Kelru," she demanded in the language of Windhome. "How do you want to use us?"

After a moment, Kelru walked to the hearth, picked up his bowl, and took a deep swallow. "As my brother, Pierre is not mine to use," he said. "As my guests, neither are you." Vika was sure she could detect reproach in his voice. Pierre certainly looked reproachful. Anke only shook her head.

"You are our host, and Pierre's brother," Vika said, looking steadily into his eyes. "Your friends are not."

Kelru's ears went still, then flicked slowly. "As you say." He sipped again from his bowl. "What my friends see in Pierre—and will see in you, if you stay—is proof that our people can live as people again. Come out from the shadows. Achieve great things again. As you did, making your journey across the darkness." He inclined his head politely.

Grudgingly, in response to the urgent plea in Pierre's eyes, Vika bowed her own head in acknowledgment. Then raised her eyes to Kelru's again. "But what if the Anokothu are right? What if the Destroyers return, and you lose even what you have now?" She spread her hands. "I've seen your city, your farms. Is this life so hard?" Her gesture took in the small, neat room, the fire, the fur rugs and woven hangings.

"You've seen summer, and harvest," Kelru said. His eyes were remote and did not see her. "You've seen a wealthy sisterhold. Our largest city. Our richest farmholds—from the outside." His red-gold gaze turned to her. "You should learn our life better before you judge it. Before you judge *me*."

Vika sighed. "So, then. What is it that *you* want us to do? Deny Lady Dethun before the Council?"

"Of course you must speak truth, always," Kelru said. "But first you must learn it. The Council of Eight convenes after the Last Feast, at the rise of first winter. There are more than four eightdays between that day and this one. I ask only that you let Pierre tell you what he has learned. And that you listen to him."

Vika had her voice under command now. "And he to me."

"Of course." Kelru looked at her, his ears upright. "We will have many fascinating disputes, the four of us." In his face, in his eyes, in his stance, Vika could read only honest pleasure. She glanced at Pierre.

He was looking at Anke, and she at him. And she was smiling.

In the last light of evening, Pierre watched from the hearthroom window as Kelru left to escort Vika—Vika alone—back to Dethun's house. He remembered Vika's bitter words as she refused his order to stay. *One* of them, she had said, needed to keep the Lady's trust. And access to her records. Anke could stay if she must—

"I wish she had stayed," Anke said behind him.

He turned, and she moved closer to him. He felt a strong impulse to take her hands in his—to touch another human again—but he controlled it. He saw her face dimly in the firelight, pale, strained. "You're tired," he said. "Was it so hard living in the Lady's house?"

"You might not think so," she said bleakly. "Vika had her work. The biology. And—"

"And you, the records," Pierre said.

"Those were Vika's, too," Anke said. "One tragic story after another. Almost none of it very useful. She's afraid; she thinks that's seeing the truth, the only truth." She looked away. "I didn't come here to read stories, Pierre. I came here to solve this. To find a way to fight those things."

"And we will have that chance," he said, and now he did take her hands—it would have been awkward not to touch her, as close as she was. Close enough now that he felt her warmth through his tunic.

She looked down at their hands. "What I need now," she said quietly, "is something to hope for."

"From me?" Disbelief shook his voice.

She looked up at him, then down at their joined hands. "I understand you better now."

He could not move away from her now. He could feel his heartbeat, his breath quickening. But he shook his head. "You and I, we are too different. It didn't take us long to learn that."

"Shut up, Pierre," she said. Her hands slid up to his shoulders. A human touch, *her* touch, after all this time. "Listen to me," she said quietly, and he looked down into her face. "Stop fighting, just for a while. Rest."

He touched her face, blindly, gingerly, as if she could burn him. Then he drew her to him, and they kissed. Her hands, hard and strong, slid along his body, urged him onward. He needed her. He did not know if she was speaking those words, or if it was his own thought.

It was warm there, on the floor by the fire, her skin warm against his, her gasping breaths warm, her hands gripping his shoulders warm. But in a dark place in his mind one cold thought lingered. *This is a mistake.*

EIGHT

The next morning, Vika emerged from Dethun's courtyard into raw morning frost. The clouds overhead burned with the bitter fires of dawn, and each breath was a wisp of fog, taken by the wind that sought out even these deep streets.

She tugged her thessach closer around herself and eased the door shut behind her. From a recessed doorway across the frozen mud of the street, a shadow in night-blue stepped forward, both hands stretched out palm up in greeting and the promise of peace.

Vika moved to meet Kelru and clutched the datapad bag under one arm so she could hold her mittened palms over his. Over, but not touching; she and Kelru must not touch, just as they must avoid speaking each other's name. So many rules here, for the young.

They started out. Kelru didn't speak, and Vika let the silence stretch on. At this hour no one was about. It was so cold that the icy air stung in her throat and chest as she breathed. She set her attention to moving as quickly as she could over the rutted, frozen mud. Kelru moved beside her, tall and silent, striding easily in rhythm with the swing of his thessach.

Vika had spent most of the night in Dethun's study, organizing the records of the Destroyers in her datapad. Thiain had helped her silently, keeping to the privacy in which she had cloaked herself since they left the sisterhold.

It was a relief to leave Dethun's house, if only for the day. At

Kelru's house she had felt more free, even if it was only to argue with
Kelru. There was no one at Kelru's house to whom she need submit,
before whom she must be silent. She even looked forward to seeing
Pierre again.

As for Anke—there would be little need to speak to Anke.

Vika moved the bag from one shoulder to the other. Reading all those
records again, feeling again their writers' hopeless anguish, their questions
that burned unanswered—it had been painful. Pierre would see that pain,
too. He would understand that this world had suffered enough—that the
best course was to do as the Lady asked and keep their place, keep safe. Safe
by the fire, far from the shadows, from the cold—

Then Kelru spoke. "I beg a gift from you."

"Name it," Vika said, surprised, but adhering to good manners.

Kelru looked away over the rooftops, toward the broad glassy
sweep of the Mother-River where it curved past the city's quays. "I
ask advice," he said. "And a favor."

Uncomfortable, Vika studied him, but he kept his face turned
away. "Of course," she said.

"Pierre has done something foolish," Kelru said. "I think he
believes I don't know of it, and I think he is ashamed. And therefore I
can't speak of it to him." He turned and his eyes met hers. "But I can
tell you."

She frowned at him. "What has he done?"

"He's mated with—with the other woman of your people."

Vika stopped there in the street, looking up at Kelru, looming
dark against the cold metallic blaze of the sky. *I was right.* "I see," she
said, and her voice came from far away. "I thought that might be what
happened." And it was true—though the thought had only come clear
at this moment. Her anger surprised her.

"I wish you'd warned me," Kelru said, sounding irritated. "It's
clear he doesn't understand what this means to *me*."

She could walk again now, and she did, Kelru beside her like a
shadow. "What do you mean?"

Kelru made a noise low in his throat—not a laugh. A hard, bitter sound. "I can watch Pierre—most of the time, if he wishes to cooperate. I can't watch you all."

"Why should you watch us?"

"As Pierre's mate," Kelru said, "*she*—" he hesitated, then said, "Anke—is of his family. And therefore also of my own. I must guard her, and if she is harmed, I must avenge her if Pierre cannot."

"Are we likely to be harmed?" Her thoughts were settling now, clearing. Pierre and Anke. It was natural enough that they would turn to each other again, for comfort if nothing else—

"Of course there is danger," Kelru said. "You are all so ignorant of our world, of our ways. To keep you safe is a great responsibility, and—" He shrugged. "Among my people, a woman has power, power that a man is right to fear. When she's present, at certain times, she takes from him his mind, and his will, and his words. By her presence, she takes choice from him, and he comes out of the Red Mind bound to her, and to any children that come." He cocked an ear at Vika. "Your ways are different, Pierre says. But I wish he weren't bound to her. I don't know her. I cannot trust her."

Vika looked blindly toward the sunrise. "Anke will give you no trouble," she said. "Pierre will see to that." She cleared her throat and said, "How did you find out about them?"

"I *have* a nose," Kelru said, now openly annoyed. "When I came back from taking you to the Lady's house last night, he was by the fire, and she was upstairs asleep. And he said nothing, so I knew it was a private matter. But there was no doubt." His ears flicked angrily. "I thought I understood your ways. I thought you could *choose* whether to mate. But if Pierre has chosen this, then he's a fool." He looked down at her. "That is why I spoke to you now."

"Why? Do you want me to talk to him?" She looked away. "That wouldn't be—right, by our customs."

He stopped her and looked down at her. Inside the hood of his thessach his face was sharp-shadowed, his eyes glittering. "And it's too late now," he said. "Their bond has been formed. Pierre tells me that none of you can bear children, that your physicians—"

"We were all made sterile," Vika said. "That's true."

"But even so," Kelru said, "It must go no farther."

She looked up at him. "What do you mean?"

Kelru looked stern. "Pierre must not mate with *you*."

She looked away from him, and laughed, a bright, cold sound in the bright, cold morning. When she could speak she said, "Then rest. There is no danger at all of that."

"Good," Kelru said. "For there is one thought I cannot turn aside."

Vika looked up at him, uneasy. "What thought?"

"Danger," Kelru said. "Danger will come of this, and grief."

They walked in silence the rest of the way.

Two days later, Vika stood in Kelru's hearthroom beside one of the narrow windows, her fingers resting on the thick, chilly glass. Outside, the long afternoon darkened. Slate-colored clouds loomed overhead, heavy with snow. A message had come this morning from Thiain that if she wished to keep the Lady's good will, she must return today—or never. So of course she would leave; there was work for her there, at least.

But not until Pierre finished reading the last of the scanned records.

She kept her fingers still on the glass. Pierre's choices were clear. He could agree with her assessment that continued access to these records was vital, worth the risk of Vika returning to the Sisterhold with Dethun after the Council meeting. Or, Pierre would insist that Vika remain at Kelru's house—enraging his mother, and costing them all further access to the records. There was no other archive that could rival Dethun's. Dethun had seen to that.

Vika pushed that thought away. Her datapad contained all the most powerful and evocative records from the time of the attack—the ones that had haunted her, and that would give Earth knowledge of the Destroyers that was as important as any assessment of their technology. Vika was certain that it was as essential to discover *why* they had done what they did here as to understand *how* they had done it. And this was their only possible source for that knowledge.

Repressing a shiver, she turned back to face Kelru's hearthroom. It was small, its wooden boards and beams dark with age and ingrained smoke. The walls were covered with old woolen hangings of time-faded red, embroidered in indigo with abstract leafy branches. The room had little other decoration—one plain brass candle stand, empty; several battered lamps; a few lovingly polished metal bowls arranged along a shelf. It was all clean, cleaner even than the sisterhold was kept under Lady Dethun's strict direction. But the bareness of poverty was there.

Pierre sat cross-legged on the floor beside Kelru's low worktable. Vika could see him frowning as he concentrated on the alien script. She'd offered to help him, but it was Anke who sat beside him, ready to interpret.

Kelru sat by the table as well, closer to the lamp. He was weaving new rawhide thongs onto the long wooden frames of a pair of snowshoes. Vika's fingers itched to try it; it was the kind of intricate, fascinating task she had loved as a child, and had used to fill the hours of quiet her parents' work demanded.

Now Pierre looked up at her. "I've come to the last one," he said. "You note it as especially interesting."

"It is," she said. "It was written by one of Kelru's ancestors."

Kelru set down his work and touched the datapad, tilting it toward himself. "*Ai!*" he said, his ears flicking forward in surprise. "That's the record that was preserved in my birth family. We thought it was lost." He looked at Vika and took a slow breath. "So Dethun has it?" There was a deep note of anger in his voice.

Vika hesitated. "I suppose Dethun believes it's safest with her."

"It was treasured in our house for many generations," Kelru said. His ears still flicked forward and back: mistrust, displeasure. Pierre looked down at the screen and touched it with gentle fingers, as if it were one of the real pages Vika had seen, thick and rough and old.

Kelru seemed to gather himself, and picked up his work again. "That record was written in the mountains above our farm, ten sixty-fours of years ago, by a woman called Ekhnan Therrin." He looked at Vika. "She founded our farm and family, after the attack. Ekhnan is still the name of both. Still my name, unless I find a family of my own."

"I know," Vika said, and turned to Pierre. "Read it, please." And the room was quiet, except for the faint hiss of the fire.

These records were rough going, Vika knew. Not just the strong, angular alien script, written right to left and in a poetic style very different from the spoken language. The problem, as Anke had said more than once, was the alien cultural referents of those who had written them. What did Therrin mean when she wrote, *I saw a bowl of silver against the sunrise, and the bowl was filled with death*? Was it a literal description of something? A metaphor? Or a hallucination, recalled in detail?

Pierre stopped and read out part of it: "'They came swiftly over the land like a fog rolling up from the sea; they were all of ice, and even their teeth were ice, and where they came we lay in fragments, our blood steaming in the cold.' What does that even mean?"

"Some of the carvings from Kishar show toothed flying creatures," Anke said. "But of course their dating is less certain than this, and they could have been a reference to an earlier era. Or a legend. Even fiction. The Kisharans were apparently an imaginative race."

"So are the people of this world," Pierre said, frowning.

"It does reflect some of the other records," Vika said.

"But not all of them," Anke said. "I wonder if they simply didn't understand what they were seeing."

Pierre was nodding. "It does make me question the value of this kind of archive. A terrible thing happened. We know that. What we need to learn is how it was *done*. Get some—objective picture, something that might contribute to an actual defense against them. What did their astronomers see? Or a soldier who fought them?"

"Read the next passage," Vika said woodenly. It had troubled Vika's dreams now for many weeks. *I saw them all: all our children, our children and all the stones of our house, our house and all my bondmates. Stone, all stone in the ice and the dark, their eyes sealed with frozen blood. And no kind fire can take them. For there are lights in the sky, and sounds in the hollows of the hills; and that which was here, and accomplished this cruelty, that thing lingers still—and watches.*

"Lingers still—and watches...." Vika moved away from the window, from the sight of the sky, and took a place by the fire.

Night was falling when Pierre finished the last page and set the screen down gently. He looked across the table at Vika, and shook his head. "These stories tell us of the people's fear," Pierre said. "But we can only guess about the, the *technology*"—he used the Standard word—"of the attackers. Your summaries tell me that you have found no records of anyone who survived the attacks who truly understood what they were seeing."

"There might still be some like that in Dethun's collection," Vika said.

"Except that these are the most complete records," Anke said. "Even if the fragments that we still have not reviewed—and there are hundreds of them, Vika is right—even if they contain a few pieces of objective information—" She shrugged. "Without any context, how will we know?"

"Your analysis," Vika said.

But Anke shook her head. "No analysis can turn a single data point, or a whole range of similar data points, into a model."

"I agree," Pierre said. He rubbed his eyes wearily. "I'm sorry, Vika. We need to see actual artifacts of the Destroyers, if these exist. You are certain that none would have been preserved here in Kheosseth, or in any of the other towns?"

"Not by the Anokothu," Anke said. "They destroyed even their own technology. Why would they keep anything that came from the Destroyers?"

Kelru looked up from the dried fish he was slicing into chunks for the stewpot. "And if anyone who is not Anokothu possesses or knows of such a thing, I have heard no rumor of it."

Pierre glanced at Anke, who sat frowning down at the table. She did not look up. He sighed and said, "Vika, I'm sorry. Nothing you have shown me can compare with what we would learn from seeing the ruins with our own eyes, investigating them with our own equipment. I can't risk our freedom of movement to gain access to more of that."

"I see," Vika said flatly.

"These records are unclear," Pierre said. She could sense him groping for words, frustrated by Kelru's language. "They are not enough knowledge. The last ones especially—they could have been written by people who had lost right thinking." *Gone mad*, Vika translated. Pierre shrugged. "I am sorry. None of this tells us whether the danger is still present, on this world. None of this tells us anything objective about these beings themselves." He straightened. "No. We cannot yield to Dethun's will before the Council of Eight. We must hope instead that Kelru prevails. We must carry our investigation south next spring and summer. And I will not give up hope of helping Kelru's people, when we've achieved our mission."

Anke came forward and touched Pierre's arm, but her serious look was for Vika. "Pierre and I have discussed this," she said in Standard. "And I agree. You should stay with us. Don't go back to Dethun's house tonight."

Without replying, Vika turned back to Pierre. "Are you ordering me to abandon Dethun?" She used Kelru's language.

"I would prefer that we not be divided," Pierre said austerely.

"It would be wiser for all of us to work within Anokothu laws," Vika said. "That's where the power is, here. It isn't with Kelru and his friends. If you work against that power, you risk all our lives, and with them our mission."

"I trust Kelru to keep us safe," Pierre said.

Vika turned to Kelru. "Do you accept this? Can you protect both Pierre and Anke?"

Kelru did not answer at first. Then he said, "I will protect them, because I must. But it is true that Pierre does not understand what the cost might be."

"Our world is at stake here, too," Pierre said. "I have my duty. I can't consider the cost."

"Your duty," Kelru said quietly. "My cost."

Pierre flushed, and said nothing.

Vika clenched her hands into fists. "You say we must try to find their technology," she said to Pierre. "Piece together what it was like, how it did the damage it did." She pointed at her datapad. "But that, in those records—that *is* what happened. What people saw. That is an important piece of the puzzle." She lifted her chin. "Pierre, I'm going back to Dethun's. One of us must."

"I would prefer that you stay here," Pierre said. "We need so much more information, of all kinds. It will take all of us to even begin to—"

"All the children died in the attack, did you read that?" Vika knew she was letting anger take her too far, but she went on, "*All*. And most of those born afterward. The adults, the ones who survived—they thought they were the end of their race. The last." She kept her eyes on Pierre's. "They weren't writing for us to read, far down the years," she said. "They were writing for themselves. And to leave their words behind them when they went into the dark."

Silence followed her words. It was Pierre who looked away at last from Vika's steady gaze—to turn to Anke. Who said, "Let her go, Pierre. She may learn something of real value at the sisterhold. It's certainly possible." She looked sidelong at Vika. "And certainly she'll be safer at the Lady's side."

Safer. The weight of Vika's failure descended on her then, and fully. She wanted to be away from there, far from the silent understanding between Pierre and Anke. She turned away and lifted her thessach from its peg near the door to the anteroom. "It's time I went," she said stiffly.

Kelru was already up, burrowing into his thessach of shaggy night-blue. "You'll be late," he said.

Pierre came forward. "Vika. I thank you for your hard work. I am sorry we do not agree."

She straightened Dethun's gift, the green woolen thessach, down over her body. "I'll go on with my work at Dethun's house. And she may know of some archives in Kheosseth I could study."

"Of course," Pierre said. "Of course. There are still almost four eightdays before the Council sits, and if you find anything that affects my decision—"

"I'll tell you," she said, her traitorous voice trembling. "But now I have to decide what to tell Dethun."

"Tell her nothing," Pierre said sharply. "It's better that she imagine you succeeded." He moved closer and set a comradely hand on her shoulder. "We don't have time to work from within, to persuade and change. We must work freely. Help us in that much."

She only nodded, and he smiled and looked away.

Now she could turn from him, move out from under his hand. Now she followed Kelru into the darkness of the anteroom and out into the cold. As she climbed down the steep, too-high steps, her body remembered Pierre's touch on her shoulder. He should not have touched her. If this was to be her life for now, to work alone—then it was better, easier, never to be touched.

She would have to remember to tell him.

"So," Dethun said. "Tell me how matters stand with your friends." It was late, and the fire in her splendid hearthroom had burned almost to embers. The red light glimmered on heavy hangings, new and brightly embroidered in wool; on low cylindrical candlesticks that bore plump, greasy candles, unlit; on cups and decanters; on paper books, rolled, or pressed flat between heavy boards.

Vika had arrived with her thessach crusted with wet snow, and her decision still unmade after the long walk home beside a silent, brooding Kelru. Dethun had been waiting here, alone—Thiain, she said, had long since gone up to bed. Until that moment Vika had thought only of being alone to think over what had just happened; yet when it came to the point, she was glad to accept Dethun's invitation to linger and have a cup of *khevodh*, the rough berry brandy of Kheosseth. The hand comm had not signaled from her pack; she knew that Pierre would not reach out to her. No doubt he had other matters on his mind just now.... She took the last swallow of her khevodh and set down the little cup.

"Pierre was moved, Lady." She stretched out her stiff hands to the waves of heat billowing out from the firebed. "He was shocked. I think—I'm nearly sure that I persuaded him. He's going to talk to Kelru tonight." The lie was easy.

Dethun sighed heavily. "So yours will not be the last voice he listens to."

"Kelru is persuasive," Vika said, "but he is not one of our people."

"I don't mean Kelru," Dethun said. "I mean Anke. She turned from you. Now she can speak against me with Pierre."

"The decision is Pierre's, not hers," Vika said. "He'll listen to me."

"Will he," Dethun said flatly. She bent to pick up Vika's cup, and refilled it from the same small flask. She gave the cup to Vika. Then she sat again, on a low, padded stool rather than the floor, and looked down at her. "You have such power, over Pierre?"

Vika took another swallow. The second cup of khevodh was as rough as the first, with the same astringent aftertaste. "He likes honesty. And I don't care whether what I say pleases him or not. Anke wants to please him."

"And he to please her?" Dethun's voice came from far away, soft as her fur, soft as the warm bed of ashes where the embers lay gleaming red and black, quick liquid sparks, red and black and the white ash. It looked soft enough to sleep in, warm enough to sleep in. Like Dethun's fur. "Why does she want to please him?" Dethun asked.

Vika sighed, keeping her eyes on the shifting ember-lights. "Because he's her mate."

Dethun's voice sharpened. "They've *mated?*"

"Yes." Vika rubbed her eyes with the heels of her hands, then blinked at the fire. Where was her cup? Here, beside her. It was full again. "They mated. I think it's changed her."

"Odd," Dethun said. "Among us, it's the men who change."

Vika looked up. Dethun sat straight on her stool, tall and severe as a tree in winter, staring down into the fire, her eyes glinting with unguessable thoughts. Red-gold eyes, Kelru's eyes—but cold as Tlankharu in the sky of winter.

Dethun moved to a shelf, chose a different decanter, poured something into a little cup, and sipped it thoughtfully. "Tell me, then," she said, still looming over Vika. Shadows swirled behind her, huge, engulfing. "Tell me what Pierre has offered to Kelru and his friends. Your machines?"

"Not those," Vika said, and grinned for a moment, imagining some rough-clawed man of Windhome trying to make sense of neuroid circuitry: pink viscous liquid, gray fibers, lumps of black nanocrystal. He might try to cook it.... She giggled.

"They want your knowledge, then," Dethun said, still patient. She had always been patient. See how patient she was now, kneeling down by Vika, steadying the cup so Vika could drink a little more. A little more would steady her, take the strange glare out of her eyes. A little more would make the shadows keep still in the corners. Dethun's fingers holding the cup were long and bony, the claws hidden except for their neatly clipped brown tips. "There," Dethun said. "What is it they want?"

Vika closed her eyes and the world slid sideways. She opened them and stared at the fire, and the world slowed, steadied, stopped. Strange stuff, khevodh. Being drunk had never felt like this before— the room pulsing with wavering intensity, a bitter taste in her throat, cold sweat prickling her back and shoulders and scalp.

She shouldn't be drunk. How much had she had?

She shouldn't be drunk, and so—

But the thought would only finish "and so she was," and she said aloud, in Standard, "Typical screwup," and the succession of sounds, harsh and hissing and strange now to her ear, made her laugh. Then she said, "I can only guess what Kelru's friends want. They won't tell *me*."

Dethun's padded stool was very close and very tall, and Dethun looked down at Vika from very far away. "Guess, then," Dethun said.

"The babies," Vika said. "All the little babies who die. I don't think Pierre likes that. He used to have a son—" She swallowed hard. "Oh. I don't feel well."

Dethun lifted the cup from Vika's hand and set it high, high, out of her sight. "The babies," she prompted.

"You have so many sick babies," Vika said. "We know why. We can find out which parents will make the sick ones, and stop it."

"Keep your eyes open," Dethun said. "You'll feel better."

Vika opened her eyes and lurched upright. "We can find the mothers who make the sick babies," she said, enunciating.

"So can we," Dethun said impatiently.

"We can find them before their babies are born," Vika said. "Before they're even conceived." The ashes still looked soft, softer than the cold bed waiting upstairs. She should go upstairs.

"So all the unhealthy women can be packed off to the sisterholds," Dethun said. "That gains us nothing."

"We can tell about the fathers as well," Vika said.

"Excellent," Dethun said. "So we will also tear half the men from their homes and turn them out onto the streets of the towns, or let them roam the back country in packs as the primitives did long ago. That will do much for our order and peace."

"No, Dethun," Vika said. She swallowed, then said very carefully, "We know how to keep the damaged ones from having babies at all. So they can still mate. Still live in families."

Silence, except for the fire, and faintly in Vika's ears the rhythmic rush of her own blood. Then Dethun set down her cup on a small table at her elbow. "I see. Tell me, then. What other plans do Pierre and his mate have for us?"

This was wrong. Dangerous, she knew that, though the knowledge was formless, vague as Dethun's shadow, vast as Dethun's shadow behind and above her, like dark wings, like something floating there. But Vika's voice went on, small and far away. "He pities you. As I pity Thiain. So sad, your lives. Pierre wants to give you hope. Maybe he's right."

"He does not offer us hope," Dethun said. "Only sterility like your own."

Vika swallowed hard. "My people don't like death. Needless death."

"No death is needless," Dethun said. "No life, however short, is without purpose. Your people don't know that, I see."

"Thiain said—" Vika began.

"Thiain!" Dethun's ears flicked flat, then upright again. "Thiain hasn't learned that lesson, either. She's sentimental. Many young ones like her are sentimental. 'If only I had never suffered! If only my children had never been born!' What they don't see is that the failure is *theirs*—not our world's, not their children's." She sat upright. "Life is hard. It requires strength."

Vika rubbed her eyes. "All those damaged babies—"

"I bore my share of them, in the years I lived with men," Dethun said. "The midwife showed them to me, and I said, 'Let it happen as it must.' And here I am, accomplishing my work."

Vika's head ached. "Too much," she mumbled. "Too high a price."

"Ten sixty-fours of years of life, ten generations, dragged from the teeth of death," Dethun said. "Yet after half a summer here, you and this *Pierre* know what is best for us." She sat very still. "You judge us by the standards of your own world. You have told Thiain of it. A soft place, with summers that never end, and food and shelter for everyone." She leaned forward, looming. "I have a suggestion. Judge us, if that pleases you—but first live with us through one winter. If you can."

The winter seemed far away just then, by this muttering fire, in this swirl of heat. But winter lived in Dethun's eyes, and night in the corners of the room; and Vika saw death hanging over her. "We're stronger than we look." Her voice shook, but she formed the words doggedly. "We'll live."

"But will my son?" Dethun's voice was soft.

Confused, Vika stared up at her.

"Pierre has put my son in a difficult position," Dethun said. "I wonder if you can see it."

"He's poor," Vika said. "But he shares what he has like a rich man."

"Kelru could *be* rich," Dethun said. "He could have anything he wanted. I would give it to him, I and my allies. My youngest child, and my only son in Kheosseth. I would support him in a life as a scholar, help him toward a seat on the Council where his gifts could be used to help his people. He's capable and intelligent, and his honor cannot be questioned." Her ears flicked back in displeasure. "But he has always walked his own blind path, following the dreams they taught him at the men's school. Without my help, he will die without any meaningful position, and unfamilied."

"Maybe," Vika said. Her own voice sounded far away, speaking in a hollow place. She was so tired. "But if he let you help him, what would you want from him in return?"

"Right thinking," Dethun said heavily. "This is not a world for dreams."

"No," Vika said. "This world is for pain. And you like it that way. That's what Kelru thinks."

Dethun set her cup down with a sharp rap. "Kelru and his friends are ignorant of the past. Anything new, any change, they're wild for it. That is why he came to where you touched the soil, and met you there, before any prudent action could be taken. He was curious. You made such a *noise*.... He misjudged. I have written to him about it. He should have come to me instead."

"He doesn't trust you," Vika said. "Neither does Pierre. You wanted Pierre to die."

"A mistake," Dethun said. "I grant you that point. What I did forced my son to intervene, and thus he won Pierre's loyalty."

"You suffer." Her hands were knotted in her lap, and her temples pounded with each surge of her blood. "Your people *suffer*. You just brush it all aside. Pierre can't. He should. We're supposed to be, we're supposed to, to, to be objective. But it isn't our people's way."

"Pierre should educate his tongue before he speaks to the Council of Eight," Dethun said. "One thing those old men fear, every one of them, is a meddler. We have found a way to live in spite of the cold, in spite of the deaths of our children—and those deaths matter to us, however it may seem to you." Her voice deepened and roughened. "If our lives could be better, they would be. We would make them so. But *we* cannot forget the destruction. We're a small spark, we who survive, and a feeble one. We will keep burning like that, rather than go out, or be snuffed out by the Destroyers."

The Destroyers. "They have cold hands," Vika said thinly. "I remember...."

Darkness came over her then, like a black cloak, and the shadows took her. This time there were no dreams at all.

NINE

Vika woke in darkness, shivering, with a thin ringing in her ears. Cold, dark—in a burst of panic she struck out and her hands found wood, the latticed wood screen of a cupboard bed. She went still. Dethun's house. She was in her bed at Dethun's winter house. She reached out and slid the screen aside. The little room was dim and empty. The one tiny window let in the gray, chill glow of a snowy dawn.

Vika sat up slowly and swung her feet out of the bed. The ringing in her ears faded, but not the tingling restlessness in her hands and feet, or the bitter taste in the back of her throat. What had happened last night? She remembered Kelru's cool farewell, remembered coming into the house and finding Dethun in the hearthroom. But then it became confused.

Wait. Dethun had offered her khevodh. That was it. Dethun had offered it, and Vika had accepted—and she had made a fool of herself. That was the only clear impression that remained: Dethun looking down at her from a great height, listening, listening, while Vika talked on and on about—

About what? She could not remember. She only hoped she had lapsed into Standard.

She rubbed her tingling hands, then stood up carefully. She was still in the shift she had worn yesterday, a girl's cast-off from the sisterhold, dun-gray and threadbare. Someone had pulled off her boots and her

overdress, but her socks and the shipboard trousers she'd worn with
the shift were still on her body. The clothes stank. She stank. Smoke
and sweat, and the stale miasma of khevodh. At least she wasn't sick.
She deserved to be sick.

She went to the wash-jug beside the brick chimney wall that
warmed the room. She filled a bowl, stripped, and washed herself
carefully. Her head cleared a little.

She was sealing the front seam of her cleanest coverall when the
door creaked open on its leather hinge, and Thiain peered in. "You're
awake!" Her voice was pitched very soft. She moved into the room
and closed the door gently. "Are you well?"

"Well enough," Vika said. She could feel her cheeks burning with
embarrassment. At least Thiain had missed last night's events, asleep
in her room.

Thiain seemed reluctant to speak. She was holding something
half-hidden in the folds of her tunic. "I—" Her ears flicked rapidly,
and she went on, her soft voice pitched a little high, as if she were
frightened. "I put you to bed last night."

"Thank you," Vika said. She felt the blood rise in her cheeks. "It
can't have been pleasant."

"I went into the hearthroom this morning," Thiain said. "I found
this." She held out the thing she had been concealing: a flask, such as
was used to contain medicines or wine.

Vika took the flask and frowned down at it. It was pottery, with
a pale green glaze and a pebbled texture, unusual. She had seen it
before. She had seen it last night. Dethun's hand, pouring—then
steadying the cup on its way to Vika's mouth. Now why would she do
that? "Thiain," Vika said, "what is this?"

"Open it and smell," Thiain said.

Vika did so. Nothing. It was almost empty; she shook a few drops
out onto her palm, tasted them. "Water. So?"

"Dethun rinsed it," Thiain said tensely. "It must have been after
she called me to take you to bed."

Now why— "She said you were asleep," Vika said. The ringing in her ears was louder now. She sat down again on the edge of the bed. "This is the flask she poured from," she said. "For me."

"Did she drink from it?"

Vika blinked at Thiain. "I don't know."

"She told me you were drunk," Thiain said. "But you weren't. She put herbs in your drink. Something to make you talk freely."

Vika's breath caught. "Are you sure?"

"Sisterholds know these things. Herbs to ease pain, to bring on a late birth, to end a pregnancy—or to cause unwisdom." Thiain's voice was still quiet, still calm, but her eyes glittered. "I know this one. I smelled it when—" She stopped, looking uncomfortable.

"When what?"

"She gave you over to me," Thiain said, "and I saw how it was with you. When we left her, I took you out to the midden and put a twig down your throat." She straightened her green overdress a little primly. "You would be much sicker now if I hadn't done that. The herb takes days to work through the body."

"Thank you, then," Vika said slowly. She could remember only short flashes of the night before. The fire, the fire. Long, looping dreams of Dethun leaning over her, Dethun furling black wings and looking down at her, Dethun saying strange things—

Then with an icy rush of clarity, like a black wing lifting, Vika remembered what she had told Dethun. That Pierre and Anke were lovers. That Pierre would oppose Dethun. That Vika would not be able to sway him.

And now, sitting there as the gray light grew in the window like the creeping horror along her spine, she remembered the last of it. Pierre's ideas. The gifts, he had called them, that humans could bring to this world. Freedom for women, among other things.

But Dethun wanted no gifts. And she preferred order to freedom— that was clear.

Vika looked up. Thiain was still there, her eyes dark and sober.

"Why have you told me this?" Vika asked harshly.

"Because I heard what you told Dethun," Thiain said. "That your people might be able to give us...what we lost. Power over our lives." Her eyes narrowed. "You're in danger now."

She's not calling Dethun "Lady." Vika rubbed the back of her neck wearily. "I know." A bitter knowing.

Thiain knelt on the floor, folded her hands in her lap, and spoke softly. "Dethun knows that freedom for women is a gift only she can give, at the price of their service to her. She and other Lady Mothers she controls. And she likes that. She does not want it to change. She talks of the risk of the Destroyers returning if our lives became better—but how would they know that, from the sky?" Thiain raised her hands in a shrug. "Her true concern is power. And she will act to protect it."

Vika sat up straighter. "You mean, she intends to stop Pierre."

"Not only Pierre," Thiain said. "She expects you to be very sick today, and to remember nothing. But, Vika—the memory will come to you in time. And Dethun knows it will. Do you scent my meaning?"

"No," Vika said. "She promised—" she hesitated, remembering Anke's argument at Kelru's house, but then went on, "She promised to guard and protect me as she does you." She looked up at Thiain. "And yet she brought you here."

"Yes," Thiain said firmly. "To a city of men. I was safe in the sisterhold. But we're here for the winter. If we don't leave before spring, I'll come to the Red Mind here."

Vika frowned. "Is there no refuge here for women?"

"None that's truly safe," Thiain said. "Young women don't live in the city, in winter. Or if they do, and the time comes, they and their bondmates must be locked high in a house, with strong, foul smells kept around them to hide their scent. And if the woman has no bondmates, so that the Red Mind lasts many days, then sometimes—she's found by unfamilied men, and taken." Her dark eyes met Vika's. "No. Dethun is not protecting me. Her promise to you meant nothing. She's used you for the last time—drained you of what you know. She is finished with you." She looked down. "You should not have come back here."

Vika got up and went to the high window, looked out. Flakes of falling snow swarmed gray against the clouds to the east. A gray world, dark gray and light, soft and chilly. "Then I have to leave," she said.

"You do," Thiain said. "But you must wait until evening. You can't walk alone through the city in daylight."

"Kelru was to come for me in two days," Vika said.

"Don't wait," Thiain said. Vika heard the urgency in her voice.

"I'll tell Pierre." Vika went to her pack and slid her hand into the comm pocket.

It was empty. She opened the pack and scrabbled through it. Her datapad was here, and other things, but not the comm. "Thiain," she said sharply. "One of my tools is missing."

"I did not take it," Thiain said.

Vika fought back panicked thoughts. What mattered was the fact that she could not reach Pierre. She could not get help. Only Thiain could help her.

Perhaps they could help each other. "Thiain," she said, "come away with me."

"*And go where?*"

Startled by the bitterness, Vika turned and looked at Thiain. She stood very straight in her green tunic, her dark-furred face serious in the faint and growing light. "I'm unfamilied," she said. "A woman like me can find a home, and pride, only in a sisterhold."

"There are other sisterholds," Vika said.

"And all their Lady Mothers follow Dethun, or fear her," Thiain said. "No. I'm safe nowhere. But here my word is pledged. Here I stay." She looked at Vika, who was stuffing her possessions into her pack. "Don't do that yet. Dethun expects you to be sick. Stay in this room all day. Stay quiet. Before evening I'll return and tell you the way out, and the way to her son's house. And I'll pretend to the Lady that you're sleeping. That should give you time to reach it."

Vika felt cold. "Thiain—why?"

"Because I cannot let you be silenced," she said, and left before Vika could thank her.

Vika left Dethun's house when the street was filled with shadows, and nearly empty of people. Thiain let her out. But before she turned to go in again, she took Vika's head between her hands and leaned down and took a long breath, then another. "I'll remember your scent," she said softly. "Journey well." She stepped back.

Vika caught Thiain's hand. This woman could have been her friend. But it seemed unlikely that they would meet again. She released Thiain, turned, and moved away, keeping close to the walls of the houses on the near side of the street in case Dethun was looking out her study window above. Soon cold and darkness would close the trade-houses, close the schools and exchanges, send the workers home. But in this place, unlike the bright cities of Earth, the homes were hidden, and the fires within. It was a city of blank walls, walls of gray stone and yellowish brick and thick squared timbers. Walls that hid the city's heart, and its thoughts.

Vika was to move south, Thiain had said, parallel to the river, until she reached the end of the wharf district. Then she would have to travel west, away from the river, toward Kelru's house. She must keep the concealing hood over her face, move in the shadows, and speak to no one. Thiain had been clear about that. "If you come to the river itself," she said, "veer away. The last of the riverboats are leaving for the south before the ice comes, and the docks are filled with their crews. Country men about to go home, looking about them for one last new thing to see."

As Vika passed one courtyard door it opened, and a woman stepped out carrying a lamp, a woman visibly pregnant, with a bright plaid shawl over her shoulders and black tassels bobbing at her knees from the fringe of her overdress. She gave Vika a startled look. Vika hurried on.

Three streets farther on a trade-house was closing; through its open double door Vika saw wooden bins stacked with shriveled tubers, dark woody lengths of salted fish, some shaggy bales of brown and gray fleeces. A man shook out a cloth and laid it over the fish, and from farther inside a child's voice said, "Tavaru promised us half the blood if we hurry." Then she was beyond hearing. Another street, two more streets. Here was a men's inn Thiain had warned her of, with its stylized fire-symbol splashed over the door in orange paint. As she passed under the windows she heard men singing, a wordless, droning rumble that pulsed like a heart beating, shaping a close and twisted chord that shifted, shifted again, and faded as she moved on.

She was crossing the street beyond, lifting her green thessach a little to step over the gutter in the center of the street, when a voice behind her spoke, a man's voice: "A long cry aren't *you*, though, from your sisters at Thanen River?"

Vika jumped over the rimy, stinking trickle in the gutter, then hitched her pack higher on her shoulders and moved on. And the voice said, "That's poor courtesy," and another said, "She looks odd. Let's see her face."

Vika broke into a run. The heavy thessach hampered her, the pack hampered her—it was off-balance. And she was afraid her hood would fall back. She dodged into a side street and ran. Perhaps they were behind her; perhaps not. They could follow her scent in the air, they could hear her three streets ahead. They could take their time. She ran. If she vanished tonight, it would serve Dethun well. Perhaps there were men who knew it. Perhaps there were men who wished it for their own reasons.

Fish, she smelled fish, rotting. She was nearing the river, and she saw no break in the buildings, no alleyway that would let her dodge south before she reached the bank. Ahead through the darkness she saw a fire, and shadows passing before it, and beyond it a lamplit window that bobbed gently—a barge-house. The river. *Right is south.* She slowed her pace, gasping—the air was too bitter. She let herself walk. Even in the cold, the smells were thick and layered: fish, wool, leather. Juices souring into wine or vinegar. The men following her wouldn't be able to—

Some distance behind her a voice said clearly, "The stranger passed here, there she passed," and she ran. The riverside was lined with the fronts of warehouses, high and unbroken; maybe some of the dark doorways were passages through them, but she did not know which. She heard no pursuit, no cries. But Pierre had told her that was not how they hunted here. They ran silent, listening for their quarry.

It was night now; when she came at last to a side street she saw it only as a glimmer of dirty snow between the dark bulk of two buildings. But it led away from the river. She hurried along it, trying to control her gasping breath—running was hard after months sealed up in the sisterhold. She would take the next street that led south, toward Kelru's house. There was the first corner, lit by a flickering lamp hung over a courtyard gate. She quickened her pace. It would be good to be moving in the right direction again—

As she rounded the corner strong hands caught and pinned her, and someone tugged her hood down over her face, blinding her. "I guessed it," a man's voice said, satisfied. "Tell Nakhalru we have her."

TEN

Pierre stood at Kelru's window, looking out at nothing, at the night, at his own reflection and the room behind him, distorted in the small rippled panes. His neck and shoulders ached, stiff with tension. No word had come from Vika since Kelru left her at Dethun's house last night. Pierre had commed her this morning, but she hadn't accepted it. Or was sleeping. Or sick. *Or Dethun has turned on her.*

"Kelru's been hours," Anke said from her place by the fire.

Kelru had agreed to go to Dethun's house, to make sure that Vika was all right. "He'll be here soon," Pierre said.

"Maybe he stayed for tea."

Pierre swung around. "It is no joke!"

"Sorry," Anke said, her blue eyes blank.

Pierre turned away from her. They had had another bitter argument this afternoon. He should not have touched Anke. It was wrong for them both, wrong for the mission, wrong in every way. She seemed to need him only physically. Twice they had been alone together, these past two days. Both times they'd made love. And he had begun to see what it was for her, what *he* was for her: a convenience, a kind of drug. As he had been before.

It was wrong. He should end this.

He closed his eyes. *Oh, yes.* He could resolve to renounce her. But he would fail. He would turn to her again, when his need was too great, when human touch, physical release were worth the cost to his pride. And he knew, bitterly, that those times would come often, over the years.

He clenched his fist against the cold glass. Now that they had resumed this path together, every hopeless step of it was clear. It had cost him his remaining authority over Anke. It would cost him Vika's respect, and the hope of her friendship, when she found out—if she did not know already.

And the worst of it was Kelru. Kelru was angry with him. He had seen it for the past three days, seen it when Kelru had left this afternoon with so few words. "I'll fetch Vika home for you," he had said. "Perhaps with someone else here, you'll get more rest." Pierre had looked away, only to see Anke smiling slightly.

He could not restore things to the way they had been. But even so, he could hate being a fool. As he hated this waiting, not knowing what Dethun or her Anokothu allies might have chosen to do to Vika. Who was young, and alone, and his responsibility....

Voices outside, below, in the courtyard.

Pierre moved swiftly to the window. He could see nothing below—it was blocked by the wooden stairway. But he could hear men's voices, many of them, muttering together. Angrily.

Pierre slid Kelru's hunting knife from its sheath where it hung near the door, and moved into the chilly darkness of the anteroom. He opened the door a crack, letting in a gust of icy air, and saw a dark figure on the porch.

Pierre moved to shut the door, bar it, call for Anke—but then Kelru's voice spoke. He was turned away, facing down toward the yard. "I'll see there's a good fire," he called. "A moment, and you can all come up."

Pierre opened the door wide. "You're safe," he said.

"Are you safe, too, brother?" Pierre heard the acid in the words.

"Kelru," he said, "where is Vika?"

But Kelru swept past him into the hearthroom and looked around. "Anke," he said, "build up the fire. We have guests."

Pierre stayed in the doorway. "Kelru. *Where is Vika?*"

"Here," her voice said quietly, and he whirled to see her coming into the room. She was dirty, bedraggled, her expression bleak and exhausted—but she was here.

He took two steps toward her and seized her shoulders. "Vika," he said, his voice rough. "Thank God." But she stiffened and drew back from him. He released her. "What happened?"

She was shivering, her green thessach mud-smeared and wet. "I wanted to c-comm you," she said. "But Dethun took it. She must have taken it,"

"Come in by the fire," Pierre said. He felt steadier now. Vika was safe. He had failed her, but she had come through. He steered her to a cushion on the warm slate near the flames, helped her out of her thessach, and began building up the fire. Anke wrapped a blanket around Vika's shoulders, but her expression was tight.

Kelru loomed over Vika, his ears still, his eyes dark. "Now. Tell me. What happened?"

Vika looked up at him, her face dark with anger. "Dethun drugged me last night. And I told her everything."

Pierre sat back on his heels. "'Everything.' Do you mean—"

She looked at him. "She knows you've decided we won't help her. She knows I'm of no use to her." Kelru swore and turned away. Vika took a breath. "And she knows what the next mission could do to help the women here. Give them back what they had before the Destroyers. Control over their mating, free lives—" She shook her head.

"She knows you're a threat to her power." Kelru's voice was a growl.

"All right," Pierre said. "Vika. Just rest. You're safe here." She was almost gray with exhaustion, blue shadows under her eyes. She must not guess his worry over what had happened. She must only see that he was concerned for her.

Behind him as he worked on the fire, Pierre heard others coming into the room, heard Kelru moving around pouring bowls of hot water, saying, "Share this. Share my fire. With thanks I welcome you." When the fire had caught, Pierre rose to help. Six men, seven, snowy and wet, squatted against the walls of the room, blinking at the fire and cradling the steaming bowls in their long clawed hands. Their bulk filled the room, men shaggy with the coming winter, and heavily cloaked. They smelled of wet wool, stale woodsmoke, the distinctive musky odor of their wet fur. They dripped on the bare boards of the floor, and their eyes glittered in the firelight as they studied the humans.

"Friends," Kelru said, and Pierre turned to look at him. He stood at ease in the center of the room. "Friends, you are welcome here, and I thank you again for your help. As my brother Pierre will thank you, when he understands what you've done—finding this woman, and bringing her to safety this night."

Pierre rose to his feet. "Tell me of it," he said.

But it was Nakhalru who spoke, not Kelru—one of Kelru's neighbors, and some kind of cousin. He was a lean, sour-faced, sandy-furred man, tall like Kelru; Pierre had spoken with him once or twice before. "Kelru came to the inn—"

"The one near the men's school, where some of us still meet," Kelru said.

Nakhalru's ears went back. "I'll give him the news," he said, "and waste no words. Kelru came and said, this stranger woman is in Dethun's house; I must fetch her out. *Nothing simpler*, we all cried. A woman's house, a Lady Mother, *his* mother. Well, I went—men trust my face—and found it all in a roar, the Lady herself in the street before her door, swollen up like a stormcloud, *Ah, ah, fools*, she was saying—"

"To the men she employs," Kelru said. "They watch her house, they do her bidding."

"Unless they slip away to an inn to piss," Nakhalru said, "and then top themselves off again with khevodh. These did." He jerked a thumb at Vika. "And just then, it seems, off she went. Her luck."

"Not luck," Vika said quietly. "Thiain gave them coins for the inn."

Nakhalru's ear twitched impatiently. "So off Dethun sent them, and half their inn-companions, to bring her back," Nakhalru said. "And off I went, and then all of us, to find her first. And we did." He looked pleased. "We guessed first where she was going, you see."

Pierre looked around at them all. "I thank you," he said.

"She led us a chase, that woman," Nakhalru said. "Who'd have thought anything so small could move so fast? If Ghelu here hadn't had the wit to pin her against the river and drive her south, and send the rest of us around to lie for her at the end of the next street—"

"Those others would have found her first," another man said. His eyes glittered. "And then the river, I think." Pierre saw it for an instant: Vika's corpse sliding into the dark water, to be frozen all winter down in the dark mud among the slimy pilings, to emerge in the spring, swollen and shapeless. He swallowed hard and forced the image aside. Vika was there, safe, by the fire—looking up at the man who had spoken, with her eyes full of darkness.

"Better it had been the river," someone muttered. "She'll end there anyway, with Dethun for an enemy."

"It's worse than that," Kelru said to Nakhalru and the rest. "Dethun drugged her. We must assume that Dethun knows all our hopes, all the arguments we planned to make before the Council of Eight, to help our people, and to keep my brother free. She can prepare against them, poison them before we speak them." He looked around at them all, his ears still. "So, then. Those arguments must change. I propose this."

"We will listen, cousin," Nakhalru said, and Pierre heard scattered mutters of agreement.

"I will speak alone before the Council," Kelru said. "I'll say nothing of Pierre's ideas, or of his world. I'll speak instead of his rights as a man. With a man's right of choice in shelter, a man's right of choice in speech—"

"And Dethun will faint from the force of your arguments," Nakhalru said, "and the Council of Eight will weep. Rights! You want to talk of rights to the Old Anokothu!"

A husky-voiced man began to chant. *"Against the Destroyers' darkness, there is no fire—against their voice, there is no word—in their shadow, light flees, and there is no mind, no choosing—"* Listening, Pierre shivered. Vika sat with her head bowed, her face turned away.

"Ah, Bekhireg," Kelru crooned, "how you frighten me. Let us all go and hide over the mountains, for fear the Council might speak an angry word. Or—" He looked around at them. "Or choose to believe as I do, that there is still hope for these strangers, these friends of mine. And so for us, and for our world. The risk is a little more, true. But you need not stand with me. Let the risk be mine."

Pierre drew a breath to protest. But Nakhalru was rising to speak. "If you lose," he said, "and the Council orders your exile, these strangers will die. Little soft things, bare-skinned as a newborn baby. Can Pierre shoot? Can any of them build a fire?"

"We must hope that I succeed with the Council," Kelru said. "But we will also prepare. I'll teach my brother and his mate, and the woman who is my guest. They'll learn to ride my beasts. They'll learn the Rules of Winter—know them as we do, as we know the scent of our own breath. And they'll gather their strength."

"What they have of strength," Nakhalru said. "How far will you ride? And where?"

"South, of course," Pierre said. "Toward the ruins we wish to study."

"Toward the skull places," Nakhalru said. "That is really your wish?"

"My—necessity," Pierre said. "Anke needs to study them, and we will help her. There must be somewhere we could find refuge—friends of your cause?"

One of the other men said, "It would be death to them to take you in, if you were exiled."

"And in any case we cannot turn south," Kelru said. "To move south, we would have to travel past many farms, many towns. I think you do not understand what exile means, Pierre. Anyone who sees us would be not just allowed to kill us, but expected to do it."

Pierre frowned and looked down at his hands. "Then where can we go?"

Kelru leaned back. "There are places in the north where exiles can find shelter," he said. "Places where warm water rises from the ground, or where the hills block the wind. Trappers live in such places. We'll find one, and wait there for spring."

Nakhalru looked gloomy. "There are skull places there, too. Poisoned lands. But perhaps that will make Pierre happy."

"Not at all, cousin," Pierre said drily.

Kelru stood up and looked around at the others. "Are we agreed, then? That only I will speak?"

Nakhalru gave a gusty sigh. "*I* agree," he said. "You'll argue from birth-family, and that lets us out. Even me. Good enough. Free, we can help you. A little."

Pierre looked around the room, but Nakhalru had spoken for them, it seemed. They were all getting to their feet. "Wait," Pierre said. "Kelru, you cannot give up these men's help, or their backing. What can you do alone, in front of the Council of Eight?"

"What I must," Kelru said quietly.

"Kelru, I warned you of this road you've chosen," Nakhalru said. "Dangerous. I said it. You remember."

"Cousin," Kelru said, "you were wise. But I've passed the last turning. It's too late."

Nakhalru stared into his eyes a moment longer, then turned away. The door closed behind him. Pierre looked at Kelru, stricken.

"Don't fear for me," Kelru said. He seemed calm, assured.

Pierre looked again at the closed door, and through it, beyond it, at the night, the winter, the years to come. "I wish," he said bitterly, "that you had let me die in Dethun's sisterhold."

"Ah, no," Kelru said. "I know you are not so unwise. There's a book I studied once. *Better breath choked with snow, better words of despair, than the silence of death—which is beyond all regret only because it is beyond all choice....* Now we should rest." He was looking at Vika, who had hidden her face in her hands.

Pierre knelt beside her. "Vika—"

Before he could touch her she straightened, letting him see her face, dirty and streaked with tears. But her expression was stern, controlled. "It's my fault," she said. "If I hadn't been a fool last night at Dethun's house, we would still be safe."

"You did nothing wrong," Pierre said. "She drugged you without your knowledge. You were her guest. You were at her mercy."

"I was a fool," she said roughly. "Let me feel like a fool." After a moment she looked up at Kelru and said, "I must be your guest now, for there is no other home for me."

"You are welcome," Kelru said. "Come, you're hungry. Share this bread before you rest." He took the bread-case of stiffened leather down from its high peg, opened it, and held it out to her.

Pierre watched Vika take the rough, dry round of bread and taste a little. "Eat all of it," he said. "You'll need your strength."

"More than strength," Anke said, reaching out to the bread-case and taking a piece for herself. "To survive in the open here, in winter—it can't be done."

"It can be done," Kelru said, "though of course it is best not to *be* in the open. And we'll begin easily, with the Rules of Winter all children learn. For example, you've eaten your supper, and so you must not eat that bread."

Anke looked up at him in surprise. "Even one piece of bread?"

His ears flicked back, then forward again. "This is winter. Even here in the city, you must form new habits."

"Tell me," Anke said, putting the bread back in the case.

Kelru straightened. "As I said—the Winter Rules. Before you go outside, you must be sure your feet are dry and well-covered, your hands protected, your ears covered unless you're hunting—can your ears be frostbitten? They're so flat." He looked questioningly at Pierre.

"They can," Pierre said, remembering winter hunts in the hills around his mother's village.

Pierre saw Vika rub her face surreptitiously with her sleeve. She had finished the bread and was gathering the crumbs from her lap into her palm. "What else, Kelru?" Her voice was steady now. She could be so strong, Pierre thought—not young at all in some ways.

"Never be cold when you can be warm." Kelru began to tick the items off on his brown claws. "If you cannot be warm, keep moving. Stay out of the wind. In the Deep Cold, never go out at night. Eat your share when food is offered, and while it's hot. If there is no food, sleep as much as you can. Never waste heat—keep your piss in the house until it cools off." Anke snorted, and Kelru looked reproachful. "A old country custom," he said, "but a useful one."

Vika shook her head slowly. "Different rules," she said. "I grew up in a city called Kolkata, where it was never cold enough for water to freeze."

Kelru stared at her. "No winter? No seasons at all?"

"Not like this," she said. "Even winters were hot. The summer was even hotter, and it rained so hard there were floods." Her voice was sad. Pierre remembered with a jolt that Kolkata was one of the cities that had been declared doomed by the sea in the last message from TFE—by now its streets would be flooded, its silent buildings crumbling into the water....

"A strange place," Kelru said. "At least Pierre knows what snow is like."

"Yes," Pierre said. Snow on Christmas Day, dusting the tangles of diseased trees on the hills around his mother's house, a week before she died. Snow crusting his old boots as he went out to gather deadwood for an illegal fire, the last she would see.

"Our world is warm almost everywhere now," Vika said. "When the ice melted, whole cities drowned. In my district, my country—India—some of the biggest cities were lost. My home—by now it is one of them."

Kelru looked at her, his long arms folded. "Pierre has told me some of that. How strange your world must be. Here you'll need more strength than it has given you."

Pierre saw Vika's mouth tighten. Perhaps she disliked being called weak. He spoke. "Many of us died as the world changed," he said, "in the dry times, and the storms and floods. We fought over water and food. Old farms turned into deserts. New farms had to be made from dying forests, and the old tundras weren't ready to become forests. My people have been tested, too."

"A slow testing," Kelru said. "We'll waste no more time, brother. Tomorrow we'll make a beginning. Tomorrow we'll see what you are. You must all rest." He pointed with his thumb at Anke. "And I mean rest, Pierre. Apart from *her*."

Pierre was conscious of Vika looking at the floor, her face flushed, embarrassed. He wondered why it mattered to her. Or to him.

In the silence of Kelru's sleeping loft, in the gentle warmth that breathed from the bricks of the chimney, Kelru lay watching and listening as the strangers slept. In the far corner Anke huddled alone in her blankets, smelling of anger even in sleep. She must be cold, but she had refused to share her bed with anyone tonight. On the other pallet Pierre sprawled out beside Vika, the tightness that never left him, waking, all gone now. Asleep, they all sounded like children—their quick light breath, their restless turning. Poor little creatures, so far from their home.

Kelru thought about Vika—the one who spoke most clearly, yet was silent and listened when that choice was right. Kelru honored her for her grasp of the hospitable customs, her loyalty to the one who had first sheltered her. Vika had had a rough waking this day. Now she understood: Dethun put her beliefs ahead of every consideration. Dethun was so careful of her great principles that she trod on any person who might thwart her, any consideration that slowed her in her path. Kelru wondered if there were people like Dethun on the world called Earth.

He stirred on his pallet, turned onto his side on the old, thinning fur. So far down the road of expediency his mother had gone. Kelru could no longer imagine what she would hesitate to do. She was a dangerous enemy.

He gazed at the little horizontal sliver of pale-yellow light that touched the rough bricks—chilly light from the moon, from far out in the clear, still night. He, Kelru, was dangerous as well—to himself and to his friends. In making Pierre his brother, he'd struck at Dethun's pride where it was most tender. Struck with the glee of a boy just come to manhood, angry at the home that had turned him out. A man grown, he was—had been one for years now. Yet Dethun could make him an angry boy again with a word, with the flick of an ear.

And now again Dethun held his life in her hands, as she had when she gave him birth: the child of her age, her last before she finally took the place she had prepared for herself at the sisterhold. If, by the fire in the birthing hut, those cold eyes of hers had seen this day, would Kelru have breathed twice?

ELEVEN

Vika woke with something warm against her back, someone's breath tickling her scalp. She realized first how strange this was—and then, fleetingly, how good it felt. And then she was awake, and knew it was only Pierre.

A small, thick-paned window let in enough gray morning light that she could see the bricks of the chimney in the center of the room, and in the space beyond it, another pallet like this one. Anke lay there, her head pillowed on a wadded blanket. Her habitual tense expression was gone, leaving only the precise beauty of her bones, and her fair skin delicately flushed with warmth. Strange, this defenseless prettiness. Awake, she had always had the cold glitter of an unsheathed knife.

As if sensing the thought, Anke opened her eyes. "Good morning," she said in Standard. "Don't you two look comfortable."

Pierre stirred at Vika's back, then sat up quickly. Anke laughed. "You forgot the bit about putting a naked sword between you," she said. "But don't worry, Pierre—I know you were a perfect gentleman."

"Leave it," Pierre said.

He pulled a plain black sweater from his pack and tugged it on. But he didn't change out of the woolen trousers he had slept in. When he stood up, Anke said, "I take it back about the sword. You didn't need it with those things on."

He looked at her with bleak patience. "I have a word for both of you. Are you prepared to listen?" Anke shrugged angrily. "Good,"

Pierre said. "We have much to learn in the coming weeks. You will both do as Kelru asks, and learn what he teaches you. Without mockery. This is his world. He can save us. Without his help, our mission will fail."

"God forbid," Anke said, smiling faintly.

Pierre took a hissing breath, his dark eyes stark, and Vika looked at him, startled. "Without mockery," he repeated, in a low, trembling voice. Then he turned abruptly and climbed down the ladder.

Vika shook her head at Anke. "That was odd. Why should that old swear word make him angry?"

"One of his holy words," Anke said. "A lot of those Québecers are half-Catholic. But some go all the way. Like Pierre." She looked up from pulling on her socks and lifted an eyebrow. "Didn't you know?"

"He's always been odd," Vika said. "But—if he follows one of the outlaw religions, then he can't have signed the Covenant. How did he get on the team?"

"Maybe he lied," Anke said. "You could ask Dr. Kozlov. If he weren't dead." She bent to straighten the toe of her sock. "It's not a bad religion, really, in our position."

"Why's that?"

"You're Gaian, aren't you? Well, after you die, you'll never reintegrate into Gaia. You've left the cycle, Vika. The end of the road. When Pierre dies, though, he'll go floating straight up to God. Twenty-six light-years is nothing when you're omnipresent."

Vika didn't laugh. She was still absorbing this. Pierre—stuffy, conventional Pierre—was an outlaw. He believed things the world-rapers had believed. Absolute morality, and the divine mandate to exploit....

She had little time to consider the matter over the next days. They all had much to do, and much to learn. The snow fell often now, and thickly, creeping higher against the walls of Kelru's courtyard. The three of them helped keep the door to the stable under his house shoveled clear, and with Kelru, they took his riding animals out daily for exercise—Thonn, his favorite, a pale-furred, middle-aged male, untrustworthy with anyone but Kelru; gray-furred Feth, old and stolid, content to be dominated by both Kelru and Thonn; and Nukh, dark-furred and too small for Kelru to ride, but useful for carrying packs, and now Pierre.

The beasts made Vika nervous. But Kelru insisted that she and Anke learn to ride—Pierre already could manage it. After a solid eightday of practice, Vika could control old Feth well enough to ride him at a walk, in town. She still hated country rides, running full tilt along the snowy roads. She didn't trust her grip on Feth's fur. The saddle had stirrups, so a bowman could stand up to shoot, but even after Kelru shortened them as far as possible, they were still just out of reach of her feet. Kelru said she needed a smaller saddle, a child's, but such things had to be made specially, and cost more than he could afford. She did her best to hold on with her legs. Her muscles burned at the end of each day.

Kelru also taught them how to care for the animals. Vika took her turns cleaning their shared stable, and brushing smooth their thick winter coats. It had to be done every day, or the thickening fur would become matted and untidy. The beasts seemed to like it, pressing close against her as she worked—solid walls of thick, coarse hair. She couldn't help being afraid of them. The teeth, the claws.... Kelru took all three beasts hunting in the hills every eightday or so, an all-day trip from which they came back muddy, bloody, and replete.

The Peace of Winter was coming, and with it the first meeting of the Council of Eight. Vika trusted Kelru's intentions, but she was not at all sure of his ability to carry them out. He would be arguing for their mission—and, since exile might well kill them, for their lives. Yet the votes he had counted on were drifting away. Kelru worked for Yradhu, the Judge of the Roads—the man who determined when travel was safe enough that contracts were officially in force. Yradhu was one of the younger members of the Council; but now he avoided Kelru, claiming that he wanted to avoid even the appearance of bias.

Even Pierre's pose of confidence was eroding.

Secretly, Vika was beginning to pity Pierre. The whole disastrous course of this mission had been out of his control. Yet he was still responsible for it. Stiff, stuffy Pierre, smug Pierre, was hollow-eyed now with worry. Vika shared a pallet with him, because Anke still refused to share with anyone, and Kelru took up all of his. So she knew that Pierre slept badly these days. Long days of preparation for disaster were followed by long nights of lonely thought, about which he never spoke.

Part of Pierre's trouble must be worry over Anke. In the past few days, she had withdrawn completely—even her mockery had fallen silent. She sat for hours on end, eating little, rarely stirring from the fire. Worn out with tension, Vika had no patience left, and she made Anke no allowances. Anke turned nowhere but inward, to no one but herself.

Vika took up meditation again, for the first time since she was seventeen. She was looking for solitude, if not for peace. And several times, coming suddenly up the ladder to the loft, she came upon Pierre praying—encounters from which they both retreated with embarrassment. In fireside conversation he fended off questions about his beliefs. Vika could guess that this was a habit formed in his childhood. However half-heartedly, Québec was a Covenant subdistrict, with the Covenant laws against proselytizing for the old faiths. Even objective discussion of the world-rapers' religions was against custom, if not quite against the law.

Kelru, however, seemed to have overcome his own doubts— or passed through them to a calm fatalism. His somber mood had lifted. He sold the few valuables left in his house to provide them all with the essentials—another winter tent in addition to his own; thick woolen bedrolls; oiled ground cloths; felt boots and liners; fur hats and mittens; well-made packs for spare clothing and food. Day by day, he added to their supply of dried meat, tubers, and fruit. He insisted that they keep everything essential in their packs, ready to be snatched up at a moment's notice. He brought home extra meat for his animals, feeding them up for a hard push.

Vika knew how to knit—one of her silent childhood hobbies— and taught both Anke and Pierre. Kelru traded for some skeins of brown woolen yarn, and while they listened to Kelru's teaching in the evening, they made themselves more socks, scarves to wrap around their faces in the cold, hats to cover their heads under the hoods. Kelru remarked that he found having fur much more convenient.

In time, Vika came to see the value of this calm preparation for the worst. Her own anxiety faded a little as she pitched in to help Kelru. He also had his work for the Judge of the Roads: he rode out into the countryside daily now, as the snow lay deeper and deeper. She went with him once, on Feth, for riding practice. They took the main road north, up the valley, riding into the wind, and stopped at midday at a sort of inn. For a small fee, they tethered their animals in a frigid, gloomy barn. For a larger fee, they were admitted to the inn itself, a large plain room with straw on the floor and a sleeping loft for men. At least there was a good fire. For a last bit of copper, they were allowed to heat up the food they had brought. But they didn't linger, once they had eaten and warmed up slightly. Several groups of travelers were there already; their silent watchfulness was oppressive.

They headed south again as the afternoon drew on. A thin overcast cut the glare of the sun on the snow, and it was good to have the wind behind them. The road was almost empty of travelers, and the farmholds they passed had a sealed look, with firewood stacked neatly around the walls of the houses and barns. It was getting colder every day. The snow that fell now was like dust in the air, and the wind stirred it up the same way, dashing it along the road ahead of them. The wind was the only sound, and Kelru's blue thessach the only color.

Kelru dropped back to ride beside her. "Four days until the meeting." His voice sounded small in the vastness.

"You've sworn to serve the Council," Vika said. "If they rule against us, won't you be breaking that oath by saving us?"

"Pierre is my brother," he said. "They cannot order me to let him die."

"I'm glad to hear it," she said. "So. Where will we go? To those outlaw settlements you mentioned? Do you know where they are?"

"I've never ridden so far." Kelru let out a breath, a quick puff of freezing fog. "And they are not on maps. But we will find one. Some who live in those places are hunters and trappers—unfamilied people, uneducated, uncouth. But some are exiles. They might listen to us."

She looked up at him. "And we'll stay there until spring?"

"Until spring, yes." He raised his hand in greeting to a rider headed north, then went on, "On the way we may pass some of the ruins the Destroyers left. The skull places. Pierre says that in such a place, with fortune, you might learn what you need to learn. Then a fast journey south, and Pierre can send his message."

"So there's hope." She was honestly surprised.

"Hope, yes," Kelru said. "A little." And then he was silent, as if speaking of hope was a danger, too. They rode in silence all the way back to the city gates.

That evening, Kelru taught them a game called "snatch" that involved some bone dice and a pile of wooden counters of various shapes. Anke withdrew to a corner with her datapad and put in her audio plugs. Pierre and Kelru both seemed to enjoy themselves, laughing as they fought for the counters. But Vika was pretending— the hollow woman. She could only vaguely remember how she'd felt during training—the soaring ecstasy of being chosen to be part of this adventure. How sure of herself she had been, with the comforting support of Dr. Kozlov, the sly jokes shared with Lucas, Fadma's patience, Isamu's warm friendship. All gone, all gone. All she could think of was her last real-time conversation with her parents, by commscreen, during the transit to the Moon. Her mother rising abruptly and walking out of the room. Her father sighing, and then telling Vika, "We've said all there is to say. Let's just make it a clean farewell, shall we?" The sadness in his eyes then had planted a sliver of ice in her heart.

The game ended with all the counters in a heap in front of Kelru. Anke had long since gone upstairs to sleep. The three of them moved nearer the fire, and Kelru took out some mending, though he did not seem in a rush to begin it. They sat in silence, warming their feet. Vika listened to the hollow hoot of the wind around the eaves of the house. Cold. It was beginning.

She looked down at the hearthstones beside her. Kelru's long, powerful hand rested, slightly curled, on the frayed gray wool of his tunic. The reddish fur on his fingers looked like velvet, with little tufts over the knuckles. She knew that the skin of his palms was bare and brown, that it would feel hard and cool to her touch. If she dared to touch him.

Then the moment was over. Kelru picked up his work. He had turned out his leather bag of old winter clothing and was trying to piece together enough for the women. It didn't seem possible to Vika, even with everything that was nearly worn out, and everything too small, pressed into service. They could not buy new clothing: keeping wool-beasts alive through the winter was expensive, so cloth was scarce and high-priced. Vika realized now that the spinning and weaving and dyeing done at Dethun's sisterhold supported everyone there.

Now Kelru sat frowning at a tunic he'd turned inside out. "These seams are especially fine," he said to Vika. "My mother-sister Akhian's work. It would be a pity to take them out just to make the tunic smaller." He looked speculatively at her body. "No. I see it. If you fold the tunic at the sides and belt it in, the way Pierre does, you can wear it. No one will care that you wear it like a man; they'll just think you're a boy."

"I don't really need this," she said. "You've given us so much already."

Kelru seemed surprised. "I share what I have. The Judge of the Roads pays me for my services."

"You had little chance to work last summer," Pierre said.

"My word was pledged," Kelru said. "And the Judge never has much work for me in the summer. I could have been copying out documents for suits that will come before the Council of Eight this winter. But that pays nothing, hearth sweepings. It's the riding in rough weather that keeps me."

"But now you have three of us to support," Vika said.

He looked at her, both ears flat back—exasperation, she judged. "Does it matter? If one of my fathers came here, poor and ill, would I turn from him?"

"Dethun has turned from you," Pierre said.

"She saw that I don't need her." Kelru seemed to brood for a moment. "And she—if she believes that an action, or a way of thinking, is right, then no other way exists. She is certain that she sees through to the true foundation of things. Of course it can be painful to those who don't see." He picked up the poker and turned a log over. A shower of sparks shot up from it. "That is why she left our farm, a few years before I was turned out, and went to the sisterhold."

"She has freedom there," Vika said.

Kelru snorted. "Now that she is Lady. But for most who live there, freedom is the Lady's gift, and she can withdraw it. So is it freedom at all? I would call it safety."

"It's a kind of safety that matters." She was thinking of Thiain.

"It's good that such places exist," Kelru said. "But there are other good places for women. In families, for example."

Vika caught her breath, then asked the question that had been troubling her now for weeks. "Will you ever join a family?"

Kelru's ears flicked back, then up again. Pierre shook his head. "That is a rude question," he murmured.

"I'm sorry," Vika said.

"No matter." Kelru stared into the fire, the tunic bunched forgotten in his lap. "I was born late, Dethun's last child. And I had no womb-sibling. My people fear that a child born alone will produce damaged children. I won't be asked to join a family. And my mother has no interest in arranging it." His voice was tranquil. "Or I in asking her for the favor."

"Do you ever wish you could?" She swallowed in a dry throat. "Do you ever feel any desire to mate?"

Kelru looked at her austerely. "We aren't like you," he said. "I'm not like Pierre. Half ice, half fire, all the time. Mating is always there for Pierre. He can always do it, he can always think of it. Or not do it, and not think of it." He brushed away Pierre's attempt to interrupt. "My people keep all things in their proper place and time. Nothing spills over." His red-gold eyes glittered in the firelight. "But at the proper time, nothing is denied."

"Very neat," Pierre said, staring at the fire. His cheeks were flushed. "Still, I would not want to change what I am."

Vika looked away. She would have liked to change, just then. To sidestep the narrow, sterile future that stretched out before her. At best, preparing their report for Earth, and then nothing. Living as a burden on Kelru. Able to help his people only if the Council of Eight permitted it. If not—sitting by the fire, winter after endless winter, with Pierre and Anke—if one of them didn't kill the other, eventually. And Kelru—but he would be dead of old age, in thirty or forty years. People did not live long here.

And all this was the best possible future, if the Council of Eight voted in their favor. If they failed there, they would die, whether or not it was officially ordered. Or they would live in hiding, on the run, at the cost of Kelru's honor and position.

"I'm tired," she said abruptly. "I'm going up to bed."

Kelru stood and stretched, claws spread. "And I, to the privy. Sleep well."

"Sleep well, Kelru," she said. A gust of bitter air from the anteroom made the fire flare up as the door closed behind him.

"A moment, Vika," Pierre said, in French.

Her heart sank. "I'm tired. Can it wait?"

"No, it can't." Yet he hesitated a moment before going on. "I wondered if—if perhaps Anke has told you what has been troubling her in the past two weeks."

She shook her head. "I asked her once or twice. It wasn't worth it. Ask her yourself."

"But she has shut me out." He grimaced. "She will not accept that I am simply concerned. That I am genuinely responsible for her welfare."

Vika tilted her head skeptically. "Responsible to whom?"

He sighed. "To myself, I suppose. Vika, whatever you may think of me, I am in command here. I am responsible for the mission, even if no one else ever learns what happened to us. Will you try again to talk to her?"

Vika felt herself flush. So he wanted her to mediate—Vika, with her expendable pride. *No.* "I'm sorry, Pierre. Truly, it's none of my business."

He stared at her, scratching his beard thoughtfully. "Was it as hard as that, this past summer?"

She looked away from him. Tears stung her eyes. Ridiculous. Ridiculous!

She heard Pierre get to his feet. He laid a hand on her shoulder— no more than that. "Perhaps it was," he said. He wasn't looking at her. "I will speak to Anke again tomorrow." And he went up the ladder.

Vika watched the fire. Listened to the wind. So damned alone, so lonely here. Thiain had been a friend, but only while Vika shared her prison. And Kelru—he was elusive, he kept drawing back. After all, she was a woman. An alien woman, with no power over him—but still to be avoided, still not to be touched.

No one would ever touch her again. Not with love.

She heard Kelru's boots on the stairs, and climbed quickly up the ladder before he came in at the door. Pierre lay still against the wall, his back to the room. Vika heard nothing from Anke's end of the loft.

Vika scowled, staring into the dark. She could go to Anke and ask her what was wrong, ask her if she could help. She could wake Pierre, and they could have it out, once and for all. It would ease everyone's tension. It would show compassion for Anke.

And yet...Anke was not a child. If she needed help, she could simply say so. If she would not, and if that meant that her pain was hers to keep—well, she had chosen it. Vika pulled off her clothes and climbed in beside Pierre.

That night was long, in the silent city waiting for winter and death.

TWELVE

Hood up, head down, Pierre rode toward home on Nukh at the end of another day of riding and target shooting. The last. Today was the traditional last day of autumn. Tomorrow at dawn, the Council of Eight would take their seats in the ancient warrior-barrow dug into the square in the center of Kheosseth. And Kelru's battle—Pierre's battle, too—would begin.

Pierre had forgotten that a sky could be such a clear, rich blue. The late-afternoon light tinged the shadows with purple. But the wind met them as they rode north toward Kheosseth. Pierre knew this wind well by now: the world-wind, vast, cold, streaming south from the barren places, from the eternal ice beyond. Even Kelru, leading on Thonn, hunched down against it. The beasts moved slowly, their thick fur fluffed out, their heads tucked low to protect their eyes from the particles of ice the wind kicked up from the road. Pierre peered out from under his thessach at the sun sinking over the mountains to the west. He had to squint against its raw reddish light. It was late. Anke would be wondering where they were.

Or perhaps not. He lifted his head and looked at Vika, riding ahead of him on old Feth. She had been very quiet all day. He'd wanted her to stay home, but Anke had made it clear to all of them that she wished to be left alone today. So Vika had come out with Pierre and Kelru—and all to no point. She was strong for such a small woman, but she could not string even Pierre's bow—a boy's bow, by Windhome standards. After his afternoon's shooting the muscles of Pierre's arms and shoulders ached dully. They would be worse by morning.

At intervals all day, Pierre had heard the thin cold wail of the Calling Tongue, relaying the Council's summons from district to district, giving the threefold call that those with business before the Council of Eight should prepare, prepare, prepare. That warning Kelru had not needed: he had received a formal summons at dawn, while he and Pierre were silently devouring their sparse breakfast in the hearthroom. A gust of raw air, a flurry of snow; instantly on their feet Kelru and Pierre faced the man who had come in. His midnight blue thessach marked him as a messenger of the Council, by law free of any house in the City where no young woman lived.

Pierre felt a stab of worry at that thought. If the Council did not consider Anke or Vika to be women, then—

The messenger, a very young man, reached into his leather bag and held out a small square of folded paper to Kelru. "Ekhnan Kelru," he said formally, "accept this command." His thessach was so newly dyed that it had a pungent smell; his broad, brown-furred face was impassive. He had barely glanced at Pierre.

Kelru had accepted the paper just as impassively. With a strong claw he tore open the glued fold scribed over by some Councilman's signature. Pierre moved to Kelru's shoulder and read with him.

The summons was written in red-brown ink, in a harsh square hand. *At the hour of the Great Call, at the first dawn of winter, Ekhnan Kelru will present himself with the witnesses named beneath before the Council of Eight in the house of their assembly. Those named being the stranger Ekhnan Pierre; the stranger the woman Ekhnan Anke his mate; and the stranger the unfamilied woman Vika; this call being a charge upon them all, to attend and speak as the Council may require and permit, at peril of their shelter and their bodies' warmth.*

The messenger had left, and Kelru said, "Don't fear. Always the words are the same. They will only give the order of the cases tomorrow; we may wait for many eightdays."

"We must still be prepared," Pierre said.

"We are prepared," Kelru said. "Though, brother, I wish your shooting were something better."

And so the three of them rode home through streets beginning to fill with people from surrounding farms, and from the houses of the city itself. Even young women who were not pregnant, as long as they were nowhere near the Red Mind; custom allowed it for this night of festival, the last before the long austerity of winter. Tonight Tlankharu would rise at midnight to take possession of the night sky he would dominate throughout the winter. Tlankharu, the Old Man's Eye, that called up the souls of the burned dead on the wind.

Here was the courtyard. They were home. Pierre slid down from Nukh and led him after Thonn and Feth into their warm, musky stable under Kelru's house. "Brother," Kelru said, "take your friend up to the fire, will you? She's let herself get chilled again. I'll tend to the beasts."

Pierre did not argue; even stuffed awkwardly into an old pair of four-fingered gloves, his hands were stiff with cold, aching from gripping Nukh's neck-fur and from shooting. And Vika had already gone out to the stairs. As Pierre left Kelru called, "And just set some water to the fire—Anke always forgets."

When Pierre came in from the anteroom, Vika was already hanging the copper pot on its swiveling arm. She swung it in over the few scattered embers, then turned to the woodbin and began pulling out sticks. The hearthroom had a chill that would take an hour or more to dissipate. Pierre touched the bricks above the hearth and swore under his breath. They had cooled. He glanced toward the ladder to the loft. "Anke's sleeping?"

"She must be." Vika kept her eyes on her hands feeding the fire.

Pierre took off his thessach and hung it on its peg. "She sleeps so much. Perhaps she's ill."

"She's worried," Vika said. "Like all of us. I'm sure that's all it is." But she did not sound sure.

Pierre looked at her. "*Is* she ill?"

Vika hesitated. "She's very private. I haven't asked."

And that was a hint, of course: he was Anke's lover; he should go to her and ask, and of course she would tell him. Pierre, whom she had not touched in many days, to whom she would no longer speak. With a bitter taste in his mouth Pierre said, "I will talk to her."

The sleeping loft was colder than the room below, and dark—a shutter covered its one window. Pierre stood near the top of the ladder, head and shoulders into the darkness, and said, "Anke?"

Silence.

Steadily, he climbed to his feet, went to the shutter and opened it, letting in the sunset light, red-orange, showing him clearly what was there to be seen. But it was not as he had feared: she was not lying there dead, a suicide. She was not there at all.

Here was Kelru, peering up at him. Pierre's voice sounded strange in his own ears as he said, "Kelru. Did you see Anke outside?"

"No," Kelru said. "I didn't see her, or scent her."

"Check the privy," Pierre said to Vika, below with Kelru. She nodded and went out, and he knelt by Anke's pallet and picked up her pack. Her spare clothing and datapad were still in it.

He set the pack down, climbed down the ladder. Of course her thessach was gone, the green one Dethun had given her; he should have noticed that before. He went out the door and onto the porch, Kelru following silently. In the courtyard below, Vika emerged from the low stone privy against the street wall. She stretched out her hands in a shrug.

Pierre felt his anger take fire. Now, of all times, Anke chose to be unaccountable. "She's gone," he said bitterly. "She will come back when it pleases her. Too late for us, of course."

Kelru touched Pierre's back. "Easy, brother."

"I will not be easy," Pierre snapped. "We don't even know where she is."

Kelru tossed his head. "Exactly. Where can she go? My friends and I will find her before full dark. Her scent is strange; even in a thessach she'll be noticed, and remembered."

Vika came hurrying up the stairs. "Kelru," she said, "if some of the Old Anokothu catch her—"

"It will not happen," Kelru said quickly, in a strong voice. "The winter festival begins tonight. The streets are full. There are public fires for warmth, and crowds. No one will harm her tonight. But—" he looked at Vika—"you must stay here and wait, in case she comes home. She'll need the fire, and some tea."

Now that Kelru's warm reassurance was turned toward Vika, Pierre could sense its hollowness. Kelru was deeply worried.... Pierre stood silent, suddenly caught on thorns of doubt, and fear, and the guilt that lurked always ready within himself.

Kelru turned back to him. "Pierre, put on your other tunic and trousers, and your dry boots. Bring a lantern, in case we must search in the alleys. I'll go talk to Nakhalru." And as Kelru hurried down the steps, Pierre saw his apprehension in the set of his shoulders, in the stillness of his usually expressive ears.

With a sick, dropping feeling, Pierre turned back to Vika. "If you know anything about where Anke is," he said, his voice coming out harsh, "anything at all, you must tell me now."

But Vika only shook her head. Under its cap of black hair, her thin dark face was troubled. "I'll stay here, in case she returns," Vika said. "One of us must."

The rest of them left within minutes: Nakhalru and a friend to gather more searchers; Pierre with Kelru. Riding animals were not permitted in the evening streets during festivals such as this, so they were forced to go on foot. Anke had several hours' lead, most likely— and they could not even guess which way she had gone.

The sun had set, and the evening, cold and crystalline, smelled of woodsmoke. The city murmured all around them in the darkness. Fifty thousand people—that was a city, on this world. But it was more than enough to hide Anke. Pierre followed Kelru through the courtyard gate. A small fire crackled and sparked in the street just outside. Several men stood or sat around it, passing a flask.

"Kelru," one of them said in greeting. "And Kelru's brother." Someone else made a rude noise.

"Joy of the festival, Kelru," a third voice said.

"And for you," Kelru answered. "Has one of the strangers passed you?"

"We're no watchmen," one of them said. "Which one?"

"Pierre's mate," Kelru said.

"We're in festival," the man said, "and if she passed, we might not scent her." Pierre could smell the fruity reek of raw berry brandy. The man held out a flask in an unsteady hand. "Drink joy to us, Kelru."

But Kelru waved the flask away and moved on. Pierre followed. One of the men at the fire called after him, "Keep your mate by the hearth next time!"

As they hurried along over the frozen ruts of the street, Kelru said, "Pierre, you must keep near me. Especially where men are dancing, or fighting." Pierre bent his head in acknowledgment. People feared him for his strangeness, he knew that well. But he also knew something Kelru had concealed from Vika: many men would be drunk tonight, beyond fear, beyond judgment. And many might find the festival a convenient excuse for violence.

The narrow side street opened onto a broader road at the foot of the slope. The bonfires began there, and the crowds. Pierre heard singing clearly now: many deep, strong voices, in rough unison. He could not understand the words. The group of singers was surrounded by a larger group of listeners, swaying in time to the music. Some were women, their thessachs folded back over their shoulders to display bright plaid linings, tassels bobbing around their knees from the hems of their unbelted overdresses. Most of the women were unhooded; none of the rest were small enough to be Anke. Pierre saw Kelru speak to several men, but none gave him the news he sought.

Singing at the first fire, dancing at the next. This was a men's dance, accompanied by thin music from a bowed string instrument and a small slap-drum. Kelru stopped Pierre near one of the musicians, a man white-furred with age, who held his little viol propped on his crooked knees, sawing at it with a one-string bow, wheezing in time with the hard strokes. It was a circle dance—ten or twelve men near the fire, leaping and crouching, their heavy-booted feet pounding the street. Anke was not there. Pierre heard Kelru speak to a man in the crowd, who raised his palms in a shrug. No, he had not seen or smelled such a person.

Kelru came back to Pierre. "She must be in one of these crowds. She can only be both warm and cloaked if she is outside by a fire."

"You assume she's well," Pierre said. His anger had dulled; the thread of worry was tightening inside him.

"I assume nothing," Kelru said evenly. "Nakhalru and the others will check the inns. If Anke was taken anywhere against her will, if she struggled at all, we will at least hear a rumor of it. We can begin from there."

At the next fire was a storyteller, surrounded by a group of intent children—small, hooded figures. Pierre hung back as Kelru moved along the front of the line of listeners, peering down into their little soft-furred faces. The storyteller glanced at him, flicked an ear, then went on with his story. "But when the sun rose again," he said, "Fyakh took a needle and some thread, and he sewed all day, and he sewed, and he sewed—and when the red-clawed beast came to his door at sunset, there was Fyakh!—all in one piece again!" Now Kelru was hurrying Pierre away, and they heard no more of that story.

They passed women's dances—slow, intricate, dignified, women touching palm to palm as they passed each other, tassels bobbing at their knees. They passed an inn that had set benches in the street, and the high tables that were used where floors were not clean enough to sit on. Here they were set in a square, for a formal argument. Two men offered position and counter-position; their listeners pounded agreement on the tables with their fists and drinking bowls. One stroke, in unison, at the conclusion of every successful point.

Beyond that Kelru changed streets to avoid a fight; then they passed more men's dances. And then they came to the student district,

Kheosseth's only enclave for scholars. Kelru had studied there for two years; he had told Pierre about it. The students, all unfamilied men, were not all young, but like Kelru, all had the young man's view of life. They were educated as far as the Anokothu permitted, but they stayed on the fringes of power. They could be soldiers, clerks, advisers. But unfamilied men had no place on any council, no right to any position of real authority. They served, they explored, they studied, they argued.

And they sang. Only here, on all of Windhome, was music studied as an art. Here the crowds were smaller, but they stood in silence to listen. The music troubled Pierre. The men's deep, warm voices shaped long, curving branches of melody over a firm ground. It was music potent with mystery, heavy with the considered grief of years. The strange scale, like and yet unlike any music of Earth—the sense of searching, searching, for a center, for return, and just as it seemed the music might come to rest there, the voices would fade....

Pierre knew what he was hearing in that music, and behind that music. He could not allow the dark, ravenous longing for home to begin again. Yet the memories came: The songs and dances in his village, handed down from generation to generation on the fringe of the Covenant world. The singing in the church at Christmas. And at last, his own son's face, pinched with distress—*Why are you going away? Was I bad?*

Pierre knotted his hands together, gripped until the bones hurt. He could not allow himself to remember that now. He straightened, stood firm, watching Kelru's tall figure moving through the crowd, always looking down. And still he listened to the music. The words were simpler than the harmonies that carried them. Perhaps if he concentrated on the words—

The singers' faces were intent, disciplined. *Over those mountains is my home*, they sang. *In this broad valley is the land where I will die. World-wind, carry my ashes high. Carry them higher than those mountains, O wind.*

Pierre's breath caught in his throat and he looked up, up at the stars, which trembled at first, trembled and then stilled as he won his battle yet again. Thousands of stars burned there, a bitter glory. He had never seen such stars in the dusty skies of Earth. Here the night was a flawless emptiness between himself and infinity. He stood exposed on the backbone of an alien world, waiting for death to find him. To find them all.

Kelru returned sooner than Pierre expected. "Word," he said briefly as they stepped away into the dark. "She was seen near here, before sunset, moving upriver."

"Going where?"

Kelru looked away. "Nakhalru has gone on ahead," he said. "Breathe slowly. Anke will be safe." But he started off again, faster, so that Pierre had to run to keep up.

Nakhalru was waiting for them outside an inn. His bony face looked disturbed in the weak yellow light of the door-lantern. "She was seen again just at sunset," he said without preamble. "Alone, three streets east of this inn. Moving north. She was chased—some men on a street-corner, they smelled her and guessed what she was. But they were too drunk to catch her."

"But she was moving north." Pierre looked uneasily at Kelru. "Could she be headed for Dethun's house?"

"That at least is a place she knows," Kelru said. "But what could she want there?"

Pierre had no answer, though he felt sick with a sourceless dread. "Let's go there," he said.

All around them as they moved through the streets, Pierre half-trotting to keep up with Kelru and Nakhalru's long strides, the music was stopping; the singers and dancers and drinkers and arguers were melting away from the bonfires, climbing up walls, into trees, onto roofs, all looking east. Tlankharu was coming. Winter was coming. A hush fell on the city. Even the wind had dropped to an icy breath.

As they rounded a corner Pierre looked eastward, across the roofs of the houses between this street and the river, and he saw it. Tlankharu rose, a sudden harsh brilliance over the shoulder of a distant hill. The city around them was silent. On Earth there would have been cheers, applause, firecrackers for the spectacle. Here there was nothing. Tlankharu hung fierce and red, low over the rooftops, like a trapped spark.

Now the street was full of people walking quietly homeward, huddled against the wakening wind. Here and there Pierre heard a burst of song, quickly stifled. He smelled smoke from bonfires and the familiar cold-dirt scent of coming snow.

"The festival is over for tonight," Kelru said quietly. "This was the end of autumn. Tomorrow at sunrise, the Council sits to mark the beginning of winter. But tonight—tonight is the silence between."

As they walked, Kelru and Nakhalru asked those who passed them for word of any disturbance. The answer was the same. No, no word, no stranger; nothing strange at all, cousin.

Kelru turned to Pierre and said, "Well, we must still hope. She might have—"

But his words were cut off by a cry. Not the thin wail of the Calling Tongue; a man raising an alarm in the distance. "*There! Follow! Take her!*"

Kelru and Nakhalru began to run. Pierre pounded along behind them, unsteady in his too-large boots. Another cry, more cries—"*There! There she passed!*"—confused shouting. Trailing the others Pierre came to a wide, muddy square still dimly lit by fading bonfires, faced by the blank walls of large houses; and from an alley in the opposite corner a figure burst, running, running. Behind it the voices of men, the gleam of torches. The figure's hood flew back, showing a pale face, pale ruffled hair. *Anke.*

Terror for her drove Pierre forward, shouting. "Anke! Here! To us!" Kelru and Nakhalru were running ahead. Then men spilled from the alley behind her, bowmen in the green of Dethun's sisterhold. Pierre saw several stop and raise their bows, ready-drawn; he took a breath to warn Anke. But then an eerie buzzing hum whipped past his ear, making his scalp crawl, and then another overhead, and the breath went out of him as Kelru threw him down into the trampled, half-frozen mud. When Pierre raised his head he saw that Anke was down. Down alone, in the center of the square. He struggled to his knees. The men had stopped shooting; Nakhalru had plunged into the middle of them, swearing at them passionately.

Kelru helped Pierre stand—odd that he needed help.... Anke did not get up. She lay motionless on her stomach, her face turned away. Pierre felt lightheaded, strange as he walked up to her, Kelru slow and almost reluctant at his side. "Anke," Pierre said, "it's all right."

Kelru knelt beside Anke on the dark, churned mud, glistening in the light, and someone brought up a lantern. Gently, but without hesitation—as if he knew he could not hurt her now—Kelru rolled Anke over. Her face, blank and still, stared up at the chilly stars.

Pierre saw the wound that had felled her, a torn place at the center of a huge wet stain on Dethun's green thessach. The sharp, metallic smell of blood filled his nostrils—how could he have missed it before? He dropped to his knees beside her and took her thin wrist in his hand, but of course she was dead. Dead before she fell. He held her hand in both of his as he knelt there, frigid mud soaking his trousers. Anke was dead. Anke was dead, and it was his fault. If he had seen— If he had tried—

Here was Nakhalru beside him, and others, Dethun's bowmen. "*Another* of these strangers," he heard someone growl. He looked up at a face he dimly recognized. Dethun's man. Ganarh, scarred and sullen.

"This woman was not a stranger," Kelru said, rising to his full height. Pierre tried to stand, too, but this time he could not. He settled again beside Anke. Kelru said, "She was my brother's mate."

"You still call that thing your brother?" Ganarh held out an arrow. "Then give this to him."

Pierre set down Anke's hand and reluctantly took the arrow. It gleamed dirty yellow in the fading firelight: one of their meter-long, barbed arrows, the fletching stained with blood and flecks of tissue.

"She was little," Ganarh said. "It passed through her. We found it well beyond her. But I know the markings."

"How did it happen?" Pierre heard Kelru ask roughly.

Ganarh faced him. "She tried to break into the Lady's house. I caught her creeping over the courtyard wall."

Pierre realized he was turning the arrow in his hands, turning and turning it, and he set it down on the ground. Of course he would never know why Anke had been where she was. But he knew with fierce certainty that she had chosen this death. She had gone the last little distance into silence. She was alone now, as she had wished to be.

"Pierre, you must stand up now," Kelru said. There was a hand under Pierre's arm, and now he was standing.

Ganarh faced him. "Choose swiftly," he said. "It was my man Yekhiru who shot her."

Pierre stared at him, struggling to understand. Kelru waited and then said, "This would best be settled before the Council, tomorrow." He bent and picked up the arrow, handed it to Ganarh. "My brother does not know our customs."

"I see that," Ganarh said, staring at Pierre. "A *man* would have claimed his right at once." He turned to Kelru. "Drag this to the Council if you like. But in the country we like to settle things more quickly than that." With a contemptuous glance at Pierre, he gathered his men with a word and was gone.

Pierre was shaking now, though he did not feel cold. "I want to take Anke home," he said.

"We will, brother," Kelru said. "Ease yourself, brother, Pierre. Nakhalru has gone for a cart. We'll take her home."

Pierre clenched his teeth and took a breath, then another. His fault. Always—and now forever—his fault. He bent down unsteadily to close her eyes, but Kelru stopped his hand, appalled. "Let her see," he said. "She must see until she is burned—until she's free."

Pierre straightened. After all, it did not matter. Let her see. Let him see her. They would put her in a fire soon enough, swallowed up, gone. Dust.

He stood, then, with Anke's pale gaze before him in the lamplight, chilly and blank as if she were dismissing the world from her notice.

Yet he must be strong now—he must not fail again. He must not fail
Vika and Kelru, the last ones left to trust in him.

Kelru touched him again, said again, "Ease yourself. You must,"
and he understood at last that Kelru wanted him to weep. But he could
not, must not weep; he must be clear-headed, to think, to plan. He
took a struggling breath, and then another that was easier. Another
that was easier still. "I told her to be careful," he muttered to himself,
and then said to Kelru more clearly, "I told her to be careful, do you
see? But she wouldn't listen."

"Brother," Kelru said, very gently, "I don't understand you."

Pierre shivered. Of course. He had been speaking in French. "It
will be all right," he said in Kelru's language, standing there over
Anke's corpse. Standing straight and dry-eyed, while Tlankharu rose
higher in the silent sky, while the cold wind shook the stars. The
universe was black, and bleak, and empty; and the face of God was
turned from him.

THIRTEEN

The night had nearly passed before Vika finally heard voices in the courtyard below Kelru's house. Men's voices, speaking quietly. Cold with sudden fear, she snatched her thessach from its peg and, clutching it around herself, walked out onto the porch. She saw Nakhalru's door close, and she heard heavy feet on the wooden stairs that led to this door. She waited. Pierre came first, with a torch; he looked up at her with a strange, remote expression that did not ease her dread. Then came Kelru, carrying something long and heavy wrapped in a blanket. When he saw her, Kelru stopped and stood looking up at her, cradling his burden, his ears twitching slowly.

"No," Vika said in a reed-thin voice.

"Vika," Kelru said heavily, "Anke is dead." He did not seem to notice that he had spoken Vika's name.

She had no breath to speak properly, but finally stammered, "How did it happen?"

"We won't discuss this on the stairs," Pierre said. He touched her arm. "We—we should go inside."

She found herself in the hearthroom, watching Kelru lay his burden carefully in the corner of the room farthest from the fire. He was telling her how it had happened, but the words drifted around her without touching her. Kelru folded back the thessach from Anke's face, from her open eyes and the emptiness of death.

Pierre stood by the fire, his back to Kelru and to her. She'd seen

the blood on the front of his thessach, but he seemed unhurt. She went
to him and took his hand in hers. It was cold, and sticky with blood.
"Pierre," she said carefully in French, "tell me how I can help."

He turned his head to look at her, and in his living eyes was the
look of Anke in death: weariness, hopelessness—and anger. His hand
slid from hers. "I'm well. And Kelru and I have matters to discuss."

And so she stepped back, leaving him to his pain. Kelru had gone
out for wood; the room was empty except for the two of them. And
it was not for Pierre's comfort that she had touched him. Not only
for that.... She clenched her fists, breathing carefully, drawing herself
inward toward calm. When she had collected herself, she turned back
to Pierre. But he was looking at Anke, his eyes black and lightless as a
fire that had gone out.

When Kelru came in, Vika knelt down near the fire, arranged
her hands neatly on her knees, and calmed her mind as she had been
taught in school. Breath by breath. The familiar discipline kept her
here in this moment—it reminded her that she, at least, was alive. She
was not like Pierre, talking so calmly to Kelru. Talking calmly while
Anke his lover lay dead, there in the corner by the ash pail, bundled
in her green thessach soaked with blood. It seemed easy for him, that
calm. Maybe he had not felt much for his son after all. Pierre's strange
faith and Anke's hard skepticism had shut them both out from Gaia,
from the web of life that had formed them, that linked them to all
people, whether they believed in it or not. And now Vika was as alone
as if she, too, did not believe. Her shameful anger fed on that.

No. She began again with the first breath of the meditation.

Now Pierre was sitting cross-legged by the low table, talking with
Kelru, whose own calm, Vika sensed, concealed a ready compassion
for them both. "What will this mean for our case tomorrow?" Pierre
asked.

Kelru scratched behind his ear. "It gives you power, of a sort,
against Dethun," he said finally. "Her household committed a crime
that harmed you."

"How was it a crime?" Pierre asked. "He was Dethun's guard, acting to protect her."

"But he should not have *killed* Anke," Kelru said. "There are not so many of us that we kill each other lightly. No, you were wronged. And you must now seek justice."

"What do you mean by justice?" Pierre asked. Vika had never heard him speak Kelru's language so precisely before.

"A life," Kelru said.

"Whose life? The man who shot her?"

"It can be anyone," Kelru said. "Any servant of Dethun, at the sisterhold or here. It's a law to stop blood feuds, you see: If a family is wronged by murder, they can choose any life in the murderer's own family, or company of servants, in exchange. Anyone, even an innocent, and after that death the matter is closed. So people mostly do not kill each other."

"What if I chose Dethun herself?" Pierre asked calmly.

Shocked, Vika turned to look at them both. Kelru's ears were laid back. "No, brother," he said. "Her guards shot without orders. Dethun was not responsible. You cannot touch her."

"So the custom only goes so far," Pierre said. "I might have expected that." He seemed to have found his strength again.

"It's a custom between equals," Kelru said. "You and I are not equals of someone like Dethun. None of us is." He dropped his clenched hands on the table, so heavily that it rattled. "Pierre, you must not delay this matter tomorrow. You must end it, or we have no hope of being listened to further—no hope that you and this woman will be allowed to carry out your mission. If you still must."

Pierre seemed to gather himself. "We still must." Listening, Vika felt only deep weariness. *Of course. Of course he would say that.*

"Then choose the man who killed her," Kelru said patiently, "and there let it end. I advise you thus as your brother. If I must, I'll beg you."

"You need not beg," Pierre said stiffly.

"Good." Kelru rose to his feet. "Rest now. Both of you."

They obeyed, climbing silently to the loft and into the pallet they still shared; Vika had no wish to sleep in Anke's, and Pierre must feel the same. But once Pierre was still, Vika lay awake. Her pain at Anke's death, her anger at Pierre, had faded to exhausted numbness, but still she could not sleep. She watched the thin yellow moonlight crawl across the floor, listened to the wordless cry of the wind. Thought about death, and her parents, and Dr. Kozlov. She thought about Anke's empty pallet. Anke's death was as cruel and arbitrary as Isamu's had been. She had come so far for nothing. How much farther could Vika and Pierre carry this? Even if they were allowed to do so?

Beside Vika Pierre breathed steadily, unmoving, unmoved. She was the last human left on this world, it seemed. She thought about the bitter, endless sky, and about Ekhnan Therrin, turning over rubble looking for the corpses of her children. Listening for the thin whine of the Destroyers' skyships returning. Earth, home, was vulnerable too....

Finally she rolled over against Pierre's back. He didn't move or speak, though she guessed he was still awake. His silence was a wall between them. But his body, at least, was warm. Comforted by that warmth, Vika slept at last.

When she woke, just before dawn, Pierre was sleeping soundly. She rose silently and went down to the hearthroom. Kelru was there already, his back to the wall near the fire, his long legs stretched out before him. When he looked up at her in the dimness, she saw the red-gold gleam of his eyes. "How is Pierre?" he asked quietly.

"Sleeping. We didn't talk." She looked down at him. "You stayed here all night?"

He spread his hands in a shrug. "Thinking," he said. "And then it was too late to try to sleep." He peered up at her. "And you, Vika. You're well?"

She gazed at him, her slow-waking thoughts moving from pain to pain, like touching and discovering new wounds. "I'm well," she said at last. Someone had to be well now; it had better be her. She made herself look around the room for Anke's body.

Kelru followed her glance. "I moved her down to the cold cellar," he said. "She'll last there until Pierre is ready to decide what is best."

Vika took a breath, then let it out in a sigh. "Let me decide," she said. "What's usually done here? I know you burn them."

"More than just that," he said. "The night before the burning, we hold the watch-feast."

She moved to the fire and held her hands out to it. "What is that?"

Kelru scratched himself under his tunic. "A meal eaten in the presence of the dead. It's shared by all who knew her. They speak of her, so that before she's burned, and the world-wind takes her, she knows the truth." His ears flicked. "All that we thought of the dead one. All that we remember. We forgive her quarrels with us, and confess if we have wronged her. But mostly what is remembered—" he closed his eyes and tipped his head back against the wall— "mostly we remember what was best, in the time we had."

Vika looked down at her hands. "No one knew Anke," she said bitterly. "Not even Pierre. And she never cared what we thought of her." She shook her head. "Arrange to have her burned. That will be enough."

"Your people have no ceremonies for the dead?" He looked distressed.

"Most people wish them," she said. "But Anke was not one of them. And if Pierre has words to say for her, he can say them alone."

"It's as well." Kelru's voice was quiet. "I doubt we will have time for a feast."

Vika shivered. Today they would go before the Council of Eight. And as Kelru had made clear last night, Anke's death at the hands of Dethun's servants made them an urgent matter for the Council. By noon today they would know their fate. Kelru clearly had little hope that they would be granted their freedom.

Pierre came down soon after, and in the frigid dawn they made their last preparations. They checked the beasts' saddles, loaded the packs with the last of the food they had gathered and their few personal possessions, tied their essential equipment securely on a small sledge that Feth could pull. They could leave the house forever within moments of returning from the Council. If they were allowed to return.

They walked to the Council's hall at the center of Kheosseth, through the deep, winding streets, while the sun rose somewhere behind the heavy, blue-gray clouds rolling slowly southward on the bitter wind. The Council met in a long, low building that stood alone in a square at the center of the city: a place like an ancient barracks— which it was, Kelru had told them.

When they entered, stepping cautiously in the gloom, the crowded petitioners fell silent. Vika saw dozens of faces turned toward Kelru and Pierre and herself—eyes intent, noses twitching at their scent; ears flicking forward and back in nervousness, fear, hostility. The long room nearly filled the building. It was windowless, the only light coming from smoke-holes in the roof and a few inadequate oil lamps in the rafters, stinking of fish oil and soot. Petitioners sat on the shelves that ran along both walls, shelves two meters deep and more, where soldiers had slept in earlier times. This place had been almost a thousand years old when the Destroyers came, six hundred years ago....

An ash-filled trench, a firepit, ran the length of the room, but a fire had been lit only at the far end, where the Council was seated. The long chamber was cold and stuffy, smelling of stale ashes and wet wool, and the sharp tang of unwashed people.

The other petitioners gave them a wide space to stand in. Looking toward the lighted end of the room twenty meters away, Vika got her first view of the Council: eight old men in dark-blue robes, sitting behind a long table, turning over pieces of paper. Then they rose to their feet.

With a rustle, and a faint buzz of excitement, all the petitioners stood as well. Kelru pointed out the Council's eldest and leader, Vakhar: a heavy man, fur almost white with age, who called out in a powerful voice for silence.

Silence fell at once. "We are the Council," Vakhar said less loudly. "We are met in accordance with law, at the time and the place required. We find that petitions have been placed before us, and we declare that we will meet in this place each day, barring the last of each eightday, until all petitioners have been heard, or until the Peace of Winter ends." He stopped to cough. Vika saw Kelru fold his arms tensely around himself, his ears erect and still. Deep worry.

Vakhar set down the paper and picked up another. "But before any man is heard," he said, "a matter of blood has arisen, and must be laid down." And he raised his voice, so that even those nearest the door could hear him clearly. "Ekhnan Kelru," he said. "Come forward, with those who stand with you."

They obeyed. Vika followed Kelru and Pierre, keeping her eyes down as a young, unfamilied woman must, picking her way carefully between the fire-pit and the crowded petitioners to stand, at last, across the table from the eight men who would decide so much. An eight-pointed star of hammered copper hung on the wall behind the Council. It glinted in the lamplight, bitter as Tlankharu itself.

Then Vika saw Ganarh come forward as well, bringing with him a stumpy, middle-aged man in sisterhold green, a man with the scars of a fighter. "Yekhiru," Kelru muttered. Vika looked at him more closely. Anke's killer: the one Pierre must choose for death.

"Now," Vakhar said. "Let us examine this sad matter."

Kelru glanced over his shoulder at the crowded chamber. "My brother is in sorrow," he said, "and our customs are strange to him. It would be better to settle this in private."

"The choice is not yours," Vakhar said. "This matter involves more than your own honor, Kelru." He coughed. "We now inquire," he said formally, "into the death of the woman known as An-keh, bondmate of Ekhnan Pierre. Let those who know of this matter come forward and speak."

Ganarh was the only witness. He said little: that he and his men had been guarding Dethun's house, as they must on a festival night; Ganarh had been making the rounds of his watchmen. Then someone had shouted, and Ganarh had looked up in time to see Anke drop into the alley from Dethun's courtyard wall and run. Ganarh raised the alarm, and the chase had ended in the square, where the stranger was shot. Dead at once, certainly, her breastbone split by the arrow. Yes, Ganarh had it. He produced it from his thessach. Yes, those were Yekhiru's markings. Vika stared at the long arrow in horror. It was dark with dried blood and—other things.

"Well," Vakhar said. "A regrettable occurrence. Our laws are clear." He glanced along the table at the other Council members, who gravely signaled agreement. Vakhar turned to Pierre. "You, who are a member by adoption of the family Ekhnan, have been greatly harmed by this death of your bondmate. We grieve with you. I have spoken with the Lady Dethun, and she accepts the guilt of her servant." He stopped and went on less formally, "Has Kelru explained our law?"

"Yes," Pierre said. In icy calm his voice matched Vakhar's. "A life for a life."

"Exactly," Vakhar said, after a slight hesitation. "Now you must choose that life from among Dethun's servants. And then, in a place that has been prepared, you must take it."

Vika gasped, saw Pierre flinch. But he said evenly, "Kelru has told me this." Vika looked up at Kelru, but his eyes were on Vakhar.

In the lamplight and firelight Pierre's sharp profile was chiseled and still as stone. Vika swallowed in a dry throat, waiting for what he must say. She looked sidelong at Yekhiru, sullen and stiff-furred at Ganarh's side.

The arrow that had killed Anke now lay in the center of the table. After a moment, to Vika's shock, Pierre picked up the stained arrow and balanced it on his hands. For a moment Vika saw his chilly control waver, an instant of something like pain. Then it was gone, and he was calm again. "In the world where I was born," he said, "we have a different idea of justice."

"Surely there can be only one just decision, given the facts of the case," Vakhar said.

"Not so," Pierre said. With sudden strength he broke the arrow over his knee, and let the pieces fall to the floor. Vika watched, her breath caught in her throat. Angry muttering rose from the crowd behind them.

"What is your choice?" Vakhar asked, looking puzzled.

"No choice," Pierre said. "No more death. That man was doing his duty—protecting the Lady Dethun. By all the justice I understand, all the truth I know, if I take his life in exchange for Anke's, I become a murderer myself." He straightened. "I will not do it." He stepped back and stood again by Vika. She could sense the quick light tremor of his body, and she heard the growing stir and murmur of the crowd behind them. This was dangerous, so dangerous—

Kelru stepped from his place, faced Pierre, and gripped the human's shoulders. Silence fell. "You cannot do this," he said hotly. "You cannot let a blood debt stand. It threatens the city's peace. The Council will exile you."

Vika saw something kindle in Pierre's eyes, a spark of answering anger. "Then let them," he said, his face dark. "That at least is freedom."

"It's death delayed," Kelru said, anguish in his voice. Vika saw his grip tighten on Pierre's shoulders, saw the brown claws dig into the fabric of Pierre's thessach. "Blood debts must be settled. They must *always* be settled."

Pierre did not stir in Kelru's grip. "Nevertheless," he said, "I am commanded by—by a higher authority than Vakhar. Even for Anke, I will not kill, in cold blood, a man who was doing his duty."

Kelru released him with a despairing gesture and turned to Vika. "Then *you* choose," he said urgently. "I cannot act if Pierre will not— his wrong was the greater, under our law. But you may have your own right in this. She was your sister, near enough—I can argue it. This matter cannot be left open."

Vika looked at Pierre. His face was calm, but his eyes were filled with an unreadable urgency. She stood with her hands folded tightly together, knowing that Kelru, Pierre, the Council, the room waited for her decision. She was unsure. If it was only that Pierre could not make himself choose the one to die, well, she could take that burden from him...or could she? However he may have acted last night, Pierre was not inhuman; his words today showed that he was clinging to his humanness at any cost. If she killed this man, would she leave that humanness behind? In his view?

In her own?

All at once she knew what her decision was, what it had to be—because she *was* human. Born into Gaia, linked through Gaia to her own heritage—and even to Pierre, whatever he might believe. She glanced at the crowd, and then turned to address the Council, careful not to meet their eyes, as the unfamilied woman she was. "I stand with Pierre," she said. "Whatever the consequences. You have sheltered us and taught us much, and we respect your ways. Yet we are different people. Your laws are not ours."

Pierre closed his eyes. Vakhar looked at Vika for a long moment, then got to his feet. "Yekhiru is dismissed," he said. "The blood debt remains." In his heavy-jowled old face his eyes glittered strangely—almost as if he were pleased. He raised his voice. "I speak for the Council," he said, and paused ceremonially, but no other man moved or spoke in dissent. He went on, "Ekhnan Pierre and the woman Vika are forbidden from this moment to shelter in Kheosseth, or in any farmhold that abides in the law. They are forbidden to receive aid from any servant of this Council. Including Ekhnan Kelru, who is sworn to the Judge of the Roads." He kept his dark gaze on Kelru. "Ekhnan Kelru's petition, of course, is denied."

Vika saw the fur on Kelru's neck rising. But Kelru's voice was calm. "Then I will join them in their exile."

"No, no," Vakhar said. "Hasty words. We will not bind you by them." The murmur of the crowd was rising to a growl. Vakhar looked at the other Council members. "We will recess briefly." They all indicated agreement. Vakhar led Kelru and the humans through a side door that had been standing open, into a windowless, low-ceilinged hearthroom lit only by its fire.

When the door was closed, Vakhar turned to face them all—Kelru and Pierre tense, Vika waiting, empty, for whatever would come. "You forced our stroke, Kelru," he said. "It was your choice, sheltering these strangers when many in this city, and outside it, believe the strangers came from the Destroyers. The bond you formed last summer was most unwise." He rocked a little on his feet, holding his robes away from the flames. "Most unwise," he said again, but again Vika sensed an odd satisfaction in him. "These strangers and their wild claims— they set custom at nothing. They would end our peace, our way of life. Whether or not they come from the Destroyers, what they offer is dangerous."

"We offered life and health for your children," Pierre said in a low voice.

"You see?" Vakhar said. "Put a certain way, it would appeal to some people. It would cause bitter feeling against the Council's laws. And to return to the methods and devices of our ancestors—we know too well what lies at the end of that path. Yet some people value their present happiness more than the future of this world."

"Vika and I did the opposite," Pierre said. "We sacrificed our happiness to come here. Our companions sacrificed their lives. All we want is to learn what you can teach us of the Destroyers, so we can warn our world. Our people."

"But your people are stronger than ours," Vakhar said, "and they are far from here. My task is to protect my own. And how am I helped in that task? One of you comes to Dethun's house in the night, to enter her courtyard and endanger those who serve her. Perhaps with the aim of harming her."

"I knew nothing of this," Pierre said. "But as Anke's bondmate, and—and as her commander, I take responsibility for what she did. And for her death." Vika heard the strain in his voice.

Vakhar straightened. "The Council cannot allow you to remain among us. Or anything that belongs to you. Your machines will be broken and burned, before they call the Destroyers down on us again."

Vika felt sick. All their equipment, lost. The Council's men probably could not harm the lander, sealed tight in its pasture near the sisterhold, but that would hardly matter. Without those devices, she and Pierre would be unable to measure or record anything, unable to upload their data to send to Earth....

"Then we have failed," Pierre said. "We cannot live without shelter. You have ordered our deaths."

"You have chosen them," Vakhar said. "Your exile is a matter of law. In some places, however, on the fringes, in the north, in the hills— in some places there is no belief in law. You might reach such a place before the Deep Cold."

Vika shivered. The Deep Cold, when trees split, burst by frozen sap; when the snow no longer fell, but ran in drifts and dunes under a hard, pitiless sky, a sterile and strengthless sun. When, Kelru said, any man caught without shelter died.

"And Kelru?" Pierre asked. "What of Kelru?"

Vakhar spread his hands wide. "It's simple. If you and the other stranger agree to leave Kheosseth, and if you free Kelru from his blood-bond to you—why, then, he can set it aside. He would be welcome then to stay. More people than I would say that."

"I free him," Pierre said immediately.

Kelru looked at Pierre, his eyes burning bright. "I thank you," he said quietly. "But I will not set aside what binds us." Vika took a sharp breath.

"Don't choose so quickly," Vakhar urged Kelru. "The cost—"

"I *have* no choice," Kelru said, an edge of anger in his voice. "How long do you think these two would survive on the trail, in winter, alone?"

"Thank you," Pierre whispered.

Vakhar lifted his hands. "Then the ruling applies to you as well. You have lost your place with the Judge of the Roads, and your house is confiscated. Your name will be cried within Kheosseth as an exile, and you will be sent out from the city before the sun rises tomorrow." Vakhar looked weary, old. "Your mother will grieve."

"Tell Dethun," Kelru said, "that I'm sorry I can be of no further use to her."

"Don't speak so bitterly," Vakhar said. "She values you more than you know." He was silent for a moment. "One more thing. I free you from your oath to the Council of Eight. The Judge of the Roads consents to this. It will let you take service in the guard of a sisterhold, if that will help."

Vika looked sharply at Vakhar. Of course—that would be an escape for Kelru. Many disgraced men served at sisterholds, without question or persecution. She had seen notch-eared, even earless men among Ganarh's bowmen: thieves, murderers. Surely some distant sisterhold would accept Kelru, innocent of such crimes.

"Vakhar, I thank you," Kelru said in a flat voice. "But I will never serve Dethun, or any of the Lady Mothers who follow her. You may tell her that as well."

An appalled silence. Then Vakhar said sharply, "No. No, Kelru, you must consider. If you choose—"

"I've chosen," Kelru said. Vika sighed.

Vakhar lifted his face in a gesture of grief. "Dethun, come forward," he said.

She stepped from the darkness that had concealed her, her eyes on Kelru, her face unreadable. And Kelru gazed back, as if he had known she would appear. Vika took a slow breath. Most likely he had scented his mother when they first came in. "Please let me speak to them alone," Dethun said to Vakhar, who went out, closing the door behind him. Dethun, swathed in her green thessach, went straight to the fire and stood there tensely, warming her back.

Vika wanted and did not want to see what would happen now. She thought Pierre might have chosen to leave them there, mother and son; but there was nowhere to go. The room had an outer door, but no doubt that was locked, or guarded. Pierre sat down on a bench in the farthest corner and appeared to give himself up to his thoughts.

But Vika chose to stand where she was, watching Dethun and Kelru. A witness. There should be a witness.

Dethun turned to her and said, "I grieve for your loss."

"It's the end," Vika said, feeling the weight of the words as she spoke them. "Our mission is over. We've failed." She saw Pierre raise his head and look at her; but she did not meet his eyes.

Dethun bowed her head. Then she looked at Kelru. "And you?"

Vika knew Kelru well now: she saw the pain that gripped him, though his words were steady enough. "I will keep my word to Pierre," he said. "In spite of all that you planned."

Vika's breath caught. Planned? How could Dethun have planned— But Dethun was speaking, her hands pressed together. "This came of your own actions," she said. "I wish, oh, I wish you had chosen your freedom."

"You would rather have an expedient man at your side, than an honorable man opposing you," Kelru said.

"I don't think that," Dethun said. "I never have. I want—I *need* your help in my work. Keeping our people safe."

"We must go," Kelru said, "if that is allowed."

"The door is open," she said. "We could leave together."

"There is nothing," Kelru said, "that could bind me to you now, or to your Anokothu laws. I left your house and your way of thinking when I was twelve winters old. I will never return to either." Dethun bent her head. Vika saw her eyes gleam strangely, but the old woman said nothing. "But there is a last service you can do for me," Kelru went on. "There is no one else I can ask, no one with land-rights."

Dethun's ears flicked forward. "Ask."

"Anke lies at my house," Kelru said. "As a kindness to my brother, who is of our family, see that she is taken to the farm, and burned there on the family pyre. Scatter her ashes from the cliff, as if they were my own." In a half-vision, feeling chilled and sick, Vika saw them, saw ashes falling. Fire and death— On the hearth a log fell heavily into its own ashes.

Dethun's eyes on Kelru were steady. "I would have given you everything," she said. "Made you my partner. Taught you all that I know. You might have had a seat on the Council someday. Served your people with honor. But these came instead, and you gave your honor to them. So I will die knowing that your bones are freezing in the mountains, that the kharag are chewing them. No clean fire for you, and no free wind. And all for nothing. For no one." Her glance shifted to Pierre, watching now silently, his eyes dark and troubled. "For that."

"It is not for nothing," Kelru said. He looked at Pierre, at Vika. "Now for the journey," he said. "Are you ready?"

"Yes," Vika said.

"And I." Pierre got to his feet.

Dethun watched silently as they adjusted their thessachs. But as Kelru turned to the outer door she said, "This cannot be the end of it." Vika knew the harsh voice Dethun used to mask strong feeling.

Kelru must know it, too. He stopped, but did not turn. "But it is," he said. "Mother."

She raised her hands as if reaching for him, then let them fall. "Live well, Kelru."

"We'll live as well as we can," he said. "You should forget me."

"No." Her voice broke. "I remember all of my children. The living, and the dead."

Kelru looked at her for a long moment. Then opened the door, and walked through it. Vika glanced back once, as she closed the outer door behind them. Dethun still stood by the fire, as if waiting. But there could be nothing to wait for now.

FOURTEEN

P ierre winced as he followed Kelru out into the gray glare of the winter morning. Tugging his hood lower over his face, he looked around. He saw no one else in this corner of the square, penned close by frowning walls, lidded with a sullen gray sky. A few flakes of snow drifted down. Vika caught up with him, settling her own hood so that it shadowed her distraught face, and they set out after Kelru.

The side door of the Council chamber was discreetly close to the opening of a small alley. Without speaking Kelru chose that way and stalked ahead, stiff and quick with obvious anger. Pierre had not expected Kelru to understand the decision he and Vika had just made. Perhaps Kelru never would understand it. Pierre glanced at Vika, hurrying along beside him, and again it struck him, as it had in the Council chamber: *she* had understood. It stunned him. He had thought Windhome justice, weighing this against that, would seem natural to Vika—a Gaian, with a Gaian's passionate concern for balance. Perhaps she was not as Gaian as he had thought.

The few people they passed gave them only the single curious glance Windhome courtesy permitted. Kelru looked back from time to time, as if checking that Pierre and Vika were following, but his face under the night-blue woolen hood was remote, shadowed. Yes, he was angry. And just now it would not do. Pierre hastened his steps and drew abreast of Kelru. "Your legs are longer than ours, brother," he said. "Can't you slow down?"

He saw Kelru's quick contemptuous breath, a puff of white in the bitter air. "No," Kelru said. "We must outrun gossip, you see. Some of the Anokothu will hear the order of exile and catch the scent of it as well as the words—they are now free to hunt us."

"I know," Pierre said. The value the Council had just set on their lives was nothing, or less than nothing; and if the Council itself could not order their deaths, it could look the other way while the Old Anokothu dealt with them. Pierre glanced around. The faces in the street seemed more alien than before; the few high, slitted windows darker and more sinister. He remembered the arrows last night, their vicious buzzing flight. And how one of them, just one, had torn the life from Anke.

He turned back to Kelru. "If they hunt us," he said, "won't they begin at your house?"

As soon as Pierre said it he regretted it. Kelru said, "It is no longer my house." His voice was low and bitter. But he went on, "If we get there before anyone from the Council, if we are in time to fetch our packs and the beasts—then we might live."

"In time?" Pierre asked. "But we've been ordered to leave now."

"Yes," Kelru said. "If tomorrow's dawn finds us inside the walls of Kheosseth, anyone who chooses may kill us all, and throw our blood and bones to the kharag outside the walls. And there are some who would prefer that end, for you and the woman with you at least."

"Then how will we leave the city? They will be watching the gates."

Kelru's sidelong stare was inimical. "True, brother. You and this woman have prepared me an excellent problem. Now leave me to solve it." And he turned back stolidly to his walking.

Vika moved up beside Pierre now. She must have heard it all, but she said nothing, and he was grateful, though he could see the fear in her dark eyes. Kelru's anger was no more than they deserved, and Pierre could pray that it would change. But the choice they had forced on Kelru—to set aside his word, or to lose his place, his work, his home—that fact would not change. Perhaps nothing would ever be the same between them again.

Pierre's heart went cold when he saw the trampled slush of the side street that led to Kelru's gate. No one spoke. The courtyard gate stood open, and they went through, Kelru leading.

They stood a moment, the three of them, staring up at Kelru's house in the grim gray light. The door had been smashed inward and now dangled from one of its leather hinges. Pierre whispered, "No," his eyes stinging. Vika looked dazed.

Kelru shook himself and walked quickly down the ramp of packed snow to the shelter under the house, where his beasts lived. Pierre hesitated, then followed. Better to face it; better to know at once.

The stable was empty. No animals, no packs, no saddles. Pierre looked around in despair as Kelru silently leaned his head against a post. Vika looked from one man to the other. She was frowning. "Kelru? Kelru, listen to me. Think. This was done before the Council even ruled. It must have been."

"Oh, no doubt," Kelru said wearily. "Dethun knew what the ruling would be."

"And arranged this? Just since last night?" Pierre swallowed. "She is a cold planner."

"Colder than you know," Kelru said, looking away. "She has long wished to close off every path for me but the one she herself walks." He threw his head back and took a deep, tasting breath of the stable's air, as if to catch the scent of his lost beasts. His eyes closed. "We cannot leave the city as we are; but we cannot stay."

Pierre calmed himself. "Surely there is something we can—"

"No." Kelru lifted his chin in negation. "Dethun has won."

Pierre stood appalled into silence. Vika stirred beside him. But before she could speak, a shadow darkened the entrance. Pierre drew his knife, saw the flash of Kelru's blade as he did the same. The man in the entrance stooped to come in, then straightened and looked around at them. It was Nakhalru, his sandy-furred, vulpine face full of questions. Pierre and Kelru sheathed their knives.

"A bad thing, cousin," Nakhalru said. "So many men. I couldn't stop them." He glanced at Pierre, then turned to Kelru. "What went wrong?"

"Pierre would not take blood for blood," Kelru said, still weary.

"That was stupid of Pierre," Nakhalru said calmly. Pierre felt his face flush as Nakhalru went on, "And the order?"

Kelru straightened and brushed at his thessach. "The order is exile. Today."

"A bad thing," Nakhalru said again. "You'll need food, and packs, and beasts."

"Nakhalru," Kelru said heavily, "I cannot let you give us anything. It would mean exile for you as well."

"I will give you nothing of mine," Nakhalru said, and the spark of hope died inside Pierre. Nakhalru examined his claws. "But, cousin— your beasts are in my shed."

Pierre caught his breath and felt Vika clutch at his arm. Kelru's ears flicked upright. "You say?"

"I moved them just after you left," Nakhalru said. "Packs and all.... Rumors were sounding bad, the last few days. I thought they might try to keep you from leaving. Separate you from the strangers—" He tilted his head. "Take you to *her*. To submit to her."

"Well, there is a chance now that we won't come to that," Kelru said. His voice sounded stronger, as if hope was growing in him as well.

Nakhalru's ears flicked once, dismissing the near-thanks. "I feared they'd search every house here, but they weren't looking for fights. They were fast—broke down your door, loaded a big sledge, went away again." He flicked a glance at Pierre. "They took the dead woman. For the kharag, I think."

Pierre closed his eyes, fighting back nausea. Then said, "Kelru. If they searched the house quickly, they may have missed something."

"You two see about that," Kelru said. "Nakhalru and I must talk."

Another dismissal. Pierre turned away silently. He should not resent this—if they were to escape, Kelru must lead. Yet he did resent it—even fear it. No voice now, no choice; the decision he had made when he faced the Council, and spared Yekhiru, might well have been the last free choice of his life.

Upstairs he hesitated at the ruined door, thinking of ambush. But Vika pushed past him before he could stop her. He did not want to call out to her, in this quiet courtyard. He followed, angry and glad of his anger: the easy cure of all fear, all doubt.

Inside the house, the anger fled; he looked around, dismayed. The old hangings lay in rucked heaps on the floor, stained with muddy bootprints. The table was tipped over, the wall shelves knocked down, the bowls all smashed. Pierre picked up a curved shard. There had been no need to do that. And no need to break the water jugs. The Council's men could have poured out the water to prove they hid nothing. The ashes of the fire had been raked out all over the floor, which was scorched in spots; in others, ashes had mixed with water to form a thick gray sludge. Ashes, death—an ending. The peace and comradeship he had once known in this room seemed farther away than home, than Earth. Dead like Anke. Like the mission.

Vika had already climbed the ladder to the sleeping loft. Numb, Pierre followed. She stood in the center of the room, her back to him, motionless. He could see that nothing was left. The equipment was all gone, the pallets slashed and spilled.

Vika turned a steady face toward him. "At least we have what Nakhalru saved," she said.

It was admirable, the self-control she was showing. And she was right that at least they would have the field equipment they had packed on the sledge. They would have their packs, as well: their datapads, and the few personal items they had brought from Earth.

Footsteps below. Pierre moved to the ladder and looked down, one hand on his hunting knife, the other gesturing Vika back. But she moved up to stand beside him. It was Kelru. "Come down," he said. "We must move now."

"Move where?" Pierre asked as he descended.

"Nakhalru's stable," Kelru said. "To keep the beasts quiet. You must both wait there until night."

"And you?"

Kelru's gaze was calm, quizzical, but Pierre could see that he was still angry. "Ah, brother," Kelru said, "you trust me so little, do you? After giving me your lives to save?"

Pierre gritted his teeth. "I trust you, brother," he said, harshly formal. "And I ask you to forgive me."

"In a while, brother," Kelru said. "When we've survived what I must forgive you for."

Pierre met Kelru's gaze. "I could not order Yekhiru's death," he said. "By the law I follow, it would have been murder."

"And you still believe your laws matter here." Kelru's lips lifted in a half-snarl, baring his sharp teeth. "Well, brother, you must learn to think differently. If today's lesson doesn't kill you, the next one will. Unless you listen to me. *Listen*, Pierre—not judge and dismiss."

"I'll listen," Pierre said. He did not look away from Kelru's angry gaze.

"You must live as my people do," Kelru said. "You cannot afford soft thinking from your soft world. If I tell you a thing must be done, then it must be done." He looked from Pierre to Vika. "I promise you that before this winter ends, we will come again to choices such as the one you and Pierre faced this morning in the Council chamber. That choice, or worse; and you must choose as I tell you hereafter. You *must*."

Vika looked at him. "I'll do as you say," she said. "You have my word."

"And yours, Pierre?" Kelru's face was intent.

Pierre looked up into Kelru's eyes. "I can't change what I am," he said.

"You must," Kelru said. "Or by my true-father's ashes I *will* cast you off, and be an oathbreaker; for I cannot keep you alive if your choice is death."

As Anke's was. Pierre nodded once, unwilling to speak. But Kelru apparently understood the human gesture, and was satisfied. "Then we will go."

In silence, Pierre and Vika followed Kelru across the empty courtyard to Nakhalru's stable, beneath his house. Pierre kept his eyes down, avoiding Kelru's anger, Vika's worry. He had failed them both, he thought bitterly.

Nakhalru must have moved his own beasts elsewhere to make room for Kelru's. Pierre blinked in the dimness. It stank in here: piss and wet fur and, faintly, the sharp coppery tang of raw meat. In the pen something stirred, something large, and made a deep-chested rumbling sound.

Kelru went to his animals. They pressed toward him with eager grunts, shoving against the barrier around their pen until it creaked. Kelru flung an arm around Thonn's neck and buried his face in the animal's fur. Pierre saw him take two deep breaths. Then he lifted his head. "Come and check your packs." They lay in a heap in the corner—Anke's, as well.

But— Pierre looked around sharply. "Where is the sledge?"

"The Council's men took it," Kelru said. "It was too heavy for Nakhalru to move. They've broken and burned it all by now."

Gone. Pierre swore. The last of their lab equipment. The emergency supplies. *The medkit*.

Kelru stood a moment longer, scratching behind Thonn's ears. Then he said, "I'm going out to look at the walls, at the ways out that I know, and see if I can find one that is unwatched this night. I'll be back before morning, and I'll bring you food. You must not eat any of the food in the packs. But sleep, if you can. I'm leaving you a lantern. Light it at dark, if you like, but don't open the cover without need." And he left them there.

Pierre stood still, his thoughts moving in tight circles. The sledge was gone. What could they learn, what could they discover, with barely more than their eyes and their hands? How could they help Earth? How could they even help themselves?

Vika touched his arm. Her expression was gentle, concerned. Well, this was not the time to discuss what had happened. He would keep at least that much of his command: he would keep his distance. He moved away from her. Then he took a steadying breath and said, with the last of his strength, "Get some rest."

She lay down silently and stretched out in the straw, and did not speak again.

Cold with humiliation and rage, Dethun strode through the morning streets back to her house, Ganarh ahead carrying the green-painted club that meant *Make way for the Lady*, two of his men behind. No doubt Ganarh thought shame drove her now; only he of all her men knew what she had hoped to accomplish today. And therefore he knew she had failed; Kelru had not come away with her.

Failed. She bared her teeth at the thought, and a man passing the other way flinched and looked down.

If the stranger man had simply killed her worthless guard, then the strangers who still lived, and Kelru, would have remained in the city all winter; there would have been no question of releasing them to wander freely, not after that kind of disruption to the city's peace. There would have been other opportunities to reason with Kelru. Other opportunities, perhaps, to remove the problem of the two strangers that were left....

But now, now, they would have the freedom they had sought. Without their packs, without their beasts—but even so, Kelru would find a way to keep them alive. He always had found a way to thwart her plans for him.

And now he had ended them.

They came to the square where the stranger Anke had died, and started across it in the pale sunlight. The stranger coming alone to her house yesterday had given her the simplest opportunity, and so the first. When Ganarh came to say that the pale stranger female had come to the rear door, that she had asked to speak to Thiain, it was

simple to order him to take her into his small sleeping shed outside
that door, and keep her silent. Then Dethun had sent Thiain away
under guard, through the front door, to make a purchase for her in
the festival market six streets away. A particular dried herb it would
take her some time to find. Dethun had known that a chance like this
would never come again.

She slowed her steps, lifting her long robe up away from the
muddy snow of the street. Ganarh knew her; Ganarh was loyal; it had
been a matter of a moment to make clear to him what was to happen.
Keep Anke silent, and then, just as the festival fell quiet for the rising
of Tlankharu, turn his back while she slipped outside. Pursue her,
shouting, calling to his men around the walls. Panic her into running.
And end it. He had done it admirably, and performed perfectly at the
Council this morning.

But it had failed. Oh, there was one fewer of those creatures in the
world; but it had failed. Kelru had turned from her for the last time.
And he might just be right. She might never see him again. As her
grief deepened, so did her anger. *Someone will pay for this.*

They reached the house, and she went inside, closing the door
solidly behind herself, closing out Ganarh, and the city whose gossip
was no doubt already mocking her. She dropped her thessach on the
floor in the hearthroom and stalked to the fire. Her foul temper did not
diminish when she turned to see Thiain patiently shaking the thessach
straight and hanging it on its peg. "You!" she snarled.

Thiain turned and faced her, head down, hands still along the
neat folds of her overdress. "What have I done, Khesit?"

In the face of that almost insolent patience, words fled. Finally
Dethun said, "Wine. Warmed and spiced," and sat down heavily in
her chair near the fire.

And the woman had it standing ready. Standing *ready*. As Thiain
set the cup on the small table by her left hand, Dethun looked up at
her. "Who told you? Who has already told you?"

"The gate-guard heard in the street, Khesit," she said quietly.

"That things had not gone as you—as we all had hoped. That your son was exiled, and the others. He told the cook, and she told me."

Rage choked Dethun. She picked up the cup in a trembling hand, then set it down again. "If you had kept better watch—"

"I was not here last night, Khesit," she said. "You sent me away."

"I meant the woman Vika," she said. "If you had kept better watch that day, the day after she was so disgustingly drunk in my hearthroom, she would still be here. There would be only one of the strangers loose in the world to corrupt my son."

"Ganarh keeps the watch, Khesit," Thiain said. Her voice was low but unmoved. Insolent.

Dethun rose to her feet. "You contradict me?"

Thiain stepped back, her head still down. "No, Khesit."

Dethun stepped forward and gripped her arms, shook her. "Raise your head."

"Khesit, I did not—"

Dethun shook her again and hissed, "Raise your head!" When Thiain obeyed, her eyes were wide, her ears flicking uncertainly. "Now," Dethun said. "Assure me, by the gift-vow you made me, that you did not betray me. That it was not *you* who let the woman Vika out of my house. Assure me of that. Then I will know that I did not waste my shelter and protection and honor on you. That I can trust you still."

Thiain said, an instant too late, "I have never lied to you, Khesit."

"Not yet," Dethun said, and waited.

"Khesit—" Thiain's eyes were wide, but her ears were still now. She took another breath, but said nothing.

Dethun released her grip, and Thiain sank to her knees. Dethun cuffed her on the side of her head, stalked to the door of the house, and opened it. "Ganarh," she said. "Come inside. And bring two men with you."

Vika jerked awake. She was sitting cross-legged in a pile of straw, in near darkness. Their lamp, hooded, cast one thin gleam of light against the blank stone wall of the stable. She smelled straw and dirt and beast-fur, and heard Pierre's slow, sleeping breath behind her. For a moment she did not know where she was, or why.

Then she realized what had waked her. The stable door was creaking slowly open. "Pierre," she whispered, and touched him.

He stirred and sat up, then jumped to his feet. She saw him snatch up his knife, and gesture her behind him. She rose and obeyed silently.

A dark figure slipped into the stable. Someone small, in a ragged woman's thessach, Vika saw; and she saw Pierre's knife hand tighten. Then the woman put back her hood, and Vika gasped.

"Vika," Thiain said. Her dark fur was untidy, her black eyes dull with fear. "You must help me. Dethun—"

"Has sent you to spy on us," Pierre said. The knife was steady in his hand.

Thiain started, but did not turn. "No," she said. "Dethun has turned me out of her house. Turned me out to die." She kept her dark gaze on Vika. "I came here to find you. I followed your scent, Vika. I wanted you to see this." She put back her hood, let her thessach fall, and Vika gasped. The fine green overdress that Thiain had worn as Dethun's personal aide was gone. Under her thessach she wore only an old woolen undershift, stained here and there with blood. Blood streaked and stiffened the fine fur of her arms and shoulders. "She had them beat me," Thiain said, her voice trembling. "Her men beat me. She let her *men* touch me, Vika!"

Vika could only guess at the horror of that—to a woman who had found refuge, thought herself safe. "Why?"

"Because I helped you escape her house," Thiain said. "Because I told you what she had done to you. She guessed it, and this is what she did." Thiain straightened. "And now you are my only hope. When you leave Kheosseth, I must come with you."

"She cannot," Pierre said to Vika, and his voice was flat, absolute.

"It is impossible. Kelru will forbid it."

"Vika," Thiain said, "will you help me? As I helped you, when you were in danger from Dethun?" Her black eyes shone with fear. "Please."

Vika looked from Thiain's pleading face to Pierre's frown. But before she could choose her next words, the stable door opened again. "Pierre," Kelru said angrily as he came in, "I told you to keep the lantern covered—" Then he stopped still, as he saw Thiain. Pierre closed the door quietly behind him.

Vika found words. "This is my friend Thiain," she said. "Who is coming with us into exile."

FIFTEEN

When Kelru heard Vika's words, his anger fled, replaced by disbelief. Of course this woman would not come with them. That was beyond all dispute. Kelru wondered how Vika could even propose it. She and Pierre, they were so strange, so strange, blundering through life as if they had no sense of smell, no eyes to see with, no ears to hear....

Kelru averted his eyes from the woman, for fear she would turn and meet his gaze, shaming them both. "No," he said to Vika when at last he could speak. "She cannot come." He would speak reasonably; there would be no argument, no anger.

But Vika chose to argue. "She must. She has nowhere else to go." Her small voice, thin as a child's, carried no force, and her flat face showed little to Kelru's eyes; she was not like Pierre, whose feelings Kelru could guess by listening to his words—or to what he was *not* saying. But Kelru felt sure Vika was angry. "Listen to her," she said. "Look at her, Kelru. She was beaten."

Kelru's gaze did not shift. Still he hoped to keep this discussion reasonable, and part with the woman with no one shamed. "You know, of course, that I cannot look at her," he said. "Or speak to her. Or speak her name."

"You speak to me," Vika said.

"Yes," he said patiently. "But you're unfamilied. You cannot be shamed." It was true, and so could not offend her.

"Vika isn't unfamilied," Pierre said angrily. Strange, Kelru thought, for what was Vika to him?

"She became unfamilied when she came to my house and lived there," Kelru said. "She is not your mate, not your sister; nor is she mine."

The strange woman spoke then. "I'm unfamilied as well," she said. "I lose nothing by traveling with you."

Kelru addressed his words to Vika. "If I had a sister who spoke in this way," he said, "I would tell her that the wild lands, the dark hills, are no place for a woman brought up at the hearthside, to quiet thoughts. I would tell her to seek another sisterhold, or failing that, to have her mothers find a new family in need of a young wife, and take place among them."

Then the woman did turn—and moved to stand before him, staring up into his eyes.

Kelru's belly went cold with shock, but he had to meet her gaze. To look away now, to evade her challenge, would signal his surrender. And he was in the right in this matter.

So he looked down into her face. The lamplight shone bright on it—a woman's face, soft-furred and short-nosed. He could scent her clearly: a woman-smell, like smoke and salt. Her eyes, black as night between stars, held bright sparks of anger, and hope, and not a little fear.

He felt the fur rise on his neck, but she did not look away. "I served your mother for five winters," she said, in familiar address. "Today she gave me to her guardsmen for a beating, and she turned me out of her house and her protection."

"As she has turned me out of her city," Kelru said. "But for me and those with me, there is no sisterhold to welcome us."

"Nor for me," the woman said. Her voice was steady, uncomplaining. Her steady gaze unnerved him. Only once had a woman of his own people talked this openly with him. She had been unfamilied and barren; and she had told him what he could pay her to join in her next mating—matter-of-factly, as if it were not the proof of her life's failure. But she had looked down when he refused her.

Yet this woman, this Thiain who served and spied for Dethun, did not look down. "I have no place in any sisterhold," she said. "Dethun has declared me an oathbreaker. My name will go before me on the Calling Tongue. All sisterholds will know that I have no word to give to anyone."

Kelru shrugged. "Then mate."

Her ears moved delicately, signing an old grief. "I was mated," she said. "I bore children who died. I left my family."

"Then you've chosen your road," Kelru said. "To live unfamilied— to be taken without promise or friendship, and bear unfamilied children. A hard road. But we will not walk it with you."

Vika turned to him. "Why can't we help her? We're exiles. So are you. You can't still tie yourself by Anokothu rules."

Kelru felt relief in his belly, along with his anger, and his frustration at Vika's stupidity. Relief because now that Vika had addressed him, he could turn to her, and breaking the gaze with Thiain meant nothing. "They aren't Anokothu rules," he said. "They are the necessary rules of life, as real as the Rules of Winter. This woman is young. Once a year, perhaps, the Red Mind comes to young women. And do you know what will happen to her, on the road, on the trail, when her time comes? Even if we find shelter at a settlement?"

"I'll face it then," Thiain said.

"You've never met a northern trapper, I see," Kelru said. "They kill each other over matings sometimes, did you know that? The winners fuck the woman. Then they go off into the woods again. Leaving the woman there still unfamilied, and pregnant."

Vika moved to stand beside Thiain. "But this is different," she said. "Pierre and I aren't like you. When the time comes, we can take her off alone, and care for her until it's over."

Kelru saw Thiain look away in quick shame at Vika's ignorance. "She will be in the Red Mind," Kelru said. "Mad to mate. Fighting to get away from you. And any man with a nose will scent her from three ridges away. There are hunters and trappers in those mountains. In one day, or two, before the Red Mind ends, one of them at least will find you. And if you try to stop his joining with your friend, he will turn aside from it just long enough to kill you." He looked at Pierre. "In the Red Mind *I* would kill you, if you interfered."

"I know all these things," Thiain said to Kelru in a low voice. "I'm no child. I've lived through more than twenty winters, and I've mated and borne children."

"But not to me," Kelru said, not meeting her eyes. "Be unfamilied if you choose; but I will not pay your mating price."

He turned then to Pierre. "We must leave now to cross the wall in darkness. Cloak yourselves. As for this woman, she can wait here until Nakhalru comes, and set her problem before him. He may not scruple as I did. Men have bought matings before. For some unfamilied women it is a way to live."

"I will die first," Thiain said. Her voice was dry and tight.

"But at least *we* will not," Kelru said. "Now come."

"No," Vika said. "Not without Thiain."

Then Pierre took hold of her, hard, by both arms, and Kelru saw with relief that he was at last going to set her right. "Listen," Pierre said. "I am sorry for your friend, but Kelru is right. She must not come with us."

"Then I cannot come either," Vika said. "Thiain is in this position because she freed me from Dethun's house. I might have died there."

"As Anke did," Thiain said without expression.

Anke's death—so well-timed, so convenient for Dethun's purposes. Kelru could not stop himself. "Dethun ordered Anke's death?"

"If it is true," Thiain said, looking at him, "Ganarh will never admit it. The Lady owns him. But *I* could prove it. Though only if I live."

Kelru's hope that Pierre would not understand this passed at once when Pierre said, "Kelru—if Dethun ordered Anke's death, then she lied to the Council. If we can prove that, she'll be disgraced."

"And all the world will be made right," Kelru said bitterly. He slashed out at the wall of Nakhalru's stable, claws unsheathed, tearing raw yellow stripes in the old, silvered wood. He could feel dark jaws closing on his bones. He scented his own death. But in it, beyond it—a victory of sorts.

"Let the woman come," he said. "But we will all regret it before the end."

Vika struggled with a sense of unreality as she and the others prepared to leave. She was beginning to understand how unready she was to begin a long journey now. It must be well past the middle of the night. She had had no real rest since the night before last, and even that sleep had been troubled. Remembering her fears then, she could almost laugh. The truth was so much worse.

Kelru and Pierre crouched by the lantern, checking the contents of the packs, both people's and animals'. They had quickly dispatched the bowls of stew Nakhalru, wordless and watchful, had brought for them all. Vika took another grateful bite of her own stew, savoring it all, even the meat. She was dressed in Windhome clothing for winter travel: a light inner layer of loosely woven wool; heavy woolen shirt and over-tunic and trousers; woolen leggings; thick felt boots over woolen socks she and Pierre had knitted for themselves; and over all the thessach, the sleeved and hooded cloak of thick wool, left oily and woven tightly to resist water, cut loose to drape over a beast while riding, but with a belt that could be tied for walking in windy weather. Near at hand were a matted fur hat and old fur mittens, which she would wear over the gloves she had brought from Earth. She hoped it would be enough.

Nakhalru had supplied Thiain with worn clothing out of his own stock, and she squatted now near the door, lost in a too-large thessach, her empty bowl on the ground before her, her thoughtful gaze on Kelru's back.

Kelru closed the last pack and set it aside. He rose and bent toward Nakhalru in formal thanks, guest to host. "Cousin. If I live, I will repay what we have taken from you."

Nakhalru blinked at him. "It is nothing that matters."

"You'll be in danger for us tomorrow," Kelru said.

But Nakhalru only shrugged. "A little price, for long friendship. But when you return in safety, I'll name the gift that settles your debt." The words were formal, Vika knew. Then Nakhalru stepped forward and set his hands on Kelru's shoulders. "Live well, cousin," he said, and drew him into an embrace, one shoulder then the other. To Vika's surprise he then did the same with Pierre, saying, "Strange little people, you are, but tough as roots. If Kelru comes back, you will, too. Cousin."

"Cousin," Pierre said, and touched the other man's shoulder lightly, tentatively. His eyes were sad.

"Now go," Nakhalru said. "All of you. Dawn must not find you in the open." Vika tied her thessach snugly at her waist, then set the fur hat on her head, brought the hood up over it, put on her heavy mittens.

They left silently, taking only their own packs. The animals stayed behind with Nakhalru. Vika had gathered that he and Kelru had worked out a way—a risky one—to bring them out of the city at dawn, just as the gates opened.

As she crossed Kelru's courtyard for the last time, she looked up at the black, bitter sky. Tlankharu, Arcturus, was approaching the zenith, staring down at them through scudding clouds. She smelled snow, and smoke, and faintly the stables and privy; lately this mingling had come to be the smell of home. How much more so for Kelru? She saw him, a dark shape against the pale gleam of fresh snow. He seemed to hesitate, looking around him; she heard him take a quick breath. Then he went out the courtyard gate, Pierre just behind him.

Vika and Thiain followed. At this hour the streets were empty, the few windows dark. The wind whined thinly overhead, above the roofs, and stirred the snow in the street. The reddish glow of Tlankharu, and of the small yellow moon, nearly full, gave them light enough to see their way. Soon she was beyond the parts of the city she had known. She was tired, and shaky with the longing to be safe. Impossible now. She took a stinging breath of the night air and concentrated on walking.

At last they came to a little square set against the western wall of Kheosseth. Kelru gestured them to silence. They waited, and listened. Vika looked out across the square. She knew that nothing was supposed to be built against the city wall, an important defense long ago against roving packs of unfamilied men, and still vital against wild beasts. But someone had put up a shed at the far end of this square, against the wall.

"Wait," Kelru muttered to Pierre. "When I signal, all of you come across. Send the women up to me, one at a time, then follow." He loped across the square, scrambled up onto the steep roof of the shed, and climbed carefully up toward the wall. At the top of the roof, Vika saw him feel around in the snow, then creep along the beam there, digging something out. A long pole. He raised it with an obvious effort, and braced it carefully at a certain place along the roof beam. The pole reached upward five meters, almost to the top of the city wall. Now he turned and raised a mittened hand.

They hurried across. When they reached the shed, Vika could hear dim animal snores from inside—khaltenu, perhaps. Then Pierre gave her a boost, and she climbed carefully up the roof. The snow was only a few centimeters' accumulation since the last time it had been cleared, and as long as she moved carefully, it stayed in place. The roof felt strong, built to bear much more snow than this. As she moved to stand beside Kelru she could see that deep notches had been cut into the pole, handholds and footholds.

When they all stood beside Kelru, he said, "Pierre. Up." He steadied the pole as Pierre went up, climbing with wiry strength, and swung himself out of sight onto the top of the wall. Vika slid her gloved hands out of her over-mittens and followed, carefully fitting her hands and feet into the notches. Once she slipped, and froze for an instant, clinging to the pole. At the top she had to climb upward with only the shallow stones as handholds. With her feet in the uppermost notches she could barely reach the top of the wall. "Pierre!" she hissed.

He took her wrists and hauled her up the rest of the way, over a low parapet and onto a walkway about two meters wide. It was drifted with snow, except for a trampled path against the high outward parapet. She got up and dusted herself off quickly so the snow wouldn't melt. Thiain almost landed on her, and Kelru heaved himself over the edge a moment later. Vika glanced over the outer wall. The ground was far away here—seven meters, or eight. Wearily, she wondered whether Kelru expected them to climb down the old cracked stones. It didn't seem possible.

"Where now?" Pierre asked.

"Come." Kelru led them along the path. About a hundred meters farther on, he stopped and fished around in the drifted snow. He came up with a coil of knotted rope. Vika stared at it. "That," she said, "and the pole. How?"

"An old way," he said. "City people always have their own ways in and out, for winter hunting, to avoid the gate tax on food."

She had trouble getting down the rope—no strength in her arms or hands. She fell the last three meters, but landed unhurt in the deep drift of dry snow against the base of the wall. As they slogged away from the city wall, westward across the open field, the world-wind met them in all its strength. The right side of her face went numb almost at once. Remembering Kelru's teaching, she stopped to wrap her hood more closely around it. The others waited silently. Then they were off again. The snow looked smooth and firm in the dim starlight and moonlight, but Vika found at once that it was like powder, or fine sand, and she sank in with every step. It was slow going. But at least the wind would quickly erase their tracks.

At last they came to a steep bank, and below it a road—drifted with snow, but not as deeply as the field. Kelru scrambled down first, then waited while the others joined him. Vika was trembling, near her limit, worn down by two days of dread and disaster. Kelru must have sensed it. "Only a little farther," he said, almost gently, and touched her shoulder. She nodded mechanically, and they set out northward. The wind in Vika's face flattened her thessach against her and dashed away the ice-cloud of her breath.

The city lay to their right as they traveled, the wall less than half a kilometer away. Kelru's words to her had been a kindly fiction: they had more than a little farther to go. They passed almost all of Kheosseth before they came to a small group of buildings clumped on the south slope of a low hill, under a grove of trees. All the windows were shuttered, wooden flaps let down from above, but light gleamed through a few cracks. Smoke rose from several chimneys. A barn loomed behind, and she could see two sledges under a shed roof in the center courtyard. An inn. Not for them the bright fires within, the warm box-beds stuffed soft with straw. Kelru led them to the barn, and she staggered after the others down a ramp of trampled snow to the door. Inside, in the beast-smell and the darkness, she felt Pierre's touch guiding her to a small, enclosed place. It was frigid and dank, but there was straw to lie on, and no wind; and as soon as her aching limbs were settled, she slept.

Kelru had to shake her awake. She stared up at him, barely recognizing him in the weak gray light from the open door of the barn. He had already turned to Pierre, who was sitting up, about to speak. With a sharp clenching gesture of one hand, Kelru cut him off. Then he sniffed—the signal for silence and watchfulness. There was some kind of commotion going on in the yard outside the barn, and a squeal from a riding animal. It roused others inside the barn.

Thiain touched Vika's arm and drew her back with the men, into the shadows at the back of the small beast-pen where they had slept. The door of the barn swung inward.

It was Nakhalru. He strode into the barn with his narrow snout lifted to sniff the air. Kelru stood up. "Cousin," he said in a quiet voice.

Nakhalru's ears twitched, but he did not glance toward them. "Too bad the barn is empty," he said reflectively. "I'll have to stable those beasts of mine in here. Might be stolen the very next minute, by someone in a hurry to get up the road before this barn is searched by Vakhar's men." He went out, and returned leading Thonn, with Feth and Nukh following. All three were saddled. Behind their saddles, all three carried packs—ones that Vika recognized. With a few experienced hisses and grunts, Nakhalru persuaded the animals into an empty pen near the one where Kelru still stood, grave and silent, watching. Then Nakhalru left, without once glancing in Kelru's direction.

Pierre moved quickly to the rail of the pen. "It all seems to be there," he said softly.

"Good," Kelru said. "We must move out of here at once. The hunt is up."

"How will we ride out of here in daylight?" Pierre asked.

"Muffled up," Kelru said. "Keep your heads down, don't talk, and you might pass for children."

"Children don't travel during the Peace of Winter," Thiain said.

"No one travels during the Peace of Winter." Kelru sighed and turned to Vika. "I'll ride Thonn, with you up behind. The other woman will ride Feth—he's gentle enough to carry a stranger. Pierre will have Nukh."

They rode away from the inn in a freshening wind, with heavy snow lashing down toward them out of the north. No one tried to stop them; they saw no one at all. Vika turned once to look back. The buildings of the inn loomed gray-white behind the curtain of snow. She wondered how soon she would long for the chance to sleep in a barn again, on a pile of straw. They rode on in silence except for the *crump* of the animals' wide feet on the fresh snow, the creak of leather, the endless rush of the world-wind in the conifers that crouched low beside the road. Pierre, then Thiain, then Kelru and Vika. Kelru sat stiffly. His blue-cloaked back smelled of wet wool, and faintly of woodsmoke. She couldn't find the courage to speak to him. Everything she could have said was too important. Or perhaps none of it was. They rode in the center of a dome of whiteness that extinguished words and, finally, thought.

Sixteen

For Vika, the days that followed blended into a long, formless dream of cold and weariness. They traveled northward slowly, taking care not to be seen. Kelru led them on hill paths that no one used, paths made by the horned *gherrau* in their cautious migrations. He knew the lay of the land, how to find a sheltered spot each night where they could risk a fire. He kept their minds on the path to be followed, and on the Rules of Winter.

Vika grew to hate the Rules even as she absorbed them, lived by them, knew her life depended on them. At first Kelru let everyone ride, gaining speed at the cost of the beasts' strength. But when they were well clear of the Mother-River plain, and into rougher land that was thinly settled even by Windhome standards, he insisted that all of them walk. "If we ride, in this weather, the beasts need meat every second day," he said, "and we dare not stop to hunt, not for days yet."

Vika learned how to walk in snow—to follow carefully, close at Thonn's tail; to breathe through a layer of wool to spare her lungs the worst of the cold; to adjust her clothing to cool herself so she would not sweat with exertion and risk a chill. That was the lesson Kelru came back to again and again: to be wet was to die. To make any mistake, or any wrong choice, was to die.

The winter was still young enough that they did not need snowshoes in the forest; Kelru had told them he preferred this, as they might need to climb trees if they encountered a pack of kharag.

Kharag were cowards, Kelru said, carrion-eaters; but they would try for anything small enough—Pierre's size, for example. The riding beasts would try to fight them off, of course, and Kelru and Pierre with their bows; but all their lives would still depend on a quick retreat to safety.

In spite of Vika's weariness, she learned to watch all around as she walked, to know at any instant which tree she would run to if Kelru gave the order to climb. Kharag could climb, too, that was the worst of it; but some defense would be possible.

Sometimes at dawn or dusk she heard the kharags' voices, a resonant rattling bark that seemed to come from no direction, or all directions. "Good," Kelru said once. "We know where they are." *Too close*, Vika thought.

For the first few days of travel, Vika woke every morning so stiff and sore that she could barely move. That passed, but not the weariness that grew every day—a weariness of body and mind. Hardship was draining her, but so was her isolation. The silences among them saddened her. Silence between Thiain and Kelru, who avoided naming or glancing at each other; Thiain rarely spoke even to Vika. Silence between Pierre and Kelru, in whom she sensed deep anger still smoldering, buried. And silence between Pierre and herself.

She would so have welcomed any sign of warmth from him, any sense of companionship. But, she guessed, for Pierre to open himself to her would threaten his strength; and she knew he needed that strength desperately. He was her commanding officer, still bound to the mission, to which he would give his life until it succeeded, or until he died. She could no longer ridicule him for that. She wished her own life had a goal beyond the next stop for rest, the next bowl of hot food. She wished she could even pretend to hope.

She saw that Pierre still grieved for Anke, or for his failure that had allowed her death. She did not try to comfort him. She'd learned that Pierre was a man who needed to fight his own internal battles; no reassurance from anyone else could reach him.

The days went on unchanging. The trapper settlements, the shelter Kelru had talked of, were marked on no map; they could only hope to find one by the logic of the land—places in the shelter of ridges, and near water. Kelru said that there were valleys in the northern mountains where warm water bubbled out of the earth. People might well settle in such a place, make use of that warmth to survive the Deep Cold. It was some kind of hope. He'd chosen a route that would take them to that part of the mountains, but it would be a long journey.

Kelru had ruled that a midday meal was necessary for winter travelers, and so they always stopped at high sun to eat—*khishtuh*, a gruel of pounded dried tubers, cold from the morning; and *gakht*, a stiff paste of minced dried meat and animal fat that tasted of the leather bags it was kept in. Vika found herself eating hungrily. She was always hungry, though so far there had been enough food. "Food is warmth," Kelru had said, and she knew it was true. But still she dreamed of another kind of warmth, of the sun in open skies beating down on her, warming her to the bone. *Never again.*

One day at their midday meal she sat apart from the rest. Thiain slumped against her pack, perhaps sleeping. Pierre and Kelru were arguing, drawing maps in the snow with sticks. Sick of them both, she left camp, trudging through shallow snowdrifts toward a bush where she could piss. It was farther than it had seemed, but finally she passed around it—

She heard the thick indrawn hiss of animal breath, and even in the bitter chill she smelled blood. She saw the corpse of something big, a gherrau, maybe, lying splayed and broken in the underbrush, blood frozen, stripped ribs glistening. In a nightmare frozen moment she thought of Isamu, Isamu on the ship—

—then the kharag's pale triangular head lifted from the prey it was guarding. Eyes at the knobbed corners of the skull swiveled toward her, black slits in orange—

—purple-black lips slipped back from needle teeth, teeth for tearing carrion, or living flesh—

—the muscles of the thing's shoulders shifted, gathered—

Vika bolted, crying, "Kharag! Kharag!" As she reached the fire the riding beasts rose to their feet, teeth bared, black tongues tasting the air. She flung herself onto Feth's back and clung there shaking. Kelru and Pierre stood with drawn bows between Nukh and Thonn, Thiain behind them.

From her height she watched the kharag. It did not approach. It slid silently away into denser brush. Even to protect its kill it would not face the riding beasts—killers larger than itself, predatory carnivores from the south, strong and well-fed.

Shivering with adrenaline reaction, Vika slid down from Feth's back. Strong hands gripped her and turned her. Kelru looked down at her, his ears flat back. "You have learned nothing," he said scornfully. "If Pierre had done this, I would beat him. If you were Pierre's mate I would tell him to beat you, by my word and my blood I swear it." He let go of her with a shove. "If you ever go so far from camp again, I will set aside custom and pay you out. Remember that." And he turned away and stood stiffly by Thonn, his head bowed.

Pierre came up to her and said in Standard, "I will not let him harm you. But I cannot let you harm yourself. Learn from this, Vika." His gentleness hurt more than Kelru's open anger. And beyond Pierre she could see Thiain, gazing at her reproachfully. Vika had endangered them all.

Vika could give them no answer. She had made a mistake. She had caused another silence, built another wall.

But now she knew the voices that called from the dark forest; now the kharag were real to her. She no longer left camp for any reason. She learned, of necessity, a Windhome person's casual acceptance of necessary bodily functions; safety was also necessary.

At least they slept warm, while the good weather held. Vika and Thiain shared one *avartha*, and the men the other. The avarthu were small shelters made of thick, tight-woven wool, oiled to shed water, made to be set up easily among trees. They were triangular, slanting down from a high-peaked opening in front—designed to lean over a fire—to a low wall in back. An avartha captured heat well—and smoke, but it was worth it. They spread their beds inside on soft branches stripped from conifer limbs. Rolled up tightly in her blankets, Vika was fairly comfortable.

Kelru and Thiain split the night watches, which Kelru would not trust to the humans' weak hearing and negligible sense of smell. Vika was relieved to see that Kelru valued Thiain's help, however grudgingly he admitted it. But Vika always slept better in the part of the night when Thiain shared her bed. Thiain's body gave off little warmth, through her fur and her carefully efficient clothing, but her nearness comforted Vika. At no other time did anyone ever touch her.

It was a loneliness that seemed to fit, in this vast and winter-shrouded landscape. The mountains rose all around them now, white and silent, blind watchers in the day; at night the stars, a trembling immensity, whispered of death. And always they heard the wind—empty, cold, eternal. One night by the fire Kelru told them stories of the world-wind: that the unavenged dead mingled their voices in it, crying for justice, crying to be freed. Pierre, listening, looked pale. Vika knew he was thinking of Anke. She knew Kelru had meant him to—an angry gesture. Vika was sorry for that. Pierre did not need to be punished. He was punishing himself relentlessly.

Three days later, crossing a little valley, they came to a frozen river—one of the many tributaries of the Mother-River itself, and larger than any they had crossed before. Vika rode numbly behind as Kelru led them downstream until the valley widened and turned south, and the river swept down it in a broad curve. "We'll cross here," Kelru said, "where the ice is thickest. Then we'll make for the trees." He glanced up at the sky. Vika looked as well. A wall of sullen blue-black clouds hung in the northern sky, the low sun outlining their

towers with blood. Heavy snow before morning, Vika knew. Their
good weather-luck was ending. And they would find no shelter near
the river in this flat little valley, among the clumps of dead bracken
and thorns. To find a good place to camp they must turn back, or
move on; and Kelru always chose to move on, toward the rumor of
hot springs and their faint hope of refuge. Still at least two eightdays'
travel away, he said.

They set out to cross the river. It was Pierre's turn to go first.
Vika watched him lead Nukh down the bank and start out onto the
windswept ice.

She was halfway down the bank, picking her footing carefully,
when she heard Pierre shout. She looked up and saw Nukh shying
back toward shore, the ice crazing and crackling around his feet. And
where Pierre had been, a great black shattered place. And something
dark and wet, clinging to the downstream end. The ice there was
crumbling away.

The world stopped for an instant. Then the cry ripped from her,
tearing her throat—"*Pierre!*"

Kelru passed her headlong, half-sliding down, and she found she
could move and plunged after him. He had a rope, that was good—

She could still see Pierre's head above water. She caught Kelru
just before he started out onto the ice. "No!" she shouted. "I'm light,
I'll go. Rope!"

Kelru instantly gave her the end of the rope in his hands. She knotted
it around her waist and crawled out onto the cracked ice. It creaked under
her, and she lowered herself to her belly and began to creep. Pierre looked
beyond reach. A wet black head, now frosting over with white. He had
minutes, seconds, to live. "Pierre!" she cried. "Hold on!"

Closer now. The rope was in her way, but she had no time to stop
and shift it. She could feel the broken ice sagging under her, pressing
down into the frigid black water. Pierre still clung to the edge of the
hole. "Hold on," she said again, gasping for breath. She slid toward
him very carefully now. She did not take her eyes off him. If she

looked away, he would be gone when she looked back, sucked down to drown in darkness, scrape downriver under the ice. Lost.

She reached him. He tried once more to raise himself onto the edge of the hole, but the edge only crumbled away under him. "Pierre," she said, willing a response. "I'm here. Pierre, look at me!"

He looked at her dully. His lips were already blue. She tore the mitten off her right hand with her teeth and stretched her hand out toward him. "Take it!"

He flailed toward her with his left hand, bare, and she caught it. But he could not grip her hand, and she lost hold. "Try again!" she said. This time she caught his wrist, not his hand, and she was able to hold on. With an effort she brought up her other hand and got a better grip. Then she stopped, agonized. He was too heavy. All those clothes, saturated with water. She could not possibly hold him.

She looked back toward shore. Kelru had secured the other end of the rope to Thonn, and stood ready to lead him back up the bank. He saw her motion and called to her, "Now?"

"Not yet!" she shouted, desperation shredding her voice.

She slid closer to Pierre. He was no longer looking at her; his eyes were dull. "Pierre," she said. "I'm going to tie this rope around you— hang on...*Gaia's death!*" One-handed, numb-fingered, she could not untie the knot at her waist.

Well, then. The ice cracked under her, but still held her up as she threw a loop of her rope over Pierre's head and worked it down under his arms. "Pierre, for Gaia's sake, help me!" He did not stir. Frigid water soaked her arms, her chest. Her breastbone and ribs ached. It didn't matter. Pierre's eyes were closed now. "Pierre!" she shouted at him. "Pierre, you coward! *Wake up!*"

He sagged in her hold. She snugged the loop around his body, then gripped both bights tightly. "Kelru!" she screamed. "*Now!*"

The drag came, but Pierre did not move. It was too late, he was frozen in— Then the wet, limp weight of him began to slide forward. Vika took a sobbing breath and tried to help. He caught on the jagged edge of the ice, raw against the bare flesh of his hands and wrists. She pulled savagely, swearing, and he came free again. He looked like a sodden corpse, emerging from the water centimeter by centimeter. His ice-scraped face, his bluish hands oozed blood, diluted to a cold pink by water. Fear set cold claws on her neck.

They reached the bank, and Vika struggled to her knees to help pull Pierre the last couple of meters. Panting, Kelru untangled them from the rope. Beyond him Thiain knelt, feverishly working to start a fire in a pile of sticks. "Hurry," Vika croaked. "Oh, hurry."

"We must get these clothes off him," Kelru said. His voice was strange, hoarse with anguish. Vika helped shift Pierre onto a blanket spread on the snow. He seemed unconscious, but shivered so violently that it was hard to strip off the wet clothes, which were already beginning to freeze. As soon as he was bare, she scrubbed at him savagely with another blanket to dry him, and Kelru wrapped him in two more. They turned him onto his side and he convulsed at once, vomiting river water while Vika held him steady. Then he went still, and she laid him down on a dry part of the blanket.

"He's going to die," Kelru said. "Even with a fire."

She tugged off her hat and pulled it onto Pierre's head. "He's not going to die," she said fiercely. "He's not like you, he doesn't have fur. We can raise his core temperature. We can save him." She shivered in her wet thessach—she needed help as well. Soon, soon.

"We'll try," Kelru said. "He needs shelter from the wind first. Then a fire. Hot water with sugar in it. We still have root-sugar, don't we?"

"A little," Thiain said. "Ah." The fire had caught. She looked up at Kelru. "Make Thonn lie down upwind of Pierre. Then go and get some wood."

Kelru maneuvered the beast into place, then went off with the axe toward a clump of scrubby trees. Vika bent to drag one of the avarthu from its covering, but Thiain touched her. "Stop." Vika straightened. Thiain stripped off her own thessach, set it aside, pulled Vika's off over her head and dropped it in the snow. Then the warm, dry folds of

Thiain's thessach covered Vika's sodden tunic. "Now you have a little time," Thiain said. "I'll help." She quickly unfolded her old thessach, the one she had worn from Dethun's, and threw it on.

It was a nightmare struggle to set up the avartha in the bitter, steady wind, with no tall trees about. At last it was ready, low-roofed and sagging but adequate. Vika spread out the ground mat. The fire had grown, giving light to the purple dusk. The avartha, leaning over it, caught the heat and held it. "Let's get him in there," Vika said.

She and Thiain laid Pierre down inside the shelter and covered him with more blankets. Then Vika began to undress. "No," Thiain said in a shocked voice. "You've lost right thinking. You'll die."

"I know what I'm doing," Vika said through chattering teeth. "I can warm him. I don't have fur to insulate me from him." She tore off her undertunic and slid into the cocoon of blankets with Pierre, naked as he was, right against him.

He was as cold as a dead man would be. She wrapped her arms and legs around him, pulled him against her, willed him to warm up, to live. "Pierre. Wake up. Listen to me, Pierre!"

He still seemed unconscious, but after a while he said something in a blurred voice.

"That's right," she said. "Wait just a moment. We're getting you something hot to drink." Her throat ached with pent-up tears— reaction, fear—

He began to shiver again. "Gabrielle," he said. "Gabrielle, I'm cold." He spoke in French.

Gabrielle, once his wife. Anke had told her about Gabrielle and his son, at the sisterhold. "Soon you'll be warm again," Vika said, also in French, tears filling her eyes. "Wait now. Try to stay awake."

"Where is Thierry?"

"In the next room," she said unsteadily.

"Liar!" He began to sob. "Bitch! He's gone. He's dead. I left him to die. They'll come and find him, they'll kill him—" He broke off, helpless between coughing and weeping.

Fear tightened within her. Pierre would die—he would leave her here alone— She pulled his head down onto her shoulder and rocked him until the hot water was ready, rocked him with her face turned away from the fire, stiff, distorted. She must not cry now.

Then Kelru raised them both, blankets and all, and Vika held Pierre's head while Thiain, her eyes dark with concern, touched a bowl of hot sweetened water to his lips. At first the sticky-sweet liquid dribbled down through his beard. Then he coughed and began to try to swallow. Thiain gave him as much as he would take, and then Kelru laid him down with Vika again.

While she was up, she had seen that it was a poor campsite, far too exposed. But there was nowhere else; they could go no farther tonight. She tightened her hold on Pierre, lay still, tried to rest.

A long time later she felt him shift against her. She pulled back and looked at him. He blinked at her. "Vika—what—" Then he broke off, coughing.

Kelru shadowed them, squatting down beside them. He spoke cautiously. "He's awake?"

"He's conscious," she said. "And he's started to sweat. I think he'll live." Relief swallowed her voice, and she hid her face in Pierre's hair. Steady, steady. She felt Kelru's hand brush lightly against her shoulder.

Vika slept then, the long, stunned sleep of exhaustion. She woke much later, confused in the dark and cold—confused by a dream of a past lover, long past. A warm hand cupped her breast, the thumb moving gently over her nipple. Heat beside her, cold all around—

"Vika," a voice murmured. Pierre's voice.

She turned so that his hand slipped from her breast, and gathered him close. "Hush," she said, looking past him toward the fire. Past midnight, she guessed. It was snowing hard, thick flakes that hissed faintly in the fire. She could see Thiain's hood burrowed down into her blankets in the other shelter. Kelru sat motionless by the fire, his bow at his side, looking out over the river with his back to her and Pierre.

Pierre sighed. His breath was warm against her neck. She could not move away from him, could not move at all. His body was warm now, almost too warm. His hand slid down her body, caressing.

"Pierre, don't." She caught his hand, held tight. "You're confused. You need more sleep."

"No, I don't," he said. "Come closer." His breathing had changed, slowed, deepened. His hand freed itself and drifted again over her body.

He wanted her. And under his touch she was melting—the ice inside her was melting. She turned her head, tried to catch her breath, but when she turned back he kissed her, and she found herself responding, her arms tightening around him. Everything was all right....

No, it wasn't. She broke away, turning her head. "We can't," she whispered. "Kelru and Thiain—"

He looked down at her, his black eyes gleaming. "No. We can do anything." He kissed her, drawing the whole length of her body strongly against his. She felt him against her, felt his readiness. Warm against her cheek he breathed her name, and his hands moved boldly, caressing her.

She stopped trying to think. Pierre was there with her, alive and safe. He had not died. *She was not alone.* Nothing else mattered.

She turned toward him, shifting herself carefully in their wrappings, and with one fierce motion they were joined. They were so swathed in blankets that it was hard to move. It was a slow, dreamlike time, lit for Vika by a strange burning joy that made her weep silently, shaking. He was with her. He wanted her, needed her, as she did him. She was human—they were human together.

He kissed the corners of her eyes where her tears spilled over, kissed her mouth and she tasted salt. For that moment the camp was gone. Kelru and Thiain were gone. The Destroyers were gone. She and Pierre were alone at the center of the world. They slept there until dawn.

SEVENTEEN

Kelru tended the fire carefully as morning approached, building it up to heat water for khishtuh and drinking. The heavy snowfall had passed in the night. Dawn burned pale gold behind the clouds across the river, and the new drifts were a deep-shadowed blue. The wind had fallen almost to stillness. All the country around—the treed hillsides, the snow-hummocked valley floor—lay in a listening silence.

They had heard no kharag voice last night. Perhaps none lived in this valley. Or perhaps a pack was out there now, belly-crawling silently upwind through the brush and the drifts. Kelru touched his bow, ready at his side. He put back his hood and listened again. Wind rattled the bare scrubby branches that still showed above the snowdrifts. He heard no other sounds but their own. But in those far dark trees anything might wait now, watching, scenting the air. Anything, or anyone....

Anger at himself soured his blood—anger at more than his own misjudgment of the ice. He was angry that his mistake had stopped them *here*. It was an exposed and shelterless place from which they could not retreat, and of them all, only Kelru was able to shoot. But the worst of it was something he had kept to himself, so as not to frighten the others: they had entered a skull place.

Kelru felt the fur on his neck lift a little at the thought. The Destroyers had poisoned this land long ago, hunting and burning from the sky. Such lands were left untouched—left for the scattered bones of the unburned dead, and the deep scars where entire towns, entire farmholds had vanished into silent light.

Kelru had never trespassed in such a place before. But he had known from the start that it was inevitable. This stretch of forbidden land was barely two days' travel across, but it was centered around one of the old roadways that extended far to the northeast and to the southwest. There was no way around it except to journey south toward inhabited lands, or to curve far to the north, weeks out of their way.

By Anokothu law, the penalty for entering a skull place was death. His hope had been to pass through quickly, so that the others would not guess the truth. But now they were trapped; they could travel only very slowly until Pierre recovered—or died.

Another thought made Kelru restless as well: Sometimes the Anokothu law did not need to be invoked; sometimes men who entered a skull place died of the poison left by the Destroyers. Kelru had heard how they died—wasted, furless, shitting blood and water....

Yet they had more to fear than the skull place itself. Yesterday, cutting wood, Kelru had found some bones in the woods, a gherrau, kharag-stripped; and caught in the ribs was a hunting arrow, its shaft broken off and frayed. Some men, outlaws, did live in skull places, taking advantage of the unhunted game, the easy trapping. Dangerous men, who preyed on lost travelers and the helpless. And while Pierre's life hung in the balance, they were all helpless.

Looking out at the river Kelru could see it now—the place where Pierre had nearly died. The broken place was skinned over with a glassy film of new ice. It shone pale gold like the sky. The rest of the surface was blue-white, snow-covered.

Kelru had never doubted that the ice would hold. He stared at it now, remembering an old saying: *Winter slays the confident man—and those who trust him.*

Kelru got to his feet with an effort, holding his thessach close in the still, chill air. He moved around the fire to the sticks where Pierre's wet clothes, and Vika's, were draped to dry. He rearranged the stiff-frozen wool, bending it down over the sticks until the ice in the fabric crackled.

That, at least, had been well done—Vika's rescue of Pierre. After her panic when she saw the kharag, it was good to know that she could also meet danger with a still belly and steady eyes. A strong woman, a bondmate with courage, would help Pierre on the hard road ahead. If Pierre lived. If any of them lived.

Kelru went a little way upwind from the fire, and sniffed the air. Thonn would wake if he smelled a strange man or riding beast, but still— Kelru smelled nothing suspicious. Ridiculous anyway—as if men who lived here would stalk downwind. No, the first sign of them would be an arrow in someone's throat.

Kelru went back to the fire and turned the pot of melting snow. In the avartha behind him Vika stirred and muttered. He wondered if she and Pierre would expect him to pretend nothing had happened the night before—pretend he had not heard them or scented them. They were strange people: so secretive about matters of mating, as if hiding a truth could change it. Kelru added more snow to the pot. He would pretend nothing; that was a luxury left behind in Kheosseth.

He was glad that Vika was now of his family. Though he knew well how that thought would have surprised him only yesterday. Oh, Vika was an excellent woman, that had always been clear—she had an alert and listening ear, and a good mind. She had quickly mastered the polite art of when to speak, and when to keep silence.... But Kelru had never thought she would be useful, or indeed anything but another burden, on a journey such as this.

Kelru owed her a word: to say he regretted the threat he had made after her foolish escapade in the woods. And he must speak that word soon, if he wished to be sure she heard it in life.

He tugged his hood forward over his face and looked down into the fire, listening to the wind, and to Thonn's deep rumbling snore behind Pierre's avartha. He owed Pierre a word as well. Strange how that had only become clear in Kelru's mind after yesterday's disaster. He had known Pierre's history for a long time. Yet only now did he understand: Pierre had given his word years ago and far away, and he could not swerve from the way he had sworn to follow. It was that word that kept him from avenging Anke. It was that word that kept him moving forward even after all hope was gone.

Kelru set another stick in the base of the fire and bent his head. "*Iyahhhh*," he muttered—denial, grief, regret. If Pierre lived, if they all escaped this place, Kelru would help him keep his word.

Once Thiain had been left behind.

He glanced over at her, still sleeping soundly, snow caked on her hood. She was a good woman, too, he had to admit. Clear-thinking in an emergency, and honorable. It would be a pity to leave her among rough, lawless men as the Red Mind came near to her.

But Kelru could not mate with her himself, not even as one of many men. No. He wondered if Pierre or Vika had thought of it, or would understand if they did. As his bondmate, Thiain would be nearer to Kelru than Pierre—because she would bear in her body what might be Kelru's children. Kelru would have to keep her safe, at any price—to give his life for her, if that was required. Pierre, and Vika, and their mission would weigh nothing in that balance.

No. He could not mate with Thiain, even to save her from an unfamilied fate in the far north. She had chosen to come this far. The consequence, however heavy, was hers.

He had leaned forward to stir the melting snow in the pot when Vika called softly to him. "Kelru!" She sounded afraid.

He took a breath, then rose and went to her, his belly cold—sure that Pierre had died in the night, as he had dreaded. But Pierre breathed, still bundled in blankets. Kelru knelt and saw that the black hair on his face and scalp was wet with sweat, and his skin was gray. Vika squatted beside him, Thiain's thessach clutched hastily around her; one hand rested on Pierre's face. She said something that sounded like a curse, and then said, "He's sick." Her voice was rough, angry, but Kelru could still smell her fear, as strong on her as the strange musty scent of their brief mating.

Kelru knelt down and touched Pierre's cheek. It was hot as a stone in a fire, and fine shuddering tremors shook the sick man's body. "Pierre," Kelru said urgently. "Wake, Pierre!"

Pierre did not wake. His breathing was harsh. Kelru leaned closer and listened, and heard the little whistling sound the air made as it passed into Pierre's lungs. He opened Pierre's mouth and sniffed. Foulness, and a hint of blood. "He hasn't coughed," Kelru said, through the worry like a sick weight in his belly. "A good sign."

"Speak the truth," Vika said, looking straight into Kelru's eyes. "Some of the river water got into his, what is your word, his lungs. This could be a sickness growing in his lungs. From the water." Her voice was steady now.

She had asked for the truth. "Yes. I know this illness," Kelru said carefully, after a moment. "Fever, and a strong cough with blood, and difficult breathing; and finally, often, they die." He saw Vika's face change, saw the fear deepen in her eyes. Pity for her burned like a knife in his belly, and he said, "But, Vika—your people have so much we lack. You must know how to cure this."

"I know how," Vika said. "But the things I need to save Pierre were on the sledge. They're gone. The tools that could discover exactly what medicine he needs, and then make it for us." She dragged her woolen sleeve across her face and looked down at Pierre. "Without that, I can do no more than you can." Her face was dark and stiff with anger, or with grief held under rigid control.

"Let me see him," Thiain's voice said, and Kelru moved aside for her. She had lived at a sisterhold, might have worked at the hospital there—perhaps she would know what to do.

Gentle, graceful, Thiain sank down beside Pierre, touched and listened and sniffed, and said at last, "Yes. The lung sickness." Her voice was calm and steady. "But we can save him."

"How?" Vika said. Her odd face looked twisted.

"First he must have better shelter," Thiain said. "A warm room, where we can cool his fever safely."

"We can build a shelter with—" Kelru began.

"Not in time," Thiain said, her ears twitching with impatience. "We must take him to a place where people live." She looked up at him. "You served the Judge of the Roads. You must know something of this land. Where will we find people?"

Kelru breathed out sharply to calm himself. "Nowhere near here," he said harshly. The lie tasted foul in his mouth, but the truth would be fouler.

Thiain rose and looked into his face. "I saw you this morning," she said. "How you watched and listened. There's something here you fear more than kharag. Outlaws?"

"If we did find outlaws here," Kelru said, "we could not ask their help."

"Why not?" Vika demanded. "Do you want Pierre to die?" She looked up at Kelru with a hot light in her eyes. "It would solve your problem, wouldn't it? If we died, you could go home to Dethun."

Kelru's rage burst, flaring his neck fur, baring his claws and teeth. "You dare!" he said. "You dare *speak* such a thing!"

Thiain stepped between them, laid her hands on Kelru's chest. "Peace!" she said. "Vika is afraid for Pierre. Forgive her." Kelru snarled and slapped her hands away. But she did not turn away from him or look down. "And you must not lie again," she said steadily.

He faced her, and Vika beyond her, at Pierre's side. "As you wish, then," he said bitterly. "I'll tell you where we are. Look around you. Under this snow lie the bones of our people. Above this land the Destroyers walked in the air. This is a skull place."

He saw Thiain's glance flick aside, saw Vika's mouth tighten. "You understand, then," he said. "Poison in the air, and lights in the night, lights that burn without fire. And voices under the ground, that tell you the way of your death."

"Children's stories," Thiain said, but her voice shook.

"And everywhere the unburned bones. Trapped spirits calling for release."

Thiain's ears went flat back. "Nevertheless," she said, "we must save Pierre. If people live here, we must find them."

"Yes," Vika said. She still knelt beside Pierre, her bare hand laid along his cheek. "Please, Kelru. I'm not afraid." Her anger seemed gone. But her cheeks were wet with tears. "I ask you to forgive what I said. I know what you've given up for Pierre."

"We both know you will not let him die," Thiain said to Kelru. "He is of your family. And Vika, too, since last night."

Kelru saw the naked brown skin of Vika's face darken. "I think he was already getting sick. Confused. He might not have—chosen this, if he'd been clear in his mind."

"My people also mate with unclear minds," Thiain said. "But the result is the same."

"Not with us," Vika said. "It's a choice, with us. And I don't think he chose freely."

Kelru laid his hand on her shoulder, and she looked up at him in surprise. "Vika, you are among my people," he said, "and mating means what it means to *us*. You are my brother's bondmate, and my friend, and of my family." Suddenly, powerfully, he wanted her to understand that she was no longer unfamilied. No longer alone. "Even if Pierre dies," Kelru said, "the bond has been formed. That is our law."

She nodded in acceptance, but did not seem comforted. She picked up Pierre's wrist in her fingers, bowed her head over his hand.

Kelru looked up and into Thiain's eyes. "You and I must build a travois Thonn can pull."

"Where will we go?" Thiain's dark gaze was steady.

He tightened his hands, feeling the claws dig into his palms, and then spoke the words of his surrender. "Downriver," he said. "It's our best chance of finding people. And it's downwind, so they'll scent us coming. Perhaps then they won't kill us."

"I'm not afraid," Thiain said.

"No?" Kelru laid his ears flat back. "You should be."

Vika knew this journey from nightmares: progress so slow it seemed no progress at all, danger all around, blind hurry chewing at her guts. She saw nothing but her own stumbling feet, and Pierre, a limp bundle of ragged blankets tied in place on the travois. Sometimes he coughed so violently that they had to halt until it ended. Then Vika would wipe the bloody phlegm from his mouth, and they would move on until the next time.

Pierre talked in his fever, sometimes pleading incoherently, sometimes raging. He spoke to his son, to Gabrielle, to Anke—sometimes to Kelru, Vika thought, judging from the shifts in language. After a while Pierre's voice hoarsened and roughened, until he could no longer speak; then she was grateful.

Thiain took turns with Vika to walk beside Pierre, tend to his needs, and help to lift the travois when it caught on brush or uneven ground. Kelru rode Feth so he could shoot from a height. Thonn, the strongest of the beasts, pulled the travois, but as a riding beast he had never been trained to harness, and it made him unsteady and snappish. When it was Vika's turn to rest she rode Nukh, but she always had to be ready to leap off and set Thonn free so he could fight. Kharag were a constant threat—but not the only one.

By day's end Vika was exhausted in every way, body and spirit drained flat. The insidious cold ached in her lungs and slowed her thoughts; walking and riding both hurt; and above all, she was afraid. Not of the skull place, anonymous under deep snow; not of the men who might live here. She was terrified that Pierre would die.

She knew, with anguish, how dangerously ill he was—how thin a thread held him to life. Held them both. If Pierre died, how long would she live, alone in this world, and without hope? Grief waited with every break in Pierre's breath. Like a dark, frozen wave it hung over her, immense, inevitable.

As she walked she studied his sharp-boned face, sallow under the untidy black beard. She remembered how she had doubted his abilities. But now even those, his human weaknesses, had value; now that his death was near, she clung fiercely to every moment, every memory. She saw those memories differently now; she saw how hard he had always tried—how far he had come from the awkward, imperious Pierre of the first days after they woke from cold sleep. What a hard blow it must have been, to be made responsible for a hopeless mission, knowing that command was neither his training nor his gift. Yet he had not turned aside from the burden. He had tried with his whole heart to carry it.

By the time they stopped for the night, Pierre was deeply unconscious. After she cleaned him and settled him for the night, she placed the diagnostic patch—all that remained of their medical equipment—on his body while the others watched. It gave her bad news, confirming the rattle of fluid in his infected lungs and the thin, rapid stammer of his heart; proclaiming the burning height of his fever. Its readout on her datapad listed medications Pierre required, in order of urgency, with recommended dosages; but from first to last she had none of them. She keyed in a request for alternatives. *Fluids, rest, warmth*, it said. *Oxygen*.

They could no longer rouse him enough to give him water. But rest and warmth he could have, for a while. She slept beside him again, because it let her help him when he coughed in the night, and because it assured her he was still alive. His fever smoldered on. His breathing rasped; the cough was less frequent now, but worse, bringing up fresh blood.

He lived through the night. In the morning, the diagnostic patch demanded still more medicines, a list that began with rehydration fluids. Bark tea with root sugar was all they had to give, and it took Thiain, with all her grim experience, many minutes to rouse Pierre enough that he could drink it.

It was snowing heavily again, but Vika sensed that the sun was high. Higher than it should be. "We should get moving," she said.

She became conscious of a painful silence. Kelru and Thiain looked at each other. Then Kelru turned to her. "Thiain and I talked last night," he said. "She does not believe we should travel today."

Vika felt a flicker of fright. "But we have to get Pierre to shelter!"

"No," Kelru said gently. "No, Vika. I'm sorry. We must make him as comfortable as we can, and wait."

"Wait?" She looked up at him, at his pitying eyes, and her spine turned to ice. "Wait for him to die. Is that what you mean?"

He took her shoulders in his mittened hands, and his breath was warm on her face. "You did well, trying to save him," he said. "You pulled him from the water. You mated with him, and that was the good that came of all you risked—your gift to each other. But sometimes death has a long arm."

"He suffers when we travel," Thiain said, close beside her. "You saw that yesterday. We must let him die in peace, and give him to the wind. And then go on."

"*Go on where?*" The words tore Vika's throat. Go on forever, alone—even with Kelru and Thiain, alone. They were alien. They could not know her life, or her world, or her mind.

Pierre knew. But nothing would be left of Pierre.

She flung out her arms, pushing their kindness away. "So you won't try to save his life." Her voice was brittle as old ice.

"We all wanted to save him," Kelru said. "Peace, now. This is best."

She kept herself rigid. "But it isn't your choice, Kelru."

Thiain folded her arms across her chest. "If we move on," she said calmly, "Pierre *will* die, and in pain."

"He would risk that," Vika said, "for even a small chance to live, and complete his mission."

"A tiny chance," Thiain said. "If we go on, and find no shelter, no help, Pierre will be dead by nightfall." Her eyes in the shadow of the hood were dark with pity. "It would be cruel to move him now."

Vika hardened herself against Kelru's compassion, Thiain's gentle and sensible arguments. "If we can't take Pierre to find help," she said, "we must call help to us." She licked her dry lips and said, "You must use the Calling Tongue."

They stared at her for a moment in silence. Then Kelru shook himself, and set the back of his spread hand on his forehead in the gesture of utter rejection. "No," he said. "We would only be calling our death."

"Pierre is dying already," Vika said.

"But you and Thiain will live," Kelru said. "I will not risk your lives for nothing. There never was much chance that men of a skull place would help us."

"They'll come," Vika said, "if Thiain calls them."

Kelru's ears went back. "Thiain!"

"And if they come," Vika went on steadily, "you can save us all. You're Dethun's son. You have her gift of argument. Use it to save your brother." She folded her arms across her chest. "If you refuse, then you admit that you will not risk as much for Pierre as I did. And he wasn't my bondmate then."

"*I have risked everything for Pierre*," Kelru said, his voice low and raw. "Is it not enough? When will it be enough?"

"You chose to bind yourself to him," she said. The words hurt her as she spoke them.

Kelru closed his eyes and took an anguished breath. Then he faced her. "You can lead me by my promise," he said. "But nothing binds Thiain. You cannot compel *her*."

Vika turned to Thiain. "Listen to me," she said, before Thiain could speak. "I can't speak the Calling Tongue, and my voice is too weak anyway. You must do it for me. If they hear you call—a woman's voice—they'll come from any distance to help you. If Kelru calls, they won't come at all. Or they'll come to kill us."

"I will call them," Thiain said harshly.

"No," Kelru said, then, "*Why?*"

"For my children," Thiain said. "When I have them." She faced Vika. "I was your friend. I betrayed you when I let Dethun drug you. Then while you were drugged, I heard you tell Dethun what your people can give us. Life, life for our children." Her eyes burned. "For that, I would dare anything. I will help you."

Kelru walked to the edge of camp and stood with his back to them, his head bowed. Thiain climbed the low rock outcropping that sheltered the camp. Vika looked up at her, a gray shadow in the heavy snow. Thiain pushed back her hood, took a long breath, threw back her head and cried out—a soaring wail in a high, eerie register. She breathed and called again, and again.

Vika could not follow the words. The Calling Tongue conveyed meaning with tone, rising and falling; consonants were trills or stops, and little else. But to Vika, the sound itself conveyed fear, loneliness, despair.

In his bedroll Pierre groaned and muttered. Vika knelt to calm him before he set off another fit of coughing. His skin was hot and dry, his lips cracked and peeling. His eyes were partly open, white slits. She held him until Thiain fell silent, climbed down and joined them at the fire.

They all waited, and listened; but they heard no answering call. "No reason to expect an answer," Kelru said. "If they come, they will come like kharag. Silently, and from downwind."

Thiain sat quietly, but Vika knew she must be afraid. Kelru had explained it last night: Men of a skull place—outlaws—would keep Thiain prisoner until the Red Mind came, and they could mate with her. She would be equally valuable afterward: pregnant, but still able to work. Most likely she would never leave their encampment again. The cycles of her body would bind her there—and the needs of her children. If any lived.

Vika sat beside Pierre. If no one had heard Thiain's call, Pierre would die in this place after all, today, or tonight, or tomorrow. And if someone *had* heard....

But there was no other choice. No other way. Pierre would surely have done the same for her—would have forced Kelru and Thiain as she had done. She knew it. For her, he would have endured this silence, and the anger in Kelru's eyes. She could do the same. She would.

But when, toward noon, the riding beasts heaved to their feet, rumbling a warning deep in their chests—when Kelru rose, his hand on his knife, and threw back his hood—when under the trees gray shadows shifted, and a hard voice spoke, saying, "*Set down your weapons*"—then she saw fear plain on Thiain's face, fear and the knowledge of what would come. Vika looked away, sick with sudden regret, cold with her own fear that Pierre would die anyway. That Thiain's sacrifice would be for nothing.

EIGHTEEN

Pierre woke in darkness, enfolded in warmth like strong red light striking through his bones. The warmth was good. Yet something about it was wrong—strange and wrong—it nibbled at his exhausted mind, kept him awake. No place was warm anymore. So where was he? Was he even alive? Darkness pressed against his eyes.

He tried to move, to sit up, but he could not. He had no strength at all. And at that the familiar cold-sleep nightmare struck: Paralysis in darkness. Cold blue light. Chilly voices like sheets of shivering metal, shaping words that terrified him, because they meant nothing.... He cried out, a hoarse whisper that burned his throat.

Then someone moved beside him, and a woman's arms gathered him close, and a woman's voice soothed him in French. Not Gabrielle; the accent was wrong. And Gabrielle was lost. He had lost her years ago, long before he left Earth. Lost her—and Thierry.... A sob shook him, tearing his chest, and he tasted blood.

"Hush," the woman said. "Hush, Pierre. Rest." And he quieted, there in her arms. He knew, from his heart he knew that he was safe while she was with him. The nightmare faded, and he slept.

The second time he woke, his eyes opened on firelight. When he stirred, a dark shape above him moved, and a face looked down at him. His vision cleared. It was Kelru, winter-shaggy and unkempt. His eyes were tired, but his ears pricked up in a smile. "Brother," his deep voice said softly. "Welcome to the day."

Pierre blinked. His mind was clearer now, and he knew that he had been ill. Memory and fever dream danced and shifted in his mind. Through it all he remembered a quiet voice, a calm face, strong and gentle hands: the woman last night. He could name her now. Vika. Where was she? "Where?" he rasped, but could get no farther. It hurt to speak. Torn by days of coughing, the muscles of his chest burned with every breath, and his throat was raw.

Kelru set a long, cool hand on his shoulder and said kindly, "You are safe. Thiain says you'll live. You need not worry about anything."

Then another figure moved between Pierre and the light. A man like Kelru, but older. His yellow eyes were narrowed; a scar drew one side of his mouth up in a perpetual snarl, baring broken teeth. One of his ears was missing. He looked down at Pierre, but spoke to Kelru. "Awake, ah? He's even uglier than the other one."

In the lamplight Kelru's face went still. "Pierre must rest now, Talakh," he said.

The other man grunted. "Rest so he can work later," he said, and moved away.

"Vika," Pierre said, pleading.

"She's sleeping," Kelru said. "Thiain said not to wake her. She's been tending you for days."

Pierre closed his eyes. Vika was safe. Wherever they were, whatever had happened, she was safe.

His memory was clearing; his heart beat heavily, slowly. He remembered frigid water clawing him, dragging him down. He remembered strong arms encircling him, and then warmth against his body, like dark fire, bringing him to life. With joy he had known her: Vika, with her deep-buried strength, her stubborn courage. She had used both to save him from the river. And then she had given him an even greater gift. Hope....

Kelru moved away to fetch something, giving Pierre a clear view toward the fire. It burned in a pit at the center of the room, its smoke rising into shadows overhead. Around the fire he saw people, strangers:

four men clothed in work-soiled animal pelts; a woman silver-furred with age, tending a pot set near the flames; another woman, young and untidy, her body swollen with pregnancy, squatting with her dirty hands stretched out toward the warmth. As if she sensed his eyes on her she turned and looked at him—then struggled to her feet. Her hands twisted into some kind of warding sign before her belly.

Kelru, returning, lifted Pierre and held a wooden bowl to his lips. "Drink this, brother."

Pierre drank thirstily. It was cool water, with a faint strange taste, some herb. Or else the reek of this place was affecting him: smoke, leather, wet wool, charred meat, stale piss. Pierre finished the water and found that he could speak. "Where are we?"

Kelru bent close. "A trappers' encampment," he said in a low voice. "Outlaws. We called them to us because you were dying. They saved you because of Thiain. But now I must speak to you."

"I want to see Vika when she wakes," Pierre said.

Kelru touched Pierre's mouth with a firm finger. "As I said. I must speak to you as an elder brother, and as a younger brother you must listen." The finger pressed down, its claw sharp and cool against his flesh.

When Pierre lay quiet, Kelru took the finger away and said, "Listen, brother. I know you. I know you think that as your bondmate Vika threatens your mission. I know you were fevered when you took her. *But you cannot turn from her as you turned from Anke.*"

Pierre stared up at him, shocked. "I don't—"

"Be silent!" Kelru's red-gold eyes flared. "I told the people here that Vika is your bondmate. You must accept that—call her by name, share a bowl at meals. You must hunt for her, when you're strong enough. Both your lives are in danger until these people accept *you* as people. And they will not, unless you live by patterns they know. You and Vika must go on together as if you were friends, and glad of your mating. She saved your life, and then she was kind to you. She must not suffer for it." He laid Pierre down again and rose. "Now you must sleep."

Pierre wanted to argue, to tell Kelru that he had no wish to deny

Vika; but Kelru's words stopped him, filling him with sudden doubt. Kind, Kelru said—she had been *kind*. Was that what she'd told Kelru...?

Vika knelt beside Pierre, watching him sleep. It was late in the morning, but of course he needed rest to rebuild his strength. When his fever had finally broken the day before, she had felt only deep, exhausted relief, and an aimless sense of gratitude. He would live. After all the days of work and worry, she could not think beyond that. But now she knelt down beside him and considered him, brooding.

It was time to think of what came next. Pierre might still believe they could carry out the mission—study the ruins the Destroyers had left behind, and then somehow return to the south, reach their lander in the heart of Dethun's lands, and send off their warning to Earth. Vika had always had doubts, and they were much stronger now.

Doubts about the mission, and about this new path she and Pierre had taken. Her few earlier lovers, men and women at the university, had been pleasant companions who kept their distance, with ambitions that did not parallel her own. And that had been as well. Vika had never had any thought of a permanent relationship, even before she had signed on to this mission. She wondered how well she and Pierre would manage, living together for the rest of their lives. Of course they could never achieve the wordless, hermetic closeness of her parents' partnership—a union so complete that it excluded even their child.... If there was a middle path between her own early choices and her parents', she did not know how to find it. Bleakly, she rose and went to join Thiain.

Vika spent the rest of the day following Thiain's lead, helping with the women's work: mending, carrying wood, and pounding dried tubers into flour to be baked into flat cakes for the evening meal. Kelru worked in the barn all day, tending their beasts, whom he said he had been neglecting. At midday, Vika brought him hot bark tea and found him checking the pads of Thonn's feet for cracks and ice cuts, rubbing thick, warmed animal fat into them. He rose, wiping his hands on his thessach, took the wooden bowl of rapidly cooling tea, and sipped it. "That's good."

Vika leaned over the woven-twig fence of the beasts' enclosure and sighed. No one else was in the barn at the moment—none of the sullen, filthy trappers, and neither of the women. "Kelru," she said. "Are we safe here?"

Kelru drained the bowl and passed it to her. "For a time," he said. "If you do as I tell you. But we must leave as soon as Pierre can travel."

"It's almost the Deep Cold," Vika said, frowning.

"Yes, and still more than an eightday's travel to the next possibility of shelter," Kelru said. He stroked Thonn's fur, then stopped to pick at the rough, hard flesh of his palm, to free the coarse hairs snagged there. "We must risk it. This rest has been good for the beasts. Without the other woman, we can all ride more often, and conserve our strength."

Jolted, she looked up at him. "Without Thiain? But—"

"It's necessary," Kelru said. "Remember, she chose this path. And in fact we must leave quite soon, if my nose is any judge, to escape before she mates."

"Because if you mate with her, you'll have to stay with her."

"Yes," he said. "But it's dangerous even before a mating. The men here are eager."

She blinked. "You said your people didn't think about mating until the time came."

"Well," Kelru said. "Not as much as your people do, perhaps. But that isn't what I mean. Dakhiru, the senior man here—he's old. Losing his strength. The other three are watching him. Talakh is the one I fear might move against him. The one with one ear, and bad teeth. He's been here long enough, and he's strong enough. And I think he is a killer."

She thought about Thiain in Talakh's power. Thiain in Talakh's bed. Dakhiru was dirty and ignorant, but Talakh— She fought a surge of nausea. "Why would Talakh move against Dakhiru now?"

Kelru's ears twitched. "In the last few eightdays before a mating, there's something—" He hesitated, then went on. "In established families the men are friends, loyal to each other. Custom sets precedence. But in places like this—with no friendship, no bond among those who mate—here, custom is weak. People have animal ways." He picked at a claw, as if to avoid Vika's eyes. "When the Red Mind is near in a place such as this, a younger man sometimes challenges the senior man. Tries to kill him, or drive him out. The winner is first to mate with the woman."

Talakh, and Thiain. And Vika had brought it about, thinking only of Pierre. Of herself.... There had to be a way to save Thiain. "What if you were still here?"

Kelru's eyes were clear, gazing far into shadows. "I would have to submit to the others, and mate with her last. But in the Red Mind I might fight for a higher place. And if I fought Talakh, I think he would kill me. He's older than I am, but he's been fighting all his life."

"Then how could Dakhiru hope to win?" A gaunt, aging man, who worked hard all day, then groaned in the night with arthritic pain; whose hands were twisted with old burn scars.

"He has a chance," Kelru said. "He's lived to be old in this place." But Vika could hear that the words were empty.

At supper, Pierre still slept. Vika watched the trappers eat. They used the tuber-cakes to scoop up brown gakht, glistening with grease, from a central bowl on the floor. Talakh stared at Thiain all through the meal, his permanent snarl giving him the look of a lurking animal. Thiain appeared not to notice. Perhaps working for Dethun had taught her this calm.

Dakhiru watched Talakh. The other two trappers simply ate, grunting as they crammed the food in. Then one by one the men pissed loudly into a clay jug in the corner, and stalked off to lounge in their places on the sleeping shelf near the fire. The young pregnant woman—very young, Vika realized—carried the jug out of the house to empty it. Then the women ate, from their own bowl; and Kelru as well, silent and aside from the rest.

Ghetha, the old woman—small and bony, with a claw-scarred face—seemed to have accepted Thiain. The younger one appeared indifferent. She called herself Ushal. Kelru had said that was the name of a tragic heroine from one of the epic chants. At supper Ushal sat near Vika and whispered questions to her. How many children had Vika had? How old was she? Twenty-five! So old to have no children! But then, the men of Vika's people were probably not strong enough to father them. Judging from Pierre. He was so thin! And the fur in patches all over him. Was that his illness, or were they all like that?

After supper Vika took some of her own mending and sat near the fire to finish it. She watched Thiain move about at her work. Vika remembered her at the sisterhold, proud and quiet at Dethun's side. Tonight Thiain knelt at Dakhiru's feet and sewed up the hem of his tunic, her quick hands deft with the stiff, grimy cloth. Her face seemed calm and untroubled. Vika wondered what her thoughts were. She must have noticed Talakh's avid yellow gaze.

The work of the day was ending even for the women when Pierre finally woke. Vika did not go to him at once, because he insisted that Kelru, not Vika, help him piss. His odd, formal ways again; he must be feeling better. Maybe it wouldn't occur to him who had helped him, and how, through all the days of his illness.

Then at last she could go to him. Kelru moved discreetly away, placing himself as if by chance so as to block Talakh's view of Pierre and Vika.

She knelt beside him. He looked up at her, pale with apprehension.

And now that the moment had come, she could not gather her thoughts, or steady herself to speak. Because at the sight of him, so serious, with his hair and beard rumpled with sleep, with his thin hands tense on the coarse blanket—at the sight of him, her heart turned over inside her. She did not know what this feeling was, so much like pity and yet shot through with happiness. She took his hand and gave him an unsteady smile.

He drew a sharp breath. "I don't know what I should say to you."

"Kelru lectured me thoroughly," she said. "*Seem to be glad that you mated*, he said. But I *am* glad."

To her astonishment he broke into a smile of pure delight. "I, too," he said. His grip on her hand tightened. "It is not sensible. But it is right."

She nodded, her heart beating unsteadily, her breath short. "And now—"

He lay looking up at her with an expression of calm pleasure that bordered on smugness. "And now I need to get my strength back."

She couldn't help grinning at him. "Why? We're never alone."

"To protect you," he said.

At that, she sobered. "No," she said. "We'll never be safe if you think of me that way. Think as they do here. We're partners in all dangers. Bondmates."

He gazed at her for a long, considering moment—then squeezed her hand and said, "Bondmates. That, at least."

She bent down and kissed him gently on the lips.

Behind her someone spat into the fire. She straightened and looked. Talakh had moved to stand just beyond Kelru, watching them—malignant, powerful. She shifted her body so Pierre would not see him. "Rest, now," she said. And she watched beside him until he closed his eyes.

Kelru saw the quiet happiness between Pierre and Vika with surprise and relief. He had always heard that mating eased and settled a man, but that had not happened when Pierre and Anke mated. Yet in the days that followed his waking, Pierre seemed at peace. And as for Vika—Kelru had never seen her happy before. But now she was, in her quiet way. In the crowded house she and Pierre were never alone; but there was speech without words between them from morning until night, and after, when they slept wrapped in their shared blankets like two babies in a basket.

The sight of them was Kelru's only pleasure. Around Thiain tension was mounting, and always there was Talakh's silent menace. They must leave, and soon. The danger grew each day.

Kelru struggled to hold his peace during Pierre's slow recovery. Vika hovered over her bondmate, waiting and watching and testing his health. Of course she knew her own people's needs better than Kelru could; but time, time....

The Deep Cold set in, and with it came heavy snow, a blizzard so severe that the few beast-lengths between the house and the barn could be traveled safely only by a strong man clinging to a rope.

But it was worse when the sky cleared, and the true cold crept from the north, from the shadowed lands. The wind rose, and rose, and rose again. Often, now, the smoke from the fire could not pass through the hole in the roof, and everyone moved in a reeking haze. There was no escape from it, except to cross through the knife-chill to the barn, where the beasts huddled together, their breath quick fog in the light of Kelru's lantern. Even there it was too frigid to stay long; and Kelru always worried about the others, left back in the house with Talakh.

On such nights Kelru thought of the endless, lightless forest that surrounded this house. Out there on the icy ridges, in the black, shelterless hollows, trees cracked in the cold; the wind tore at their branches. Anyone caught out in that would die.

No, they could not leave until the weather eased. And not until Pierre was strong. Ten days' travel, even in open weather—with Pierre and Vika, so inexperienced— Kelru shuddered and recited to himself the Discourse to Children that counseled patience.

Pierre had been out of bed for an eightday, sallow and unsteady but gaining strength, before Vika pronounced him well enough to go outside. Kelru took him, bundled in his thessach, one afternoon when the wind had dropped for a time. Kelru had to keep a strong grip on his arm as they climbed up the trampled ramp in the snow to the surface.

The trappers' place, a few buildings surrounded by a low palisade of logs, lay in a narrow east-west slash in the hills. Kelru watched Pierre look around, blinking in the glare of the hazy sunlight. "See where we are," he said. "The house behind us. The barn ahead. To the side here, the meat shed, and the one where furs are stored. See how they both stand on stone posts, to keep the food and skins cold, and to keep out the feotheg."

"The house and barn are low," Pierre said.

"Yes," Kelru said. "An old way of building. It works. They're half in the ground for warmth, and to protect them from wind. Shallow-roofed, so the snow stays on."

"No windows," Pierre said.

"In summer they do their work outside. In winter, as you see, by the fire. One door, so the house can be defended. One room inside, so one fire will warm it."

"And the small building beyond the barn," Pierre said. "What is that?"

"For matings," Kelru said. "And births. And deaths. They often go together." He wondered if Thiain had yet begun to fear.

Pierre said nothing, but looked past Kelru toward the door of the house. Kelru turned. Ushal stood brushing fresh snow from the roof into a wooden bucket. Even under her draggled fur thessach her swollen belly was obvious. Kelru lowered his voice. "Her first mating," Kelru said. "It may not end well. She's very young."

"How did she come here?"

"She was born here," Kelru said, "to a woman now dead. Last summer she mated for the first time. And so you see her."

"How old is she?" Pierre asked very quietly.

Kelru shrugged. "Thirteen, fourteen. In a family, a woman that young would be held aside from mating for a time, maybe sent to school at a sisterhold. Here—" He raised his hands in a shrug. Pierre's eyes narrowed, as if in pain, but he said nothing more.

The next day the good weather still held, and Dakhiru commanded a gherrau hunt. For the first time Kelru rode along. It went as he hoped; he shot a gherrau from Thonn's back before the herd was even fully encircled. And after Thonn was turned loose, the big beast killed another on his own, and headed off a third so Dakhiru's beast could bring it down.

Dakhiru returned home full of strength, talking of a last hunt, a big one, before the next storm. A full meat-house for winter. "We've not had the men and beasts to manage it, not for ten years at least. But that Thonn, his nose is even better than Kelru said it was. And his jaws! A grip like tree-roots."

"He does well," Talakh said. "I wonder how he would hunt for me?"

Kelru felt Pierre stir beside him, and touched his arm in silent warning. Dakhiru eyed Talakh, perhaps unwilling to speak a word that might be taken as a challenge. But Kelru had no place among the men here; his word was no challenge even to Talakh. He coughed politely, claiming speech, and said, "Thonn hunts by his own choosing. And his jaws are strong. He's never chosen to turn them on *me*." He kept his eyes on Talakh's for a moment, then let them drop.

Vika woke with Thiain's claws brushing lightly over her cheek. Dimness, the fire banked to embers. She raised her head. "What is it?"

"Ushal," Thiain said softly. "She's begun her labor."

Vika disentangled herself carefully from Pierre and slid from the blankets. The raw night air tore a gasp from her as she flung her shift and overdress over her naked body. In the blankets Pierre muttered something and turned over. She looked down at him fondly. Privacy they could not have, but at least they could sleep—just sleep—together.

Thiain handed Vika a bowl of bark tea. The first astringent swallow cleared her head a little. "I thought she had a few eightdays still to wait."

"It's hard to say," Thiain whispered. "She can't count very well."

Vika looked past Thiain toward the fireside, where Ushal was pacing back and forth, visibly glorying in the drama of the moment. Her belly had a fine high arch, and above it her four full breasts pressed against the greasy wool of her overdress. Her eyes were bright.

Thiain followed Vika's glance. "There can't be much pain yet," she said dryly.

Vika tied on some ragged trousers, then sat down to pull on houseboots. "What will happen now?"

"Ghetha has gone out to the mating hut to build a fire," Thiain said. "When it's warm enough, you and I will go out there with Ushal."

"Me?" Vika's belly knotted. "No. I ought to start the khishtuh. I wouldn't be any use to Ushal."

"You must be there," Thiain said. "All the women gather, always. If you stay here with the men, you'll be telling them you're an outsider. Not a woman, not even a person. And you know the danger in that."

Vika sighed and rubbed her eyes. "All right. But why? Why do I have to be there?"

"Because sometimes," Thiain said, "a decision must be made. And every woman's voice is heard." She leaned closer. "And you will speak after I do, and as I do. Do you understand? Will you do it?"

A chill slid along Vika's spine. She'd known this was coming, of course—that she could not avoid it. She owed a great debt to Thiain for saving Pierre's life. And she'd given Kelru her word that she would follow the ways of his people. So there was nothing she could say except, "I will."

When Ghetha reported that the hut was warm, Vika and Thiain took Ushal there. The hut was low and round, with a smoke-hole at the peak of its conical roof. Inside was a single room with a large stone-lined pit where a fire now roared.

Vika released Ushal's arm and looked around. Half of the circular space was taken up by a low split-wood sleeping shelf covered by an enormous fur rug, a riding animal's skin, matted and patchy with age. Ghetha had spread clean blankets over it. A round rush basket stood nearby, lined with more blankets. For the babies. And there was a good supply of dry wood. It must have been stacked here days ago. All these preparations, made so silently—dread stirred again in Vika.

In the room's oppressive heat, Vika soon joined the others in stripping off her outer clothes. Ghetha and Thiain held Ushal up between them, walking her slowly back and forth across the dirt floor by the fire, though she wept and begged to lie down. Vika kept the fire roaring. This was a bitter world. She remembered Thiain's lost children. A common thing here, an ordinary thing; considered sad, but necessary. Even in the heat, she shivered.

An endless time later Ghetha let Ushal down onto the sleeping shelf. "Get a blanket for the baby," Thiain said to Vika, over Ushal's hoarse grunts. When Vika turned back, the first baby had nearly been born. Thiain stood on the shelf, gripping Ushal under the arms, holding her in a squat, and Ghetha knelt in front of her, saying, "Gently, Ushal, gently...." Between her hands was a dark little head. Then a slippery rush, and a gush of musty-smelling fluid, and the first baby lay on the blanket. A boy. Thiain let Ushal lie back on the matted fur. Ushal's eyes were tightly closed. The cord between her and the baby pulsed unsteadily. The baby did not move.

Ghetha and Thiain watched it intently. Vika wanted to shout at them to pick up the baby, slap him, get him breathing. His furless skin was purplish-blue. The cord pulsed once more, then stopped. Ghetha tied it in two places with animal sinew, and Thiain handed her a knife. Ghetha reached down and cut the cord, then lifted the baby away. He still did not move. She laid him near the fire, not far from Vika, and turned back to Ushal.

"Ghetha," Vika said in disbelief, "is that all you're going to do?" There was nothing visibly wrong with the child. They were denying hope, denying the chance of life.

But Thiain muttered, "Keep silent!" Vika remembered her debt, and obeyed.

Thiain was kneeling by Ushal, gently stroking her face. "Ushal," she said, "there is another one. The pains will begin again soon. You did everything right. Just do it again. We'll help you. No, don't open your eyes."

The second baby breathed at once, then struggled and cried. But still Ghetha and Thiain were silent; and Ushal, whimpering now, would not look. Thiain cut the cord, picked up the baby—a girl—and handed her carefully to Ghetha.

The old woman dried her with a scrap of blanket and carried her over to the light of the fire. Vika studied her. Hands, feet, all were perfect—except the face. At first she thought it was distorted with crying, but then she realized that the baby's long upper jaw was split to the nose. Cleft palate. Correctable, on Earth; but here...she knew what would happen here.

Ghetha sighed. Then she carried the baby, who was still squalling, back to Ushal. "Open your eyes." Her voice was flat.

Ushal looked at the baby. "Oh, Mother," she said thinly, and sobbed once.

"Come, girl. Say it." Ghetha sounded irritated.

Thiain gripped Ushal's shoulder. "You must say it. Then you can rest."

"L-let it happen as it must," Ushal whispered. The baby's loud crying continued.

Ghetha turned from Ushal and laid the baby in Thiain's arms. Thiain looked down at her, and her arms tightened for an instant. But then she said quietly, "Let it happen as it must." Ghetha took the child—and brought it to Vika.

The baby yelled more loudly as she took its weight. The small squirming body felt so warm. And with a surge of grief, and anger, she knew that her principles were no match for this reality. She looked down at the child. *No*. The word burned inside her—*no* to Thiain, *no* to Ghetha, *no* to this world. *This baby could live.*

But she had promised Kelru. And how could she, alone, save this child? She was shaking. Unconsciously she pulled the baby closer, to keep her warm, close against her breasts.

A strong hand caught her by the chin. "Say it," Ghetha snarled, over the baby's frantic yells.

She mouthed the words, voiceless, hating them, hating herself. Then her arms were empty, and Ghetha turned away. A moment later, the baby's cries stopped. The silence was like an explosion.

Vika sobbed once, her hand pressed to her mouth. She was still human, no matter what she had just done. She was human, not like these—

Thiain was with her now, helping her put on her thessach. "Peace," she was saying. "You only make it worse for Ushal." Vika tried silently, hopelessly, to pull away from her—she could not bear Thiain's touch. Thiain was alien. All of them were alien, as chilly and inimical as the Destroyers. And Vika hated them.

NINETEEN

For Pierre, waiting for word of Ushal and her children, the morning stretched out endlessly. The men of the household, the trappers, showed no concern. Kelru sat cross-legged near the fire, calmly patching a boot. But Pierre had to struggle against the urge to pace back and forth. He knew what Vika feared. He knew the danger of this time for her—the decision she might face.

He was thankful when the hide covering the entry passage stirred, and Thiain and Vika came in. But then he saw Vika, her face streaked with tears, clutching her thessach tightly around herself. He got to his feet, but beside him Kelru muttered, "Wait."

Dakhiru did not get up from his place on the fur rug nearest the fire. "Tell us."

"Ushal is well," Thiain said, her voice low. "But there are no children."

The room was silent. Then Dakhiru sighed. "Well. It often goes that way with the first. The next will be fine and healthy."

Talakh sat near Pierre and Kelru, rubbing his long hunting knife slowly down and down a smooth stone. He caught Pierre's eye and said in a low voice, "It goes that way more often when the senior man is old. Never much use, planting withered seeds first." His mouth opened and he laughed silently.

Pierre turned his back on Talakh as the other men returned to their occupations—mending a saddle, making snares, scraping the raw sides of fresh pelts clean. Pierre went to Vika. She said nothing, but she leaned on him as he guided her back to their place on the sleeping shelf. For the first time since his illness he felt that he was stronger than she was.

He looked around the room. It was as if nothing had happened. Thiain was gone—back to help Ghetha with Ushal, of course. Pierre settled Vika on their blankets—she did not want to take off her thessach—and fetched her some bark tea.

Vika's fingers, touching his as he gave her the bowl of tea, were cold. She thanked him stiffly. He sat down across from her and said, "I'm sorry, Vika."

She sat rigidly straight, balancing the bowl in her fingers, and his heart ached for her. "They made me agree to it," she said in a low voice. "To killing the baby. I kept my promise. I agreed. But it's wrong. They don't try hard enough to save them." She stopped, her face stiff, as Kelru came over to them.

He sat down beside them and looked at Vika with obvious concern. "I know it was hard for you to see that. But you did well."

She raised her head and met his look. "You don't understand." Her voice shook, and in that moment Pierre understood why. This was not grief. It was anger.

Kelru took a sharp breath and let it out slowly. "Pierre told me something once. He said that the people of your world have been rich, and safe, for many generations. And so you can no longer imagine anything more important than mercy."

Vika straightened, and now the anger was clear. "Pierre knows better than that. I understand the dangers here. But I cannot accept that death without caring. I cannot say that that this is how things should be." Pierre took her hand firmly, though he was conscious of Talakh's yellow stare.

"Death *can* be caring," Kelru said. "That child you saw killed—it would not have been able to suckle. Your friend told me. It would have been dead in an eightday in any case."

Pierre saw tears spring to Vika's eyes, and looked away. He had learned long ago that the idea of fighting, always, to offer the best chance of life meant little here. Now, at least. Perhaps someday, with help, that might change....

Kelru cupped his jaw in his hand and looked at Vika. "You've seen people hurt by our ways. You've been hurt by them. But you've never seen the families, the bonded families, at home on their farms in year after year of peace."

"I don't need to see it," Vika said bitterly. "Thiain's told me what it was like."

"They do have sorrows," Kelru said. "Like your friend's, and worse. And there's never abundance of anything. But in our families we care for each other. Because that is all there is, ourselves and the cold. And if the Destroyers return, as some believe they will—there will only be the cold."

Vika was calmer now. Her eyes were hard as she looked at Kelru. "You care for each other? You care for your children?"

"We care," Kelru said. "But we are poor. Most of us work hard just to survive. We can't spare our strength to help children like Ushal's. Or the ones your friend lost."

"But—" Vika seemed to struggle for words. "There should be a way."

"Once there was," Kelru said. "The Destroyers took that from us. And left our world poisoned, so that these things happen far more often than they once did." His fur was ruffled now. "Whatever I and my friends might wish for the future, whatever gift of hope your people might someday give us, our world is a hard place now. You cannot live here and still follow your own, soft rules. You know it. You showed today that you know it. Now you must stop feeling sorry for yourself."

Pierre tightened his hold on Vika's hand. "Kelru, we can't help being what we are."

"Then you shouldn't have come here!" Kelru seemed to take hold of himself. He went on more quietly, "What Vika did was necessary for our safety. And it was right. Remember that." He rose and went back to the fire.

Pierre raised Vika's fingers to his lips and kissed them. "You did do well," he said quietly in French. "We are in such danger—you could have done nothing else."

"Don't lecture me, Pierre," she said. "I know you think you have to *motivate* me. But that's a game. It was always a game. And it's over."

He had to stop this. He faced her, gripped her hands hard. "Listen to me," he said. She gasped and he loosened his hold slightly, but did not let go. "We are in danger, and it's getting worse. Kelru is right. You cannot indulge yourself in this."

She shook off his hands and looked up at him, her eyes burning. "Pierre. You would have tried to save those children. You know what I did was wrong."

He closed his eyes, and sighed, and told her the truth. "I know there is no way, here, to do the right thing."

That night Vika lay between Pierre and the wall. Thiain slept with Ushal, who cried all night long. Vika lay awake listening to that, and to the wind, and to the timbers of the house groaning and popping as they shrank in the bitter cold. The next day, at noon, she went out with the household, bundled in thessachs and blankets, to burn the babies' bodies and scatter their ashes on the world-wind.

It seemed too bright for the middle of winter. The world-wind blew from a bare, hard cobalt sky, and the high sun blazed without heat. Dakhiru laid both small, wrapped bodies on a fire-mound freshly piled on the ice-crusted snow. Vika watched as Ushal bent, trembling, and lit the fire with a torch, then straightened and pulled her thessach close around her. She stood alone. The world-wind whined in the emptiness above her.

The fire was quick; but then, the bodies were small. Vika watched it all, barely conscious of Pierre standing close by her side: the dwindling mounds; the moment when Ghetha picked through the ashes to make sure all was consumed; the moment when Dakhiru took a small bowlful of the still-hot ashes, limped downwind and flung them into the air, where the wind took them and spun them away. Ushal wept again.

Vika did not weep. She was part of those ashes. That death had been by her choice.

Inside, afterwards, she could sense tension all around her, an avid waiting. As Thiain moved around the room at her tasks, all the men watched her now—not just Talakh. Even Kelru's eyes followed her, until he got up restlessly and left the house, muttering something about tending the beasts.

Vika got out her datapad and tried again to read one of the books she kept in it. But by now the most ordinary passage was an unbearable reminder of the unattainable—of home. The little memories hurt the most. Flowers, grass under bare feet, birdsong. The serene face of the full moon. All things soft, subtle, fragile, intricate. She set the datapad aside at last and sat in the dimness, far from the fire, alone. When Pierre approached, she turned her face away. Under Talakh's eye, she knew, he would not dare to touch her. He did not stay, or speak to her.

At the evening meal, Ghetha and Thiain served everyone silently. Ushal had cried herself to sleep on the rug by the fire. Talakh finished quickly, then sat motionless, watching Dakhiru, who ignored him.

The instant Dakhiru's bowl was empty, Talakh stood up. "I claim the right to speak and be heard," he rasped.

At the words, so ominously formal, Vika's heart lurched. She sat up straight in her place in the shadows. Pierre joined her at once and stood beside her, half-sheltering her, his hand on his knife. But his eyes, like everyone's eyes, were on Talakh.

Talakh knew it. He scratched the jagged stump of his left ear and looked around, his eyes glittering. "We all know what happened this morning," he said. "Weak children. That comes when an old man's seed goes in first. You saw. And Ghetha, he fucked her for years, and she never bore any children at all. So it was always sour seed. It dried her up. We can't let it dry up Thiain."

Kelru was on his feet at once. "You don't yet have the right to speak her name."

"City ways," Talakh said. "This isn't the city. You're soft-minded. You must have lived a little too long with your mother."

Vika saw Pierre's hand tighten on his knife. The insult was a common one between men. But it was the wrong thing to say to Kelru.

Kelru's ears went flat, and he seemed to swell as his fur stood up. The Red Mind— "Pierre," she whispered, "Kelru might fight. Stop him!"

Before Kelru could answer Talakh, Pierre stepped between them. "Peace in the house," he said. But he was so much shorter than either of the others that their gazes stayed locked over his head.

Pierre reached up and laid his hand on Kelru's shoulder. "Kelru, we're travelers. We have no rights here. What happens between Talakh and Dakhiru isn't our concern."

Vika held her breath. Then, slowly, Kelru dropped his gaze, looked down at Pierre. He did not speak, but he stepped back from the fire, into the shadows where the others watched.

Now Dakhiru stalked into the light, Ghetha at his elbow. "Sit down, Talakh." His hand gripped the hilt of his hunting knife. Vika could see his knuckles through the thinning fur, swollen with arthritis. But Dakhiru's hand was steady, and his voice. "Sit down and be silent."

Talakh's one ear twitched, then stilled. "They've agreed to hear me," he said mildly. "They know my words are important."

"You're a kharag," Dakhiru said. "You would tear my throat in the dark. But you won't face me now, in this house, before these men who follow me. We don't fear kharag, and we don't fear you."

"A mistake," Talakh said. "But I'll overlook it. You can live here in peace, old man. All you have to do is bend to me now."

"Never in this house I built," Dakhiru said, trembling.

"Strong words," Talakh mocked. "But hollow. You know I'm right, old man. You're too weak to fight me." A quick, smooth motion, and his knife was in his hand, blade up, pointing at Dakhiru. "You should've done as I told you."

Everyone was on their feet now, even Ushal, shivering and blinking beside Ghetha. Kelru led Thiain to stand beside Pierre and Vika. "He won't kill him," Vika stammered. "He won't just kill him!"

"All of you, stay here," Kelru said grimly. And he moved closer to the two men.

Dakhiru was staring at the knife, dazed, or entranced, or lost to death already. "I gave you that," he said in a strange, calm voice.

"Come and have it back," Talakh said, with a little upward thrusting motion of the blade. He stood lightly, ready to spring.

Ghetha shouted, "Bend to him, Dakhiru!" Others took up the call.

"No!" Talakh kept his eyes on Dakhiru, but spoke to all who watched. "No. It's too late. He's Dakhiru, the proud one. Will he offer the back of his neck to me? When Thiain mates, will he wait until I'm finished with her, until I have no seed left to plant in her?" He waved the knife. "The proud one. Will he carry my pot to the privy every morning?"

Without a word, without a cry, Dakhiru sprang, his knife trying for Talakh's throat. Talakh danced aside, slashing, and blood sprang bright along the front of Dakhiru's tunic. Another pass, with no one hurt. Then another—and Talakh set his knife in Dakhiru's chest, neatly and surely, a solid, final blow. Vika stared, numb, as Dakhiru fell. Someone wailed, high and lost-sounding—Ghetha, or Ushal. Then silence. Vika raised her head and looked. Dakhiru writhed at Talakh's feet, a little on his side—the knife was still in him, its hilt jammed in the dirt floor. He was trying to lift himself, trying to take the pressure off the blade. His mouth worked, but he made no sound. In the weak light his dark blood glistened, spreading out over the churned dirt and filth.

Then he went limp. His breath rattled out. He twitched, fluttered, and was still. His knife, unblooded, lay near his open hand.

"Well, then," Talakh said. He looked around. "Anyone else?"

Silence.

"I'm watching you," he said. "I know you all."

Ushal went up to him, walking slowly. He watched her come. She stopped before him, then dropped to her knees. At first Vika thought she was mourning Dakhiru, bending forward over his body. Then it became clear: she was offering Talakh the back of her neck. The gesture of utter submission.

He acknowledged it, running the claws of his left hand lightly along her nape. Ushal rose and looked down at herself. Her trousers and the tattered hem of her overdress were shiny with Dakhiru's blood. She took two steps toward Ghetha, stumbled, then vomited. Expressionless, Ghetha looked away. Thiain, still outwardly calm, led Ushal away.

Vika found that her arms were clamped around Pierre. Gently he pushed her a little away, keeping his eyes on Talakh, who reached down cautiously and picked up Dakhiru's knife. Then, armed again, he stepped forward over the body. "All of you," he said, looking around the room. "Submit. Now. Or fight me, and die."

One by one, they went to him. One by one, they gave him the backs of their necks: the two other men, Ghetha—even Thiain, stiff and trembling. Vika shuddered as Talakh's claws touched Thiain's neck.

Then Talakh pointed at Pierre and Vika—using his forefinger, as if they were animals, or objects. "Come here, you." They went forward, close beside each other but not touching.

He studied them. "You're no use, either of you. Especially this one." Vika smothered a cry as he gripped her arm, claws digging, and pulled her against him. "No reason not to kill her now." He pressed the point of Dakhiru's knife against her throat.

Terror numbed her, slowed her. She reached up with her free hand and took hold of his knife arm. But she could not move it, left arm against left arm, her weakness against his strength. She saw Pierre's face, drawn, shocked. "Talakh," he said hoarsely. "Stop!" But she felt the knife begin to bite.

Then Kelru faced Talakh. "Let her go." His voice was flat.

The knife stopped, but Talakh kept the pressure on the tip, burning into Vika's flesh. "Why should I?" His breath was hot and foul. "Have you decided to bend your neck to me?"

Through the white fog of her fear, Vika realized that he was trying to goad Kelru, and perhaps Pierre, into attacking him. And at this moment of strength, backed by two men loyal to him, Talakh would certainly kill them both. The knife at her throat kept her silent. Surely Kelru saw the trap—

Kelru moved forward into the firelight. He was wearing his night-blue tunic, and his red-brown fur shone. "I'll bend to you, Talakh," he said. As if it were a simple thing.

The knife's pressure vanished, and Talakh roughly pushed Vika away. She stumbled into Pierre's arms, touched her throat. Her fingers came away bloody. She turned to watch Kelru and Talakh.

As Kelru approached, she saw Talakh's hand tighten on Dakhiru's knife, saw the blade wink as it moved. Suddenly she was sure that when Kelru knelt, Talakh would kill him. Nothing could change it. She had no voice to cry out against it. She felt a trickle of blood run down her neck from the mark Talakh had set on her.

In the center of the silent ring of watchers, Kelru knelt, and then slowly bowed his head. His ears were still. Talakh stood a moment looking down at the man at his feet. The knife was in his left hand, his fighting hand. If he did not shift it—to touch Kelru, to acknowledge his homage—then she would know he was about to use it.

He did not shift the knife. He reached down with his right hand—the tainted hand, the hand for giving lying gifts and swearing false oaths. And he pressed down, down. Pressed Kelru's face into a puddle of Dakhiru's blood.

Then Talakh let him straighten. "Remember what you've done here," he said.

"Oh, I'll remember this," Kelru said. Blood streaked his face. He rose to his feet and rubbed his sleeve across the stain.

Talakh turned and looked down at Dakhiru's body. No one had touched it. "I want him washed and laid out," he said. He tried to slide Dakhiru's knife into the sheath at his own belt, but the knife was too large. The other men, Dunail and Rosharu, rolled Dakhiru onto his back. With a quick, sharp effort, Dunail pulled Talakh's knife free and held it up to him. Talakh did not move to touch the dark blade. "Let Dakhiru keep it," he said. "I never liked it much. I'll have this one instead."

He balanced Dakhiru's knife in his hands as the body was carried away. Then his yellow eyes turned again toward Vika and Pierre. "Those," he said. "I want them out of this house."

Vika took a shaking breath and drew closer to Pierre, as if they could protect each other. She felt Pierre's heartbeat, quick and strong. Somehow, somehow, there had to be a way—

Kelru faced Talakh. "Pierre is my brother," he said, "and Vika is his mate. If I have a place in this house, so do they."

"Your place is the lowest place," Talakh said. He seemed to be gaining confidence, now that Dakhiru's corpse was out of his sight. "Those *things* have no place at all. They aren't people. Anyone who looks at them can see that. Pierre can't be your brother. And as for the other one, thinking about them fucking makes me want to vomit." He flourished Dakhiru's knife. "They go. Tonight."

"They'll die," Kelru said. "They're guests in your house. You can't turn them out."

"But I can, city man," Talakh said. "This isn't Kheosseth. No fine Kheosseth rules. I will waste no more food on those things. Their mothers should have twisted their necks for them, like Ghetha this morning." And he made a wrenching gesture so vivid that Vika's stomach lurched. She clenched her teeth.

Then Thiain appeared, and knelt by Talakh. Calm and steady as ever, she bent and touched the hem of his filthy tunic to her forehead. "Talakh," she said. "If you hurt Vika, or her mate, I will bear no children for this house."

He blinked down at her. "But you will. I'll see to that." He made a thrusting motion with his hips.

"No," she said. "You can fuck me, and make me pregnant. But I will never give birth. I was in a sisterhold. I know how it's done." Her voice was slow, dreaming. Vika saw a flash of shock on Pierre's face.

Talakh glared down at Thiain, who kept her gaze on the floor. He seemed to think, while Vika's pulse throbbed in her temples.

Then he raised his eyes to Kelru's. "Put them in the mating shed," he said. "I'll settle this in the morning." He turned and stared directly into Vika's eyes, his one ear flicking forward and back. "As I choose."

Vika stared back into his eyes until Pierre took her arm and led her away.

TWENTY

Shivering, Vika clung close to Pierre's warmth as they followed Kelru around the barn to the mating hut. Around and above them the dark wind keened. Flecks of ice skittered along the hard surface of the snow, stinging her face. Overhead the stars glowed, their hard brilliance diffused by the ice in the wind. Above the eastern hills, Tlankharu floated in the center of a faint reddish ring. Watching as Talakh had watched, with the same cold patience. Vika shivered. She was so tired that she felt sick. And she could not forget Thiain's threat—could not stop imagining Thiain's fate. Fucked by Talakh, in Talakh's power.... Ahead of them Kelru trudged head-down, carrying an ember pail.

When they entered the dank and lightless hut, Vika put back her hood with unsteady hands. Kelru lit a spill from the embers in the pail, and its weak flare showed her no sign of what had happened here this morning. The blankets and baskets were gone. Only the matted fur rug remained on the sleeping platform.

There was still wood. Vika sat shuddering with cold on the old fur as Pierre helped Kelru lay and start the fire. She tried closing her eyes, but the world spun faster then. She watched the flame instead, imagining her own calm growing as it did. Calm. She could be calm. The nausea eased a little.

Finally she could look up at the men. Kelru was studying her. "Are you all right?"

"Yes," she said. "Tired." Her voice broke on the word, and she covered her mouth.

Pierre came to her, sat beside her, pulled her against him. He rubbed her back gently and said to Kelru, "She needs rest."

"We all do," Kelru said. "The next days will be hard ones." He touched Vika's throat, lightly, with a clawed finger. "You should clean that knife cut. It might fester."

From the shelter of Pierre's embrace, Vika looked up at Kelru. "Thank you for what you did for me tonight," she said quietly. "I know it was hard."

"It was your right," Kelru said. His air of leashed anger seemed to ease a little. "You're my family. Not just the words. You *are*." He lifted a corner of his thessach and touched it to her cheek. "Dry your tears," he said. "Dry your tears, because now we must plan."

She sensed Pierre and Kelru exchanging a look over her head, and she took a fold of the rough wool and wiped her face with it. "Plan what?" she asked tensely.

Kelru looked at her, then at Pierre, his ears flicking. "We must leave. Tomorrow, if possible. Or Talakh will kill you."

"But Thiain's threat—"

"He will break her down," Kelru said. "Or in his arrogance he believes that he will. For you, the result will be the same."

"All right," Vika said. "Can't we kill him?"

"It would be no use," Pierre said with exasperation.

"Pierre," she said wearily, "there comes a time—"

"Pierre is right," Kelru said. "It wouldn't save you. Talakh's successor would certainly kill you. Unless you killed all the men, and left the women to starve."

"What if *you* were Talakh's successor?" Pierre asked.

Kelru looked away. "I can't fight them all. No, only leaving this place will save us."

"Leaving," Vika said dully. This was no home, but it was shelter. To leave, now— "In the Deep Cold? How can we?"

"This is a skull place," Kelru said. "There are ruins in the hills. Houses dug into the ground."

"We'll freeze to death," Vika said. "We'll starve."

"I promise you that you would die sooner here than out there," Kelru said. "We can find food. Feotheg sleeping in burrows, and other things. And we'll steal enough from this house to start us on our way."

"Thiain can help with that," Vika said.

"No," Kelru said, calmly but firmly. "We cannot tell her. She's too close to mating. Her mind isn't clear. She might try to come with us."

Vika looked away. Looked straight at Pierre, who was watching her with pity clear on his face.

Kelru sighed and said, "I must go back to the house. Bar the door. I'll come in the morning with food. Try to sleep." The fire flared in a gust of bitter air as he went out.

Pierre barred the door solidly behind him, then dropped down cross-legged on the animal fur. Back straight, he faced her, regarding her steadily, waiting. As if he knew what she had to say now. She pushed back a strand of her filthy hair and said it. "I want Thiain to come with us. I can't leave her to Talakh."

"Vika," he said, "that's how it has to be. It is hard. If we try to save her, we'll die. And you and I must survive. Our people must learn of the Destroyers. We *must* carry out our mission."

"And Thiain is the sacrifice," she said. "This time."

At the bitter words she saw his expression harden, but he did not look away. "Yes," he said quietly. "But the last. Or so I pray."

Vika folded her hands in her lap. *Reason, reason.* "Remember why she's in this position. She called these people to us to save you. She knew what would happen." She swallowed in a dry throat and said, "We have to save her."

He shook his head. "Kelru leads us, here in the wilderness. And he will never allow it. I have a boy's bow to shoot with, and that would be all our defense, while he and Thiain mated. We would die the first night, all of us."

She wrapped her arms tightly around herself to still her trembling. But she could no longer keep her voice steady. "I can't," she said. "I can't consent to let Thiain die, Pierre. She will die. The herbs they use to end pregnancy—they're dangerous, used too often. Thiain told me, in the sisterhold. Sooner or later, after enough matings, enough pregnancies, she'll bleed to death."

Pierre's jaw tightened, but he said nothing.

"Your choice put us in danger," she said. "Now I—after what I did this morning, if I agree to leave Thiain behind—Pierre, I won't be human anymore." Her face twisted in anguish. "I want to stay human. Even for the mission, even for Earth, I can't give up myself. What I am. What *we are*." She looked at him, at his eyes dark with pain. "Help me," she whispered. "Please. Help me save Thiain."

At first it seemed he could not speak. Then he said unsteadily, "You ask much."

"Because I must," she said. "Because you understand me. Kelru can't. If you agree, we can save her, whether Kelru agrees or not."

"He's my friend," Pierre said. "He saved my life."

She reached out and took his hands in hers. "So did Thiain."

He sighed. Then his hands tightened around hers. "I'll do it," he said. "But, Vika—this world punishes mercy. You've seen."

"I'll risk it," she said steadily.

Vika let Kelru in the next morning, soon after dawn. She and Pierre had slept comfortably enough, wrapped in both their thessachs—but they had not slept long. Kelru looked at her sharply. "Are you well?"

She looked away, conscious of her cheeks darkening. Pierre grinned. Easing the long physical tension between them seemed to have eased his mind, too. "We're well," he said to Kelru. "How are matters in the house?"

"Quiet, for now," Kelru said. "Talakh wants a watch-feast for

Dakhiru tonight. They'll drink, and stuff themselves with meat and khishtuh, and sleep far into the morning. And by then we will be gone. Talakh will say they're well rid of us."

He had brought them the saddle-packs from the barn. After he returned to the house, Pierre and Vika barred the door and checked the packs, opening and inspecting the avarthu and other equipment, making sure it was all clean and in good repair. No one came near them. After dark, Pierre helped Kelru drag a carcass from the meat-house to the barn for Thonn and Feth and Nukh. Pierre looked half-frozen when he came in. Vika looked up at him tensely. "Did you see her?"

"For a moment," he said. "Long enough. She will come."

"And you told her what to do?"

"I told her." He held his chapped, dirty hands out to the fire. She waited, but he did not share his thoughts with her. She understood him now: his sense of honor would not allow him to speak of doubts after he had given his word.

They shared their scant supper in proper Windhome silence. Then they went to bed, alone together and in shelter for perhaps the last time.

Far on in the night—long after their urgent lovemaking, long after Pierre had gone to sleep—Vika lay staring into the fire. Pierre's body was warm against her back. They'd had one last day of fragile happiness. But it was over now. Now they had only the mission. Afterward, if they survived— No. It was a waste of time to plan for that now.

They woke in the dark before dawn and dressed carefully in their warmest clothes. Vika was tying her thessach snugly shut when she heard a scratch at the door. Three scratches, as arranged. Pierre unbarred it. Kelru's head appeared around the edge of the door. Snow glinted in his fur. "Ready?"

"Ready," Vika said. "You brought them?"

He handed her a sack. She opened it and winced at the stench.

"They're old, some of them," Kelru said. "I had to dig down into the pile to find big ones."

Vika had already laid out an old blanket on the fur rug. She dumped the sack onto it. Bones, some picked or boiled clean, others with bits of frozen meat adhering. They were gherrau, mostly—some ribs, some long bones from legs, a few plates of skullbone. She arranged them on the blanket—rib cages, arms, legs, a bit of head at the top of each. Then she spread another old blanket on the wooden floor near the fire-pit—and tossed a fold of it into the fire. The cloth was dry, as dry as the wood of the hut, and it ignited at once, spreading avidly. She watched it for a moment, then ducked to the door and out. Pierre and Kelru were waiting outside. "Done," she said.

The three riding beasts loomed behind the men in the snow-swept darkness. Feth rumbled in his chest when he scented Vika. She rubbed his forehead as Kelru tossed on the saddle-pack and strapped it in place.

"We'll ride until we're well up the ridge," Kelru said. "I drove the other beasts that way when I emptied the barn." He helped her up onto Feth. Pierre had already mounted. She felt behind her to make sure her pack had been tied on over the saddle-pack. She was worried about Thiain. This heavy snow would help their plan by concealing her tracks. But would it slow her too much?

Kelru mounted last, and they paced away into the woods. Vika put her trust in him and in Feth, and held on. The snow lay thin under the trees, but as they climbed the face of the ridge behind the compound, Feth had to breast deep snow with awkward leaps that almost threw her off. When they reached the ridge-top, she looked back. The sun still had not risen, but the dawn light was steely blue all around them, and the wind blew fitfully, heavy with snow. And the smell of smoke. Kelru had assured them that the barn and house would not burn. But the fire would keep the men busy, and the bones might fool them for a while. They might believe only Kelru had escaped, and that one mounted man would move too quickly to be worth chasing.

"Keep moving," Kelru said. "We don't want a kharag to scent us." He carried his bow strung and ready, slung under a fold of his thessach to keep the string dry.

They had gone perhaps two kilometers down the next valley when Kelru abruptly raised his hand, snapping a command that halted the beasts in their tracks. It was full day now. He put back his hood and turned his head, ears flicking carefully forward and back, mouth open to taste the air. Vika watched, her heart beating unsteadily. Pierre gave her a dark glance. "Kharag?" he said to Kelru.

"Another scent," Kelru said. He turned and looked at Vika. "You told her." He sounded tired.

"No, I did," Pierre said. And upslope from them, from the shelter of a snowbound evergreen, Thiain emerged. She moved tentatively, a loaded pack slung from her shoulder.

Kelru looked from her to Pierre. "*You* told her? I thought better of your mind, Pierre!" He looked at Thiain. "I should send you back. You had good luck to get this far, with kharag in the valley."

"I was willing to risk it," she said. "I won't stay in that house." Her dark eyes burned.

"You risk us all," Kelru said. But to Vika, his words sounded mechanical. His gaze was fixed on Thiain, his eyes deep red-gold. His fur had risen slightly.

Then he shook his head and looked away. "Ride with Vika," he said, and started off without waiting for Thiain to load her pack on Feth. As she helped Thiain, Vika watched Kelru, worry stirring deep inside her. He had barely resisted at all. The Red Mind must be nearer than any of them had thought.

They started out, Vika riding behind Thiain. Pierre drew close on Nukh and said, in Standard, "Time is running out."

"I agree," she said. "We need to find shelter as soon as we can. A defensible place to camp. Can you make him understand?"

"I can try," Pierre said. "Vika, I'm worried."

She glanced at Pierre's bow, tied unstrung behind his saddle. It was a good size for a tall human man, but a boy's bow by Windhome standards. Half of his arrows were boy's arrows, slender and barbed, with loops for attaching a line. They were meant for hunting feotheg, small animals that lived in the ice palisades between the ground and the snow. They would not even annoy a kharag. "I'm worried, too," she said.

The snow had stopped, though the clouds remained heavy and threatening. Soon they reached a larger branch of the valley and turned north, into the wind. At midday they ate a chilly meal standing in the lee of the animals, who huddled head-down, facing the wind. Kelru kept well away from Thiain.

The valley floor rose and roughened as they rode north, following the direction Kelru had laid out last night—the shortest path across the skull place. Trees grew more thickly in the higher, better-drained ground. Vika kept glancing nervously behind, downwind. Their scent would not carry far in such cold, but they had no hope of hearing or scenting anything that followed them. In that broken country, with every tree trembling in the wind, Vika kept thinking she saw something, someone, following far behind. Kelru still appeared to keep watch, but she could not trust him.

By late afternoon Thiain was far gone inside herself, and Vika began to realize just how close she was to the Red Mind—how close they all were to disaster. She and Pierre sharpened their watch for any kind of shelter—ruins, a cave, anything. When they stopped to rest the beasts and drink warm, leathery-tasting water from the bags they all kept next to their skin, Kelru stayed upwind of Thiain—his last, desperate defense. She was drawing him in. He could not resist much longer.

Vika laid a hand on Pierre's shoulder. "We're out of time," she said quietly.

He bit his lip and nodded. "You're right. How is Feth?"

"Well enough. Those hills aren't far—there might be shelter there."

"Let's go." He put away his water-bag and turned to Thiain, who was leaning against Feth, her eyes vacant, her breath quick. "Thiain," he said. "Get up on Feth now."

But she did not stir, and Pierre and Vika together could not lift her. Suddenly Kelru stepped between them and boosted her up.

That was almost the end. Kelru stood at Feth's side, his face buried in Thiain's thessach, his arms tight around her.

"No!" Pierre shouted. He tugged at Kelru's arm. "Vika, help!" She took hold as well, but could not budge Kelru. Thiain wrapped her arms around Kelru's shoulders and bent down over him, rubbed her cheek against the top of his head. Her eyes stared, unfocused.

Pierre twisted Kelru's ear savagely. Vika scooped up a double handful of snow and plastered it onto the side of Kelru's face. "Wake up!" she shouted.

Something must have reached him—the icy bite of the snow, or the pain from the ear. He released Thiain and staggered back a step or two. Vika dodged him, and he looked down at her with a weird light in his eyes. Then he back-handed her across the face.

The world spun around and slammed her in the back. Deep green water over her—No. Blue sky. Snow in her ear. Her head hurt. Pierre was leaning over her. "Don't try to move," he gasped, then lurched to his feet. Kelru and Thiain were both staring stupidly down at her.

Keeping well back, Pierre pitched more snow into Kelru's face. "Think!" he yelled. "Think with your *brain*, you animal! Get up on Thonn!"

Kelru shook his head slowly, brushing feebly at the snow on his face. Then he staggered to Thonn and swung up. Pierre knelt again by Vika. "Are you all right?"

"Yes." She sat up slowly and winced.

"We have to move." Pierre helped her to her feet. "Thiain and I will ride ahead. I'll look for shelter, anything defensible. You ride with Kelru on Thonn. Slow him a bit. But keep us in sight."

"I'll try," she said, her hand on her bruised cheek.

They labored on. Thiain rode Feth with Pierre on Nukh leading. Vika rode behind Kelru, as she had so many times before. Under her light, careful grip she could feel the tension in his muscles, his deep, quick breaths. If they did not find shelter soon— She closed her eyes. Her headache pulsed. Thonn surged onward.

Toward evening, they found ruins.

It was Pierre who saw them, back in the shadow of a low hill, and called a halt. Thonn came up beside him, and Vika looked where Pierre was pointing. She saw a circular formation perhaps ten meters across—a low wall of square lichen-stained stones, well overgrown with tough, crabbed shrubs, leafless at this time of year. The circle lay against the base of a low bank, and snow had drifted over part of it. But in that random, broken country, the regularity of the arrangement was obvious.

Pierre dismounted and slogged over to the ring of stones. Kelru and Vika stayed well back. Thiain sat dully on Feth, her head down, looking more tired than the beast.

Then Pierre called out exultantly, "In here!"

Vika patted Kelru's back. "Stay here," she said. He grunted. She slid down from Thonn's back and crunched over to Pierre. "What?"

It was a doorway in the hillside, inside the ring and overhung with matted roots. It gaped, black as death. Pierre pulled their one carefully kept handlight out of his pocket. "Follow me."

"There might be something asleep in there." But she followed him, her blood beating in her temples. It was a straight passage, walled with rough but neatly laid stone, and it went only about ten meters before ending in a rockfall. Pierre looked discouraged.

"It will do," Vika said. "Anything will do."

His eyes glinted in the dimness. "Will it do for two or three days? Can we defend it?"

"Pierre," she said, "we don't have a choice anymore. If we don't get back out there, they'll mate in the snow."

They made their way back to the mouth of the tunnel. Vika went to Thiain and helped her dismount. Holding the handlight in her teeth, she dragged Thiain's pack and one of the avarthu to the inner end of the passage. Thiain followed, then stood passively and watched her work. Spread out flat, then folded, the avartha insulated part of the stone floor with four layers of heavy, tightly woven wool. Vika topped it with Thiain's blankets. Then she went to Thiain and touched her face gently. "Thiain?"

She raised her head. In the weak, frigid light she looked already spent.

"Thiain, there are some blankets here. And your water pouch, and mine. Is there anything else you need?"

Her breath caught. "Nothing." It was the first word she had spoken since morning.

"Should we let Kelru come to you?"

She reached out to Vika. Their hands met and clasped. Thiain's breathing deepened and roughened. After a moment Vika squeezed her hands, let go, and left her there. Outside, Pierre waited. Beyond him, Kelru stood looking past her at the doorway.

"He can go in," Vika said, suddenly reluctant to speak to Kelru.

Pierre nodded, then turned. Kelru brushed past them and disappeared into the tunnel.

Vika looked after him for a moment. Then she turned to Pierre. "I'll get a fire going, if you'll get these beasts unsaddled."

By nightfall they had a good fire just outside the tunnel mouth, with a night's supply of wood stacked in the shelter of the tunnel. They kept up a steady stream of talk—the sounds from the tunnel made any silence awkward. Hearing them, Thonn and Feth and Nukh stirred and snorted. But at last they settled to sleep on the drifted snow, in the shelter of the little hill. Pierre cooked supper while Vika sat with her knife, stripping twigs for a bed just inside the mouth of the tunnel. "I wish I'd had time to do this for them," she said. "They'll be bruised."

Pierre grinned faintly. "I don't think it will worry them."

As they ate their khishtuh and dried meat, Vika looked around at the dark, twisted trees and shivered. The feeling of being stalked was returning, now that the known world had shrunk to the edge of the circle of firelight. "I wish we had a better weapon than your bow," she said.

He studied her for a moment. Then dug into his pack and came up with a cloth-wrapped bundle. "I found this in Anke's pack, the night she died." He unwrapped the bundle with careful fingers, and Vika saw with shock that it was one of the projectile weapons from the lander—the ones that had been left there at Pierre's order. Pierre went on, "She must have taken it from the lander when she went there alone, while you were at the sisterhold."

Vika shook her head. "Pierre—why have you kept this hidden?" Both of them had trained with these, knew how to use them fairly well. "If we'd had this when we faced Talakh—"

"You know better than that, Vika," he said quietly. "If Talakh knew we had such a thing, he would have taken it. Killed me to take it, if he had to. And you, and I, and Kelru would be dead. But now—" He held it out to her, carefully.

Vika took it, checked that it was unloaded, and hefted it. She had forgotten its cold weight, the dark metal's slickness. It brought back memories of target practice on Earth—the fierce kick as it fired, the stunning noise, the stink of the chemical propellant.

"Ammunition." Pierre laid a small, heavy packet in her hand.

Forty rounds. "Is this all we have?"

"One or two shots will do for anything. Even if you miss, the sound will frighten kharag away." He sounded confident. Vika wished she could be sure the confidence was real.

She loaded the weapon and laid it, with the safety on, on a pack near her right hand. Pierre yawned and got to his feet. Then he listened for a moment. "I think they've gone to sleep."

"For now," she said. "Enjoy it while you can."

"Should we put some food where they can get it?"

"Maybe tomorrow," she said. "I don't trust Kelru's temper."

"All right." He went to the edge of the firelight to piss, then came back. "Wake me about an hour past midnight."

She nodded, glancing upward and estimating where Tlankharu would be by then. Pierre touched the bruise on her cheekbone. "I hope that eye doesn't swell shut. Does it hurt much?"

"Not now. It's lucky he didn't claw me."

Pierre winced. "It certainly is." He bent and kissed her.

She touched his shoulder. "Sleep well."

She heard the rustle as Pierre stretched out, then nothing but his even breathing and the crackle of the fire. The trees nearby were stiff and stunted, and the wind barely rustled their sparse branches. She looked up through them into the night sky. Tlankharu—old man's eye. A merciless old man. One who could look on death after death without turning away, without even blinking. If the God Pierre believed in truly existed, that was what he would be like. He had watched this world die, and now he watched the survivors scratch for life in the rubble, and he would change none of it. Even when they broke babies' necks. Even when men and women mated blindly, without love or tenderness—unless they were able to build it together, afterwards.

She looked at Pierre, who was already asleep, the blankets clutched tightly around him, his knitted woolen cap pulled low over his ears. Everything fine about him, and everything ridiculous, combined to make him what he was. And Vika could hope to know all of it someday, to know his mind and heart as well as she was beginning to know his body. There were no barriers between them, as there were between the men and women of Windhome. They were lucky, so lucky, to be human—

A faint sliding sound on the bank, behind and above her. She whirled and stared up into the darkness there. A little snow rolled down, clumping into powdery balls. "Pierre!"

In the corner of her eye she saw him sit up and reach for his bow. The snow stopped coming down, but something snapped, well back in the leafless brush. Pierre was bracing his bow on the top of his boot, sliding the loop of the string into place. And at last Vika realized that she had not picked up the gun. She sidled toward it, keeping her eyes on the brush above her. She started to call out, "Up the—"

Something leaped. She saw the flash of a knife and dodged to her left, jumping over the fire. The figure landed on its feet, the knife aimed out at Pierre and Vika. The stance, the knife, so familiar— Terror slammed the breath from her body. It was Talakh.

TWENTY-ONE

Pierre stood in the mouth of the tunnel, his drawn bow aimed at Talakh. He breathed carefully to keep himself calm, keep his aim steady. The trapper, torn and filthy, half-crouched on the other side of the fire.

Pierre could see Vika, unarmed, her eyes wide with fear. She could not reach him or the gun without passing close to Talakh.

Talakh looked only at Pierre, standing between him and Thiain. His yellow eyes smoldered. He moved his mouth as if to speak, but only a groan came. Pierre's stomach knotted. *He scents Thiain.* Talakh had been drawn into the Red Mind, just as Kelru had; and he wanted Thiain. He would kill to have her.

"Shoot him," Vika gasped.

In that instant Pierre realized he had let his aim drift a little—and in that instant Talakh leaped at him and tore the bow out of his hands. He had dropped his knife. He was now just an animal, claws were enough. He smelled of rotted teeth, of blood and greasy wool. He swung the bow at Pierre. It struck Pierre's ribs with a sharp crack, knocking him aside. Pierre landed hard, the broken bow beside him.

Vika stood over him, her little knife in one hand and a flaming stick from the fire in the other. Still on the ground, Pierre lunged for the gun, rolled to his knees, and aimed at Talakh.

At Pierre's motion Talakh froze for an instant, his hood fallen back. He had no cap. Pierre saw numbly that his remaining ear was gone, his face slashed—fresh wounds, barely scabbed. Talakh bared his broken teeth at them, then swung to face the tunnel.

The tunnel where Kelru and Thiain lay unknowing, oblivious. Pierre raised the gun in both hands, took steady aim, and fired twice. Both projectiles hit Talakh, one in the neck, one in the side. He fell in ruins. Fell hard, tossing an arc of dark blood against the pure snow behind him. Fell and was still. The sound of the shots echoed from the surrounding hills, a rolling crackle that took a long time to die.

Pierre got painfully to his feet, staring at the corpse. The fresh blood steamed in the icy air. Vika said weakly, "Thank you."

Pierre felt a spasm of revulsion. "I had no choice," he said. "I had to do it."

Then something nudged him in the back, and he spun around. It was Feth. And behind him, Thonn and Nukh, shouldering close, intent on Talakh. Pierre grimaced. They could smell the blood, of course. And they were hungry. He smacked Feth on the nose and shouted, and the beasts moved back. For the moment.

Vika came to him, and they embraced. She was shaking. "Was he alone?"

"He must be," Pierre said. "He'd been in a fight—you saw his ear. I think the other men drove him out. He must have a riding animal somewhere, to have kept up with us today. But no bow."

"How do you know?"

Pierre's jaw clenched. "If he'd had a bow, we would be dead."

"And he would have Thiain." She looked grim. "Why did they drive him out?"

"I think—the Red Mind," Pierre said. "The men were almost there, almost ready. And then Talakh frightened the woman away." Pierre kept his eyes on the corpse. Penance. He had never killed before, other than hunting for food. "They must have been very angry." He felt shaken, shocked, changed. "And then where could Talakh go? What could he do with what was left of his life? Nothing but—" Pierre broke off. "I'm going to be sick," he said carefully.

"Sit down." Vika helped him to the fire. "Rest for a minute." She held her trembling hands out to the fire, keeping her back to the place where Talakh lay, near the mouth of the tunnel. "We c-can't burn him. There isn't enough wood. But we have to move him away from here." Her voice was high, unnatural.

"Move him where?" Pierre buried his face in his hands. Then he raised his head. Calm. For Vika's sake, for all their sakes, he had to regain his self-command. "We must keep his body by the fire, and watch over him. Or Nukh and Thonn and Feth will eat him."

He saw her mouth twist with nausea that no doubt matched his own. After a moment she said, "At least we can get him away from our bed. At least that."

They dragged him a little farther from the tunnel entrance, but still near the fire. When that was done, Pierre turned to Vika and took her icy hands in his. Through all this she had forgotten to put her gloves on, and her fingers were almost blue. Her face was blank with exhaustion—she was tired all the time now, since his accident and illness. He had taken so much from her.

He kissed her hands gently. "You should sleep first."

She looked up at him, her eyes darker smudges in her dark face. "You're tired, too."

"No arguments," he said with mock roughness.

Once she might have smiled at that; once she might have argued further. But tonight she went immediately to the bed and wrapped herself in the blankets.

Silence fell. Pierre folded one of the saddlecloths to sit on, threw a blanket on over his thessach, and sat by the fire. The gun in his hand, he waited for silence, for his soul to settle again. For peace. But it did not come.

He could not pray. He kept hearing the crack of the shots that killed Talakh. They had deafened everyone, even God. Pierre knew he should be watchful; if any of the other men had followed Talakh, they would be drawn out of hiding to Thiain like a moth to flame. He must watch.

He watched the patterns in the flames, the sparks flashing and racing along the embers. He listened to the hiss and whisper from the center of the flames. Voices. Everything on Windhome had a voice—fire, wind, the land itself. The land that told one the manner of one's death. Pierre listened. But the land was not speaking to him. Or it was speaking very slowly, each word lasting seasons....

Vika woke cold and stiff, with light in her eyes. Light from the rising sun lanced through the trees. She rubbed her face, then gasped. Pierre should have waked her after midnight. She sat up. "Pierre!"

He was there, by the fire. Asleep with his head on his knees. She called him again, fright in her voice. He stirred, then sat up straight and swore. "The fire!"

The fire was a pile of soft gray ash, faintly smoking. Pierre snatched up a handful of tinder. He worked feverishly to rebuild the fire as Vika stuffed her feet into her filthy felt boots. She could not stop shivering. And a queasy smell, stale and coppery, hung in the air.

She got to her feet and came out of the tunnel, looked at once at the place where Talakh had lain. A shudder rippled through her. Only a red stain on the snow. He was gone. He had been dragged away—dragged toward where the animals now lay sleeping.

Vika looked at them, curled up together on the snow. There was quite a lot of blood. And some torn things like rags—wool, or furry skin.... She turned away until she was sure she was not going to vomit. She could hear stirrings at the back of the tunnel. Too soon to hope that it was over. Down the tunnel, Thiain gave a wild cry, and Kelru began to grunt rhythmically. "Pierre," she said in a shaking voice. "The beasts took Talakh."

"God—no!" He lurched to his feet and stood looking at the beasts, his hands spread, helpless. "When Kelru finds out—"

She nodded wearily. Kelru had explained it once. A riding animal who ate the flesh of a person was killed at once, always. It could no longer be trusted: the next time it was hungry, it might turn on its rider.

Pierre's face was pale but steady. "They're safe enough for now. We can't afford to kill them."

"I know." She shivered.

Pierre left her and went over to the animals. They were snug, full-fed, pleased. They lifted their big fanged heads to sniff at him. He moved around between them, bending and collecting things in a fold of his thessach. Then he came back to the fire and pitched them in, one at a time. Vika winced when she saw them. Bones. Talakh's bones. They were glistening fresh and pinkish-yellow, most of them split and leaking remnants of bloody marrow. They hissed as they landed among the flames. "Pierre, that's our cooking fire!"

"I won't leave them for the kharag," he said grimly.

That day was long. In the tunnel, Kelru and Thiain slept much of the day away, but toward sunset they woke and began another bout. Vika took a long, slow breath. *Let this one be the last.* She was exhausted.

And so was Pierre. Vika looked up from building up the fire to cook their khishtuh for supper and saw him cradling his broken bow in his lap, fitting the splinters together, smoothing them down so the bow looked almost whole.

Apprehensive, she got up and went to him. He looked up as she knelt beside him. "I should know how to do this," he complained. "Why didn't Kelru teach me how to do this?"

Her heart cold with pity and terror, she said gently, "Because it can't be done. You know that." He frowned at her for a moment, and then nodded slowly.

She touched his forehead, but anything at all warm felt hot to her icy hands. "Wait a moment." She turned to her pack, her hands unsteady as she dug through it for the diagnostic patch. "Pierre, I'm worried that your fever might be back. Can I just—"

"There's nothing wrong with me that a week of sleep in a warm place would not correct," he said wearily.

"Hush," she said, and reached up under his thessach to spread the patch out against his ribs. If the infection had returned—

She opened her datapad and called up the readings from the patch, and her heart went cold. It complained of a shadow at the base of his left lung.

"What is it?" he asked irritably.

"Just something residual from your pneumonia," she said. It had to be. His body temperature was normal. But did this reading fit? Where had the worst of the infection been? Those days had been so terrible, she could not remember. She flipped down the list of previous readings to the first one—and took a long breath of relief. The same patchy shadow, but much larger than it was now. "You're all right. I'll just—"

It was then that she noticed the reading before that, at the bottom of the screen. The name at the left was Anke's. And the time—the day before her death.

"Vika. What are you doing?"

"Wait," she said tensely, and opened the file. Anke was dead—it could not matter to her. She read the summary at the top. Then read it again, her heart pounding. *Normal pregnancy. Gestational age 23 days.*

She looked up at him, and he frowned at her, irritated. "What is it?"

At last she was sure she could speak. "Pierre," she said thinly. "When Anke died—she was pregnant. Very early."

He stared at her. "That can't be. We were both—we were all—it was done surgically, it was permanent. There could be no mistake!"

She showed him the screen. And the other readings, including the magnified scan of the embryo, a tiny thing curled up tightly. He looked at it, aghast. "Oh, Christ."

Vika knelt beside him on the unsteady ground, trying to think.

"She must have been so afraid," Pierre said, anguish in his voice. "Why didn't she tell me?"

Vika's thoughts were racing now. "She wouldn't have wanted to tell you until it was over," she said. "Until she'd solved it." She took a breath. "That's why she went to Dethun's house. Not to harm Dethun. Not to get herself killed. To see *Thiain.*"

Pierre was silent. Then he said, "And end it. As she must."

"It would be the only thing to do," Vika said. *If it didn't kill her. If it worked at all.*

But Pierre was looking at Vika now, his eyes shadowed. "Vika— what about you?"

She rocked back on her heels. *No.* She and Pierre had coupled only three times, four— She could not possibly—

Her hands shaking, she peeled the diagnostic patch carefully off of Pierre's ribs. Lifted her tunic and set it on the bare flesh of her abdomen, ignoring the bite of the frosty air. Picked up her datapad in an unsteady hand and tapped out the command for *anomaly search.* Then waited.

Waited until the answer came, and closed her eyes. "It's normal," she said, her voice raw. "I'm not pregnant."

He caught her hands and said, "Thank God."

But she was looking at him. "Pierre—you know what this means."

"We can't live as we have been," Pierre said bleakly. "We can't risk this happening to you." He buried his face in his hands and said, "I am so sorry."

"I am, too," she said numbly. "But we can still be lovers. Not everything is a risk."

"I know," he said. "When we're safe again. Maybe then...."

As darkness fell, she stretched out on the rustling bed of boughs. Silence from the tunnel—they were sleeping again. *Please—let it be over.* She closed her eyes, wishing that Pierre lay beside her in peace, that they could absorb this news together. Sleep evaded her for a long time.

After half a night's restless sleep she woke with Pierre shaking her shoulder. She sat up blinking and gasped at the cold.

"The wind has picked up," he said. "Keep a good watch." With that, he climbed into the warm place she had made for him and rolled over to face the wall.

She spent the rest of her watch alternately huddling by the fire and pacing around it in a circle. She kept the gun in her thessach's side pocket, and it thumped against her hip as she walked. The wind blew so hard that even the stiff, thick-limbed trees rattled restlessly, a dry, hollow clatter like bones. Tlankharu blazed, sinking toward the west. The nearby trees seemed to lean toward her, and everything looked sinister in the faint and flickering light. Just there, Talakh had fallen— there was the spray of blood that had come from his neck. Here were the marks they made when they dragged him to the fire. And there Pierre had sat and slept while one of the beasts, Thonn probably, had come and set his teeth in the corpse, dragged it off into the dark, and taken the first great crunching bite.

And now Pierre would keep his distance from her again. She saw it clearly, bleakly. It was practical. It was sensible. It was safe. She got up, restless, and stood alone by the fire until dawn.

Kelru came back to himself like a klakurr returning to its hollow tree after a storm: lost, driven, exhausted. He was not sure that he had been sleeping, only that now he was lying in chill darkness, on a blanket over stone, with his eyes open and his thoughts circling, circling. A woman lay beside him, and the place was thick with the scent of mating. His body ached, spent. His body, his belly knew what had happened, and slowly as he lay there the knowledge flowed all through him, and he remembered. It was not a forgetfulness like that after drinking too much khevodh. It was a matter of finding where the memories had been laid, far down at the foundation of his spirit.

He was a man, a mated and familied man. He belonged to the woman beside him, and to the children she almost certainly carried within her. It was as if the Mother-River had reversed her flow, as if the sun were rising in the west. He did not know his way through this new world. All that he was, all that he believed, seemed strange now, changed now, as if he saw it in the light of a different sun.

He was the bondmate of Thiain, a woman he scarcely knew. He must guard and protect her, and prepare with her a place of safety where she could live in peace and bear their children. And he knew, as his fathers had taught him in boyhood, that their physical joining had only begun the bond between them; if they were to be bondmates, people of honor, they must build a friendship, a deep one, that would perfect that bond.

He reached out tentatively and touched Thiain, as was now his right. But she was deeply asleep and did not even move. *Let her rest.* In that moment Kelru realized he was hungry as a kharag. Gray light gleamed at the mouth of the tunnel, and he smelled smoke. A fire. And food.

He got painfully to his feet, felt around on the ground until he found the clothing and the thessach he had torn off when it began. They were crushed, creased, and they felt strange and heavy against his newborn body. Newborn Kelru, the mated man, the father. In a settled family a man or woman's first mating was marked afterward by new clothing, by the eating of risen bread, by a feast that lasted a day and a night. Here there were only the two of them—and Pierre and Vika, who had been his only family.

But now there was an inner family: Thiain and himself, and their children.

He tugged on his cold boots and stumped down the tunnel to the mouth. Outside it was dawn, or sunset—he had to sniff the air to recognize the scent of morning, and then the world turned and settled itself. Vika and Pierre rose slowly from their places by the fire and stood looking at him. Pierre spoke first. "We wish you and Thiain peace and long friendship."

He should have offered Kelru food first, but of course he would not know that. Kelru went to the fire and lifted the lid of the pot there. Khishtuh, of course. He bent and brushed windblown snow from a patch of frozen earth, then sat down on folds of his thessach. He picked up a bowl and scooped out some of the hot food. When he had tasted it he said, "Thiain and I thank you." Then he ate hungrily.

When his belly was momentarily satisfied, he set down the bowl and looked at Pierre and Vika. They were still standing at a distance, as if they were afraid of him. This time he saw that Vika's face was marked, bruised purple on one cheek. He rose and went to them, reached out to her, touched the bruise. Memory rose out of darkness. *Snow in my face. Ugly little creature pulling me away from my mate.* "I remember—" He frowned, puzzled. "I hit you. Why?"

"It doesn't matter," she said. "You couldn't have stopped yourself."

"Still I am sorry." He looked at them both. "Thank you for bringing us safely here. You did well." But they still looked at him strangely. They stood strangely, a little apart from each other, as if something had happened between them, as if they shared a secret, or a grief. "What is it?"

Pierre sighed. "Talakh came."

Kelru's belly went cold. "Talakh. You killed him?"

Vika shuddered. "Oh, yes."

Kelru looked around. There, beyond the opening of the tunnel, bright blood stained the snow. "Was he alone?"

"Yes," Pierre said. "The other men drove him out. They tore off his other ear. And he had no bow."

"They didn't want him to watch the house and pick them off one at a time." He looked around again, more sharply. "Where is he? Did you burn him?"

There was a silence. And then Pierre said harshly, "The beasts ate him. I fell asleep on watch, and Thonn and the others ate him."

Horror burned like ice in Kelru's belly. "You tell me this so calmly?" He looked from Pierre to Vika. *"Do you know what this means?"*

"We know," Vika said, looking frightened. "We didn't want it to happen."

Kelru's grief burst then, and he threw back his head and cried out, a long, shuddering wail of loss and denial. His beasts stirred and rose to their feet. Kelru went to them, his eyes blurred by tears. Thonn gave a chuffing snort of pleasure and stretched his head toward Kelru, asking for a scratch. Kelru dug his fingers into the thick fur of the beast's neck. "Cousin," he said, "cousin, I wasn't there. I'm sorry I wasn't there." He threw his arms around the beast's neck and buried his face in the thick pale fur. Thonn twisted around to rub his big cheek against Kelru's thessach.

Calmer, Kelru turned to face Pierre and Vika again. "I asked much of you," he said to them both. "I understand your failure. But you do not know what this has cost me."

Pierre frowned at him. "We have to let them live," he said. "Perhaps this can be forgotten."

"It cannot," Kelru said flatly. "When these beasts have saved us, when we come to safety again, I must reward them with death. And until then we must watch without fail, especially when the beasts are hungry." He did not try to hide his anger and sorrow. Pierre accepted it quietly, but Vika turned away abruptly, went to the mouth of the tunnel and stood there. From the way her body shook Kelru could see she was weeping.

He walked back to the fire and stood warming his hands. Pierre lifted the lid of the khishtuh pot and stirred it mechanically. "Brother," Kelru said, irritated, "doesn't she need you?

"It will pass," he said. "Kelru—we've learned something." He looked up. "When the Destroyers came to our ship, they interfered with us more than we knew.... I told you that before we left our world we were all made unable to have children. Well, while we slept in our ship on the journey here, it seems that was undone." He looked down at his hands. "Anke was pregnant when she died."

Kelru heard the sadness in the words. "Brother, I'm sorry that you lost more than you knew." And then, after a moment, he understood. He looked at Vika. She stood looking away but clearly listening.

Pierre was looking at her, too. "Vika is not pregnant," he said. "And now that we know, we won't take that risk again."

"You will not live as bondmates," Kelru said, and sat down beside Pierre. From somewhere he did not yet understand, pity welled up so strongly that he could say nothing more. He set his hand on his brother's shoulder, and they sat silent there for a long while.

To Vika's relief, they traveled northward slowly, taking shelter in ruins where they could. Pierre still slept close beside her when he was not on watch; but there was a distance again. He had remembered that he was her commander, that they had a mission. In every ruin they both combed the ground for traces of the attack, but trappers and outlaws had cleared out anything useful long ago. If the Destroyers had ever walked this land, they had left no trace. Or it was hidden under meters of snow.

The weather grew still more bitter as they moved north, nearer to the place where the land opened out into tundra, with eternal ice beyond. Kelru's knowledge of winter travel saved them. He permitted no mistakes; if Pierre or Vika so much as shivered, Kelru began looking for shelter immediately. He was even more protective of Thiain. Because of Thiain, they still traveled within the borders of the skull place, where they could be sure of finding shelter among the scattered ruins.

Kelru and Pierre hunted several times with the beasts. The meat— scrawny feotheg, tough and wasted gherrau—eked out their dwindling supply of tuber flour. Thiain found reeds standing bleakly in frozen ponds, reeds whose pith could be cooked into a gummy, flavorless paste. It was food, but it made khishtuh seem like a treat.

Several times they camped in the ruins of isolated houses, once

Pierre had determined that the radiation level was safe. Dwellings this far north tended to be built on hillsides where possible, or on upthrusts of granite, to avoid summer flooding. The foundations were carved into stone or built of stone blocks, and these had endured when the wooden structures burned or rotted away. Sometimes they found tunnels or underground rooms, but typically they pitched their avarthu on drifted snow within foundation walls, in a hole in the ground that was open to the sky. The animals slept on the surface above, trampling out hollows in the snow and letting blown snow cover them.

There was beauty even here. Vika sometimes sat her watch at night under a shimmering green or red curtain of aurora. Once or twice she thought she could hear it—a faint, cold sizzle.

Kelru and Thiain were drawing closer together, building a friendship. Vika hoped that someday the two of them would find a place to settle together and form the core of a new family. As for her own life, and Pierre's—she did not let herself imagine what might never be. Kelru talked of the land over the mountains to the west, along the coast, far out of reach of Kheosseth; not a place for outlaws, but for new settlers founding new families. Like the four of them. Vika carefully did not look at anyone when Kelru talked this way. Not even Thiain.

They traveled now through wider country, where the trees clustered on high ground. Kelru told them that in summer in country such as this, the low ground was covered with bogs, with moss and small ground-hugging plants that bore bright flowers. And there would be huge clouds of little insectlike flying creatures, whose bites could drive a large animal mad. Listening to Kelru, Vika shuddered. Pierre took her hand and said, "But we will be far from here by summer." She wondered, emptily, what he was imagining.

One night they found especially good shelter, an underground room with a hearth and a clear chimney. It was bare and plain, a round room with stone walls and floor. It was not five meters across, and it smelled musty. In the back they found a few relics of its former inhabitants: a corroded metal tub, and a jumble of baskets that crumbled to powder when Vika touched them. But Pierre's handlight also showed them scorches on the stone walls, black starred bursts. Vika did not let herself try to imagine what had made them. Or what might lie under the smooth hummocks of snow they had crossed to come in here.

As they set up camp they were startled once by a sound from Pierre's pack, a muffled crackle of static. He pulled out the hand comm, and Vika came to him and looked down at it. "It's on," he said. The burst of static faded to silence as they listened.

"Did a stray signal turn it on?" Vika asked.

"From where? No, something in my pack must have touched the control pad." He set it down on top of his pack and turned back to spreading out the ground-cloth for their bed.

That night the dead were all around, a silent, crowding presence that pressed on Vika. She slept restlessly, waking to see Kelru outlined in firelight, his eyes thoughtful; waking again after midnight to see Pierre, the gun at his side, leafing through the little book he always carried with him. She wondered again what comfort he found there, and drifted back to sleep.

Deeper this time, far, far down, swimming in warmth and darkness. Then she saw light farther down, below her, light and drifting color; and then she was standing on the earth. Standing on Earth, bathed in golden light. It was the Denver TFE campus, where she had trained and studied for so long. The sky burned hot blue above her, and the Rockies cut the horizon to the shape of home. She looked around. Eucalyptus leaves rustled gently. She was home. She was forgiven. She could begin again.

Then her heart was full to breaking, for a man stood near her in the shadows of the trees. It was Dr. Kozlov. Alive and whole. He was smiling warmly, his gray eyes soft. He was speaking to her, though she could not quite make out the words. Something was strange about them. At first she thought he was speaking Russian. But she could understand Russian. She walked toward him, but he backed away, still muttering, muttering. He smiled at her, but he kept moving away. She tried to run toward him, but he receded as she approached. Faster and faster. She called out to him. Then someone touched her shoulder.

And it was all a lie, all a dream. She looked up at Pierre blearily. *This* was real, this frigid room, and the whistle of the wind outside, and that soft muttering voice—

That voice—

Pierre's eyes were dark, apprehensive. He held something in his hand, something that frightened him, she could see that it did. "Do you hear it?" he said.

Awake now, she sat up slowly. The others still slept. The first deep-blue light of a snowy dawn was filtering in from the opening above. She looked at the thing in Pierre's hand. The hand comm. It was speaking. Muttering, like the voice in her dream. Words that were almost nonsense. "*—assessment of reserves as Eleni has said many times this morning we met at seven to discuss how can I tell them the truth with luck we will not see them I am afraid but Eleni would not—*"

The voice was Dr. Kozlov's.

TWENTY-TWO

Vika said slowly, "They're alive. We've—we've found them."

Pierre shook his head. "Listen to the words, Vika. It's nonsense."

She listened for a while, her apprehension growing as the words flowed on without meaning. "It could still be him," she said. "He could be sick—"

"Or insane," Pierre said. "Or it could be something assembled from recordings of his voice. Perhaps his journals—I know he spoke them."

She looked away. *Let me hope, this once, Pierre.* "He must be close, if that's his comm implant." She reached for the comm.

He caught her hand, stopping her, and said to the flare of anger in her eyes, "We don't know where he is. We don't know—who is with him. We don't even know that it *is* Dr. Kozlov. And if it is not—"

She looked up at him. "We have to find out."

"We must find—the source of this, if we can," Pierre said. "But we must see the situation from outside first. We dare not signal back; that might be all the aliens need to find us."

"If any of our people are alive on this planet, they need our help," Vika said emphatically.

Pierre hesitated, and she heard Dr. Kozlov's voice, continuing without breath or pause. "*—into the all of us halfway to Helsinki in and of itself—*" A chill stirred along her spine.

Pierre said, "We'll talk to Kelru." She only nodded.

That morning's discussion with Kelru was long and bitter. They must change course, Pierre insisted; find the direction of the signal, and travel toward it. No, Kelru insisted with equal force; they must move on toward the thermal springs near the northwest mountains, toward real shelter and safety for Thiain, before they did anything else.

At first Vika left the argument to Pierre; she monitored the comm, recording the transmission, listening for any change, any sign of sense. There was none. Thiain sat near the fire, listening to Kelru and Pierre, her expression darkening. Finally she got to her feet, and both men stopped and looked at her. "Will you not see," she said sharply, "either of you, that this is a matter of family? For Vika *and* for you, Pierre." Pierre looked down as Thiain went on, "You've talked of your lost friends. What if they're near? And alive?" She turned to Kelru. "And you! Is it right to tell Pierre and Vika that they must pass by without learning more? Should they leave their friends, their family without help in this wilderness so *I* can be warm and safe?" She stood very straight and still, anger clear in her eyes. "I don't agree. We're bondmates now. You don't decide this for me. Or for Vika."

"Thiain is right," Vika said, cradling the comm in her hand. She looked up at Kelru. "Grant us a few days' travel north toward the signal, to see if we can find any trace of them. And if we don't, we turn west toward that refuge you want to find." Kelru opened his mouth to answer, but Pierre spoke first.

"Four days' travel, no more," he said to Vika, and reluctantly, she nodded. He turned to Kelru and said, "Then we find shelter for the winter, and return south in the spring."

That, at last, drew grudging agreement from Kelru, and they turned to breaking camp. As Vika settled her pack on Feth's back, Thiain appeared beside her and took Vika's gloved hand in both her own. "This will end," she said. Her dark eyes were gentle. "Whether we find your friends, or not. At the end we *will* find a place where we can live in peace. The four of us together, and the children."

"I hope so," Vika said, with more feeling than she intended. It seemed far away, like something that would never happen. As beautiful, and as unreachable, as Earth. And Kelru's silence worried her.

As they moved on that day, Pierre settled the signal's direction: almost due north, in the direction of a low outcrop of snow-covered mountains. Dr. Kozlov's voice never stopped—not even for breath. But they had to listen, in case that changed. She knew that listening wore on Pierre, too, judging from his look of relief as he handed her the comm when they stopped to eat their sparse midday meal.

Vika no longer knew what to hope. If the voice was Dr. Kozlov's, then he was not sane. If that condition was permanent, how could they help him, here? And, they heard no voice other than his.

And how did he come to be there? And what might be guarding him? Her thoughts shied away from that.

The third day dawned clear, with high streamers of cloud shining gold against deep blue. The world-wind, fanged with cold, flung dry snow and chips of ice in their faces; the beasts walked head down, pressing against it like an enemy. At midmorning they came to a frozen river that ran north and south, and at first they traveled on it; but then Kelru, always watchful now, saw signs that the ice was thinning. They traveled instead along the bank, through a tangle of brush that thickened as they moved northward.

The signal was stronger now. And the ice on the river thinned still further, until at last they saw open water out in the center. Vika regarded it with wonder. "There must be a hot spring upstream," she said.

Kelru's ears flicked back. "I've never heard of one so large, in this land or anywhere," he said. There was dread in his voice.

They journeyed on up the river. Wide patches of rough ice, with bare trees and shrubs sticking up forlornly here and there, showed where water had spilled over and then frozen at night. The air stayed cold all day. They moved through a thick white fog, under branches fuzzed and spined with frost. The rocks of the stream bed glistened, skimmed over with white, bearded with ice stalactites. Their hoods and the humans' woolen scarves frosted over, and water condensed on their faces, froze on their thessachs and the beasts' noses. Pierre's beard turned white, as did Kelru's muzzle and Thiain's. Vika had to break bits of ice off her face-scarf to breathe.

The valley turned east and steepened toward a waterfall that they heard for a long time before they came to it. The sound of flowing water was strange, haunting in the winter stillness. The fall itself was dreamlike, an echoing thunder of falling water in a high palisade of ice-covered rock, white within white.

Kelru found a way up, though the ice made it treacherous. They had to unload the animals and carry the packs up themselves in several trips. Finally Kelru and Pierre persuaded the unladen beasts to follow.

The path—cut by migrating gherrau, Vika guessed—moved upward along the river through a steep cleft of stone. At the top, she saw that the cleft opened out. Kelru was ahead of her leading Thonn. Vika saw him come up to the opening—and stop short. He stood still, unspeaking.

Cold with apprehension, Vika struggled to the top with Thiain at her side. Pierre, following with the other beasts, stopped beside her, and together they looked out, dazed, at the impossible.

The cleft opened into a small, round valley a few hundred meters across. And all the little pocket of land was green, thick with trees and undergrowth, leafed out and living, and a grassy meadow just below the slope on which they stood. Impossible, this far north, at this time of year. Yet there it was, glowing in the diffuse white light that penetrated the low ceiling of clouds.

Thiain pointed silently. At the far end of the valley a dark opening, perfectly round, pierced a wall of stone. Springing from the hillside above it, a slender pillar of copper-colored metal stretched at least a hundred meters into the sky, topped by a thick knob of the same metal. Below the black opening, a broad, dark pool of water roiled, overflowing into the channel of the river. Vika stared, stunned. "The source of the river," she said.

"What is this place?" Pierre breathed.

"We shouldn't be here," Thiain said sharply. "It's not for us. We're not wanted."

Vika shivered. She had the same feeling. The profusion of life, the moist warmth of the air seemed oppressive, sinister. She told herself that she had become used to bare, plain landscapes, leafless trees, the cold, bleached world of winter. That was all....

Pierre came up beside her, his face taut with apprehension. "That structure—Vika, was there anything in the records that described such a thing?"

"Not in the ones I read," she said unsteadily.

"Or in any of them," Thiain said.

Pierre moved to Nukh's side, opened one of his saddle-packs, and pulled out a datapad. "Anke's notes from her Kishar work," he said. "We need to see if there were any similar images in the inscriptions there."

"Give it to me," Vika said. "I know how she organized them." She found the archive, opened it, and searched it based on a visual scan of the tower.

The first image to appear was a simple painting in black, on stone, of a spire rising from low hills. There might have been a slight thickening at the top.... Vika scanned the accompanying notes and said to Pierre, "Remember the cave called Jackpot, in the far southern hemisphere. The one where some of the images had inscriptions associated?" She showed it to Pierre, but he only shook his head. "That does look like this," Vika said. "But there's not enough detail. And the inscription hasn't been translated. I wish—I wish Anke could see this."

"I, too," Pierre said austerely. He looked down at his datapad. "From here I detect no radiation above background. We'll continue monitoring as we approach it." He held out his hand, and Vika gave him Anke's datapad, which he returned to the saddle-pack. Then he turned back toward the reality across the valley. "This isn't simply a hot spring," he said. "That couldn't melt all the snow, keep all these plants and trees green and growing in the middle of winter. Even at thermal sites in Iceland, there is snow on the ground in winter. There must be some stronger source of heat in the ground itself."

Vika nodded. Something that warmed the water, and the soil, and the plants that grew there. And more than that. There were animal sounds—feotheg whistles, and the harsh scraping croak of klakurr. Vika felt prickles of sweat under her heavy woolen clothes.

Pierre wiped sweat from his forehead, then dropped his pack, tugged off his hat, and started unwinding the scarf from his neck.

"Brother," Kelru said sharply. "Think a minute. This could be a Destroyer place. A living one." He gripped Pierre's arm. "Wait here and watch. If this is a snare, we should not spring it. If your friends are alive and free, they will come to you."

"But they may not be free," Pierre said. "Or know that we're here."

"They know," Kelru said, with dread in his voice. "Listen."

At Vika's side, the comm had fallen silent. Dr. Kozlov's voice had stopped.

Pierre shook his head. "We can learn nothing from here. My duty is clear."

"Your duty is to Vika," Kelru said sharply. "As mine is to Thiain."

"No." Vika began stripping off her own winter coverings. "Pierre's right. They're our family. We'll go. You and Thiain should stay here." The air felt almost balmy.

Pierre dropped his thessach in a heap. Then he turned to Vika. "We should get a closer look at that opening," he said. "Are you ready?"

She went to his side, then turned to look back at Kelru and Thiain, standing close together on the stone shelf. "Vika," Thiain said unsteadily. "Don't go down there. Whatever this place is—it's something from the Destroyers." Her ears were flat back. "If your friends are here, you may not be able to help them."

"I agree," Kelru said. He stood with his arm around Thiain's shoulders.

"We heard our brother's voice," Pierre said. "If he is here, we must try to find him. Stay back. Protect Thiain. We'll return." Kelru lowered his eyes.

Pierre pulled his datapad from his pack and activated it as a recorder. Vika did the same, and they descended the short slope. The ground was bare and hard, solid rock under a thin layer of scrabbly soil, until they stepped out onto the grassy ground below.

It was then that Vika began to feel it—a throbbing tremor under her feet. A deep pulsation of power, like a vast and distant engine. She bent and touched the ground. "It's warm," she said. She looked back at Thiain, who clutched at Kelru. Beyond them, the beasts stirred nervously.

"I can't tell where the sound is coming from," Pierre said, turning in a slow circle with his datapad held out. "Just—below."

She nodded. "All around us. I can't—" She broke off. "I hear something else. In the woods, over there." She pointed. Creaking and popping and a sound like wind in the branches. But there was no wind. *How can there be no wind?*

Pierre drew the gun. "I don't see anything—no." He pointed. "Movement out there."

She stared into the gloom under a distant stand of trees. Movement, yes. But not an animal. The trees were swaying. She saw a tall one a hundred meters away rise, rise from the ground, then sag over sideways with a crackle of breaking branches. Then another one, closer, rising as the ground bulged beneath it. "Something is coming," Pierre said. "Something under the ground."

An explosion of dirt and pebbles, and it erupted from the soil before them. Vika staggered back and almost fell, and she heard Kelru shout something, but she could not take her eyes from the thing. It glistened, flecked with grit and leaves. It was hard to see, the same color as the trees behind it. No, she realized—it was clear, like glass, except for a cloudy knob at its upper end. It was like a snake. A snake half a meter thick. And how long? No way to tell; only part had emerged from the ground.

Pierre came to her side. "Steady," he said. But she was staring past him at the thing that had come from the ground. She cringed as it turned, swaying, aiming the knob all around. Then, with a wet sound, part of the knob's cloudy surface irised open, and a milky gray globe appeared, like an eye, a featureless eye. The knob turned until the eye faced them, and then it stopped.

"It sees us," she said in a cracked voice.

"Are you recording?" Pierre asked evenly.

"Of course I am!"

"We'll want two good records," he said. "Now. Move away to the right as I circle left." He passed her the gun. "Shoot only if it attacks."

For a wild moment she thought of running. But she could not leave Pierre. She moved off to the right, keeping ten meters between herself and the thing.

It turned its eye to follow her, then swung to look at Pierre. Then with another wet pop a second eye appeared on the surface facing her.

"I am going to approach it," Pierre called. "Stay where you are." And he took a step toward the thing, then another—

It struck like a snake, so fast it seemed to blur. It knocked Pierre off his feet and arched down over him. Its eye was only centimeters from his face. "*Christ*," Pierre moaned. Through the thing's body, watery and distorted, she saw him struggling to rise. The thing pressed down on him.

And then she smelled ozone. Something was growing quickly out of the side of the thing, clear like its body, visible only because it glistened slightly. A kind of hand, with three or four loose curling tentacles.

It reached down and tore the datapad from Pierre's equipment harness. The hand, holding the datapad, flexed oddly and then seemed to swallow it. Vika saw the little rectangle begin to move through the middle of the arm, back toward the main body.

Not a hand, then. A mouth.

Shaking with horror, she raised the gun and fired. One, two, three, four. Explosions, whistling ricochets, three cloudy patches on the clear body of the alien thing—but the fourth projectile hit it in one of the eyes.

It splattered, spraying gray fluid. The thing lifted away from Pierre, swayed toward her. Then stopped—and began to sink silently back into the hole from which it had emerged.

They watched it go. Vika kept the gun trained on it. The knob disappeared into the ground, and the smooth sides of the tube crumbled in. Gone. It was gone. Stiff with shock, Vika turned to Pierre. She wanted to say, *Let's go back—let's go somewhere safe—* But there was no such place.

She looked around for Kelru and Thiain. They had moved far back, with the beasts, up onto the rocky shelf above the river where it spilled out of the valley. "Up there, onto the stone," Pierre said. "For now." Shaky, breathless, Vika climbed away from the meadow and up the steep, rubbly slope, off the floor of the valley, with Pierre close behind.

Kelru and Thiain waited for them at a level place about fifty meters above the valley floor. Vika paused and looked back. Behind and below her, the woods were silent now—no animal sounds. For Vika, all the beauty of the place was gone. Something lay beneath it—something alien to them all.

They reached the others and stopped. Kelru spoke. "It wasn't far enough for you, to come all that long journey to my world," he said. "No, you had to come even farther—to find *this*...." He seemed dazed. "You *wanted* to find them. To find the Destroyers. Didn't you, Pierre?"

"We came here to find our brothers and sisters," he said. "And we will." He was streaked with dirt from his fall, and his equipment harness was torn where the datapad had come free. But he regarded Kelru calmly.

"There is no hope for your friends," Kelru said. "The Destroyers are here." He looked down at the valley, his ears flat back. "Dethun is *right*," he said slowly. "The Anokothu are right. The Destroyers are still here. Making sure that we never try to rise from the dirt. Generation after generation, forever." There was a note of despair in his voice that Vika had never heard before.

"We can't leave until we know more," Pierre said. "Until we know that we cannot reach our friends and help them." He took Vika's hand. "I want go down there again, and try to get farther."

"You might as well try the comm now," Vika said. "They obviously know where we are."

But the comm stayed stubbornly silent. Pierre finally set it down, turned to Vika, and said again, "I must go back down there."

"Both of us," Vika said steadily. "But tomorrow. We're losing the light." Around them the daylight had begun to fade to bronze twilight under a clearing sky. Below, the dark woods were deepening into gloom. She shivered at the thought of going down there in the dark, with something alien moving in the ground under her feet.

Pierre shook his head. "Nevertheless—"

Kelru snorted. "Pierre, Vika is afraid, and so is Thiain. And so are you. I can smell it." Thiain stood straight beside him; he laid his arm around her shoulders. "We must leave this place. You must not risk Vika in this."

Vika's jaw clenched. "It's my decision," she said. "Not Pierre's. Certainly not yours." She met Pierre's look, held it until he nodded. *Good.*

Their sparse supper was grim. No one had much appetite. Afterward, Kelru took the first watch. Pierre and Vika spread out their blankets and lay down together on their backs, looking up at the profound depths of the sky. Pierre took her hand. She could feel his warmth beside her, holding her to the ground. Otherwise she would tip forward, tumble into emptiness, up and up and up, like a soul on the world-wind. Lost.

She saw the quick bright furrow of a meteor, and made a hopeless wish—that tomorrow night she would lie beside Pierre in safety. She fought the grief, fought it down silently, and slept.

She woke when Pierre touched her shoulder. He laid a finger on her lips as soon as she opened her eyes. The stars were gone. Dawn, she thought: a ghostly orange light showed her Pierre's face taut with strain, worn with cold and hard travel. Sleepily she thought, *I must look like that, too. Ten years older*....

He bent close and said quietly, "Come to the edge of the slope." Then he was gone, back to the edge, to lie there beside Kelru looking over, looking down.

She sat up and reached for her thessach, then did not put it on. The air was warm. Warmer than yesterday, warmer than ever. They would need a fire only for cooking—

The fire was a heap of smoking ash. Thiain sat motionless beside it. She had let it go out.

Vika walked toward Pierre and Kelru. Pierre turned his head and gestured emphatically downward with an open palm. She dropped to her hands and knees, then crawled forward to lie between him and Kelru, to look down at the meadow below.

The light was not that of dawn. It came from below, from the open grassy space where the thing had come up from the ground. The light source was near the edge of the woods—an upright oval, as tall as a man, that shed a ghastly pinkish-orange glow on the meadow, on the hillside.

Standing at the foot of the slope below them, orange in the light, was a man. A human man. He stood still. He was far away, fifty meters or more, and lit from behind, so she could not make out details. He—

No. It. It stood awkwardly, as if some of its joints had been placed incorrectly.

"The light began only a little while ago," Kelru said. "Everything was just as you see it. The, the person hasn't moved."

"It's not a person," she said. "Not real."

Kelru's nostrils flared. "So Pierre says. I can't tell. I don't understand the smells."

Pierre reached for his scope and passed it to Vika. "Look at it. Look closely."

She steadied the scope and peered through the eyepiece. The face of the—image—came clear. Narrow and sharp-chiseled, even beaky, with a draggled beard. Of course. Of course. "*Your* face," she said to Pierre.

"My face," Pierre said flatly. "It had a good look at me. Vika—this is an obvious attempt to communicate with us."

"I agree," she said, tasting fear in her throat.

Kelru stared at them, his ears flat back. "You're going to go down there."

"It's our duty," Pierre said.

"I'm glad it's not mine," Kelru said with emphasis. He glanced back at Thiain, who still sat unmoving. "When you are satisfied, we all go on to find shelter somewhere else. Agreed?" There was a pleading note in his voice.

"When we have learned what we must learn," Pierre said. "I give you my word." He stood up. "Vika, get ready. Leave your datapad—we can't risk losing it as well." He saw her slide it into Feth's saddlepack. He turned to Kelru. "Brother, if—if anything happens to us, if we don't come back before midafternoon—take Thiain and get as far away from here as you can before dark."

"You'll come back," he said, but his ears were twitching as he said it. "We will wait one full day."

"Thank you," Pierre said quietly.

Kelru caught Pierre's forearms and pulled him into a formal

embrace, touch and touch with the forehead to each shoulder. Then he pulled him closer and hugged him. He repeated the process with Vika, silently. And now Thiain came up to them as well, somber-faced. Vika took her hand and said, "Thank you for all you did for me when I first came to this world."

"Thank you for guarding me and my children," Thiain said with difficulty. "Come back to us." She stopped and looked at the ground. Kelru took her hand, and she turned toward him and wrapped her arms around him.

Time to go. Vika stripped off her tunic and woolen trousers as Pierre was doing, until she stood in her last layer of clothes—the coveralls she had first put on in the ship in orbit, more than half a year ago, frayed and worn thin. First contact. Strange to think that all those months ago, she had done just this, in just these clothes, to descend from the lander and meet Kelru. Now she was about to face in truth what she had feared then—the true alien, the unknowable. The destroyers of this world—and someday, perhaps, her own.

As she turned to go, Kelru stopped her. He took her left hand and brought it to his mouth, blew a quick breath into it, and closed her fingers over the palm. "You have the gift of saving life," he said, holding her closed hand in both of his. "I give you life of my own to be with you. Good fortune to be with you. What you have saved, will save you." She felt the warmth of his breath on her palm, and she kept those fingers closed as she started down the slope.

Her thick felt boots gave poor traction on the bare rock, so she had to watch her feet. It startled her when they came to the edge of the soft ground, to the low, rough grass. She looked up. The man-thing was less than ten meters away. It still stood in the same place, but its head had swiveled toward them.

They took one uncertain step, two, and Pierre stopped, halting Vika. He reached to his shoulder and set Anke's datapad to record. "Why are you here?" he asked the man-thing, in the language of Windhome. Then repeated it more loudly.

The man-thing did not move or speak. Pierre repeated the question in Standard, then in French.

Then the man-thing opened its mouth wide and held it open, unmoving. Words came out of its mouth. Not in Pierre's voice. Thin and sweet, a child's voice, speaking rapidly in French. "Pierre," it said. "Mama says you're leaving tomorrow. I watched you boarding, on the news net. Papa says your ship is as big as an ocean ship. I remember the time you took me to see the robot freighters in Vancouver. That was fun. Mama says I should thank you for things, and say goodbye. Thank you for all the books you sent me. I'm sorry they wouldn't let you take them with you on the ship. Papa and I are going to build a shelf for them. Well, goodbye. I hope you have a good trip. Goodbye." A click, and silence.

Pierre was frowning at the thing, absorbed. "Was that Thierry?" Vika asked him.

"Yes, of course," he said abstractedly. He raised his voice and said, in French, "Can you speak for yourself? Do you understand any language?"

The man-thing's head swiveled, a meaningless gesture. The hands flexed, and the fingers straightened and splayed. It lifted its arms from its sides, stiffly. The mouth opened. This time it was music. A chorus of men's voices singing in Greek. *Kyrie eleison*, over and over.

"It doesn't know what it's saying," Pierre said. "It's—accessing things from my datapad, that's all. Like Kozlov's voice, just a jumble from his journal."

She silenced him with a hand on his arm. The man-thing was walking toward them. Awkwardly, as if walking were something it understood only theoretically. Then Vika realized that it was hobbled somehow. One foot dragged as if tied. No, a tube grew out of it, a clear tube, leading back to the place where it had been standing— leading into the ground.

So this thing was an extension as well. Vika's skin crawled. Perhaps it was the same thing as before, only in a different shape.

"I want you behind me," Pierre said evenly. "Keep recording. Don't let it get the datapad. If it tries to touch you, get away. If I am attacked, run back to Kelru and Thiain. That is an order."

It stopped in front of Pierre. They were precisely the same height—the man and the alien copy. It raised its left hand, all five fingers splayed. Pierre raised his own right hand and spread his fingers. Slowly, as if compelled, he moved it closer to the alien's palm. Then jerked his hand away. "Something stung me," he said in a strained voice, turning his palm up. Five little beads of blood. "I am—it's strange—" Vika leaped to his side and steadied him.

Too close, the man-thing watched them. She put her arms around Pierre. "I love you," she said, in utter despair, and caught him as he fell.

She lowered him to the ground and cradled him. A shadow fell over her, and she looked up. The man-thing stood there, its head bent to look down at her. The singing had stopped. The thing's mouth opened again, and words came. Vika's voice. Her words from months ago, distant and distorted as Pierre had recorded them from the lander. "I come from a planet called Earth," it said, and tilted its head to one side. Its chest heaved unnaturally, and air hissed from its mouth for the first time. Then it spoke again—not a recording. Its voice was a gassy croak. "Caaaaahm," it said. "Caaaahm."

Sick with fear, she stared up at it, clutching Pierre. He was alive, breathing, but utterly limp.

It waited a moment. Then it reached down toward them. She shrank away, weeping in fear. But she could not get away, not without abandoning Pierre. The hand touched her wrist and the fingers clamped around it. Cold and smooth. Then she felt a tiny stab where its palm touched her skin. Blackness broke over her, and she sank down under it into the dark.

TWENTY-THREE

Pierre woke blind and feverish, his mind buzzing with disordered dreams—that he was back on the ship, waking from cold sleep. But alone. The rest of the team was dead, and he was dying. He smelled mold. He knew the others lay beside him in the dark, dead, skinned over with mold. He would die, too, and rot....

Waking, he stirred, and his hand brushed a wet surface. He lay still for a moment, gathering his thoughts, then rubbed his hand along the surface. It was warm and springy, slick, yet gritty as if sprinkled with dirt. He tried to raise his hand to his face, but it hit a springy surface just above his body. He felt around with both hands. The same surface. His heart raced. He could not bend his knees—they struck against it. He could not roll over—his shoulders hit the surface above him.

He felt for his knife. It was gone from his belt. With a surge of panic he knew, *knew* that he was dead. Buried. The others thought he was dead, and they had buried him. Fear filled his throat. He worked his fists up to his chest, slammed them against the surface above him and shouted. Something swallowed the sound. He had been swallowed.

No. Forcing himself to breathe steadily, he wormed a hand to his face and wiped away sweat. *Think.* His face was gritty. Sweat and dirt. Absolute darkness. Silence, except for a deep, deep hum, too low to hear, only to be felt. After a moment, he could hear his heart beating.

But he had air. Something was giving him air, or he would be dead. Something wanted him alive.... Memory crept back, and he felt his swollen palm where the false Pierre had stung him. It ached.

"Vika?" he called, cautiously. But he heard no reply. She was dead, she was hurt, she had escaped and left him there—he fought down the flood of useless speculation. *Think.*

"I come—" He stopped to clear his throat, steady his voice. "I come from a planet called Earth."

A rush of sound, too loud at first, then cut to a bearable level. It was Vika's words again, the ones she had spoken when she first met Kelru in the pasture below the lander. Kelru's words, too. Pierre understood them now: asking Vika where her home was, and the name of her family. Then silence again.

He changed to Kelru's language. "Please. I must get out of here. I must have light."

Silence.

He tried again in Standard. Then French. No result. At the back of his mind the idea that he had been sealed in here to die began to stir again. He pressed his fists against the walls of his trap and swore. Took another breath and prayed silently, his fists clenched, for light, for release. For Vika's voice....

Calmer, he felt his clothing, his equipment harness. Anke's datapad was still mounted against his left shoulder. He peered down at it and felt a wave of relief. He could see the status lights. He was not blind.

The unit was still recording. That meant the crystal was not yet full, and so fewer than six days had passed. He could run the recording back, see what had happened—see how long it had been.... No, he had better wait. Perhaps the datapad had been overlooked. He dared not draw attention to it.

Then he saw light glowing beyond his feet. A ring of light, creeping forward, shining all around him as it slid along his body. Slowly, slowly. Here was another. At last he realized that he was moving.

Light at his feet again, and coolness. Not a ring of light this time. His feet were free. Then his knees could bend, and his feet struck a yielding floor. He slid out the rest of the way, awkwardly, and stayed there on his knees, too weak with relief to stand. He raised his head and looked around.

He had been deposited in a round compartment that arched around and above him—twenty meters across, dimly lit by a red glow from the floor and the low ceiling. Here and there along the slick wall, just above the floor, big, glistening sacs bulged out—ovals more than two meters long and one high. The opening he had come out of had vanished, or melded back into the wall. To his hands the wall felt slick and warm, and he sensed a faint vibration. *This place is alive.* Perhaps literally. Perhaps the Destroyers *grew* their installations, incorporating the life and soil of the world they were attacking. It would be efficient. He saw no other opening, no other way in or out. The air was breathable, but moist and too warm. It smelled of dirt, mold, faintly of vinegar.

"Vika," he said tentatively. Then he shouted it. "Vika!" There was no reply.

He looked down at himself. Dirt on his coveralls. His palm was a virulent red, visible even in the reddish light. He touched the datapad. Time to find out what had happened.

Fifteen hours had passed since he lost consciousness. With despair, he watched the recording of Vika's capture. *She should have run.* She should have escaped, kept herself safe. But it had been her choice from the moment he was unconscious, and she'd made the choice he feared.

The recording told him little else. Vika had collapsed across him, so from that point there were no visuals, and sound was muffled. He heard dragging and scraping that went on for a long time, until he searched for new information only. There was nothing until his waking in—wherever he had been. He resumed recording.

He touched the floor. It felt damp. If this was a partially living structure, it would need to breathe; the wet surface might be part of that system. And the red glow could be the kind of light the Destroyers' eyes needed. He had an overwhelming sense that he was in the gut of a huge animal. He wished that he had the gun, but he had chosen to leave it behind—it was irreplaceable. And it had taken four shots even to damage their first attacker.

He got unsteadily to his feet and looked around. The walls—he bent and touched one of the glistening bulges. It was smooth and elastic, but barely yielded to his fingers. He struck it with his hand to see if it sounded hollow.

An uneven patch of the yellow color disappeared, leaving darkness. The color was a coating on the other side of a thick, transparent film. He struck it again, and more of the yellowness went. It fell away in flakes, slowly, as if through liquid.

He stood up and kicked the sac, hard. A big chunk of the yellow substance broke loose. And at that moment a light came up inside the sac.

The sac was roughly cylindrical, full of fluid, which was clearing slowly in the orange light. The yellow flakes drifted down, settling on an irregular shape stretched along the bottom of the sac. Puzzled, Pierre leaned closer. Something buzzed under his feet, under the floor, and the fluid swirled, clearing quickly.

He jerked back in shock. Pressed against the inside of the clear barrier was a face. The side of a face. At first he could not understand what he was seeing. Then he realized that it was a Windhome inhabitant. All of its fur was gone. The naked flesh, pinkish-yellow, looked obscene. One eye, sealed to a slit, was pressed against the clear barrier. The face looked lopsided, as if it had been wedged there for centuries.

Perhaps it had. A corpse. Not Kelru. Not Thiain.

Then the face twitched, a lightning tremor. Pierre swore and backed away.

He was breathing quickly. "Let us see," he said aloud, in an unsteady voice. He went around the room clearing every sac. More hairless Windhome people, all ages, all sizes. He made himself look more closely at one of them, a woman. Several slick-looking, brownish tubes stretched from one end of the sac to the woman's head and shoulders. They reminded him of the brown, tubular kelp that he saw washed ashore on Vancouver Island, when he had been assigned to orbital runs out of the port there. These tubes branched and spread along the hairless flesh, gripping the woman, some seeming to disappear beneath the surface. One snaked into her mouth. There were tiny dark leaflets here and there along its length. As he watched it seemed to pulse slightly.

Pierre gagged—then turned away and moved on. He had to understand this. There were children and babies here, too—packed efficiently, two or more to a sac. Some of the smallest moved when the light struck them, kicked and turned to hide their faces from it. Pity wrenched at him.

When he had all the sacs clear—eleven of them—he tried to open one, tearing at it with his fingernails. He could not even nick it. He moved to the center of the room and sat down, hugging his knees. "Theory," he said aloud, for the datapad. "This is an alien base. Or a ship that was left behind. It contains living biological samples. It has automatic defense systems. It is programmed to investigate and neutralize technology." He chewed on a knuckle, then added, "I need more data."

He stood up and felt his way along the wall, trusting his fingers more than his eyes in this dim light to find an irregularity that might mean an opening. Then he heard a faint, wet tearing sound. He turned. Between two of the sacs, the wall had split open.

The thing, the image of himself, wormed its way into the room. Pierre noticed the arrow at once—one of Kelru's arrows, through the thing's chest. It had been shot from behind. The shaft jutted forward just where its breastbone would be, if it had been a man. "Good shot," Pierre breathed. Kelru used hunting arrows with four-bladed tips, barbed and razor-sharp. The arrowhead glistened, wet with some clear fluid.

The shaft through the thing's heart—through where its heart

should have been—did not seem to bother it. It moved forward with the same dragging step. The clear tube attached to its heel led directly into the floor and moved forward as it did.

Pierre backed away. "I come from a planet called Earth," he said steadily.

Its mouth worked. Air wheezed. "Pierre," it said in its own voice—indistinct, unhuman.

"What are you?" Pierre asked it.

"Pierre," it said again.

"No," he said. "I am Pierre."

Its mouth worked, then hung open. Dr. Kozlov's recorded voice spoke. "As for Pierre Gauthier—I have doubts as to his real abilities. But his undeniable dedication, especially since the loss of his family, may serve our purposes well."

It could not know what it was saying. "Say more."

Its chest heaved, and the croaking voice said, "Pierre." It took a step toward him, and he backed away a step. He felt the wall at his back, warm and elastic.

The thing did not drug him this time. It gripped Pierre's neck, pressing him back against the wall, pressing until blackness flickered before his eyes, until he could no longer struggle. He felt the thing's other hand rip the coveralls from his body. Then the other arm *stretched* down—impossibly far—and pulled off his boots. The pressure on his throat eased slightly, and he gasped for air. He could think—

His hand found the arrow through the thing's chest, closed around it. He worked his other hand around the shaft, gripped, bent. The arrowhead sliced his palm. The pain cleared his head, and he tightened his grip. The shaft snapped. He closed his bleeding hand around the arrowhead. He was still gasping for air. Black spots fluttered in his vision. Had it drugged him again?

Then, again, the thing forced him back against the wall, and he felt it split behind him. The thing shoved him through, twisting him, pushing him down and back into a clinging, horizontal slit barely large enough to hold him, that flexed like muscle as it closed around his body. The man-thing moved its hands swiftly along the top and bottom of the slit, and where the stroking touch passed, clear film appeared along the edges. The thing tugged both edges toward the center, and the clear film grew. Where the edges met, the film was instantly seamless. He was sealed in.

Sealed in to die. Or worse. Through the substance of the seal he saw the thing turn and move away into the shadows. Pierre kicked at the clear film. But it held.

Fluid was rising, cool against his naked back. He was sealed in, sealed away. A new sample. He had been collected.

Fear shook him, but he forced it away. The fluid rose, swirling around his shoulders. It had a musty, chalky smell. Something cold touched his ankles, then took his feet in a grip he could not break. He looked up toward the other end of the sac and saw one of the brown tubes snaking toward him through the rising fluid. It was casting around blindly. Looking for his mouth.

No. Rage filled him. He took hold of the tube, tried to push it away, but it was too strong, his hands too slippery with blood. It came on. Its blind, blunt end brushed his cheek.

He felt for the arrowhead as he wrenched his face away. His wounded right hand found it, and he slashed blindly at the film. He felt it rippling, flinching away from the cut. A slosh and gurgle—and the fluid was falling, not rising. Pierre widened the cut, then rolled out through it, into the room.

On the far side a gap in the wall was healing over. *It* had gone that way. He flung himself against the gap and wormed his way into it, feeling its rippling, muscular pressure against his body. He pushed with his shoulders and knees. Blood from his hand still gripping the arrowhead eased his passage. Darkness, pressure, and he was through.

Another room lined with sacs. One sac was clear, and lit; the thing stood facing it, watching as fluid roiled higher inside it. Sick with horror, Pierre saw Vika's hands pressed white against the inside of the sac, saw the cloudy outline of her naked body straining, straining against what held her.

He lunged forward and slashed with the arrowhead at the tube that attached the false Pierre to the floor. The thing turned, and the tube twitched under his attack. He cut, cut again, and hot strong hands gripped his hair, lifted his head, started to twist his neck. Blindly Pierre slashed a last time—

The tube parted. The hands let him go. The thing fell.

Pierre lurched to his feet, to Vika's sac, and ripped at the film with the arrowhead. Fluid gushed. "Stay back, Vika!" he said hoarsely. He pulled the gash wider, reached in and gripped her, pulled her out.

She was naked like him, wet like him, weeping like him. They clung together for a moment. He held her tightly, calming his breath, trying to slow his heart. "Are you all right?"

"All right," she said shakily.

"Thank God." Pierre made a painful sound, half-laugh, half-whimper, and buried his face in the wet tangle of her hair. "I thought I was too late."

She pulled back a little. "Where is it? The thing that looked like you?"

"I cut its connection," he said, "and it fell. There." He pointed. A glistening, undifferentiated mound lay where the thing had fallen. It diminished visibly as they watched—reabsorbing into the floor.

Vika shuddered. "It almost killed me."

"It was not killing you," Pierre said. "It was preserving you. Look." He went to one of the filled sacs and knocked away the coating on the inside of the film, as he had done before. The light came up inside, and Pierre froze with shock.

The body inside was human.

It was pale, hairless, female. Her eyes were closed. Brown, leafy tubes led into her mouth, her nose—tubes branched and spread along her limp arms and legs. Like the Windhome inhabitants in the other room. But of course this had to be—it *had* to be—

The woman's blank face twitched, and Vika cried out in shock.

"Pierre! Pierre, that's Eleni!"

He stared at the woman's face, and with cold certainty he knew Vika was right: Eleni Sadik, the team's physician. Alive. But trapped.

He turned to the next sac and cleared it. Lucas Mason. Somewhere deep in his mind, grief and horror pulsed, but for now he saw clearly, thought clearly. Lucas was alive as well. He cleared a third sac, and a fourth. Robert, from Anke's team. And—he spread his hands out on the surface of the sac. Fadma, his captain—her dark brown face twitching continually, her eyes moving restlessly under closed lids.

Vika was shaking. "We have to get them out of there."

Pierre reached out with the arrowhead—then stopped, his heart sinking. "We can't. They're alive. But what do those tubes do? How do we extract them?"

"You saved *me*," she said, tears streaking her face. "We can save them."

"You weren't attached yet," he said. "Vika, we dare not try to free them until we know more. Until we know how to save them. Vika, listen! We might kill them."

She shook her head. "Does it matter? Look at them. Don't you think they'd rather be dead than—like this?"

"Not if we might have saved them instead," he said with utter certainty. "We dare not do this. We have to know more." He started toward the next sac, and the floor lurched under him.

He fell, Vika beside him. The floor was heaving upward under them, lifting them toward the ceiling of the room. Which began to press downward.

"This way!" He crawled blindly across the heaving floor, slipping in the spilled fluid—through the wet, reeking mass where the thing had fallen. "Take my hand!" He reached back with his unhurt hand, felt Vika grip it, pulled her forward. "Through the wall," he said, and forced his way forward through the slit he had used to come in.

It admitted him. Perhaps it had to admit him—programming, or reflex. He wriggled through, dragging Vika. Yes, this was the first room—there were his boots, and his ripped coveralls.

The floor was stable in here. He staggered to the heap of fabric and tugged at it. It was stuck to the floor.

He knelt and used the arrowhead to cut away the fabric until he came to Anke's datapad. It was covered with a transparent film of the fleshy material. Pierre slit the stuff, and it jerked away. He picked up the datapad. It was no longer working. He hoped he would be able to retrieve the new data it contained. He looked up at Vika. "We must go," he said. "If we try to help the others, this place will capture us as well, and then none of us have any hope. Free—" He looked up at her. "Free, we can warn Earth. And then—later—we will find a way to help our friends."

She was shaking. "Promise me."

"You have my word," he said levelly. "Now let us go while we can."

She looked around the space where they were trapped. "Which way should we go?" She spoke in French now. Sensible, Pierre reflected; of their shared languages, French was the one this—place—could have least experience with, least chance of understanding.

"I presume that we are underground," he said. "The sounds came from underground. And that which attacked us."

"Upward, then," she said. She had control of herself now, and she looked around, wide-eyed but steady. His heart went out to her. "Think," she said, as if to herself. "This place is all tubes and cylinders and—"

"Radial symmetry." Pierre nodded. "Growth from the center outward. It is reasonable for an artifact that is grown rather than assembled."

"So there is a center somewhere."

"Which is exactly where we should not go," Pierre said. "If there is a controlling intelligence, it will be there."

Vika frowned. "Perhaps the other systems are centered, as well."

"Do you mean a sort of air intake? A tunnel?"

"Air is easy to recycle," Vika said. "So is water. But this place is warm. It produces heat. The heat must go somewhere."

"Internal cooling," Pierre said. "Not air ducts—such a system would be inefficient."

Vika shook her head. "The river."

"Of course," Pierre said. "It's too large to be meltwater from this small valley. It must come from the ground, run through this place to cool it, run up to the surface.

Vika frowned. "Would it run from the top or the bottom of this place?"

"The top," Pierre said at once. "At the center."

"So we go there. We cut our way into the water tube."

"And swim up, or be carried up," Pierre said. He did not speak the question in his mind: *How far underground are we?* "Let's go."

They pressed against the wall, and it opened for them. They passed through many chambers. In each one Pierre lifted Vika to touch the center of the ceiling. If it parted, Vika climbed through and helped Pierre follow. They found they were moving in a consistent direction. Only in that direction did they always find chambers that let them climb upward.

Finally they reached a narrow chamber that had horizontally ridged walls, as if made for climbing. The one above was the same, and the one above that. At last they came out in a warm, dim expanse that sloped downward away from them on all sides but one. The ceiling was hard and cool. It did not open when they pressed on it. And he heard a sound—

Pierre pressed his ear to the one wall, ignoring the warm, salty-smelling fluid soaking the side of his face. He heard a low, steady rushing sound. "Water!" He caught Vika's hand and kissed it. "You were right."

"It seems so." She smiled tightly. "Open that wall."

He gave her Anke's datapad. "Be ready," he said. "The flow will be strong. And we don't know how long it will take us to reach the surface."

"Suppose—" She stopped.

"Suppose what?"

"Suppose this is an intake, not an outflow," she said. Pierre knew she must be picturing what he himself feared—their bodies wedged into narrow channels inside this place. Drowned. Eaten by the system to maintain itself.

He smiled at her, a pure, unforced smile. "Dear love," he said. "They must fill the water system from the bottom, to keep bubbles out. It's a universal principle."

She blinked at him. "I see."

"Well, then. Take in several deep breaths, and empty your lungs completely each time. Then one deep breath just before we pass through. Are you ready?"

She began breathing deeply. "Yes. Go."

The wall was thick. Pierre had to dig deeply, cutting chunks of material away with the arrowhead. As they fell to the floor they melted into it almost at once. After a minute, the floor began to shudder under them. The wall trembled, twitching away from the blade. "Hurry," Vika said.

Pierre grunted and dug deeper. Then he sat back for a moment and ran his hand through his hair to dry his fingers, which were slick with his own blood. Vika stared at him. "Let me do it."

"No. My hands are stronger." He started in again, widening the hole as it tried to close around his hand. Fluid dripped from the raw edges. The shuddering in the floor became a pounding, building in intensity to a pulsing thunder. Pierre turned back to the hole, digging and slashing.

Wetness touched Pierre's hands, spread along his arm, along his body. Water, lukewarm and musty-smelling. He looked up into Vika's face. She was gripping the datapad. "Ready?"

She knelt down beside him. "Go!"

He reached into the hole again and began a steady sawing motion. Water foamed out of the hole, a trickle, then a rush, then a powerful jet. Pierre kept cutting. The wall was still trying to contract around him. Then his hand punched through into a powerful stream of water rushing upward. He shouted, "Breathe!" Then pushed forward against the pressure of the water, against the contraction of the wall around the hole. A slippery, clenching tunnel, and water beating into his face—one of Vika's hands tight on his ankle. Then he was through.

The water tore him from Vika's grip at once. It took him, flung him spinning free. He bumped the walls of the tube—rock now— once, twice, three times, raw scrapes stinging in the unclean water. Up and up, in total darkness. He had been wrong—the water was recycling, and he was going down again. *Too long, too long.* He must be going down. Through the billowing rush in his ears he heard a metallic, echoing hum that rose steadily. Fire in his chest. One more moment without breathing in. One more again. He could last still one more moment—

He burst up into air and darkness. A single instant, then back under before he had taken half a breath. But the water churned him up to the surface again. He sensed calmer water all around, and he struck out away from the bubbling rush behind him. Once he was out of the current, he rolled onto his back and swam slowly, still gasping, the buzz in his head gradually fading. Darkness. Faint yellowish light—it was the little moon, almost full. Just rising. No, just setting. It was night, but close to dawn.

He let his feet sink, and they touched gravel. He crawled out of the water, naked, shivering in the night air. "Vika!" His voice was harsh with fear. "Vika!"

No answer.

He could see well enough now in the weak moonlight. The wide outlet pond was overhung with dark, angular conifers. The center of the pond roiled where the outflow fountained up from below. Near the place where he had come ashore, the pond spilled over into the channel of the river. He staggered to that spot. If she had been knocked unconscious, perhaps he would see her wash past. "Vika!" he called again, and his voice broke on a gulping sob. He formed a prayer, blind need without words. He knew he was light-headed from shock, hunger, lack of oxygen, lack of sleep. He crouched there, staring down into the dark rushing water. Then a hand touched his naked shoulder.

He shot to his feet. It was Vika.

They held each other cautiously, because of their scrapes. Pierre pulled back first. "Are you all right?" He held her face in his hands, tracing it with trembling fingers. "I called—why didn't you answer?"

She caressed his wrist with one hand. "I was afraid they would hear," she whispered. Her other hand clutched Anke's datapad.

They were both shivering. The night breeze was chilly. "Back to camp," Pierre said. *If the camp is still there.*

They could not move fast, barefoot in poor light, over broken ground. Pierre was conscious of the ground under their feet. Conscious of a low, distant throbbing. He listened for shaking foliage, falling trees. But they encountered nothing.

The eastern sky was yellow-green when they reached the meadow where they had been captured. Raw dirt lay stirred and roiled as if it had been boiling. They skirted the edge of the meadow, leaving a dark trail behind them in the silvery, dew-wet grass. He kept a firm hold on Vika's hand. She followed steadily.

Now up the slope. The hard stone hurt Pierre's bare feet.

At last they reached the campsite. Abandoned—the ashes were cold. Pierre looked around in despair. No point in hunting for footprints in the thin soil, on the bare stone. He ran his unhurt hand through his hair. "I don't know what to do," he confessed. "I'm sorry, Vika."

"They haven't gone far," she said. "Or Kelru would have left our packs behind."

"Unless he was certain we were dead."

"He wouldn't be," she said. "Not Kelru. He would always hope."

"*For a time,*" a voice said. Pierre froze, looking up the slope.

Kelru stood there, his bow raised, an arrow on the string. Thiain stood beside him. She was holding the gun.

"It's Pierre and Vika," Pierre said, puzzled. "Thiain, put that down!"

They didn't move.

"Kelru," Pierre said. "Brother, it's me."

"So it seems," Kelru said, without moving. "But I've seen another thing that *seemed* like you...brother."

"Thiain," Vika said unsteadily, "please don't point that at us. It might go off by accident."

She didn't waver. "Prove to me," she said, "that you are Vika."

Vika sighed. "I remember the morning you dropped the tea jug, when Aghaioth bumped you. You said some words, and then you wouldn't tell me what they meant." She met Thiain's eyes. "I know now."

Kelru kept his arrow on the string. "Pierre?"

"Yes, I am Pierre," he said, exasperated. "I remember Nakhalru's womb-brother, who joined two families at once. And the Judges' Feast at the Council Hall—what you told me when you came home, after all that wine."

Kelru lowered the bow, stuck the arrow back in his quiver. "Pierre!" He came forward and embraced him. "It's good to see you alive, brother."

"You saved us, brother," Pierre said.

"I tried to," Kelru said. "I saw you both fall. And then the ground opened up. And I shot at that—thing. I hit it once at least. But it didn't stop! It took you into the earth. When I reached the place, only a hole was left, and its walls were collapsing."

Pierre nodded. "That arrow freed us both." He had lost the arrowhead, but he showed Kelru his slashed palm. "It was the only weapon we had. But it was enough."

Kelru looked at him. "Pierre. We must leave this valley. You had better agree this time."

"I do agree," Pierre said. "What we need is here." He held up Anke's datapad.

Vika moved up beside him, and he looked down into her troubled face. "But I remember my promise," Pierre said to her in French. "We will return."

TWENTY-FOUR

The return to winter shocked Pierre. He had forgotten it in the wet heat of their captivity, brief as it had been. Forgotten it in the horror of seeing their colleagues, then leaving them helpless—

It tore at Vika, too—he saw that clearly. But Pierre knew that his logic was right: he and Vika were not expendable. They must warn Earth that the destroyers of Kishar and Windhome were still active, still present on a world only twenty-six light years away.

Pierre let Kelru set the pace for their escape downriver. Kelru decided that they would ride for several days, at the risk of tiring the beasts, and camp under cover of the trees each night. Kelru and Thiain rode together on Thonn now; old Feth was weary with long winter travel, and Vika and a few almost-empty packs were burden enough for him. At midday they ate uncooked khishtuh, gritty and green-tasting. But it was food.

And they all kept glancing back the way they had come, at what they now saw framed between the twisted limbs of two trees. The copper pillar had grown upward. It rose high above the distant valley now, gleaming in the watery sunlight: a slender, unlikely structure. The knob at the top was gone—unfolded into a vast dish of netted wire. An antenna. One that could send a signal to another solar system—or anywhere. A report, or a call for backup.... Pierre did not share those thoughts with anyone.

That night they camped in a low spot among trees, out of sight of the antenna. After supper, when Thiain and Vika had gone to their beds, Pierre sat up with Kelru who had taken first watch, and told him more of what they had found inside the Destroyer installation.

"So you found some of your people, and some of ours," Kelru said, marveling. "And still living. You don't seem overjoyed, brother."

"It may not be possible to free them without killing them." Pierre watched the fire. "Vika wishes we had tried."

"Of course she does," Kelru said. "And so do you, brother, if I know you at all."

"But I don't." He reached forward and pushed a log farther into the fire. "Vika and I have talked about this. Even if severing those connections did not kill them, we would never have escaped with them by this path, in winter. They would be naked, weak, injured." He looked at Kelru. "Our first duty—Vika's and mine—is to send word to our world of what we've found here. So, brother—now we must ride south. All the way back to where we came from. It will be a hard journey, but a necessary one."

To his surprise Kelru's ears flicked assent. "I want Thiain out of the north," he said. "Even the most dangerous journey is better than wintering a few days' travel from—that." He made an oblique gesture northward.

Pierre looked away. "Once I have sent the message to my world," he said, "we can go where you like. Those new settlements on the seacoast you once talked of. Or where you choose."

"It may happen," Kelru said. His voice was remote. Then he straightened. "I have a question, brother. When you send the message, so strong and loud that it reaches your world—will the Destroyers hear it as well? Will it bring them back here in force? Not the machines we saw in that valley. The living Destroyers. And their skyships?"

Pierre closed his eyes. *Speak the truth.* "I—don't know," he said slowly. "They already know we are here. Perhaps that—place we escaped has already summoned them."

Kelru sat very still. "And will the message bring your people here, as well? Thiain believes they might help us. Is that true? Can we fight the Destroyers together?"

"Kelru, I don't know," Pierre said again, uneasy. "My people could not arrive here for many, many years—long after all of us are dead." He looked up at his brother. "Vika and I must do this. It is a matter of duty. Of an oath we both took." He took a shaking breath. *The truth.* "And for me it is a debt I owe to my son, whom I left behind. If he is alive now, he's—older than I am, physically. But perhaps he has a child of his own."

"The debt of protection to your children," Kelru said slowly. "That is a deep one, brother." He looked at Pierre, then away. He was silent for a time. Then he said, still looking at the fire, "We will return to the south."

Pierre looked down. He had asked so much of Kelru for the sake of their friendship, for the sake of their strange bond of brotherhood. Shame twisted inside him.

But this was the last sacrifice. He looked up at Kelru again, "After this is finished, you will lead us."

Kelru looked at him. "After this." His voice was quiet. They did not speak again for a long time.

Vika kept to her duty through the long weeks that followed. Kelru set the pace, and he chose what was best for Thiain, always. They traveled slowly, even stopping at midday if they found especially good shelter. Vika rested when Thiain did. Sleep buried grief.

At last the swift spring met them on its way north. The ice on the rivers broke up, forcing them out of their way to seek the narrow, railless bridges trappers built. The snow thawed each day and froze each night, forming a crust that was hard as glass, and as sharp when they broke through it, or fell. The wind became unpredictable, gusting warm from the south, then bitter cold again from the north. They began to see signs of gherrau returning north as the snow cover softened, heading for the tundra where they would feed on the rich, swift-flowering plant life and bear the young they had conceived in the first bite of autumn. Flooded out of their dens, the feotheg were everywhere, skittering nervously from shadow to shadow, eyes wide for hungry predators.

Vika and the others kept a close watch for kharag, which would be moving in packs again now that there was game in plenty. Three times they had to shoot one that came too close to their fire. One of the corpses they were able to save from its fellows, and they boiled some of the stringy meat, giving the rest to the riding beasts.

Kelru had said nothing more about what had happened to Talakh. That worried Vika.

They had to travel secretly now, which slowed them even more. They had reached country where there were roads, but they dared not use them. Fire they could not have, except at night, and carefully sheltered.

The spring rains began. The four of them were wet, always wet, even under their close-woven thessachs. The trees dripped, sodden. The kharag were pupping, and now every hollow and cave they found was occupied and fiercely defended. So at night they huddled in their avarthu, steaming where they were warm, freezing where they were cold.

Vika slept badly. She and Pierre made love a few times, in the depths of night, within the limits they had agreed on—they would not risk conceiving a child. It was a comfort, but a restrained one. One night she woke and saw Pierre sitting by the fire with his head resting on his knotted hands. Grief, or prayer. He always chose to keep this private even from her—perhaps to protect her; perhaps to protect himself. Looking at him, she wondered again what help it gave him.

But then, behind her, Thiain stirred and muttered something. Vika turned over and looked at Thiain and Kelru, sleeping nested together in their blankets. They were the seed of a new family, a frail and precious thing on Windhome. And the symbol of all that she and Pierre were placing at risk. She could guess at the source of some of Pierre's pain, because it was also the source of her own.

She closed her eyes to feign sleep, and real sleep took her at last.

"And now," Kelru said, his heart heavy, "it is time for Thiain to leave us."

It was evening, under a high, cool sky fresh with recent rain. But Kelru had not sought a place to camp. Now they stood with the beasts at the edge of a forest, looking down onto a road. A road Kelru knew. The time he dreaded had come. But first he must know that Thiain was safe.

In the half-light he looked around at the others. They all looked sadly faded. Kelru knew his own fur was matted and dull, and the flesh had sunk away beneath it, making him look half-starved. Thiain looked better—he had seen to it that she ate well. Her pregnancy, though not yet visible on her body, gave a gloss to her fur and filled out her face and breasts. But her clothes were stiff with grime, scorched and frayed. Silently he took her hand and led her aside for their farewell.

She looked up at him, a stubborn gleam in her eyes. "I tell you again, Kelru: I don't want to leave you."

Kelru brushed her cheek, tenderly, with the back of his hand. "Ekhnan is the best place for you. My birth home. Some of my mother-sisters remember me kindly, and will welcome you because of that."

"I don't want to go," she said again. "I don't want to fear for you, and not know."

He bent his head and took a deep breath of her scent. "You cannot help Pierre or Vika," he said. "Think of our children instead. As I must."

She looked into his eyes, and he guessed that she saw his meaning there. Troubled, she looked past him at Vika. But she did not speak.

"Ride to Ekhnan. Tell them whose children you carry. Wait there," Kelru said. "And I'll come for you." He caressed her cheek again. "As soon as this is over." He hoped she could not hear his grief in his voice.

This time she bowed her head in assent.

Kelru gave her Feth. Pierre helped him redistribute the packs between the remaining beasts. Thiain watched in the deepening twilight. Her eyes were lightless as ash. When Feth was ready, she turned to Vika. "Goodbye," she said. "I thank you for all you have done for me, and for my children." She did not speak to Pierre.

She went last of all to Kelru. He took her face in his hands and laid one cheek, then the other, on the top of her head. "Trust me," he whispered.

She pulled back and looked at him steadily. "I will wait to hear from you," she said in a low voice.

"I'll come for you myself," Kelru said, "and wait for you at the gate house. In an eightday, no more. Rest well."

She mounted Feth and urged him down the bank onto the road. As Kelru watched, his spirit empty, she turned Feth west, and rode away without looking back.

Vika wondered at the depth of Kelru's quiet grief. That night they traveled in silence until almost midnight. They were near now, and the country around was thick with farmholds, with fields grubbed up for planting, and pale-green pastures where huge, gaunt ashanoi and thick-fleeced khaltenu tore at the new grass, half-starved and shaky on their legs from their long winter confinement.

Kelru chose their camp in a damp hollow between two low hills. They would sleep tonight, and rest during the next day, he said; and the next night would take them to their goal. He said nothing else to them that night.

The next evening they started at sunset. It was gusty weather again, the low sun breaking through intermittently. The new-green fields, the trees with their pale dusting of new leaves, glowed in the level, golden light, then faded to gray when the sun fled. It was not far now.

Vika remembered riding this road in Dethun's train with Anke, before everything went wrong. But that had been late autumn. Now she recognized nothing. She smelled ice and wet earth, low ribbony grass, the sharp pitchy scent of conifers. The road was empty; as the hour grew later, light faded from the windows of the farmholds. Her thessach kept her warm in the bitter wind.

She rode with Pierre, in front of him on Nukh. Pierre's hand rested lightly on the back of Nukh's neck, enough to tell the beast he was in control of it; his other arm was around Vika, steadying her. She did not lean back against him. She sat straight. Kelru rode behind them, on Thonn.

Pierre talked as they rode. She heard the tension and exaltation that warred within him. They might be too late; the lander might have suffered damage from the cold, the weather. She felt Pierre's hand moving to his thessach pocket. She knew he was checking again that her datapad was still there, and the little cylinder containing the data crystals: the Anokothu records, the story of their own journey, and the data Pierre had salvaged from Anke's wrecked datapad, showing the events of their captivity.

That was all the warning they could give to their people on Earth. They would tell them all they had learned. They would tell them everything....

She felt Pierre's arm tighten around her. "I must make the upload when the ship is at its closest orbital approach to the lander. With this overcast, I can't see the ship, so I must listen for its status beam. That will give me only a few seconds' warning, and I may have to wait through another orbit so I can aim the antenna precisely."

"I understand."

"Wait below with Kelru. It will be useful to have you down there if anyone comes. You can divert them."

"I'll do what I can," Vika said. She had her duty. Fear did not matter, doubts did not matter. Kelru's silence did not matter. The mission was almost over. Darkness enfolded them.

At dawn, they were nearly there. The wind was picking up, driving low, heavy clouds before it. The pre-dawn drizzle had turned to a cold, steady, soaking rain. As the weary light came up all around them, Pierre looked around, ahead. "Where is Kelru?" She felt him turn and look back. His breath caught.

Vika twisted in the saddle and peered around him.

Someone was behind them on the road, a few hundred meters away—a mounted man riding away steadily. *Kelru*. And Vika knew this road—

"He's riding to the sisterhold," Vika said in disbelief. Then the thought, aching with grief and pity: *He's chosen his own people. His children.*

"*Kelru*," Pierre said, despair in his voice. "Nukh can't catch up to Thonn, not with two of us."

"Get down here," Vika said. "Go on to the lander. You have the command codes and the training—you *have* to do the upload and start the transmission." She looked back along the road. "I'll delay Kelru. Once you're in the lander, no one can reach you or stop you. Then it won't matter what he does."

Pierre swore foully in French. But he stopped Nukh, slid down, and unbuckled his pack from the saddle. "Go," he said tensely. "I love you."

She guided Nukh into a turn. "*Yatha!*" she snapped, and they were off.

Nukh loped forward, eager to catch up with Thonn. The road was deserted except for Kelru. Vika pulled her hood forward to shield her face from the rain.

She saw Kelru look back. He stopped Thonn and waited for her.

When she reached him, she said, "You've made a different decision, then."

Sitting very straight in the saddle, he looked at her. "My only decision was to take Thiain safely to Ekhnan," he said. "But this, your message—I cannot allow this to happen." She saw the anguish in his eyes. "I will not harm either of you. But I will ride to the sisterhold, and Dethun's men will prevent you."

She looked at him, anger and fear a tight mass in her chest. "Don't do this."

"Ride with me," Kelru said. "If you're under my protection, Dethun's men won't harm you."

"No, Kelru," she said unsteadily. "I can't let you do this."

Kelru looked at her, his sadness clear to see. "I'm only doing as you and Pierre have done," he said. "I'm protecting my people, and my family. At any cost."

She pulled her hand out of her pack, and let Kelru see the gun. "I'll stop you," she said.

His ears flicked forward and back. "You won't hurt me."

"I don't have to hurt you," she said. "I'll kill Thonn, and then Nukh. By the time you reach the sisterhold on foot, it will be too late."

Kelru's hands tightened on Thonn's neck fur. "Vika," he said, "I know you. You have doubts. Let me go. Let me stop Pierre. Then perhaps we can find another way."

"There is no way," Vika said. "No way that's right for us both." The gun, aimed at Thonn's chest, trembled as her hand trembled.

Kelru's ears went back. He hissed. Thonn gathered himself and leaped away.

"Stop!" Vika shouted, raising the gun. Kelru did not look back.

She knew, bitterly, that she should have been ready. She should already have taken steady aim, as she'd been taught, so that she could squeeze off one careful shot while Thonn was still in easy range. She fired, aiming for Thonn's legs.

She missed completely. Kelru and Thonn both jerked in surprise, and Kelru turned to look back at her. He seemed to be trying to stop Thonn, turn him, in that last instant. Too late. Her second shot struck

Thonn in the flank, splashing a wet, bloody patch on the dun fur. Thonn screamed, thin and high and breathy, and pitched forward as his legs gave under him. Then he sagged to one side, and Kelru rolled clear.

He did not get up.

Vika cried out his name, forced Nukh up the road to where Kelru lay, sprawled half in the ditch. She slid down and Nukh scrambled away, squealing. She threw herself down beside the man in the ditch. "Kelru!"

He was still conscious. He looked up at her and frowned slightly—puzzled? Dazed? She lifted his thessach aside, and her heart chilled and shrank within her. The shot that killed Thonn had first struck Kelru in the upper thigh, shattering the bone, severing an artery.

She wadded up part of the thessach and pressed it into the center of the wound, and the spurting stopped. Kelru gave a strangled sob of agony as bone fragments ground together under the pressure of her hands. She must not think about that. She had to save him. The wound was high on his leg. There must be a femoral artery—she could press on that, cut off the flow of blood. But she did not know where it was. She was afraid to lift her hands from their pressure on the wound. He was still bleeding, a slow unstoppable welling. She moved the pressure higher, into his groin. The bleeding slowed. But blood still pooled in the folds of his thessach, mixing with the rain, soaking away irretrievably into the thessach and the ground below. She was crying, saying over and over, "I'm sorry—I'm sorry—" But she was speaking in Standard, and by the time she realized it, Kelru had lost consciousness.

Later—how much later, she did not know—she realized that the bleeding had stopped. She was weak with relief, until she looked at Kelru's face again. Slack and empty, the eyes partly open. She lifted her hands away. There was no bleeding at all.

He was gone. He had bled to death.

She had killed him.

Twenty-Five

Pierre touched the screen of the comm in the lander. It pulsed beneath his palm—warm, gleaming, alien. He had forgotten about the smoothness of things made on Earth, how square and clean they were. After all the terror of their long journey, all they had risked and lost, it had been such a simple thing to transfer all their data to the lander's systems, along with a recorded message describing their journey and what they had learned; to upload it to the ship in orbit; and then to send the command codes to begin the transmission.

And now it was done. This part of their mission was done. Pierre looked blankly down at his hands—scarred, dark with ingrained dirt—resting on the clean, smooth surface in front of him. "Shut down all systems," he said, and the screen went dark. The stored power would last for years. He looked around the compartment. Some of this might be worth salvaging, if they ever had opportunity. And the other projectile weapons—

No. Let them stay here, doubly inaccessible inside the lander, in their sealed locker. He did not want them to fall into the hands of the Council of Eight.

In the end he took only a few things that he had not brought: a new medkit, another datapad for himself, a few tools. Perhaps other things would be of use in the years to come, but for now they were safest left here. Maybe some of the other humans would come here, if they lived, if he and Vika could save them. But for him the lander was too strange now. It belonged to a world he had left, that he no longer wanted to remember. With relief he pulled open the hatch, and a gust of rain spattered in. He looked out and down, expecting Vika.

Waiting below, looking up at him from the center of a ring of bowmen, was Ganarh.

They told him nothing on the way to the sisterhold. They treated him as if he were an animal, dragging him through the mud when he stumbled. Through the gate, along the wall, down a dark passage—and he was back again, back in the cell where he had waked to meet Kelru. Full circle. The end.

Except that Kelru was not there. It was Vika who waited, a small huddle under her thessach. She looked up at him with a strange, fierce expression. He saw that her face was dirty, her thessach streaked brown. With sudden fear he realized that it was blood. Even her hands were bloody—old blood, dried to a crust.

Slowly, in a soundless nightmare, he went to her and knelt beside her. Slowly, he took her cold hands in his. "Are you hurt?" He could feel his heart pounding. He knew, he knew— "What happened?" She would not look at him. He reached up and turned her face toward him. "Where is Kelru?"

"Kelru is dead," she said in a dull voice.

The words did not sound real. "Impossible," he said. "Vika—"

"He was coming here," she said. "To give us to Dethun. He told me he had to do it, for Thiain and their children. I couldn't stop him." She spoke slowly, frowning down at her bloody hands as if they puzzled her. "So I shot Thonn. I wanted to make Kelru walk. Just—to slow him down, you see? …But I hit Kelru, too. And he bled to death. I couldn't save him."

Pierre had stood up, though he did not remember it. Now he leaned heavily against the wall, his palms pressed against the rough boards. "Oh,

Jesus," he said. His legs would not hold him, he slid down the wall and sat on the floor. Then he buried his face in his arms, and wept for Kelru.

No one came for them that day. Pierre passed from blind, hopeless sorrow into an exhausted numbness that seemed much like Vika's.

Vika, whom he could not save. They were in Dethun's stronghold, in Dethun's power. And Vika had killed Dethun's son. At a word from Dethun, she would die. Perhaps there would be some kind of trial first. But Dethun's men had found Vika beside Kelru's corpse, with his blood on her hands. And she had confessed.

That night they slept close together for warmth, but separated by a silence that might never be broken again. In the morning, Ganarh came. The door rattled open, and he filled the doorway, gray and severe. He pointed a finger at Pierre. "You. Out."

Pierre looked back once as the door closed between himself and Vika. Her face was as calm and still as if she had already died.

Ganarh took Pierre to Dethun, in the secret room inside the wall where he had seen her once long before. But Vakhar was there as well this time, and one or two others of the Council. Ganarh wrenched Pierre's arm behind him, stopping him in the center of the little room. Dethun faced him, flanked by the men of the Council. Perhaps it was seeing her among men, not women—or perhaps there was another reason. But she seemed somehow diminished. Smaller, and older. She looked at him with Kelru's red-gold eyes, and Pierre caught his breath. When his eyes were clear again he said, "Why am I here? What are you going to do with Vika?"

Ganarh struck him, hard, over the ear. Pierre reeled, then straightened, his head ringing.

Vakhar spoke. "In the matter of Kelru's death," he said. "We must ask certain questions. You traveled with the woman Vika. Is she your mate?"

Pierre looked at them all, at their hard inimical faces. "What difference does it make?"

"Much," Vakhar said. "If she is unfamilied, she alone is responsible for Kelru's death, and she is the one who must die. But if you are mated, the Lady Dethun is free to choose either of you for her blood payment."

"When this law was explained to Vika," Dethun said harshly, "she claimed that you are not mated. But I don't trust her word. I require your own answer."

Pierre stared at her, then looked away. Vika had lied to Dethun.

Lied to her to save him.

He thought of Vika now, waiting in her cell. He realized he did not know how such executions were carried out—with a knife, or.... He thought about Vika, waiting for Ganarh to bring her the death she wanted. That she believed she deserved.

He looked up at Dethun. "We are bondmates," he said, and then in French, "She is my wife." As he spoke the words a weight seemed to lift from him.

Dethun turned to Vakhar. "You hear. He claims her."

"I hear," Vakhar said.

She went on harshly, "And so I claim him. *He* is the one who caused the death of my son. Last summer, when he beguiled Kelru into becoming his friend, his brother—here in this room. *He* is the one to blame." Her deep voice trembled with passion. "I choose Pierre."

"It is not quite so simple," Vakhar said. He turned to Pierre. "You freely claim Vika as your bondmate, knowing that it will mean your death?"

Knowing that Vika would live. He thought of her, going on, finding her way. He thought of her, given a chance to heal, to find peace, to make her peace with God, or Gaia, or herself. Vika would live. His eyes filled with tears and he said unsteadily, "Yes. She is my bondmate. Since last winter."

"But there are no witnesses to your mating," Vakhar said. "Dethun, I cannot consent to this unless—"

"There is a witness," Pierre said. "Thiain, once of this sisterhold. She is—she was Kelru's bondmate. She carries his children. And she is at Ekhnan now."

Dethun was before him, her strong hands gripping his shoulders. "This is true? Thiain is pregnant by my son?"

"Yes," Pierre said. "And she knows that Vika and I were mated. She can testify to it."

Dethun turned to Ganarh. "Have her brought here," she said harshly. "Now."

But Vakhar interposed. "Dethun, you do not consider: a death in a family such as yours is a matter for the Council of Eight. To be judged properly, in Kheosseth. There the testimony of Kelru's mate can be taken in the proper way, and a right decision made." He glanced at Pierre. "Then, in a few days, you will have what you desire."

Dethun took a long, shuddering breath and let go of Pierre, almost pushing him away. "Kelru must be burned," she said. "And then I will come to Kheosseth, and this matter will be settled there." She looked at Pierre, and he saw nothing of Kelru in her eyes now. "I will watch you die," she said coldly. And went out.

Vakhar turned to Pierre. "You've made your choice," he said. "If the woman you named confirms your mating with Vika, then in a matter of days you will be dead."

"What will happen to Vika?" Pierre asked quietly.

"Dethun talked of taking her as a body-servant," Vakhar said, "if she were to live." He seemed to hesitate. "I must take you to Kheosseth with me, today. Dethun hates you. I don't dare leave you in her power, until the proper time comes."

"May I see Vika once more?" Pierre asked.

"No," Vakhar said. "We leave now. She'll learn what you have done. But not until it's too late." He looked somberly at Pierre. "If she is truly your bondmate, if you are friends, that's kinder."

Pierre looked down, hiding anguish. He had wished to see Vika. He was afraid for her, alone in grief. He wanted to tell her to forgive herself. To heal, and hope—and to forget him. He had only hurt her.

But the choice was not his. He looked up at Vakhar. "I'm ready," he said. And hoped that his courage would last.

Vika knew nothing of what had happened until Ganarh came for her that afternoon. She rose, unsteady with hunger, and waited for what he would do next. But he said, "You're to come. You're to wash and have clean clothes."

She wanted to ask if this was a ritual to prepare for death. But she did not trust her voice, and she would not shame herself in front of him. She followed him, and he handed her off at the inner gate to a woman she remembered vaguely. The woman took her to a hearthroom, gave her food, helped her bathe, dressed her from the skin out in clean, worn clothes of sisterhold green—green as new grass, green as hope. She wondered if they would kill her in these good clothes. It seemed a waste. The woman answered no questions.

Then they took her into the courtyard before the main gate. She had time for one surge of shameful fear before she understood what was happening: those mounted men were an escort. That closed wagon ahead bore the eight-rayed sun, Dethun's mark—Dethun must be inside. And that cart behind—

She found herself bundled onto the cart, up beside the sullen driver, one of Ganarh's men. The gates opened, and they started out. "Where are we going?" she asked.

The driver seemed astonished that she would speak to him, or that she could speak at all. He picked his teeth with a claw and said, "To Ekhnan."

Kelru's family farmhold. "Why?" Was that where she was to die?

"Why?" the driver echoed. "Look back." He jerked a thumb over his shoulder.

She turned in her seat and looked down, and her breath caught.

In the back of the cart, Kelru lay—his face uncovered, his eyes of course open. They did not close the eyes of their dead. It would blind the trapped spirit, which waited to be freed by fire when the body was burned.

She looked down at him for a long time, as Dethun no doubt had intended. His eyes were dull, the eyes of death. They did not reflect the sky. She wondered for a moment if it might be true—if Kelru's spirit was still there, looking up at her—hating her....

They rumbled along in silence as the sun sank lower. Small, pale yellow flowers bloomed in some of the hedges; their sweet fleeting scent came and went with the shifting wind.

Vika kept her eyes rigidly forward all the way to Ekhnan. The procession turned in at the gate house, and the cart's driver climbed down. Another man, a stranger who must be one of Kelru's fathers, muttered with the driver for a moment, then climbed up beside her. Ganarh's men stayed behind, but the wagon and the cart started off again, up a narrow graveled road planted on both sides with tall, blue-green conifers.

They came to the cluster of houses when the sun was just touching the western mountains, gilding streaks of cloud in the vast, cool sky. Vika smelled riding animals. A wide bare space just showed the green of new plants coming up—a kitchen garden? Barns, storehouses, off there in the corner a mating hut, and there a substantial, two-storied house, with many windows facing outward. The cart stopped behind the wagon, in the center of the courtyard before the house. A group of women came out of the house and hurried to the wagon. The man beside Vika climbed down saying, "Go into the house," and went to the back of the wagon himself.

A thin and silent girl met Vika at the door, then led her up narrow stairs, down a passage to a small, dark room. It had one tall window facing north. The sky outside was opalescent, the last sunlight a faint glimmer on a few high clouds. The girl left Vika there, telling her, "Wait here for Dethun."

Vika waited, alone with the tall, narrow shelves of books, the low, bare worktable, the neat stacks of papers. The room was quiet, and smelled of dust. The little stove held no fire. The girl had left her no light. Vika knelt on the worn floorboards by the table. She stared at the window until the rectangle of sky was blue-black, sparkling with a drift of stars. It was cold. The cold did not matter.

Then the door opened, and Dethun came in with a lamp. Vika rose stiffly. Dethun bent to set the lamp on her worktable, and then turned, at last, to face her prisoner. She wore her green thessach still, dusty with travel. She said nothing.

Vika sighed. *Courtesy hardly matters now.* "How is Thiain?"

"She grieves bitterly for her bondmate," Dethun said. "She is resting tonight, for her children's sake. You will never see her again."

Vika nodded once, her eyes closed.

"Now we must conclude our business," Dethun said. "There are, alas, other demands on my time."

"What do you want of me?" Vika's throat ached. "I didn't want Kelru to die. I would rather have died myself."

"I would also have been satisfied with that," Dethun said.

Vika shivered. "Did you bring me here to kill me?"

Dethun looked down at her, her eyes ash. "Are you ready to die?"

"Yes," Vika said thinly. "I loved your son. I would have saved him if I could."

"Spare me your lies," Dethun said. "I am grieving for Kelru. For my youngest child." She kept her red-gold eyes, her son's eyes, on Vika. "Yet you come here expecting to be punished, do you? To hear me curse you, so you can say, *That debt is paid*, and die in peace?"

"The debt can't be paid," Vika said, tears cold on her face.

"You are partly right," Dethun said. "*You* cannot pay it. But it will be paid."

Vika looked up at her, and her breath drained away. *Pierre.*

"Yes," Dethun said with satisfaction. "I've chosen your bondmate to die in your place."

Vika knotted her hands at her sides, did not break down. Dethun looked at her almost hungrily, her eyes bright. "It was an easy choice," she said. "My son died because Pierre came to this world. My son died because all Pierre's talk of learning to understand us, studying the wealth of our history—all that was lies. Kelru died because you do *not* understand us. You do not value us. We aren't people, to you—not even Kelru, whom you say you loved. You have learned nothing. You can learn nothing. You should go home."

Vika could not look at her. "I want to go home," she said in a white whisper. "But I can't."

"Then stay in our world, and serve me," Dethun said. "But when you die, I will bury your dead flesh in the dirt. Your spirit will never be free on the wind."

At that moment it began—a thin, keening cry, joined almost at once by other cries, and more, and more, from above and below, from outside the house and inside, until the air shivered with it. It snatched Vika's breath from her. The hair on her neck stood up. Dethun was silent. She stood watching Vika calmly, and beneath that gaze Vika could not allow herself to give way. She waited, somehow, until the sound had died down far enough to permit speech. "My son is coming home," Dethun said. "Our house is ready, and Kelru's fathers have gathered to bring him inside."

Vika went to the window and looked out. People holding torches filled the courtyard below, and in the dim, hot light she saw a group of men bearing Kelru's body into the house.

"He'll lie here for a day," Kelru's mother said. "For the watch-feast, and so those who knew him have time to come here. Tomorrow at sunset, we give him to the wind. You will stay as well. You will enter my service when we return to the sisterhold. But for now, you will keep out of my sight."

Vika tried. They gave her a room to herself to sleep in, with a fire, and she sat by the hearth all that long night. She sat silently, too numb to weep for Pierre—for what she and Pierre had found, so briefly, that now was lost forever. Too numb to weep even for Kelru, lying still in the great room below.

She knew that Thiain would not come to her. No one came.

Toward dawn, Vika crept out and down the steep stairs, keeping close to the wall, and looked in at the door of the great hearthroom. Many of Kelru's family were there, some sitting silently against the wall, others standing in little groups, talking quietly. She could not see Thiain.

A space remained around the place where they had laid Kelru, still wrapped in his cloth, on the bench farthest from the fire. Vika had expected a ring of watchers, and lamplight on his face. But it was in darkness, and the body, Kelru's body, was simply *there*—as casually as if he were sleeping, a little out of the way, while others discussed important matters.

The rough wood wall pressed against her back, frigid, immovable. Real. The corpse in there was also real. But she saw, all at once, that Kelru was in that room not as a corpse, but as a person remembered—a son, a brother, a neighbor, real as long as they talked of him, remembered him. The body did not matter. It was no longer Kelru.

She slept a while in her room as the slow day dawned, rose to noon, crept toward evening. They brought her no food. She sought none. She could not have eaten it, not in that house she had wronged.

She saw them go out, at midafternoon, to bear the body up the mountain to the place where it would be burned. All of them went—women and men and children, down to the babies mewling in their slings. Vika stayed in the silent house almost until sunset. Then, taking her thessach, she went out into the courtyard and out through the gate.

She walked up the graveled road until she could see the place Kelru had once spoken of—eastward, high on the mountainside, at the brink of a sheer gray cliff. At the moment the sun sank out of sight behind her, while its long red light still warmed the face of the cliff, she saw the fire at last. She stood on the floor of a rising sea of shadow, and watched the spark grow. It was high, and distant, and it brightened as the night crept over it. She watched it burn, remembering Kelru lighting a lamp, his hand cupping and shielding the flame. She walked back and forth along the road, remembering Kelru.

After two or three hours, the dot of light dimmed, spread, lengthened into a stream down the face of the cliff—a stream of light and sparks that faded...wavered...and went out.

He was gone. Even his ashes were gone. She walked back in the dark to the empty house.

TWENTY-SIX

Vika took up her work for Dethun as the slow spring reached the hills, a late echo of the spring on the valley floor. The spring when Kelru had died. Water dripped steadily from the eaves over her window. Icicles formed at night, to melt again each morning. She was provided with a small room near Dethun's, with plain clothing and bedding, with regular meals of a quality most people in this world never experienced. She was alone. Spring became summer, and still she slept poorly. She grieved for Kelru, and for her own guilt in his death, but she kept herself from weeping. She showed Dethun only courtesy and a rigid calm; she rarely spoke to anyone else.

Near midsummer, Vika finally learned from one of the kitchen women that Pierre had not after all been killed. Her practiced numbness kept her from showing the woman, or anyone, what the news meant to her. The woman's explanation of why Dethun had not taken Pierre's life for Kelru's had been confused, obviously received at third or fourth hand. But she could ask no one for the truth of the matter. Dethun had threatened Vika with a beating if she even spoke Pierre's name. And the kitchen woman had known nothing of what had happened after that—of where Pierre had gone.

Because he must have gone. Kheosseth must still be closed to him, and there was nowhere else he might have found refuge. Unless he had gone over the mountains with Nakhalru, as Kelru had once hoped they all would.

In any case, he was far from here, and surely he was relieved to be rid of her. She had murdered Kelru, his friend and brother. She wished him peace.

Dethun required the most menial personal services of Vika, as if hoping to anger her; but Vika did not care. Dethun's disdain meant nothing. She washed Dethun's hands and feet, tended her clothing, emptied her chamber pots, and felt nothing. They rarely spoke to each other. Dethun spoke of Thiain only once in Vika's hearing, saying that she was doing well at the Ekhnan farmhold; that her children would be born in late autumn. But the words seemed to give Dethun no pleasure. Vika guessed that Dethun's heart was as empty as her own.

Summer passed, and the early autumn festival, the harvest feast, drew near. Vika worked hard, as Dethun commanded her, to help with the preparations. On the morning of the feast she was crossing the inner courtyard of the Lady's stables when she heard a riding beast's squeal. She glanced up and saw one of the stable-women cursing and wrenching at the ear of an old, grizzled animal, which was pressing against the barrier of its enclosure, straining toward Vika.

Vika stopped abruptly. It was Feth.

She dropped the Lady's clean laundry in the dust with a thump. With unsteady steps she crossed the courtyard—Feth quieted as she came. As she reached the barrier he twisted away from the stable-woman's grip on his ear and butted his huge, rough head against Vika's chest.

The stablewoman, a tall, black-furred southerner, said in her purring accent, "You know this beast?"

"I did once," Vika said, caressing his ears. Thonn was dead, Nukh was—she did not know where Nukh was. But here was Feth. "How did he come here?"

"A gift to the Lady, two days ago," the woman said. "Or so the man who brought him said. But as you see, the beast is almost worthless, old as he is."

Vika dug her fingers into the fur behind one of Feth's ears. "He's stronger than he looks."

The stable-woman lifted her hands in a shrug. "Perhaps. The Lady seemed to know him as well, and she said he's of no use alive. She wants his hide for a new bed-covering, she says, and his meat for the younger beasts."

"Poor Feth," Vika muttered, scratching him harder. Thiain must have sent him here from Ekhnan. Strange that she would give up this tie to Kelru by sending him to Dethun, her enemy. But then, perhaps it was an ill-meant gift—a gift from the right hand. After all, Feth had eaten man-flesh....

"If you're so fond of him," the woman said impatiently, "come tomorrow and say your farewells. I've work enough today."

Vika returned to her morning's work, which was harder than before. Touching Feth had waked memories of last winter—of Kelru, and of Pierre and their brief happiness—and she had to order her thoughts, concentrate on her work, to keep back a scalding tide of regret and sorrow. Better to be numb inside—to be dead inside. Maybe she would perfect it, in time.

But that night, as she walked in near-darkness, in the slow procession of women into the feast hall—it was then that someone behind her pressed a piece of folded paper into her hand. She closed her fingers over it, glanced back, but saw no one watching her. After months in a sisterhold she knew better than to look at the paper then. She slipped it into a pocket of her shabby green child's dress.

All through the feast, as she stood behind the Lady's chair, she was conscious of little but the paper in her pocket. It was a long feast, meant to last until midnight, and it nearly did. But at last the Lady dismissed her, and Vika went off to her small room, careful not to hurry.

Once there, she lit a rushlight and unfolded the paper. Black ink, bold strokes. It had been so long since she'd read the language of Windhome that at first she could not make it out. Then she could not let herself believe it. The note said, *Take Feth from the stables and come to me. Western coast. Third farmhold south of the point called the Sleeping Woman. Thiain.*

Thiain! But Thiain was at Ekhnan. Then Vika frowned at the note. Thiain was at Ekhnan—or so Dethun had told her.

Thiain would never forgive Vika. Or so Dethun had told her.

With sudden, wild hope, Vika held the note to the flame of the rushlight and burned it to ash.

Vika left the sisterhold just before dawn. Feth had come to her quietly in the dark stable, letting her saddle him as she had done so often before. Getting past the guard at the outer gate cost her two of the square copper coins she had stolen from Dethun's worktable. She paid with an inner smile.

The coming autumn hung in the air, a fresh, damp chill, smelling of turned earth. Feth moved quickly, well rested. Someone had been tending him carefully, that was certain. And then Thiain had sent him to her, and summoned her. Thiain, who had apparently left Ekhnan, left Dethun's power, and struck out into her own life again. Vika wondered how many other lies Dethun had told her.

It pleased Vika to think that Thiain had escaped. Gone west over the mountains, to the new country there, as all of them had hoped to do. A hard life, Kelru had said. But out of reach of danger. And hard work could build a farmhold there. So Kelru had said.

It had occurred to her last night, as she drifted to sleep, that perhaps—if he was alive—Pierre would be there as well. But now she knew it would be unwise to hope for that. He might well be dead, of some random cause; or drawn into some other life. And if he was there, there was no reason to hope that he would welcome her.

Vika traveled as Kelru had taught her to travel, by back roads and forest paths, in the hours around dawn and sunset. She traveled alone, trusting to the deepening cold to keep her safe from kharag. She had studied a map in Dethun's workroom, and she knew the way to the pass. In two frosty eightdays of travel she reached the mountains, crossed the pass through their vast gray silence, and found her way down to the coastal plain on the other side. There were few other travelers to avoid—the pass might be choked off by snow any day now.

The map had shown that the clean land on the coast lay to the south between the mountains and the sea. The land there was being farmed for the first time by new families moving west from the river plain. Vika traveled more quickly now. Feth's strength still held up, and through the dark rains and raw nights Vika was sustained by her hope of seeing Thiain again—her hope that Thiain was at peace.

In the late afternoon of the twentieth day, Vika passed inland of the promontory called the Sleeping Woman, and for the first time the road took her right down to the edge of the sea. She had known that the sea ruled this world's weather, the ebb and flow of its energy. But seeing it now in the wet, leaden coastal autumn, she was awed. The seas of Earth had been nearly dead, outside the seaweed farms. Now for the first time in her life she saw true wild ocean, a vastness of sullen gray water that humped itself up into greenish waves, cloudy with plankton, and fell thunderously on the steep gravel shore. She gazed at it in wonder.

From here she could reach Thiain's farm by nightfall. But now Vika found that she was afraid to go there—afraid to face Thiain, whom she had wronged so deeply. Perhaps Thiain had asked her to come so far only to tell her that, and turn her away. Vika's fear made it seem possible, even likely.

But the time had come. She ate a sparse meal of the last of the dried fish she had stolen from Dethun's kitchens. Then she mounted Feth and rode slowly south along the verge of hard sand, in the salt mist. She watched the little furry flying lizards, pale ones called *akhiakurr*, dive for fish in the waves, and thought. She would not ask Thiain's forgiveness. To burden her with that expectation would be wrong.

Feth's steps slowed and Vika allowed it. But she came to the end of her journey all the same. The third farmhold south of the point....

Thiain's farmhold looked unpromising in the murky light of a wet evening. The sea lay at least a kilometer away here, but the air was still sharp with it, the land glistening wet as if with spray. Where the track turned in off the main road, the fields were being planted with tubers. No one was working them so late in the day, but piles of cut tubers lay here and there on the raw grubbed earth, beside mounds of sodden ashes that must once have been trees and brush.

Vika dismounted for the last approach to the house. Under the low trees that lined the path, it was already night. She smelled smoke before she saw the house—small and simple, with a smoke-hole rather than a chimney. The barn was more of a shed, and the place where the mating hut should stand was only a round pit ringed with a half-laid stone wall. The pit, full of rainwater, reflected the heavy clouds that glowed greenish-gray with the last daylight.

She heard voices inside the house. Hesitantly, she scratched at the door, and the voices stopped. The door opened partway. A tall, bony adolescent peered out at her—a boy too old to be a son of the house. A bondmate, then. His knife was drawn, and he looked at Vika with suspicion.

"I ask to share your fire," Vika said.

The boy was staring at her. She put back her hood, and the boy gasped. "It's all right," Vika said. "There's a woman here who knows me."

Then Thiain appeared. Late pregnancy had changed her, more than just the high, wide burden of her belly; her face was round, her fur looked darker— Thiain flung the door wide, and warmth and firelight streamed out. "Come in," she said hoarsely. "Come in, Vika."

At a gesture from Thiain, the boy came out with obvious reluctance and took Feth, leading him away toward the barn. But Vika could not move. She was afraid. "Why did you send for me?" She had no voice to ask, *What do you want from me?*

"Come in," Thiain said again, impatiently. "You're cold. You need a fire, and some tea."

Thiain settled Vika on a skin rug by the fire and gave her tea in a wooden bowl. Vika's hands shook as she tried to drink it. She looked around. No one else was in the house just now. It was a big rectangle of rough mortared stone, with upper walls of logs snugly chinked with clay and moss. There was a loft and sleeping shelf at each end. A high worktable stood near two small glazed windows; a low table for meals stood near the fire, at Vika's elbow. Over the fire hung a copper pot like the one Kelru had once owned. Vika smelled fish, and smoke, and woolen clothes hung up to dry.

Thiain came and lowered her bulk onto a stool near Vika, leaned forward and stirred the pot. "I sent for you," she said, "for Pierre's sake."

Vika closed her eyes. "So he's here." *He's here*. She needed to stop, think this through, absorb the news—

"Oh, yes," Thiain said. "He and Nakhalru went downcoast this morning to buy more fish to dry for the winter, but they'll be home for supper."

Vika found that she was crying. She had spilled the tea—she felt the hot liquid soaking into the front of her tunic. "Does he know?" Her voice cracked. "Did you tell him I was coming?"

"*I* didn't know you were coming. I only hoped." Thiain touched Vika's cheek with one finger. "I so hoped."

"You did?" Vika said faintly. "Thiain—why? When I was the one who—" She had no voice to say more.

Thiain looked at her for a moment. "I still grieve for him."

Vika could not say, to Thiain, that she grieved, too. Instead she said, her voice low and tight, "I know."

Thiain stirred the pot again and said, "Pierre wanted you here. He and I discussed it. He said he would ride to fetch you in the spring." She sat with her knees spread wide to make room for the burden of her belly. "But I knew you could be here sooner—if you were willing to come alone. I wanted you here sooner. It isn't easy to face childbirth with no other woman in the house." Her face was shadowed for a moment.

"I think it will go well," Vika said quietly.

"It will be easier to hope, with you here to tell me that," Thiain said, her ears still. Then she seemed to gather herself. "And Pierre—he's been grieving, I've been grieving—we are a pair of useless people. With a lot of work to do.... And so I contrived a way for you to come here. A friend I made at Ekhnan, and another I still had at the sisterhold—they brought you Feth, and my message. And you came. He'll be pleased." Her ears flicked back and forth. "Why are you still crying? You're safe now."

At that moment Vika heard voices outside the house door. She looked toward it, paralyzed, voiceless. The door opened, and Pierre came in. He saw her—then leaned his weight against the doorframe, as if for support. At first it seemed that he could not speak, either. Then he said, "Vika." His voice shook.

Vika found herself on her feet. She wanted to run to him, but—He was looking at her, his face stiff with suppressed emotion. Through her tears she saw that he was not quite as thin as he had been in the spring. Where his sleeves were rolled back, his forearms were corded with muscle. His beard was neatly trimmed, but his hair had grown long. His eyes searched her face.

Vika looked down at the floor, took a breath, and said, "I didn't know where you were."

"I would have written," Pierre said. "But it would have endangered you. And the rest of us."

A tall figure loomed in the doorway, firmly guided Pierre inside, and closed the door. It was Nakhalru, dry amusement on his yellow-furred face. "I wasn't surprised," he said. "I smelled Feth as we passed the barn."

Vika stared at him, then at Thiain. "How did you all come here? How did Pierre escape from the Council of Eight?"

Pierre walked to the worktable and mechanically washed his hands in a bowl of water standing ready there. "I did not escape," he said while his back was turned. "I offered Dethun my life. But first

Vakhar insisted that I must prove that I had the right—that I was your bondmate."

"And so Pierre called on me as witness to that," Thiain said. "Dethun agreed to let me speak, because she thought I would be as bitter against Pierre as she was. I came to Kheosseth, and I told the Council that Pierre was your bondmate. But then I reminded them he had been mated to another woman as well. To Anke."

"But they knew that," Vika said. "I don't see—"

Thiain continued placidly, "And then I told them what I learned from the sisterhold guards who took me to Kheosseth. That Dethun had *ordered* Anke's death. Arranged it, when Anke came to her house asking for me."

"For you," Vika said slowly. "Because—because she was pregnant."

"I never saw her that night," Thiain said quietly. "Dethun sent me away. But I think she would have asked me to help her end it." Thiain looked past Vika. Vika turned and saw that Pierre had come to the fire. He did not approach her; he walked to the hearth and stood looking into the flames, as if searching for words.

When he looked up at Vika, his eyes were somber. "Thiain was the one most wronged by Kelru's death. More wronged than Dethun, even though Dethun had claimed right of revenge. So Thiain's words carried weight with the Council. And that changed everything. Because Dethun had ordered her servants to kill Anke, the killing was Dethun's act, not her servants'. *She* was personally liable for the blood debt, not they." He took a breath. "And...and the debt had never been paid."

No. "So, when I killed Kelru—" Vika's voice broke.

Pierre looked at her sternly. "And so, when Kelru died, by accident but at your hands, it was by right of vengeance. Dethun's son, in exchange for your fellow bondmate. There was no crime."

Vika turned to Thiain. "Why?" she asked in a choked voice. "Why did you do that for Pierre? And why did you help *me*?"

"Because I would not let Kelru's death serve Dethun's lies about us all, and about your people," Thiain said. "I was bitter. I was angry. But I know right thinking, and in time my anger passed." She gave Vika another bowl of tea. "Sit down again. Rest," she said in a gentle voice. "You've had a long journey."

Vika sank down on the rug again, drank some of the tea without tasting it. "But how did you come here? All of you?"

"I never intended to give birth at Ekhnan," Thiain said. "The people there are kind. But it was Dethun's house, too; she was free to come and go. And these children I carry are all that is left of Kelru." She looked somberly at Vika. "I knew Dethun would take my children from me, and drive me out. I did not wish to go back there after my testimony."

"And you were freed," Vika said to Pierre. "Where did you go?"

"Nakhalru's house," Pierre said. "We talked about Thiain. And he said—"

"I said I wanted to leave," Nakhalru said. "All sour, it was, serving that Council after Kelru left."

"And Thiain consented to go." Pierre looked at Vika. "Nakhalru wrote to Dethun, asking permission to visit you. She answered that you wanted to be left in peace. And I—I knew I had failed you.... And Nakhalru and I had to get Thiain across the mountains while she could still travel safely, and when there would be enough time to build shelter before autumn." He shook his head. "I would have come for you after the children were born, as soon as the pass opened in spring. I would not have returned without you."

Thiain moved to Pierre and touched his cheek with the back of one hand. "You were grieving," she said to him. "I knew Vika would be as well. I saw no reason to let it go on until next spring."

Pierre turned and faced Vika, at last. "We came here in early summer," he said. "Nakhalru had land-right from his Council service, and Thiain had Kelru's money, the bonding gift his family kept for when he joined a family. We've built all this since then—with Odhru's help. He's Nakhalru's cousin, and Kelru's brother—son of his mother-sister Akhian, who helped Thiain escape."

"And while they were all so busy, I wrote to you," Thiain said to Vika. "I gave you the chance to come to us. And you used it, as I thought you would." Her ears pricked up in a smile. "I'm glad."

But when Vika looked at Pierre, his eyes were troubled.

She sat beside Pierre at supper. Though he said little, though he still had not touched her, she was deeply conscious of his nearness—of the line of his body as he sat, and the firelight on his lean, tired face. She fought to steady her breathing. There was not quite enough air in the room. Out of the corner of her eye she saw a faint flush on Pierre's cheek, and he shifted a little as he sat. The others talked of farm matters. But Pierre was silent.

She offered to help with the washing up, but Thiain refused. "Sit and rest," she said, "and talk to Pierre. He's missed you." She collected Odhru with a smile and took him off to the worktable with her. Nakhalru went out to the shed to settle the beasts for the night.

Vika sat alone with Pierre. She found that she could not form her thoughts into words. But she knew, with passionate certainty, that she could not lose him now. He was her hope—for their comrades still trapped in the north, for the future, for herself.

He sighed and leaned forward, folding his arms on the table. "We must understand each other, you and I," he said in French.

"Yes," she said quietly.

"In the months we've been apart," he said, "I've been thinking a great deal."

"So have I," she said, before he could go on. "I think that it's a waste for us to be apart. If we're going to live together, Pierre, we should *be* together. Whatever happens." She searched his face, waiting for him to object.

He turned to face her, and looked at her seriously. "There's still great danger," he said. "There always will be. The Destroyers. The Anokothu. The primitive conditions." His dark eyes were troubled. "And yet—I think we are not so far from God after all, even here. I've thought, and prayed, and the answer that comes to me, the answer in my heart, is—that I must do what is hardest for me." He shook his head. "I must *trust*, even though I cannot know what will come." He stretched out his hands to her and she took them, her breath quick. "There is no certainty," he said. "But with you, I have hope. And on that I will build my life."

She could not speak. She brought his hands close, and kissed them. Against everything, they had found one another again. The world had changed. The world was new.

Vika woke late the next morning in their bed in one of the lofts. Pierre was gone. She stretched, smiling, enjoying the warmth of the bed. Remembering the night....

She pulled on her shift, crawled to the edge of the loft, and looked down. The house was empty and silent. She had to fight off the fear that yesterday, last night, had been a dream—the conviction was strangely compelling. She pulled on her overdress and trousers, climbed down from the loft, and went outside.

Thiain stood out in the yard, stirring a big iron kettle over a hot fire. She looked up from her work. "Vika! Welcome to the day."

The air was chilly, and there had been rain in the night, but just now sunlight trembled in every drop of water, and mist rose from the rough-shingled roof of the house. "I thank you," Vika said with feeling. "What are you cooking? Breakfast, I hope."

Thiain laughed. "That was hours ago. It's ash water. I'm boiling it down for lye. I need to make more soap, the way Pierre goes through it. And with you here as well—"

"I should at least take over that job." Vika took the stick and began stirring. "Where are the others?"

"Planting. We must get all our seed tubers in before the ground freezes, or they're wasted. Nakhalru said he was happy you're here—"

"Really!"

Thiain laughed. "Yes, because you see, with you here, Odhru doesn't have to stay with me in the house 'in case my time should come'"—she imitated Nakhalru's drawling voice. "He can work in the fields again. Next year we all will."

"Ah." Vika kept stirring.

"You need to eat something," Thiain said. "Just a moment." She went into the house and returned shortly with a bowl. "Just fish. I'm sorry."

Vika took the bowl gladly. "I don't mind. I like fish."

"For breakfast, at midday, and for supper?" Thiain smiled. "Next year it will be fish and tubers. The third year, fish and tubers and grain. So we grow rich."

It was milder and less greasy than the dried fish inland. While Vika ate, Thiain stirred the ash water. "So," she said. "You and Pierre will have children after all?"

They'd had some privacy in their loft, but of course, in a small house— Vika flushed. "It's possible."

"And that troubles you," Thiain said, her ears still.

Vika looked away. "There are good reasons for us not to have children."

"But no longer," Thiain said. "Now that you're familied."

"Familied?" She had not yet thought of it that way....

"Of course." Her eyes were bright. "You are of our new family, both of you. Of Kelruan."

Yes, of course. Vika could not speak.

"If you have children," Thiain said, "we'll all care for them together. If you must go back to the north someday—Pierre says so—your children will be safe here." She went to the pot, lifted some of the liquid out in a ladle, and watched it as she poured it back in. "That's thick enough. Now then. Just turn that jug of melted fat sitting next to the fire, so the other side warms. Careful, it's hot. The first thing you do..."

Evening closed in. Vika was helping Thiain with supper as Pierre and the others came in from the fields. Two cold arms encircled Vika from behind as she worked to saw apart the tough dried fish for the soup. She turned in Pierre's arms and kissed him—his face was chilly and smelled of dirt. "You're filthy," she said, laughing.

"I'll wash. But I had to do that first." He grinned and went off to bathe.

She brushed mud from her tunic and smiled after him. Thiain said, "Hah. Mud on your clothes. Mud across the floor. And his whole mind in the sky. Sometimes he reminds me of Kelru."

Vika flinched. She could not remember Kelru so calmly. But Thiain's clear, dark eyes were serene—and inside Vika, at that moment, something changed. "Kelru always kept a tidy house at Kheosseth," she said. "He never tracked mud in."

"That's because *he* had to sweep it." Thiain went back to chopping the tough wild greens that would also go in the soup.

Vika stood looking down at the dried fish on the table in front of her. Her eyes had filled with tears, but this time it was not grief. It was the idea, the hope that a time would come when she would be able to remember Kelru, and laugh over the memories because they were good.

And at that moment, she knew that she had begun to heal.

From the journal of Vika Jai:

We don't know what the future holds for us, Pierre and I. I know that somehow, in time, we must return to the north, and try to bring the remnant of our own people out of that dark place.

But we will not go just yet. Our people are here, as well: Thiain, and Nakhalru, and young Odhru; and now Thiain's two daughters. Thiain's, and Kelru's. When I look at them, I remember what Kelru was first to teach me: that we are all aliens, one to another. All of us, men and women, people of Earth and people of Windhome. And when we meet, all we can offer each other is kindness. Or love, if that is granted to us.

I will not risk being silenced when the time of danger does come. This is my own record, my own message against the dark, for myself and for Pierre. Our people, when they come to this world, will know what we did. Who we were. What we learned.

Even now, I stop to look at Pierre, and to wonder at how far we had to come to find each other. On Earth, we could not have become what we are.

Pierre says that this is the reason for all that we've suffered. But I disagree: I don't think there is ever a reason for pain, or that we should look for reasons.

But when I remember the terrible things that have happened, it comforts me to think of his quiet goodness, and of the peace, and often joy, we have together. It comforts me to laugh with Thiain, and help her care for her children. It comforts me to look out over our land, and to know for the first time in my life that I belong somewhere.

That I have come home.

ACKNOWLEDGMENTS

This book exists in its present form because of the love and support of my husband Tom, our children, my brother Tim Paulson, and my parents, who always believed in my writing. It exists because of the warm friendship and devastating critical insight of my longtime critique group, the Unstrung Harpies past and present (Patty Hyatt, Candy Davis, Karen Keady, Skye Blaine, Sally-Jo Bowman, and Liane Cordes). It exists because of the excellent advice and support of my agent, Caitlin McDonald. And, absolutely, it exists because of the thoughtful, thorough, and patient work of my editor, Athena Andreadis. I am grateful to you all.

ABOUT THE AUTHOR

Kristin Landon lives in Oregon with her husband Tom and an imperious Cavalier spaniel named Lucy. In addition to writing science fiction, she works as a freelance copyeditor of a wide range of scholarly and medical books. Her novelette "From the Depths" appeared in the highly acclaimed anthology *To Shape the Dark* (2016, Candlemark & Gleam). She is also the author of the Hidden Worlds trilogy—*The Hidden Worlds*, *The Cold Minds*, and *The Dark Reaches* (Ace Books). Visit her website at www.kristinlandon.com.